The Compass Rose

GAIL DAYTON

The Compass Rose

LUNA™
www.LUNA-Books.com

LUNA™

First edition March 2005

THE COMPASS ROSE

ISBN 0-373-80216-1

www.LUNA-Books.com

Printed in U.S.A.

For Robert. Thanks for all the brainstorming help
and for paying attention when I told you
how much fun fantasy was. I'm glad you're my kid.

And for Lindi. Keep at it. Dreams do come true.

CAST OF CHARACTERS

Kallista Varyl-captain in the Adaran army, naitan of the North, lightning thrower

Torchay Omvir-Adaran sergeant, Kallista's bodyguard

Stone, Warrior vo'Tsekrish-Tibran warrior

Fox, Warrior vo'Tsekrish-Tibran warrior, fighting partner to Stone

Aisse vo'Haav-Tibran woman

Obed im-Shakiri-Southron trader

Joh Suteny-Adaran guard lieutenant

Serysta Reinine-ruler of Adara, North naitan truthsayer

Viyelle Torvyll-Adaran prinsipella of Shaluine

Belandra of Arikon-the near legendary godstruck naitan who unified the first four prinsipalities to establish Adara, a thousand (or so) years ago

Huryl Kovallyk-Serysta's high steward

Erunde Nonnald-Steward's 4th undersecretary

Irysta Varyl-Kallista's birth mother, East naitan healer

Karyl & Kami Varyl-Kallista's twin sisters by blood

Mother Edyne-Mother Temple prelate in Ukiny

Huyis Uskenda-Adaran general in Ukiny

Merinda Kyndir-Adaran East naitan healer

Mother Dardra-Kallista's 5th mother, Riverside temple prelate and administrator in Turysh

Domnia Varyl-founder of the Varyl bloodline, West naitan and prelate

Oughrath, Bureaucrat vo'Haav-docks and trading official in Haav

Beltis-South naitan firethrower, Adaran trooper under Kallista's command

Hamonn-Beltis's bodyguard

Adessay-North naitan earthmover, trooper under Kallista's command

Kadrey-Adessay's bodyguard

Iranda-South naitan lightmaker, trooper under Kallista's command

Rynver-East naitan plantgrower, trooper under Kallista's command

Mora-South naitan foodspoiler, trooper under Kallista's command

Borril-Adaran guard sergeant

Smynthe-Tibran female magic hunter

Gwerie-Tibran male magic hunter

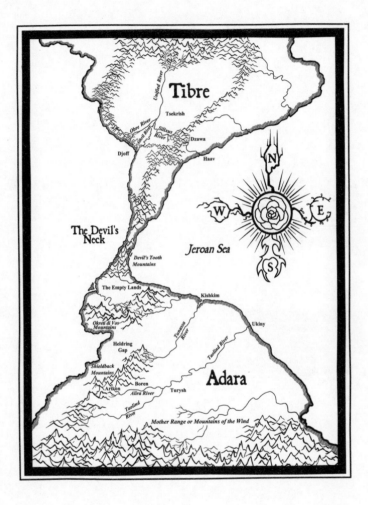

CHAPTER ONE

The wind off the sea snapped the banners to attention on the city walls. It ripped at the edges of the captain's tight queue and set the two white ribbons of her rank fluttering from her shoulders. Kallista Varyl tugged her tunic, blue for the direction of her magic, into better order. Yet one more time she wished that if she had to have North magic, she might have been given some more useful type. Directing winds, for instance.

She abhorred the way the wind here in Ukiny constantly tugged at her hair, destroying any attempt at neatness and order. And wind magic had civilian uses. Practical, productive uses. Her magic had no use other than war, so here she stood, captain of the Reinine's Own, on the walls of this besieged city waiting for the coming attack.

"What's the mood below?" Kallista continued her slow patrol of the ramparts.

"Quiet. Tense. They know what's coming." Her shadow moved forward to fall into step beside her. Torchay Omvir had been her constant companion for the past nine years. His tunic was bodyguard's black trimmed with blue to show whom he served. The folded ribbon set on his sleeve below the shoulder indicated his rank. When they went into summer uniform in a few more weeks, his tattooed rank would show on his upper arm. Most of the men making the military a career did the same.

"Not too tense I hope."

He shrugged. "Who can say until the moment comes and the battle begins?" Torchay paced alongside her, always keeping his lean height interposed between Kallista and the enemy spread out on the fields and beaches below.

Their white tents dotted the land like virulent pustules of infection as far as the unaided eye could see. Ukiny stood on the lone patch of rock floating to the surface of Adara's flat northern coast. The city's chalk-white limestone walls towered over the plains where the enemy camped. That advantage hadn't meant much so far.

"True." She neither needed nor even wanted the information she'd asked for. She asked to force Torchay to answer, to have some contact with another human at this loneliest of moments.

Torchay preferred his invisibility, claiming he could protect her better if he went unnoticed. But hair the color of Torchay's— deep, vibrant red—seldom escaped notice even when ruthlessly confined in a proper military queue. And wherever a military naitan went, everyone knew her bodyguard went also. At moments like this one, Kallista preferred company to protocol.

"Tomorrow?" Torchay stopped beside her at the northwest corner tower.

Kallista stared down at the rubble spilling from the breach in Ukiny's western wall and on down the steep slope of the carefully constructed glacis below. The setting sun gilded those broken stones, mocking the coming death they heralded.

"Likely," she said. "At dawn or just before. That's when I'd attack, when we're at our most tired."

The enemy ships had appeared unexpectedly off Ukiny just a week ago, hundreds of them. Adaran ships were built for speed and trade, not fighting. With a North magic naitan to call winds on almost every ship, they rarely had to deal with pirates or more political forms of banditry because their vessels were hard to catch. The few local ships in port when the strangers sailed up had fled. The city—still reeling with astonishment that any would dare invade Adara—had fastened itself inside stout walls.

Soldiers had poured from the clumsy ships, hundreds and hundreds of them, unloading bizarre equipment and strange-looking devices. The foreign army outnumbered the small force garrisoning Ukiny before half their ships had unloaded.

By careful listening at staff meetings, Kallista had gathered that one of the quarrelsome kings on the continent across the Jeroan Sea to the north had taken all the lands he could on his own continent and now had cast his eye toward Adara. No one seemed to know what drove Tibre on its conquest, whether greed, religion or something else. They were strange people according to the traders stranded in town when the ships fled, divided among themselves according to rank, each rank worshipping different gods.

Stranger yet, they had no naitani of their own and were known to kill those from other lands who demonstrated a visible gift of magic. That was why, despite the overwhelming numbers ranged against them, the small Adaran garrison had been confident of victory over the invading Tibrans. If they had no naitani at all, they certainly wouldn't have any attached to their army.

They had something else. Cannon.

Traders had been bringing reports for a number of years about the wars among the northern kingdoms. They told of a weapon that required no magic to break down walls and fortifications, a weapon far more effective, far more devastating than ballistae or catapults. The Adaran general staff had discounted these tales as exaggerations. The Tibrans might have *something,* but nothing without magic involved could have such a deadly effect. The generals were wrong.

Now they were paying the price for their smug assumptions. Adara was a nation of merchants, a matriarchal society that used its army primarily to control the aggression of her young men. A long succession of prelate-queens had seen little need for violent expansion. The last of the independent prinsipalities between the impassable Devil's Neck land bridge to the north and the nearly impassable Mother Range spanning the continent to the south had joined Adara two hundred years ago, the result of diplomacy and trade, not war.

The Reinines in the years since had believed Adara's superiority so obvious that no other nation would dare challenge it. And they hadn't, even though some Adaran traders skinned those they traded with a bit too close to the bone. Adara had more naitani than any other land, and the naitani were Adara's strength.

But they should have expected the other nations to develop alternatives to the magic Adara used so extravagantly. When the traders came home complaining of cloth made waterproof through the use of powders and mechanical techniques, someone should have noticed. This new stuff wasn't as good as Adaran waterproofing, but it was much cheaper. How far from there to mechanical weapons as effective at massive destruction as a soldier naitan? *More* effective, because the cannon could be used by anyone and could be forged by the hundreds. A naitan had to be born.

These terrible cannon belched forth fire and destruction. They battered the city walls hour after endless hour, day upon day. The constant *boom!-whistle-crack!* as the iron ball exploded from the mouth of the weapon, sailed through the air and smashed into stone, was enough to drive anyone into screaming fits. Anyone, that is, of lesser moral fiber than a captain of the Reinine's Own Naitani.

Kallista had destroyed one of the awful machines, the only naitan of her troop able to do so. The enemy moved them farther from the walls then, and still kept up the relentless bombardment. These cannon could fire their iron balls farther than she could throw her lightning. She could not hit what she could not see. At least her magic was line-of-sight and not touch-linked. She'd heard of some who could visualize what they aimed for and strike without seeing, but she could not.

This morning, the cannon had breached Ukiny's walls. Soon the enemy would pour through the gap and bring its advantage of numbers to bear. Kallista knew her fellow soldiers would fight bravely, but the outcome was not optimistic.

"Have you decided where to post your troop?" Torchay never looked away from his view over the wall at the enemy.

Kallista sighed. That was the supposed reason for taking this little stroll into danger. She couldn't tell her bodyguard that one more second in their austere quarters would have had her chewing holes in the furniture, even if he already knew it. "Yes. Half here—East and South. Except for Beltis. I want her fire-throwing skill with me and Adessay on the far side of the breach."

"In the tower."

"Tower's too far away. On the wall. Near the breach."

"Too close. It's not safe."

Kallista turned her head and looked at Torchay, at his bony, hawk-nosed visage silhouetted against the orange sky, waiting until he looked back at her.

"It's a battle, Sergeant," she said. "It's not supposed to be safe."

He gave a tiny nod in acknowledgment of that truth.

"We need to be as close to the breach as possible." She moved to the edge of the battlements to peer over, ignoring Torchay's hiss of displeasure. "It's going to be up to us to slow their advance, thin their numbers as they come through."

"You can't do anything if you're dead."

"If we can't stop them, everyone in the city could well be dead by this time tomorrow. And we haven't enough regular troops to do the job. It's going to require magic."

"Just—" He broke off and took a deep breath. That wasn't like him, to be fumbling for words. "Don't make my job harder than it has to be, Captain. Promise me you'll do nothing reckless."

Kallista raised an eyebrow. "You forget yourself, Sergeant."

"Probably. But if it means that you don't forget yourself when the battle begins, I'll bear the punishment." Torchay held her gaze until Kallista had to look away.

She did have a tendency to take risks in battle. Too much caution could lose a battle. Generally her risks paid off, but once... Once, she'd nearly got the both of them killed.

"I'll be as careful as I am able," she said finally. "But if my action will make the difference in winning or losing, you know I will act."

"If your lightning can turn the battle, I'll carry you into it on my back." Torchay paused then, so long that she glanced up at him. His gaze caught hers, held it. "But I won't let you throw your life away on a lost cause, Kallista." He turned away to look out over the enemy camped below. "Do you understand me, Captain? I *will* do my duty."

"I never for a second thought you would do anything else."

"Have you seen all you needed to see?"

Relieved at Torchay's return to his normal self, Kallista tugged at the wide cuffs of her supple leather gloves and wished she could take them off. It was too hot for gloves, but a military naitan could not appear in public without them. Not unless she was about to call magic.

"Let's go down." She headed for the flimsy ladder leading through the trap door in the floor and below to street level. It would be simple to remove when the time came and prevent access either up or down. "I want the troop up here tonight. If we have to stumble from our billets and stagger into place half-asleep, we'll be too late."

Torchay didn't answer, simply followed her down.

The streets were all but deserted, most shops already closed up, the owners and customers at home praying for rescue and hiding their valuables. The buildings near the wall showed signs of the enemy bombardment. Apparently, pinpoint targeting was not a strong suit of the Tibrans, but then with cannon, it didn't seem to matter. The buildings here had not been of the sturdiest construction to begin with, mostly weathered wood hovels or sheds with a tendency to lean. Now some were patched with planks or canvas. Homes too near the breach in the wall had become little more than splintered debris. Kallista hoped the residents had found new shelter.

Nearer their quarters, the buildings on either side of the narrow cobbled streets at least stood up straight. More had stone walls rather than wood, and shops displayed a better quality of goods. Flags in bright colors advertised the business operating in the buildings where they flew. Here, shops of all sorts stood hip to thigh, unlike the capital where each type of business had its own street, if not its own neighborhood.

A tailor operated next door to a jeweler, next to a shoemaker, a grocer and so on. Because of the odors they generated, the tanners and the livestock markets were relegated outside the city walls. Kallista had worried about that, about running out of food during a long siege. But that was before the cannon made themselves known. The siege hadn't been a long one.

A bakeshop along their route still displayed loaves and sweet buns on its fold-down countertop as the baker bustled about preparing to close.

"Wait." Torchay touched Kallista's arm, and when she stopped, he approached the baker. "How much for what you have left?"

"Can't you read?" She jerked a thumb toward the sign. "Two buns or one loaf for a krona."

"It's the end of the day, your customers have gone home, and your bread was baked before dawn. You don't advertise South magic preserving. It's not worth that price." Torchay spoke quietly, patiently to the baker. "I'll give you two kroni for the lot."

"Listen to me, *soldier.*" The baker spat out the word. "You got no business telling me what my wares are worth. I made these loaves with my own two hands. I don't need magic for that. What do you make? Death? What value does that have?"

Kallista stalked toward the plump baker, her foul mood flaring into sudden temper. "What value is your life? If it weren't for soldiers like him, you would already be living in a Tibran *harim* with half your iliasti dead. This man is ready to give his life for you, you ungrateful bitch, and you begrudge him a few loaves of bread?"

She knew her anger was out of proportion to the situation, but she couldn't help it. She'd had enough self-righteous scorn from the locals who looked down their lofty faces at the soldiers defending them yet screamed for help at the first sign of trouble.

But she didn't realize she'd removed one of her gloves until the shock of skin against skin made her jerk and stare down at Torchay's bare hand clasping her own.

The baker's wide eyes said she understood the threat, if not what had caused it, and she was tumbling bread into a rough sack as fast as her hands would move. "Pardon, naitan. Pardon. No offense meant."

"None taken." Though that was a small lie. Kallista had taken offense. And she knew better than to do so. She couldn't change popular opinion. Her own behavior, though unconscious and unintended, had only reinforced the impression that those who

served in the military were too wicked or too stupid to do anything else. Anything *productive.*

She considered removing her hand from Torchay's grip and replacing the glove. But that would make her inadvertent action
seem even more of a threat, withdrawn now that she had what
she wanted.

"Thank you, aila." Torchay held out two kroni. The baker waved
them away and he set them on her counter. "I pay my debts, aila.
I just mislike paying more than what is due."

With the sack gripped tight in Torchay's other hand, he and
Kallista continued down the street. Around the corner, out of
sight of the bakeshop, she jerked her hand free and rounded on
her bodyguard.

"Are you mad? Have you lost the remaining threads of the feeble wits you might once have possessed?" Kallista held her bare
hand in front of his face. "I am *ungloved.*"

"You hadn't called magic. I was safe enough. I'd have been safe
enough even if you had. You have more control than any naitan
in the entire army. Probably in all Adara."

Torchay's calm unconcern infuriated her. "You don't know that.
The sparks don't always show."

"I know when you call magic. I don't have to see the sparks.
And I know you don't have to unglove to do it. To do anything."

Kallista yanked her glove back on in short, sharp motions. "Do
not ever do that again. *Ever.* Do you understand me, Sergeant? If
you do, I'll have that chevron if I have to strip the skin off your
arm to do it, and see you flogged."

"You don't approve of flogging."

"For this I do. Never touch my bare hands. You know this. You
learned it the first day of your guard training."

Torchay gazed at her. She could see the words building up inside his head, battering at his lips in their desire to get past them.
Other naitani had trouble with their guards getting too close,

wanting more from the relationship than was possible, but Torchay had never shown any sign of the failing. Was this how it began?

She didn't want to imagine trouble where none existed. She and Torchay worked well together. She didn't want that to change, didn't want to offend him by making faulty assumptions. "If you have something to say, say it."

He shook his head. "No, I have nothing——" His mouth thinned into a straight line, lips pressed together, stubbornly holding back the words. She would get nothing more out of him, not now.

Torchay turned his back to her, scanning their surroundings for potential danger, pulling back into his familiar role.

"Give me the sack." Kallista held her hand out for it. He needed his hands free for weapons, now that she was safely gloved again. Civilian naitani weren't required to go about gloved, but military magic was considered too dangerous to risk a naitan's loss of control.

Anything covering the bare skin of the hands interfered to some degree with the magic. Leather blocked virtually all magic save for that under the most exquisite control. But Kallista didn't have to remove her gloves to use her magic. She didn't know any other naitan who could do what she could.

Torchay handed over the bread and moved down the street behind her toward the oversize home where the Third Detachment, Military Naitani, was billeted. The house towered three stories above the street, offering a view over the walls from the flat roof garden. The furnishings were elegant, gilded and ornamented to the extreme, what few furnishings there were. The table shared by the troop had curved gilded legs encrusted with more curlicues, and the top had multicolored woods inlaid in a geometric design. The mismatched chairs they used had tapestry-upholstered seats, or inlaid designs, and yet others were gilded within an inch of their lives. But most of the rooms were vacant, echoing with emptiness.

The ilian that owned it had once been much larger, a full dozen individuals all bound in temple oath to love and support each other and raise the children that resulted from their bonding. The loss of a child and his mother in an accident had fractured the family and a bare quartet of iliasti remained to finish bringing up the few children left to them. They had plenty of room for the entire troop.

Torchay bowed her into the house, but his eyes held hers as he did, watching her. It unnerved her. What did it mean? Anything?

Kallista tossed the bread sack to Torchay as he closed the door behind them. "Alert the troop. I want everyone ready to move into position by full dark. The general will be moving the regular troops into position then as well. The Tibrans won't have far-seers to spot us in the dark."

"And we hope they have no machines to do it for them."

"Bite your tongue." Kallista gave an exaggerated shudder, but it was indeed something to worry about.

Torchay opened the sack and tossed her a bun. "You missed supper." He was gone to carry out her order before she could throw it back at him.

He returned moments later, while Kallista still stared at the bread in her hand. "Everyone is ready, save for Beltis and Hamonn. They went to dinner at the public house down the street and should be back shortly."

Kallista sighed. Beltis was one of the naitani she worried about. The young South fire thrower was impulsive, romantic, and she was growing far too attached to her bodyguard. Hamonn was older, like most guards assigned to new naitani, and sensible, but—well, time enough to worry about it after the battle. If they all survived, she could talk to Hamonn then about reassignment or retirement.

"Bread is for eating." Torchay slid one of his blades into a wrist sheath and drew another to test its edge. "Not staring at. It's not a work of art. You'll need the fuel tonight for your magic."

"You're my bodyguard. Not my keeper." Kallista wanted to set the bun aside, but Torchay was right. She needed to eat. The bread tasted better than she expected for having been baked without magic and set out on display all day.

The silence caught her attention. No sound of steel on stone as Torchay sharpened one of his numberless blades. She'd tried to count them once, the dirks and daggers and short swords secreted in every place conceivable around Torchay's body. But just when she thought she had them all, he would produce another from some invisible spot. And whenever he had a spare moment, he would sharpen them. The rasping sound had played accompaniment to every quiet moment of the last nine years. Until now.

He sat in his usual place beside the street door, a wicked little blade—needle thin and razor sharp—in one hand, his whetstone forgotten in the other as he watched her.

The skin between her shoulder blades prickled. She did not have time for this now, whatever it was. They had a battle to fight, probably before dawn. She refused to encourage him. But she could not refuse to listen if he chose to speak.

"Yes, I'm your bodyguard," he said finally. "I've served you for nine years. I'd like to think I've done a good job of it."

"You have. Exemplary." Was that what had his hair on too tight? His qualifications record?

"For nine years, I've been no farther from you than a spoken word. I know you better than anyone. Better than your family. Better than your naitani." He paused and looked at his blade as if wondering why he held it. "The battle tomorrow—it's not like the bandits we've fought before. It doesn't look good, does it." He didn't ask a question.

"No. It doesn't." Kallista still didn't know where Torchay was going with this, but she had never given him anything less than the truth.

"This time tomorrow, we'll most likely be dead."

"Very probably."

He looked at her then, his clear blue eyes holding her gaze. "If I'm going to die, Kallista, I want to die with friends. The army isn't a good place for making them. You're the only person I can think of who I'd consider a friend. You're my captain, my naitan, and I'm your bodyguard. But—is it possible—could we not also be friends?"

Friendship. Was that all he wanted? Such a simple, utterly difficult thing. Someone who cared about him not because they had to, not for ties of blood or marriage, but simply because they liked him.

Did Kallista have friends? Naitani in the army were too valuable, too rare to concentrate them in large numbers, and the regular officers were often what the average citizen thought them: dim and sometimes cruel. She'd met a few fellow naitani she liked, but postings in the far corners of the Adaran continent kept her from furthering the acquaintance.

The person Kallista knew best, the one whose moods she could interpret just from the sound of steel on stone or the huff of breath through his beaked nose, the one who kept her secrets and guarded her privacy, was Torchay. Was that friendship?

She rather thought it was. "We *are* friends, Torchay," she said. "You've perhaps been a better friend to me than I have to you, but we have been friends for a long time. Why else would we have lasted nine years?"

Torchay slicked his knife along the stone, a satisfied sound. "I thought so."

"You know, you'll sharpen that knife away to nothing if you keep that up."

He grinned at the familiar comment. "Perhaps," he said in his regular response. "But it will be a very sharp nothing."

They were friends. Everything was exactly the same as before, and everything was different. She knew. At least one person in this world considered her a friend.

Torchay's head came up at the noise of doors opening and closing, boots clattering on flagstone. "That will be Beltis and Hamonn."

CHAPTER TWO

Torchay put away his blade so quickly Kallista did not see where and picked up the cloaks tossed on the bench beside him. The blue he handed to Kallista, and draped the blue-trimmed black over his forearm. It would likely get cold before dawn, she realized, and as usual, Torchay had already thought of it.

"I'll have them assemble in the courtyard," he said and disappeared into the outer rooms where the others lived.

Kallista led her troop through the dark streets of Ukiny by a pale steady light courtesy of the South naitan Iranda. Her best skill was lighting up a dark battlefield, but she could also scorch enemy soldiers, depending on how far away they were, how many they were and whether the local chickens had danced a waltz or a strut that morning. Iranda's magic was not under the best of control, but she hadn't burnt any Adaran soldiers since she'd been under Kallista's command.

Only five naitani besides herself, plus their five bodyguards, made up Kallista's troop. Three wore the yellow tunics of South naitani—Beltis the fire thrower, Iranda the scorcher and a girl from the eastern coast who could spoil the enemy's food. Kallista wasn't sure what use Mora would be in battle, but she was part of the troop, so she would be with them.

The lone naitan in the green of East magic could cause uncontrollable growth in plant life. Rynver was one of the few male naitani in the military. Men did have magic, but it was less common—perhaps one in every ten rather than the one-in-five rate of women born with magic. His parents hadn't expected their son to have magic, so Rynver had never learned to control it. His military service had already stretched beyond the required six years, but when he learned control, like Iranda, he'd be gone. Back to civilian life, working on a farm somewhere.

The other North naitan wouldn't have to wait. When Adessay turned twenty-two and finished his tour of mandatory military duty, he had a place waiting in one of the western mines. Today, he would be spilling debris from the breach down the glacis as the Tibrans tried to climb it, rolling stones in their path and generally disrupting their advance. He didn't have a great deal of power to put behind his earthmoving, but that and his excellent control was why he would be welcomed outside the army.

Beltis would spend her life in the military, like Kallista, because her fire starting was too powerful, exploding ovens and setting houses on fire even after years of working on her control. Kallista's control was so fine she could set tiny blue sparks dancing from finger to finger—and sometimes did when a staff meeting droned on and on and on. But no one had any use for her lightning, save Adara's defense forces. Defending the helpless gave her magic *some* use, gave her life a purpose.

When her troop was disposed to her satisfaction, Kallista wrapped herself in her cloak and went to stand near the arrow slit in the parapet. The lights of campfires spread down the beach as far as she could see. She'd have suspected the Tibrans of lighting more fires than they had troops to demoralize Ukiny's garrison, but she had watched them unloading. She had never seen such a vast army, never imagined a need for such a thing.

Kallista turned her face into the wind, feeling it rush past her from the shore, from the North. She squared up her shoulders, pointing them east and west so that North lay directly before her. First the Jeroan Sea, then the lower fringes of the Tibran continent. It rose to a high plateau ringed by cliffs, or so she'd been told, and beyond that, mountains. Mountains as high and wild as the Devil's Tooth range along the neck that bridged the sea, but colder. Beyond the mountains lay pure North. Cold, clear, rational. Utterly unlike Kallista's own hot-tempered, impulsive, passion-ruled nature.

Perhaps that was why the One had given her North magic, so that its icy control could provide what she did not possess in herself. Kallista opened herself to the North, calling its cold clarity into her mind and soul, filling herself with its sharp-edged magic.

She sensed Torchay's presence behind her. "You should sleep, Sergeant."

"So should you. Your rest is more important than mine. Your lightning will be needed. We guards have divided the watch."

Kallista glanced toward Beltis's stocky guard who stood over his charge. Hamonn gave her a tiny nod, acknowledging his duty, accepting it from her. "You're right," she said. "The battle will begin when it begins."

She lay down where she was, her back against the fortification, and listened to the quiet sounds Torchay made as he settled close by. "Sleep well, friend."

The silence that answered had her fearing she'd overstepped some unknown bounds, until at last he spoke, his voice even quieter than hers. "And you also…friend."

* * *

"Stop! Wait, dammit—what kind of friend are you?" Stone bent over, hands on his knees, and tried to decide whether the contents of his stomach were going to come out. He knew he'd feel better if he could just shed his jacket in this infernal heat, but the padded gray nuisance was part of the uniform. They could unbutton it, but they couldn't leave it off even in camp.

"I'm your only friend, thank you. No one else would put up with your rubbish."

Stone tilted his head and peered up at Fox who had stopped after all and was waiting, swaying slightly in the offshore wind, his face strange and shadowy in the firelight coming from the nearby crossway between tents. Stone knew that face better than his own. Both of them named Warrior, of the highest caste Tibre had to offer, below only the Rulers themselves. Both of them vo'Tsekrish, of the king's own city.

They had been partnered the day they left women's quarters to begin warrior training, when they were six years old. They were now twenty-two. Or maybe twenty-three. Stone didn't keep track of that sort of thing.

He and Fox had learned to read side by side from the same book. They had learned to fight back-to-back against the same teachers. They had even discovered the pleasures of women at the same time, though *not* with the same woman. Stone trusted Fox with his life.

But at the moment, he could cheerfully throttle him. "I thought you said you knew where women's quarters were."

"I didn't say that. You did." Fox grabbed a handful of Stone's hair and pulled him more or less upright, leaning down until they stood eye to eye.

Stone envied him those few inches that made the lean necessary. "'S not fair," he muttered. "I should be the taller. I'm lead in this pair."

"You're drunk." Fox shoved and Stone staggered back several paces.

"Am not. If I was drunk, I'd have fallen. 'Sides, Stores won't give us enough to get drunk. Just enough to get pleasantly snockered. Besides that, you're drunk too."

"Not drunk. Snockered." Fox frowned. "Why d'you suppose that is?"

"Dunno." Stone looked around for a place to sit. He didn't recognize the tents—though why he thought he should since all something-thousand of them looked exactly alike, he didn't know.

The tents were wide enough for a tall man to stretch out without getting his feet wet, long enough for six men to sleep side by side without quite touching, and high enough to stand up in if you didn't mind ducking a bit. Or ducking a bit more if you were Fox. And they were set up in identical long rows with space between them for walking and mustering.

Stone didn't recognize the warriors strolling about, either. Except for Fox. He recognized him. Worse luck. "Dunno why we're snockered," he said again, "'cept the First and Finest are always a little snockered when they go charging up through the breach. And 'cause they gave us the stuff and what else were we to do with it but drink it?"

"Maybe that's why." Fox set a small keg on its end and plopped down on it. "Give us these fancy red poufs of trousers so we'll be sure to get shot at. Get us just snockered enough we'll run like lunatics into that hellmouth, and call us a brilliant-sounding name like First and Finest so we won't realize we're something else entirely, like First and Foolishest."

"No such word as *foolishest*," Stone offered, nodding sagely. Or as sagely as he could, given that he was at least a quarter full of some truly vile liquor. "And you shouldn't talk that way. It'll get back to the Rulers. You do realize you're sitting on a keg of black powder, don't you?"

Carefully, Fox leaned to one side and peered down at his impromptu seat. "Damn me, so I am. Suppose it wouldn't do to get myself blown to bits prematurely."

"No. Won't do at all." Stone took his partner's hand and hauled him to his feet. "D'you suppose we started drinking too early? They haven't started the cannonade yet, have they?" He froze, trying to force thought through his slightly pickled brain, to hear what he ought to be hearing. "Have I gone deaf?"

Just then, the concentrated thunder of hundreds of cannon firing simultaneously at close range threatened to knock both men off none-too-steady feet.

"Did you hear that?" Fox said when the noise faded.

"Yes."

"Then you're not deaf."

"Do you know where we are?" Again Stone tried to pick out landmarks.

"Haven't a clue."

"I don't suppose you know where women's quarters are from here."

"Not a bit."

Stone shoved his hair out of his face with both hands. "Why doesn't your hair ever get in your way? It's just like mine, yellow and curly. It should get in your way like mine."

"I remember to get mine cut." Fox produced a length of string, bunched Stone's hair together on the top of his head and tied it off. "You look ridiculous. Like there's a fountain sprouting from your head."

"Don't care. It's out of my way. Thanks, *brodir*."

"Anytime." Fox paused, then pointed at the banner hanging above a nearby tent. "Isn't that the vo'Haav banner?"

Stone turned, looked. The banner was hard to see in the firelight, but he thought he recognized a black bear on the yellow flag. "If a bear is vo'Haav's emblem, then it is."

"Our camp is always just to the east of theirs."

"Don't tell me you know where east is. The sun's down. The moon's not up yet."

Fox pointed. "The city is east. Therefore east is that way. Our tent is also that way."

Stone sighed, his chest heaving in his disappointment. "I really wanted a woman tonight."

"One last time before we die."

Anger flashing like sparks in dry grass, Stone swung, his fist plowing into his partner's face, knocking him to his backside. Stone spat in the sand beside him, invoking the warrior's god. "Don't say that," he ordered, fists clenched. "Maybe we'll die, but maybe we won't. It's not up to us. You go into battle knowing you'll die, Khralsh will give you what you want. Death is easy."

Once more he reached down and pulled Fox to his feet. "You go into battle determined to live, maybe he lets you live. Life, that's not so easy, not in battle. Either way, Khralsh decides. But if you ask for what you want, maybe he gives it."

"And maybe he doesn't." Fox couldn't meet Stone's gaze.

"Maybe not." Stone shook the wrist he gripped, jarring his partner's whole body, willing him to understand, to believe. "But who guaranteed you life to begin with? Remember that Bureaucrat we saw get run down by the ale wagon? Or the Farmer who got gored by his bull? Everybody dies, Fox, sooner or later. Swear your life to Khralsh, let *him* look after it. *You* can't."

This time, Fox's sharp brown gaze locked onto Stone's. He envied Fox his eyes as well. Few others had the pale blue of Stone's eyes. Their mentors had always shuddered and called them uncanny, witchy. But he didn't mind uncanny now if it convinced Fox.

Slowly, Fox nodded. "All right. I'll swear. With you at my shoulder I believe it."

"Then swear. We swear together, we fight together, fight well, and surely Khralsh will let us live."

"I swear. I swear myself to Khralsh. I ask for life, but my life in his hands whatever happens." Fox spat in the sand, offering a body fluid precious to the warrior god.

Stone copied him. "And so I swear also. My life to Khralsh."

They stood another moment, swaying faintly when the wind gusted through, setting tent walls to flapping.

"D'you suppose we ought to try to sleep?" Stone scratched his head, careful not to disturb his new topknot.

The cannon crashed again, less in unison than before.

"In this noise?" Fox turned his partner and pushed him in the direction of their division. "You can *try.*"

"Why do you always have all the answers?"

"Because somebody has to, and you obviously don't."

Stone punched Fox in the shoulder hard enough to send him reeling to the far side of the tent street. "What is it I have then?"

"Lunatic courage."

"You have courage. Plenty of it. I've seen it."

"Ah, but I have the *sensible* sort of courage. Somebody has to be the crazy one, the one who'll charge cannon with a misfired musket or volunteer for First and Finest. And that's you."

"You were right there charging and volunteering with me."

"We're paired. Where else am I supposed to be but at your back, making sure you don't get your fool self killed."

Stone thought long enough they passed two tents, trying to work his way to Fox's meaning. The cannon's booming, now a steady rumble as the big guns fired at will, seemed to shake the alcohol from his brain. "You're pissed." He stopped in the through-way. "Not drunk pissed. Angry pissed. Because I volunteered."

"I'm not angry." Fox took his arm and got him moving again. "I was. But I'm not anymore. You convinced me we'd live through this. And if we don't, Khralsh will welcome us to his hall."

"Yes." Stone believed it. He couldn't believe anything else. "Volunteering for First and Finest will get us noticed. It could get us promoted."

Fox sighed. "Don't you ever get tired?"

"Of what?"

"This." Fox swept his arm in a half circle, indicating the camp around them, the cannon, the city with its broken walls. "Living in tents. Slogging through mud or heat or rain or all three to the next camp. Fighting. Bleeding. Healing up so we can do it all over again. Don't you wish we could rest for a little while? Go home, soak in the baths, spend some time with a woman who has all her teeth?"

"I don't know, I rather like the toothless one. The way she can wrap her mouth aro—"

Fox shoved him and Stone broke off, laughing. His laughter didn't last long. They'd reached their own tent, shared with two other pairs, all elsewhere just now. They probably knew how to find the women's tents.

Stone took advantage of their absence to speak frankly, half shouting over the cannon noise. "This is the way it is, Fox. We were born Warrior caste. We are the King's Fist. His Sword and Shield. Where our king sends, we go. It's no use wishing it was some other way, because it's not, and it won't ever be. You'll shatter your soul trying to fight it."

"You're right. I know you're right." Fox pulled his musket from the stack and sat down to clean it once more. "I think too much." He grinned at his partner. "The curse of a brilliant mind."

Stone grinned back, relief flooding him. "Crazy and stupid. That's what a good warrior ought to be. You should work on that."

"I will. Damn me! The flint's cracked already. I just replaced it this morning." Grumbling, Fox set to putting the finicky firearm back into working order.

Stone pulled out a whetstone and his bayonet. In a charge like

Gail Dayton

the one facing them, they'd only get one chance to fire their muskets. A sharp bayonet seemed more useful.

The boom of cannon fire set the walls of the women's tents to trembling. All night the bombardment had continued, a constant underpinning to the activity within the tents. The activity had ceased with the departure of the men. The women slept haphazardly wherever they found a comfortable spot, twitching when the cannon roared, but sleeping nonetheless. All save one.

Aisse vo'Haav, assigned to the Warrior caste, crept carefully from the communal areas to the tiny partitioned section where the women washed, dressed and kept their few personal belongings. If anyone woke, she would have questions, and though Aisse had answers, she couldn't afford the delay.

She took the moments necessary to stop at the shrine to Ulilianeth, healer, seductress, protector of women, the only goddess in a heaven full of gods. Aisse felt the need for her blessing before embarking on her path.

Ulilianeth had spoken to Aisse in this place, had shown her that things could be different, that she could live a life of her own choosing, free of everything that had made her existence into hell. In this place, women could say no. And Aisse intended to be one of them.

She pressed a kiss to Ulilianeth's stone skirt, then scurried to her corner where she ripped off the hated gauzy dress. She scrubbed herself until her skin felt raw, but still she didn't feel clean. Aisse pulled the brown linen tunic from beneath her box, where she'd hidden it the day she bought it from the local boy selling bread in the camp. She put it on, smoothing it down over her thighs. It left her legs bare from the knees down. Studying her exposed legs critically, Aisse decided they did not look much like boys' legs, too round and golden. She had to disguise them.

A short while later, she'd made her coverlet into a fair approximation of the leggings she'd seen Adaran soldiers wearing. Hers were lumpy and threatened to slip down because she couldn't tie the bindings tight enough, but they would have to do. She got out the scissors she'd "borrowed" from Piheko. She'd listened to Piheko bemoan their loss for days. Aisse would be sure to leave them where they could be easily found. In seconds, her waist-length mane of gold hair lay on the ground.

Her neck felt cool, tingly, strange. But she didn't have time to marvel at it or the way her head threatened to float away. Aisse gathered up the shorn hair and shoved it in with the straw of a spare pallet, scuffed the remaining strands into the dirt, and laid the scissors in a gap beside Piheko's box.

From her own, she retrieved the bag of supplies she'd been collecting—dried meat, hard cheese, biscuit, a cup, extra shoes—and knelt to peer beneath the tent wall. No one passed by. After endless hours, the cannonade was at last rising to its crescendo. The warriors would be mustering on the field before the city, preparing for the attack. No one would notice a boy slipping from the camp.

She made it past the cannon, past the endless stacks of stores, past the officers' mounts and the cattle waiting their turn to be slaughtered for rations. She could see the line of trees that marked the southern edge of the Tibran camp.

"Here! You—boy!"

Aisse froze, hesitating seconds too long before realizing she should run. Her face would never pass for a boy's at second glance. But the Farmer caste tending the beasts already had hold of her arm.

"What are you doing here, boy?" He yanked, snapping her arm painfully upward. "Spying? Off to tell your witches all our plans?"

She kept her face turned away, hoping her hacked-off hair would provide sufficient disguise.

"Look at me, boy!" He jerked her arm again.

Aisse shook her head, trying to pull away from him. He swore and backhanded her across the face. She couldn't stop the reflexive high-pitched cry. A girl's sound, not a boy's.

The farmer grabbed her face with the hand not gripping her arm and forced it upward, until he could see her. "Achz and Arilo!" He called on the Farmer caste's twin gods in his shock. "You're female."

He shook her, violently. "What in seven hells have you done? By all that's holy…" His voice trembled with horror.

And it was true horror to a Tibran male to think anyone might wish to escape his caste, to think a woman might wish to live some other life. Women lived in the women's quarters of whatever caste they were assigned, doing women's work, available to any man of any caste who might wish to use her. Most Tibran women didn't mind. It was the way life was. Aisse hated it.

She couldn't lose her chance at freedom now, not when she was so close. "Let me go!"

Her elbow punched into the farmer's stomach as she struggled. He grunted with the blow, so she did it again, kicking, scratching and biting in desperate silence.

"Witch." He shook her hard enough to rattle her eyes in their sockets. The first blow of his fist stunned her and she collapsed, held upright only by his grip. He waited till she regained her senses before he hit her again, to be sure she felt every least bit of the punishment he had in store for her. He told her so.

Torchay pressed his naitan closer into the angle between wall and walkway, his body covering hers. Not that mere flesh and blood were much defense against the cannon's iron balls, but at least if he failed her this time, he would surely die first. He put his lips next to her ear and shouted so he could be heard. "We should pull back. They're targeting the walls now."

"*And* the town."

Since the bombardment started, she had argued against leaving the walls because the Tibran missiles sailed over their heads to crash into the shops and houses of Ukiny. Then, she had been right. They were safer on the walls. But no longer.

The captain turned her head. Torchay pulled back, allowing her to find his ear.

"It's too late to pull back." Her lips brushed his skin as she spoke. "Even if we wanted to, we couldn't do it now. We're safer staying put."

Torchay gave up. She was likely right, as usual. And even if she wasn't, she was the captain.

A cannonball smacked into the crenellations behind them, sending stones tumbling to the walkway. Hands molded to his captain's head, he waited till the biggest debris settled, then lifted his head just enough to peer behind him. The other guards lay over their naitani in the space beyond his feet.

"Hamonn!" Torchay bellowed the man's name, but doubted he could be heard over the cannon's roar. He propped himself on elbows to see better, and thought something moved past the South naitan's guard.

"Status?" his captain asked.

"Checking." He nudged Hamonn with his foot. Rubble spilled from the man's back, but the man himself did not move.

"*Casualties,* Sergeant?"

"Hamonn isn't moving. Don't think he's dead, but I don't know. Don't know about Beltis either. Someone's moving beyond them, so I assume Kadrey and his naitan are unhurt." He didn't like reporting incomplete information, but his captain needed something and that was the best he had.

"Go check on Hamonn. See if Beltis is hurt. I need her with me."

Torchay flattened himself over her as another ball hit close by. "When it's safe."

"Go *now*. By the time it's safe, the battle will be over. That's an order, Sergeant."

When she said that, it meant she was beyond reasoning with. He had no choice but to obey, or risk her doing almost anything. Torchay rose onto hands and knees, but remained in place, his body still shielding hers. "Do *not* move from this spot."

They'd fought this battle out their first year or so together, but he still held his breath every time he went on one of her errands, until he returned and found her again where he'd left her.

"I won't. Now go." Her shove sent him scooting on hands and feet to the pair under the debris behind them.

Torchay moved the worst of the stones off the older man and checked for a pulse. He found it, strong and steady. "Trooper? Beltis, are you injured?" He leaned close to hear any response over the cannon fire.

"I'm fine." Her voice came muffled from beneath her guard. "Is Hamonn—"

"Breathing and well enough, given that he has a lump the size of my fist on the back of his head." Torchay probed the injury and was rewarded with reaction.

Hamonn tried to shove him away. He might have groaned but no one could hear it in the crash of a cannonball nearby. So close that bits of rock blasted from the wall spun into Torchay's face, making tiny cuts on his forehead and cheeks. Too close.

He looked up to see where it had hit in time to see the parapet above his captain begin to crumble. "Kallista!"

Torchay bellowed her name and scrambled to reach her. She was moving, getting out of the way, but not fast enough.

An enormous stone capping the structure plummeted down, striking her a glancing blow before it bounced off the town side of the walk. More stones followed. Torchay dove forward to keep them off her. He didn't quite succeed.

A fist-size stone hit her head, leaving a cut oozing blood in the fine, pale skin of her forehead. With a cry, Torchay covered her head with his hands, ignoring the battering they took. He scooted forward until he could get his head over hers. His was undoubtedly harder, could take more of a beating. But the rocks had stopped falling. The entire parapet lay on the walkway around and over them.

Torchay shoved the rocks away from her, leaving streaks of blood on their chalky surface. His hands bled from a score of cuts, and at least one finger was likely broken. He used them to cup his captain's face and turn it up to the full moon's light. He bent his head till his beak of a nose brushed her small straight one, and he felt her breath stir against his skin. "Blessed One," he whispered in gratitude.

"Is she dead?" Both young naitani peered over his shoulder, but it was Beltis who spoke.

It took Torchay a few moments before he realized Beltis sounded strange because she wasn't shouting. The bombardment had stopped. Instantly alert, Torchay looked toward the breach and saw Hamonn, slightly the worse for wear, peering around what was left of the crumbled breastworks.

"They're coming!" he shouted.

One of Iranda's bubbles burst into bright light high above the city wall, illuminating all that lay below. Torchay made note of it. The captain would want to know so she could commend her later for her prompt and proper action.

"They're coming!" Hamonn beckoned with a wave of his arm, but the two naitani still hovered.

"*Go.*" Torchay shoved at the yellow-clad girl. Adessay would follow her lead, if she only would.

"Is she dead?" Beltis asked again.

"No, but if she were, you'd still have to take command. You're ranking naitan. It's your duty to protect *them*." He jerked his head in the direction of the city and wished he hadn't. He'd taken a few too many stones to the head himself. "The enemy is coming."

He could see them over the broken wall, rushing forward in waves, hopefully to break against Ukiny's walls like the ocean on the shore. But like the ocean, they would pour through any gap they found.

"Naitan." Hamonn had returned from the hole in the wall to kneel in front of his charge. He held his hands out, palm up. "I accept your gloves."

Beltis stared at him half a second, then stripped off her gloves and laid them in Hamonn's upturned hands. "Adessay." Her voice cracked like a whip. "Come with me, Trooper. We have an army to stop."

CHAPTER THREE

Beltis had to pick her way through the rubble that had felled Kallista, rather than striding decisively, but she was moving. The young North naitan removed his gloves, handed them to his guard and followed, his blue tunic less noticeable in Iranda's light than Beltis's yellow.

Fire exploded in the plain below, turning half the lead Tibran rank into human torches. Rock tumbled down the steep slope of the glacis, mowing down the ranks behind. From the tower on the far side of the breach in the wall, more magic came, causing vines and brambles to grow instantaneously in the field, impeding the enemy's rush. Satisfied the naitani were doing their duty, Torchay turned to his own.

His muscles quivered from holding his weight off his captain for so long. He pushed himself up, gravel and dust cascading from his back, and went to his knees beside her. That she had not yet regained consciousness worried him. He had no East magic, no

healing in his touch, but he had the best nonmagical medical training available. A bodyguard needed to be able to tend his naitan if
he failed in his first duty and allowed her an injury.

Torchay cleared the area around his captain, blocking out the
shouts and screams of battle. The youngsters seemed to be holding their own, so far. He straightened her limbs, checking for injury, working his way carefully toward her torso and head. She
didn't wake under his probing, even when he pressed on bruises
he knew had to hurt.

She'd been struck in the head at least once, but he wouldn't have
thought that blow enough to render her unconscious this long.

Someone screamed. Beltis. Torchay looked up to see Hamonn
clutch his chest as if arrow struck, but no shaft protruded. He
staggered, then fell from the wall into the shattered hole where
the breach had been forced.

"They have hand cannon," Kadrey shouted back at Torchay as
he pulled both naitani down behind the broken walls. "Long, with
knives on the end like pikes, but firing tiny missiles. As bad as
archers."

Beltis screamed again, rising to her knees to fling fire at the
enemy. Looking grim, Adessay crawled up beside her. Worried,
Torchay turned his attention back to his own naitan. He had to
wake her if he could.

She looked ghost white in the eerie light. Kallista usually appeared more pale than she actually was because of the contrast
with her hair, so dark a brown it was almost black. But this pale-
ness seemed extreme. Gently, Torchay slipped his hands around
her neck to feel along her spine.

He loosened her queue, knowing she wouldn't like it, but the
tight weave of hair kept him from feeling her skull, finding injury
there. When he found the lump, she flinched and gasped. Torchay
grinned. A lump usually meant the swelling was expanding outward, rather than in against the brain. And she responded to pain.

He found no other injuries, save for the cut on her forehead and the second lump forming beneath it. He cleaned it with water from his bottle and a cloth from his pack.

"They're coming!" Kadrey shouted.

"Stop. Hurts." The captain moved her head away from his ministrations.

"I'm finished." The cut was as clean as he could make it here. Torchay took her hand in his. "Squeeze."

"Still hurts. Why?" She opened her eyes to slits, squinting against the bright illumination.

"You got smacked on the head with a great huge rock. Blame it for your headache, not me."

"No. Why squeeze?" Her hand lay limp as yesterday's fish.

"So I know you can. You might wiggle your toes while you're at it." That enormous boulder had barely brushed her, but Torchay's stomach made fear-knots over what that light blow could have done.

"Oh." She promptly squeezed his hand tight enough to hurt and waggled both feet up and down. Then she tried to roll over and sit up.

Torchay pushed her back down, realizing far later than he should have that the scuffling and shouting he heard were right on top of them. He ducked beneath the knife-on-a-pole of the nearest Tibran and buried a blade in his heart. He pulled it out and threw it at the head appearing over the wall at the breach. He just had time to see the hilt quivering in the dead man's eye socket before the next crisis was upon him.

He drew the long knife from its sheath down his back beneath his tunic and slashed across the neck of the first man rushing them, then lunged forward onto one knee and thrust it into the gut of the man behind him. That gave them a little space of time before the next enemy reached them.

Torchay stood, bringing his naitan up with him. Holding her

close, inside his protection, he surveyed the situation. Beltis lay draped over the parapet, the blood pouring from her neck denying any hope she might yet live. Adessay and his guard sprawled in a small heap, both of them gutted. Probably by the first man Torchay had just killed.

More soldiers in padded gray jackets and loose red trousers rushed down the walkway toward them, and yet more climbed onto the wall beyond.

"We should fall back." Torchay tried to draw the captain toward the town side of the wall.

"Where to?" She was already stripping off her gloves, thrusting them at him.

"Anywhere. Somewhere safer than this."

"And where is that?"

He could feel the hair-raising tingle of magic being called. Before he could tuck her gloves into his belt, lightning flashed from her hands. The massive blue-white spark leaped from man to man to man until all of them lay twitching on the walk a few moments before they fell still, their hearts stopped.

More of them climbed over the parapet, up ladders from town where shrill wavering screams tracked the progress of the Tibran sack of Ukiny. Kallista let her lightning fly in huge, jagged horizontal sheets, half toward the men on the wall, half toward the breach where countless more hordes poured through. She stood with her arms outstretched in supplication to the Source of Magic.

Again and again and again, she called on the One for power, until she was blind and deaf with it, sensing the enemy as much as seeing them. Bodies lay piled on the wall five and six deep, and still they came. They climbed over their fellows in the breach and burst onto the city streets, held back now only by Kallista's lightning and the occasional rooftop archer.

"You can't call enough magic to kill them all." Torchay crouched beside her, head swiveling as he attempted to watch in all directions. "There are too many of them. We must fall back."

"I can't!" Kallista could hear the screams of the innocent as they died, smell the smoke of homes being burnt. She couldn't save herself while they suffered. She could see gray and red on the tower where she'd stationed the rest of her troop. They had to have fallen like Beltis and Adessay.

"Kallista!" Torchay grabbed her waist with both hands, breaking her concentration. "Your death won't save them."

Sweet Goddess, he was right. But she couldn't just give up. She lifted her hands high, calling yet again on the One, the Mother and Father of All, Giver of Life, Source of Magic. "Do something!" she screamed. "They are your children! Save them. Use me—whatever you want! Whatever you need. I'll do anything, if you'll just save your people. What kind of Goddess are you?"

The wind rushed past from the sea as it had since time began. The sun crept above the eastern horizon, casting the dead into pale shadows behind the wall, painting their spilled blood brilliant scarlet and crimson and dark, dull, brown. For a moment, Kallista waited to be struck down for her defiance.

Then power filled her in a turbulent rush, enough power to fill deep oceans, to shift whole mountains and build a hundred cities. It permeated her, deep into each strand of hair, every shred of callused skin on her feet. She screamed, and power poured in through her open mouth. She couldn't contain it all. She had to rid herself of it somehow. Kallista threw her hands wide, as if throwing lightning from her fingertips, and the magic exploded from her.

Not in bright sparks, but as a shock wave of darkness, a sort of black mist, roiling out in all directions from where she stood at the epicenter. It settled over the landscape, clinging like some dark dew to everything it touched. And Tibrans began to die.

Some of them screamed, clawing at their faces as if it burned.

Others just dropped in their tracks. Others—she couldn't see clearly. A few turned and ran when they saw the opaque fog approach, but it moved as fast as the lightning she threw. There was no escape.

Panicked, Kallista tried to call it back, but the magic refused to answer. Would it kill everything it touched? She looked down at Torchay where he knelt by her side, head bent, saw the dark glitter clinging to the burnished red of his hair. She tried to brush it off, and it melted away like the mist it resembled, leaving nothing behind. Not even dampness.

Torchay turned his face up to hers, his eyes as wide and frightened as she knew her own must be. "What did you just do?"

In the high mountain pass on the southern edge of the Mother Range, huddled over a feeble fire just at dawn, the trader lifted his head. He sensed something. A new thing, strange and powerful—and oh so seductive. He straightened, searching with all his senses. Was he finally to discover what he had been seeking for so long?

When it hit him, bowing him backward in a spine-cracking convulsion, he shouted for sheer joy. Incredible power rushed through him, recognizing him, welcoming him, promising him his every dream fulfilled. It left him as quickly as it had come, but this time it left him filled with hope, with eager purpose, rather than anxious desperation.

No, not *this* time. This was as like his previous experience as the sun was like the moon. It was promise kept. It pulled at him, compelled him onward, sped his steps. His heart's desire awaited him, and the faster he traveled, the sooner he would have it.

He picked himself up from the dirt where he lay, his traveling companions hovering in a fearful circle around him. "Move, you sluggards!" he bellowed. "I want to be on my way before the sun reaches the treetops."

* * *

He hurt. All over, but especially his head. And there was dirt in his mouth. And his mouth was too dry to spit. Stone tried anyway. He succeeded in getting rid of some of it. He wiped his hand on his pants and scraped more of the grit off his tongue with his fingers.

Where was he? What had happened? They'd made it through the breach, somehow alive and—*Khralsh,* his head hurt.

Ocean was gone, incinerated by an Adaran witch. He'd taken his partner, Moon, with him. River, Wolf, Snow—too many to name—had fallen to arrows or worse. But he and Fox had made it through. He was certain of that. They'd crossed into the city, cleared the houses nearest the wall, which were mostly cleared already save for a screeching crone who'd brained him with a broom and died on Fox's bayonet. They'd reloaded, fired the houses and left them burning to advance to the next street.

Stone had killed the archer shooting at them from the roof and reloaded, then they'd checked the house. Empty. The dead archer was a woman. That had shocked him, but Fox reminded him she was dead now, paying the price of her blasphemy in the afterlife. They'd clattered back down the stairs and set the place alight. Then…

He scrubbed a hand across his face. The light hurt his eyes, even though they were still closed. It wasn't supposed to be light, was it? Wait—yes, the sun had come up. He remembered that. It had just risen over the city walls when… When what?

Stone spit more dirt from his mouth, beginning to have enough spit to do it. He should get up. Find where they'd called muster. Report in. But lifting his head seemed more than he could accomplish. He tried opening an eye and managed that. It was hard to see, his vision veiled, blurred somehow.

This didn't look like the city. Unless the city had crumbled around him. Was that what had happened? Stone opened his other eye. How could the sunlight hurt when everything seemed so dim? He lay over white stone rubble. Big rocks, little rocks, grit, gravel, bloody body parts…mighty Khralsh, he was in the breach.

Stone tried to scoot off the dead but there were too many of them. They carpeted the ground, layers deep, their limbs flopping bonelessly as he struggled to escape them. Heads lolled. Wounds gaped open. Stone's hands slipped and he fell face first into some poor soul's bloated entrails.

Retching his empty stomach even emptier, he slid farther down the slope only to fetch up against the brittle black corpse of one of the fire-witch's victims. Stone recoiled in horror, scrambling, rolling, crawling on his belly until he reached a bare rock promontory jutting from the sea of bodies. There, he curled into a tight ball and shivered uncontrollably.

What was wrong with him? He was a warrior. Death was no stranger to him. He'd climbed across bodies to capture a city numberless times before. He'd been on burial detail, collecting bodies from the battlefield and lining them up in rows to record their names before consigning them to pyres of Khralsh's flames. Granted, he'd never before seen men burst into spontaneous flame without a torch or spark to set the blaze, but fire was fire. It was natural. Not like… *What?* Why couldn't he remember?

Had it been so awful that his mind wiped the memory blank? And where was Fox?

Stone uncurled from his tight knot, just a little. Fox had been with him, he knew. Fox was always with him, just as he was always with Fox. So where was he now?

"Fox!" He tried to shout, but his throat was raw, his voice a weak, raspy, croaking thing.

How far had he rolled from the breach? Stone looked through his veiled vision up the glacis. He was no more than halfway down, but could he make the climb back up? No witches were left to set him on fire or make the earth itself move beneath his feet. So he only had to face climbing back over the cold bodies of his one-time comrades.

Fox was up there. Had to be up there. Stone would do anything for his *brodir*. Spitting once more, calling on his god with it, he started back up, doing his best not to step on the bodies. Desperately, he tried to reconstruct events. Through the breach, kill the crone, fire the houses, next street.

They'd checked the dead archer. They'd fired that house. They left the house. There was a child. An Adaran child. Boy or girl, Stone couldn't tell. Never could when they were that young, especially the way Adarans dressed them alike. The child was huddled in a doorway, terrified, staring at them with witchy pale eyes, waiting for death.

But they didn't make war on children. "Run!" Fox shouted.

"Hide." Stone opened the door behind the child, shooed it inside. Fox had marked the door when it was shut again, designating the building "Not for burning." It was far enough from the wall that they had discretion as to which building to burn, and it was—hopefully—far enough from those already burning that the wood inside the stone walls wouldn't catch. And then... Stone paused in his climb, pulled his hand back from the corpse it touched to wipe it on his filthy jacket.

And then, the air around them had exploded, the sun had gone dark and the world had come to an end.

Except that it obviously hadn't. The same sun—at least Stone thought it was the same one—still shone overhead. The same wind blew past him on its way inland from the ocean. The same bodies still lay in the same breach of the same wall around the same Adaran city.

Not...*exactly* the same bodies. He'd noticed it on his climb, but only now began to piece together what he saw. There were *more* bodies. Hundreds had fallen in the charge on the breach, but some of these dead men wore badges from divisions Stone knew were not scheduled to advance until the walls had been taken.

Many of the bodies bore no marks at all. Others looked as if their heads had exploded, or their hearts had burst, or their internal organs simply decided to crawl out through their skin. Perhaps the world had ended after all.

End of the world or not, he had to find Fox. Something drove him upward, a desperate need to find what he was searching for. And what would that be but his partner? Stone tried calling his name again, quietly this time, for he sensed movement on the walls above and inside the city. Did Tibre hold it, or had the Adarans driven off the assault with their witch magic?

He reached the place where he had regained his senses, as near as he could tell, and began turning bodies over. Most Tibrans had hair some shade of yellow, but Fox's was brighter than most, with a hint of red in the sunlight. Stone concentrated on those bodies with the brightest hair.

"Fox!" He called in a hoarse whisper, looking for some faint motion, some response. Fox had sworn to do his best to live. He couldn't be dead.

His desperation growing, Stone searched through the gray-and-red-clad fallen there in the breach. His breath rasped louder in his ears with every step he took. His vision dimmed then cleared at whim. He called to his partner, sometimes forgetting to keep his voice quiet. Body by lifeless body, he worked his way through the breadth of the breach, from one broken wall to the other.

On the south side, where ladders had been propped for warriors to reach the Adaran witches and wipe them from existence, Stone saw yet another head covered in bright curls. Heart pounding in his chest, he rushed toward it, tripping over the corpses in his path.

Fox lay on his side, curled around the base of a ladder. His face looked peaceful. No, happy. A faint smile curved his lips. Stone's vision blurred again and he wiped the wetness from his cheeks. He was afraid to touch him. Afraid to discover his partner had found Khralsh's welcome.

Swallowing hard, Stone set his hand on Fox's shoulder and tugged. Fox rolled to his back, his arm falling limp to the rubble beside him. Blood pooled on the ground from a gaping wound in his thigh. A man could bleed out in minutes from such a wound. It wasn't bleeding now.

Stone swiped his sleeve across his face again and, fingers shaking, touched his partner, searching for a heartbeat. He could feel nothing through the short, padded jacket. Stone ripped it open, sending bone buttons flying, and laid his hand flat over Fox's heart. Even the shirt could interfere, so Stone opened that as well. Nothing.

"*Damn you.*" Stone pounded on the silent chest, weeping openly now. "You swore to live. You swore to try! You broke your oath! You broke—"

The grief took him over and he sank back on his heels, crying out his pain to whatever god would hear him. He curled over until his forehead touched the rock where he knelt, and let the tears come, let them mingle with Fox's blood on the ground. Tears and blood, the most precious thing a man could offer the warrior god.

He was still there when the Adaran patrol came. They tossed the bodies of the Tibran dead—including Fox—down the slope where what was left of the Tibran Fifth Army could collect them and burn them. They put Stone in shackles and marched him away. He didn't care. He had nothing left to care about.

Aisse lay bleeding in the mud and dung of the cattle pens, waiting for the farmer to return and finish his punishment. Likely, it would finish her as well. Dawn had broken while she lay here and bled, and with the sun came a whisper of hope.

She could see her bag, the one she'd packed so carefully, lying tossed aside just beyond the rough rails of the pen. The tin cup was bent nearly flat, the biscuit crushed to powder, but perhaps the cup could be reshaped and the dirt brushed from the dried beef.

She dug her fingers into the mud and pulled herself forward. It hurt. *Ulili,* it hurt. But she moved. Focused wholly on the bag, she crept toward it bit by painful bit.

"Where do you think you're going, witch?" The farmer's harsh voice made her cry out.

But she couldn't stop, couldn't give up. Not until she had no breath left with which to whisper a prayer, no mind left with which to hope.

The farmer snatched her up by the hair and dragged her over the fence, the rough boards scraping her battered body mercilessly. "If you got life enough to move, you got life enough to feel this." He raised his fist, but before he let it fly, screams echoed through the camp. Screams coming from masculine throats.

He dropped Aisse in the dirt, spinning to face the noise, his face going pale. "What—"

She didn't care what caused the screams. He'd let her go. She stretched her arm out and forced her pain-racked fingers to close around the leather of her bag.

"Achz preserve us," the farmer whispered, and took off at a run toward the battlefront. Though what he thought he could do, Aisse didn't know. He was Farmer caste, not Warrior. But he'd left her blessedly alone.

Aisse dragged the bag close and clutched it to her chest as she crawled the few feet to her cup. It took her several minutes to fumble it into the bag, then she worked her way to the discarded beef. She didn't try to clean it. She didn't know whether she still had teeth strong enough to chew it. But she pushed as much of it as she could gather into the bag. Once that was done, she began to crawl the long, endless distance toward the cover of the trees outside camp.

The sun climbed higher in the sky while she crawled. At first, she flinched at every noise, tried to hide from the sound of running footsteps. But she couldn't move fast enough to hide, and the footsteps always ran past, toward the city. Voices shouted one to the other about witches and evil and death magic. She didn't care. As long as no one tried to stop her, they could blather about anything they liked. She was getting away.

Finally, she felt the cool shade fall across her head. Then her shoulders, her back, her legs. She kept going. She needed to find a place to hide. With so many dead—she'd understood that much, that thousands had died—they surely wouldn't try to find her. They had more important things to do. But she didn't want anyone stumbling across her accidentally and finishing the job the farmer had started.

Aisse crept off the path already formed by people walking to the nearby branch of the river. The trees were short compared to the high forests of her home, and most of the fallen wood had been collected and burned in fires over the last week. But down near the rivulet, she found a tree whose roots had been undermined by seasonal floods. The brown tangle had left a gap big enough to hide her.

She filled her bent cup with water and drank. Then she crawled into the tangle of roots. Her passage left marks in the sandy grit of the bank, but if she tried to erase them, she'd only leave more. Aisse curled into a ball and prayed that no one would find her. And if they did, she prayed for a quick death. She wouldn't go back.

"Are you hurt?" Kallista whispered, searching Torchay for signs of injury.

He shook his head. After a moment, he stood. They huddled together on the city wall, staring out at what Kallista had wrought.

Nothing moved on the walls of Ukiny. After a time, a crow fluttered up and landed with caution. No arm waved it away. It cawed and pecked at the body where it stood.

Nothing moved on the plain west of the city, as far as the beginning of the white tents in the Tibran camp. The misty wave seemed to have lost power just there, for Kallista thought she could see wounded attempting to crawl back to safety.

On the waters of Ukiny Bay, Tibran ships sat at crazy angles, their masts snapped and splintered. They'd all been anchored closer to the city than the camp had been. Some ships had already sunk, the rest sinking or so damaged they'd never sail before next spring.

Within the city, Kallista could hear shouting, some of it joyous, some frightened. The mist hadn't harmed Torchay. Could it have been so selective as to kill only Tibrans, leaving Adarans untouched?

"My gloves, Torchay. I need my gloves."

"Yes, Captain." He pulled them from his belt and helped her put them on, both of them fumbling at the task with shaking hands.

"Don't be afraid of me, Torchay." She fought to keep the quaver from her voice. "Please don't be afraid of me now."

"I am afraid *for* you. That's a different sort of thing. Blessed One, Kallista, what happened?"

"I don't know. I don't— You heard what I said. And then there was power. So much—" She shivered and Torchay wrapped his arms around her, sharing his warmth as he had before. Her shivers weren't due to cold this time, but still his presence stopped them.

"It sounds almost as if…" His voice came hesitant, fearful. "Could you have been…marked?"

Terrified, Kallista stared at him. "That's just legend. Children's stories. It isn't real."

"Isn't it?" Torchay looked over her head at the devastation on the plains below.

Kallista shivered again. Or perhaps it was more of a shudder. "Isn't it supposed to leave an actual mark? Something you can see? Or feel?"

Torchay's hand that had been absently stroking the nape of her neck came down to claim her hand. He carried it back up to where he'd been touching her. "What do you feel?"

There, beneath her untidy queue, she felt a faint raised ridge on her skin. Her fingertips followed it down to a sort of knot, where another ridge intersected the first. Cold gripped her heart.

"Can you see it?" She held her hair up, out of the way, while Torchay bent to look.

"Yes," he said. Nothing more.

"Well? What does it look like?"

"A scar. A red, raised scar." He paused and his fingers touched. He traced along her spine, then perpendicular to it. "North. South. East. West." He touched the point where the lines crossed, where Kallista had felt the knot. "And a rose in the center. It's a perfect Compass Rose."

She dropped her hair, pressed it down over the mark, over Torchay's hand. "Maybe it was there already."

"No. It wasn't."

"How can you be sure?"

"Kallista, I've braided your hair almost every day for nine years. It wasn't there."

CHAPTER FOUR

"Oh, sweet heaven, Torchay." Kallista had reached the end of her strength. She'd poured it all out and had nothing left for her precious control. A tear trickled down her cheek. "I'm a soldier. Nothing more. I don't want this."

All she'd ever wanted was an ordinary life. An ilian of her own. Family. Friends. But from the day her magic first woke when she was thirteen, and she killed one of the family's supper chickens with an out-of-control lightning bolt, she'd been destined for the military.

Her dreams had shrunk from love and family to duty and comrades. And now, even that threatened to be taken from her. Punishment for finding a friend.

On his feet again, Torchay carefully wiped the tear away with his thumb. "Nevertheless."

"I'd rather have a friend."

"Is that what you're fretting about?" His northern mountains accent came out as he teased. "You've still got that. You'll not get rid of me so easily."

"Naitan. Are you injured?" One of the regular Adaran troops put his head above the walkway, standing on a Tibran ladder. "General Uskenda has ordered every able-bodied soldier to assemble in the West Gate Square as soon as possible."

Kallista nodded stiffly. "Tell the general I'll be there. I am unharmed. My troop—" She took a deep breath. "I believe the rest of my troop is dead."

The soldier nodded back, trying to stare at all the bodies surrounding her without appearing to do so. "Thank you, Captain."

She hoped to put in an appearance at the assembly point and be dismissed to go check on her naitani in the tower. There was a chance, albeit a very faint one, that they yet lived. But the general spotted her quickly and gestured her to approach.

It had been a vain hope anyway, Kallista thought as she worked her way through the forming ranks. The blue and black she and Torchay wore made them stand out in the sea of dun-brown infantry tunics like flowers in a field of dead grass.

General Huyis Uskenda was in the midst of taking reports and giving orders when Kallista reached her side, and she didn't stop. Kallista edged closer, hoping to hear something of the battle as a whole.

"They're all dead," the captain of the lone troop of cavalry was saying, her white rank ribbons lying limp and blood-spattered against the shoulders of her gray uniform. "Every Tibran in the city. They hadn't penetrated as far as the Mother Temple, so I didn't have to ride the whole city.

"They're all dead on the plain too, at least what my troopers and I could see on a quick patrol. There may be survivors near the camp. We didn't ride that close because I know for certain there are survivors *in* the camp. They took potshots at us from the tents with those hand cannon of theirs."

"Good, good." Uskenda nodded, the layered red ribbons of rank on her brown tunic so thick they looked like fringe.

Uskenda was better than the usual run of general, her mind sharp enough to adapt to freakish enemy tactics without panicking and still young enough to walk farther than from her bed to the dinner table. Promotion in the Adaran army was based on seniority. Those who lived long enough to achieve a general's rank tended to cling to it until they died at their posts, whether they could still do the job or not.

This explained why Kallista was merely a captain at her age of thirty-four years, though promotion did tend to be a bit quicker among the naitani. She shuddered to think of some of the generals she'd served under who might have been assigned to defend this city. Uskenda was indeed a godsend in comparison.

"What about Adarans?" The general turned to an aide, a young man attached to her staff. "Did that…whatever it was…slaughter our people as well as the Tibrans?"

"No, General." He referred to his notes on the scraps of paper in his hand. "We sent out patrols immediately after—"

"I know that. Don't tell me what I already know. Are our people dead?"

"*No,* General," he repeated. "The citizens within the range of the…weapon…for the most part seem to have taken no harm, according to those patrols. The first Adarans we've found dead so far have all been known criminals. Thieves. Extortionists. That sort of thing."

Kallista leaned unobtrusively on her bodyguard as her knees threatened to buckle in relief. When Torchay had survived the dark magic, she'd begun to hope, but had been afraid to trust it.

General Uskenda nodded and turned her piercing gray glare on Kallista. "Well, Captain? What exactly did happen? What sort of—" she eyed the blue of Kallista's tunic "—of *North* magic was that?"

"I…can't say." Not because it was a naitani secret, but because she didn't know. However, generals—most of those she'd known—preferred secrets to ignorance.

The general snorted. "Never knew any North magic to behave like that."

"No, General." Not one of the naitani in the North Academy when Kallista was attending had shown any magic resembling what she had just done. No instructor had ever mentioned the possibility of anything like it. And as a mature naitan with well-established magic, Kallista should not have been able to do it. No naitan had more than one gift. Sometimes the gift manifested itself in different ways, like Iranda being able to both light and burn, but it was always the same gift.

"No?" Uskenda raised a gray-streaked eyebrow. "Are you saying you *didn't* just single-handedly wipe out an army?"

"That's not—" Kallista came to hard attention. "No, General. The enemy was destroyed by magic, and I did cast the magic. But—" She tried to keep her voice from sounding as distraught as she felt, but feared she failed. "I don't know what it was that I did—other than casting the magic—and I don't know how I did it."

The general hmmphed again, staring at her as if she could tell that Kallista kept secrets. "Very well. Maybe the naitani at the temple will know. Report for investigation."

"Now?"

"Of course now." Uskenda's scowl actually made Kallista shiver. "Do you think I mean next week? You decimated the Tibran army, you didn't annihilate it. With their ships foundered, they're trapped here. We've still got a city to defend. Our numbers might just be close to even now. If we can pin them here, keep them from shifting their cannon up the coast to Kishkim, where they've got another damn army but not so many cannon, maybe we can keep them from taking Kishkim *and* Ukiny. We need to know what you did and whether you can do it again."

"Yes, General." Kallista saluted and departed for the Mother Temple, Torchay shadowing her. She was so tired she could barely stand, much less walk straight, but General Uskenda was right. They weren't out of danger.

Torchay took her arm, supporting her, though she knew he had to be at the end of his strength as well. "You need to rest," he said. "Not answer a load of unanswerable questions."

"I'm fine." Kallista would have blamed Torchay's insubordination on their "friend" conversation yesterday, save that he'd always been on the insubordinate side. Especially when it came to generals. She saved her breath for walking and keeping her eyes open.

Ukiny was large enough to have three temples. Two devoted themselves primarily to education and healing, though they also served their areas as worship centers. The other was the first temple in the city, the Mother Temple. It provided education and healing like the others, as well as local administrative needs. It sat in the center of a vast four-petaled square in the oldest section of Ukiny.

The worship hall, the central portion of the building, soared high above the more utilitarian sections. Tall arched windows of colored glass were set into white stone walls that hardly seemed the same material of which the city fortifications were built. Though Kallista hadn't been inside the Mother Temple yet, she knew that corridors would lead from each of the four entrances to the sanctuary in the center. Every temple in Adara was built to the same plan, whether in the smallest village or the capital city.

Rooms to either side of the corridors conducted temple business; healing to the east, schools on the north, administration and records, including the city's birth, death and marriage records in the south. To the west, the direction from which they approached, the rooms served as the temple's library and archives. Centuries of records were stored in the rooms to either side of the black marble corridor they traversed.

The priests of each temple formed their own ilian—bound as mates by holy oath—and lived in a big house across the southern plaza from the temple. She'd been raised in such a house with a dozen parents and half a dozen sedili, her sisters and brothers in the ilian who were close in age. Memories swarmed Kallista's mind as they entered the sanctuary. She was too tired to keep them at bay. She'd run tame with her sedili in the temple built of gray mountain granite shipped down the rivers that joined there in Turysh. She'd been the only one of them with magic. When her magic woke in the North the way it had, it had set her apart from her sedili even more.

"Wait here." Torchay pushed her onto one of the benches against the wall in the worship center reserved for the old and infirm who couldn't stand for long periods. "I'll find the prelate."

Kallista thought about protesting, reminding him that she was neither feeble nor aged, and was his superior besides, but at the moment she didn't feel any of those things. Using her lightning often left her tired, but not drained like this. She leaned her head against the wall and watched the sunlight dance in the colored glass.

She traced its downward path till it sparkled on the floor mosaic, the compass rose depicted in every Adaran temple. A slash of blue tile lightning pointed north. To the east, the compass arm was a green twining vine. Yellow flame stretched south, a black-thorned briar pointed to the west, and in the center, uniting the four cardinal points was the red rose of the One.

The compass rose symbolized both the gifts of magic and the One Herself. Just as a rose had many petals yet formed a single flower, so the One had many aspects, yet was still One God, holding all that ever was and ever would be within Her being. All came from Her and all returned when its time was done.

Kallista had no idea how much time had passed before Torchay returned with a plump, smiling gray-haired woman dressed in a green robe over her loose white shirt and gray trousers. She struggled to her feet and bowed. "Honor to you, Mother. I am Kallista Varyl. I've been sent by General Uskenda to be examined—"

"Of course you have, dear. Come." The woman put her arm around Kallista's waist and guided her toward the leaf-and-vine-decorated entrance to the eastern corridor. "You're exhausted. You should rest."

"The general was most explicit that I be examined right away." She had never failed in her duty and didn't intend to begin now.

"How can I examine anything when you're asleep on your feet? No, you come and rest, and your ilias with you."

"He's not my ilias." It seemed as if she had to force the words past her cottony tongue. Or maybe it was her brain that was cottony. "He's my friend. I mean, my bodyguard."

"Bodyguard, ilias." The woman waved a dismissive hand. "All the same. Like aspects of the One."

She ushered Kallista into a small room containing a large bed, and pushed her onto it. "Rest. You too." She pushed Torchay after Kallista. "Sleep. I will speak with those I must. When you wake up, we'll talk."

Something was wrong here. Kallista had to think for a wide space of time before she knew what it was. "Torchay doesn't sleep with me," she mumbled. "Not in the same bed. He's my bodyguard."

"Don't talk nonsense," the prelate said as she was closing the door. "Of course he does. Now sleep."

The word must have held magic, for instantly Kallista fell into unconsciousness. She fought it. There was something she needed to do, warnings she needed to give, but her body wouldn't release her from its exhaustion.

* * *

She wandered in dreams through shining landscapes and blurring fogs, hunting something. Abruptly, she flew through the air, images blurring below her until she stood in the soot-blackened street before the broken wall around Ukiny.

The sun high in the sky near blinded her with its brilliance. Men and women swarmed the breach, clearing away rubble, stacking the salvageable stone near the wall in the space left after the Tibrans had burned the houses built against it. A small trickle of gravel spilled from the southern edge of the wall still standing.

"Back away," Kallista shouted. "It's unstable. It's going to fall!"

But no one moved. No one seemed to hear her. When the wall gave way, sending massive stones and piles of rubble crashing down, shouts and screams of warning came too late. The workers couldn't escape. The rock fell and they were beneath it.

"Quickly! Move the rock. Get it off before it crushes them. Adessay—" But he was dead. He couldn't help. Kallista ran forward to pull people out of danger.

"Kallista!" Torchay called to her, drew her back, and she was lying fully dressed in a too-soft bed in a too-dark room with Torchay gripping her shoulders.

"A dream," she breathed, rubbing her hands down her face. "It was just a dream like any other."

"Not exactly like," Torchay said, releasing her cautiously, as if he thought he might have to grab hold again. "I could always wake you from the others."

"You woke me from this one." Kallista let drowsiness claim her.

"Not till you were damned good and ready. Not till I shook you five turns and called your name five more."

"Lie down. Go back to sleep." She tugged at his sleeve and reluctantly, he did as she bid him.

"It's not proper," he grumbled. "I can take the floor. Or out in the corridor."

"Too far away. And there isn't any floor in this room. The bed's too big. Big enough for two more bodies beside ours."

"You didn't want me here before."

"Changed my mind. I need you to wake me from the dreams."

He lay quiet a moment and Kallista thought he had gone to sleep. As much as he ever slept. He woke at the slightest noise. Then he spoke. "Nightmares aren't part of a bodyguard's duty."

"I know." Kallista grinned, knowing he couldn't see it in the dark. "But they *are* in the *Handbook of Rules for Friends*. Right after 'See that your friend gets back home after drinking all night.'"

Torchay turned his back to her. "Go to sleep."

Kallista turned over and settled her back against his, as they slept in the field while hunting bandits. "Yes, Sergeant."

She slept the sun around before waking early and alone on the second morning. A smiling acolyte in the yellow-trimmed white of a South naitan-in-training led her to the baths on the floor below. Kallista paddled about in company with a trio of chubby toddlers and their pregnant minder before being escorted firmly but politely to breakfast in the prelate's office with her hair dripping down her back. There she not only found the green-robed elder, but Torchay looking entirely too comfortable. The first finger on his left hand wore a white-bandaged splint, but it didn't seem to interfere with his ease.

"Eat, child." The woman indicated a tray near overflowing with food.

Torchay picked up the plate and began filling it, ignoring Kallista's sour look.

"I am sorry, Mother," she said. "I don't know your name."

"Mother is fine. Mother Edyne, if you insist on more."

Kallista took the food Torchay handed her and began to eat, discovering an appetite she hadn't recognized.

"Your guard has told me what he observed that morning,"

Mother Edyne said without waiting. "Tell me what you experienced."

Over sweet buns, early melon and steaming cha brewed from leaves shipped over the southern mountains from the lands beyond, Kallista told her. When she had finished, the prelate frowned.

"This magic…" Mother Edyne shook her head. "It has frightened people. It smells of the mysteries of the West. That is why I've kept you here, you know. So that their fear would have no target."

"No, I didn't know that." Kallista shuddered. No one had been found with West magic in over fifty years. "But I am a North naitan. I've always been North. Not West."

"I admit it puzzles me." Edyne peered at Kallista, her eyes sharp green. "Have you found a mark somewhere on your body? One that you did not have before."

Kallista felt Torchay's gaze on her as she lied. "No. Nothing like that."

The magic she had already was enough to bear. She didn't want more. Maybe if no one knew, it would just go away. She reached back and combed her hair down closer over her neck. She didn't have to wear a queue. It wasn't regulation for officers the way it was for other ranks. She could grow her hair longer.

"Hmm," the prelate considered. "Has there been anything else? Any sign of other magic? Foreseeing perhaps? That has always been the most common sort of West magic."

"No, Mother Edyne." The dream had been merely a dream. Nothing more than that. It couldn't have been anything more.

Kallista could feel Torchay's agitation rising off him in waves. Next, Mother Edyne would be claiming *that* was a sign of West magic, and not part of knowing him so well for so long.

"Well, that's that, I suppose." Mother Edyne stood and the other two scrambled to their feet with her. "No, no. Stay. Finish your meal. And then I suppose you must return to your duties. Unless there is something more you wish to tell me?"

Kallista widened her eyes, doing her best to look as if not only did she have no secrets at this moment, but she had never had any secret in her entire life. "No, Mother. Nothing."

"Very well." She motioned them back into their chairs and let a hand rest on each head as she passed from the room. "Be well, my children."

When the door was closed and Mother Edyne gone, Torchay drew his little blade and stabbed it through a melon slice. "And why," he asked through clenched teeth, "did you not tell the prelate the truth?"

Kallista hunched her shoulders, embarrassed by her fear and by the lies she'd told to cover it. What she had done terrified her. She didn't wish it undone. Ukiny would have been taken and thousands more dead or enslaved if she had not done it. But she feared the consequences of her impulsive request.

Already, according to Mother Edyne, people whispered. West magic involved the unexplained and the unexplainable. It dealt with hidden things and with endings, including the ultimate ending: death. No wonder people feared it.

"I'm sure it's temporary." Kallista focused on the last of her meal, unable to meet his eyes. "Now that the enemy has been cut down to a reasonable size, I'll have no need for such a magic. Why bother the prelate with it?"

"When the One gives a gift, She rarely takes it back."

"But a onetime event is more common—more *likely* than my having permanent magic from two Compass points."

"You have the mark."

She refrained from smoothing her hair down over her neck only through sheer force of will. "Legend. Fable. Nothing more."

Torchay growled, a sound of utter disgust. She'd heard it countless times.

"Besides," she said, risking a glance in his direction, "talk is already circulating. I have no doubt word is already flying to the Barbs. How much quicker would they come to investigate if the Mother Temple here added its weight to the gossip?"

The Order of the Barbed Rose believed an ancient and stubborn heresy, that West magic was evil, and that if it and all its practitioners were eliminated, death itself could be eliminated. The Order had been suppressed for centuries and yet could not be entirely crushed. The fear of death and the will to conquer it was too strong. Even the One's promise of life eternal after physical death was not enough to quell this persistent falsehood.

Everyone feared the Barbs. Their secret membership fanned out through all Adara, investigating any magic that seemed the least bit out of the ordinary. It occurred to Kallista now that perhaps true West magic hadn't been seen in so long because the Barbs had somehow found a way to identify those rare ones so gifted and eliminate them before or as their power manifested.

"I can deal with any Barb who comes calling," Torchay said. "As could you. But do you really believe Mother Edyne would contribute to gossip in any way?"

She didn't, but she shrugged her shoulders. "The fewer who know a thing, the easier it is to keep it secret."

"Lying to a prelate has its own consequences."

"I'll risk it." Kallista set her plate aside and stood. "We should report in."

There were funerals to attend. Flames competed with the blaze of the setting sun as Kallista stood with General Uskenda and the honor guard in the plaza west of the Mother Temple. She let the tears flow, blaming them on the sun's glare, and commended the souls of her entire troop, all five of the naitani and their five bodyguards, into the welcoming arms of the One. Never had she lost so many.

Never had the Adaran army and its naitani been cast into a battle of such size. They fought bandits. They patrolled remote mountain passes and distant, lawless prinsipalities. They did not fight pitched battles against massive armies. They'd never had to. Until now.

Kallista fought back her grief. So many bright young lives, so full of promise, ended here. Adara could not afford such losses. She feared that they would be facing many more such funerals if changes were not made. But Blessed One, did *she* have to be the one to change?

When the sun had set and the fires burned to embers, there were letters to be written, paperwork to be done. How could she write so many at once? How could she put it off?

The breeze, not so strong inside the city where it was broken by wall and building, stirred her hair. Kallista tucked it behind her ears yet again as they walked back to quarters.

"If you will not braid your hair," Torchay said from his place at her shoulder, "you should cut it."

"Oh, that will cover my neck *so* well." She pulled her hair back from her face and held it with one gloved hand.

"Don't cut the back. Just the front, so it can't get in your face. Or you could—"

"This is not a time to be thinking about hair."

"True." He picked up his pace and took her elbow to escort her quickly through a crowd spilling out of a public house. "But it was noticed. Today it was taken as a sign of mourning for the death of your troopers. If you continue to wear it so, it could be taken as a sign of something else. Perhaps that you attempt to hide something."

Kallista sighed. She was a soldier. That had been her duty, her destiny for twenty-one years. It kept things simple. She would rather things stayed that way, but the complications kept mounting. "We'll work out some explanation later."

The sun must have hurt her eyes more than she realized. They kept watering during the short walk, even as Torchay ushered her into their too-empty billet. The setting sun must bother his eyes as well, given the way he was blinking them.

Kallista gave him the courtesy of privacy, looking away even as she briefly touched his shoulder with an ungloved hand. "I have letters to write."

She managed three, writing to the accompaniment of steel on stone, before her eyes began to cross with weariness. Torchay tumbled her into her narrow bed and took his place on the pallet in front of the door.

Once more her dreams were filled with shine and fog. Again the city wall fell and again she shouted a warning that no one heard. But the dream did not end there.

She dreamed of a man, golden-skinned and golden-haired, his hard body moving over her and in her. As she cried out in passion, he changed. His black hair tumbled around her face, and he changed yet again. His dark skin paled, his hair going bright, and it was Torchay making love to her, Torchay making her cry out.

She jerked, struggling to wake, but something caught her soul and drew her back. She went spinning across the dreamscape, colors of light and darkness flashing by and through her, until she was released to roll tumbling across a rough stone floor, fetching up against a fat table leg.

Before she could pick herself up, a blade was pressed against her throat. The woman holding it shone fierce and bright with power. She was not young, perhaps ten or even twenty years past Kallista's age. Her red hair was streaked with gray, her freckled face lined with experience. Her green-brown eyes stared deep into Kallista's.

"Who are you?" the woman demanded. "How did you get in here?"

"I…" How *did* she get here? "…I don't think I *am* here."

With a snarl, the woman sliced her knife across Kallista's throat.

CHAPTER FIVE

Kallista recoiled, hands flying up to push the madwoman away. She called for Torchay as she scrabbled backward across the stone floor, her voice a hoarse croak, surprised she still had a voice. She reached up to stanch the wound…but there was no blood pouring down over her undertunic. No pain. Carefully, Kallista felt her neck. There was no wound.

"So. You're the new one." The woman stood, tossed the knife on the table above. "How long has it been?"

Kallista ran her hands over the whole of her throat. How could that knife not have cut her? She had felt its sharpness, felt it prick her. "How long has it been since what?"

"Since I died, of course. What's your name?" The woman poured wine from a silver pitcher into an ornate cup. "I'd offer you some, but I'm afraid you couldn't drink it."

"Why not?" Kallista got awkwardly to her feet, staring at the high chamber around her. It was dark, the windows mere slits in the gray stone walls, the candles blazing from bronze candlesticks insufficient to make up for the lack of sunlight. Banners in subtle colors with strangely familiar devices attempted to soften the stone, and a fire burned on a circular hearth, the smoke finding its own way out the hole in the roof. This was the most realistic dream she'd ever had.

"I can drink in my dream if I want to," she said, recalling what the other had said about the wine.

"It's not a dream." The woman gave her a sour look. "Not exactly. You should know that— Here, what *is* your name?"

"Kallista. What's yours?"

The woman laughed and took a drink from her cup. As she drank, the smile faded from her eyes. She set the cup on the table, staring at Kallista in shock. "You really don't know me, do you?"

"Should I?"

"Yes." The woman had no small opinion of herself if she expected a complete stranger to recognize her and know her name.

"Sorry." Kallista lifted her shoulders in a tiny shrug. "I don't."

"How long *has* it been since my death? Since the death of Belandra of Arikon?"

Kallista stared. She was more than ready for this dream to end. It was becoming far too strange. "Belandra of Arikon never lived. She's a story. A tale told by the fireside to frighten children and thrill young men."

"I never lived? Never *lived?*" The woman—Belandra of her dreams—snatched up the silver cup and threw it across the room. Wine flew in all directions, none of it spotting Kallista's pale blue undertunic.

"How then did I unite the four prinsipalities into one people?" Belandra demanded. "How did I fight and defeat the enemies of the One? How did I—" Her mouth continued to move, but Kallista could not hear her. It was as if some barrier had dropped between them, cutting off all sound.

In the far distance, she could hear Torchay calling her name and turned to go, to answer him.

"Wait." Belandra caught her arm. "How long?"

Kallista felt Torchay's voice pulling at her, drawing her back, but Belandra's hand anchored her in place. "A thousand years. The four prinsipalities were united a thousand years ago. There are twenty-seven prinsipalities in Adara now. But the first Reinine was Sanda, not Belandra."

The older woman's smile showed a deep affection that made Kallista shiver. "My ilias was much better suited to governing than a hot-tempered naitan like me."

Torchay called again, stretching her thin.

"I have to go." Kallista clawed at the fingers holding her.

"Take this." Belandra pulled a ring from her forefinger and pressed it into Kallista's hand. "I will have many questions when next we meet."

Which will be never, if I have aught to say about it. Kallista closed her hand reflexively around the ring. As soon as she did, Belandra released her. She went flying back through the light and the dark and the colors to slam into her body with a force that bowed her into a high arc. She gasped, drawing air into lungs that seemed to have forgotten how.

"*Kallista.*" Torchay held her face between his hands, fear in every line of his moonlit expression.

"I am here. I'm awake." She resisted the urge to touch him in return, to be sure he was solid and real.

With a shaking hand, he brushed her hair back from her face, then sat up straight on the edge of her bed, setting his hands in his lap. "You were no' breathin'," he said, never taking his eyes from her. His thick accent showed the depth of his agitation. "You shouted, like you did before. I came to wake you, but you would no' wake. Then you quieted. I thought the dream was over so I went back to bed. But you called my name."

He stared at her, his eyes haunted. "You called my name, and you stopped breathin'. And no matter what I did, you would no' start again."

Kallista shuddered. Had that been while she was in that strange place talking to the woman who claimed to be Belandra of Arikon? Could some part of her have literally been in another place? That place? *Impossible.*

"I'm breathing now," she said.

"Aye." He was shaking, trying to hide it, but failing.

She reached for his hand. He took it, gripped it tight. But it wasn't enough. She used his hand to pull herself up. She put her arms around him and held on tight until her trembling and his went away.

"Do no' do that again," he said over and over. "Ever. Do not."

"No," she said again and again. "No. I won't. Never."

When she could let him go, Torchay picked her up and stood her beside the bed.

"What are you doing?" She had to catch his arm to keep from staggering.

"Moving your bed. I'm too far away across the room. You'll be sleeping next to me till the dreams stop." He lifted the bedding, mattress and all, from its rope frame and set it on the floor. "We can bring in a larger bed in the morning."

"It's against regulations—" Kallista began, but fell silent at the flash of his eyes.

"It's against regulations for me to allow you to die. It's against nature for you to stop breathing like that. I want you at my back." He crossed the room to collect his mattress from the doorway and laid it beside hers. He was on his knees rearranging the blankets when he paused.

"What's this?" Torchay plucked a small object from the tangle of her blankets.

"I don't know." Kallista held her hand out for it. "What?"

"It's a ring."

She could see it now as he held it up to the candlelight, examining it. Cold coursed through her veins.

"I didn't know you had a ring like this. Pretty." He set it in her hand and went back to straightening blankets.

Kallista didn't have a ring like this. It was thick and gold, bearing the marks of the hammers that had shaped it. Incised deeply into the flat crest was a rose, symbol of the One. The ring was primitive and powerful. It called to her, demanding that she put it on. Kallista curled her hand into a fist, resisting the urge. She did not own this ring. She could not. Because it had been given to her in a dream.

She opened her hand and let the ring fall to the floor. She didn't want it, didn't want what it might mean.

"Careful. You've dropped it." Torchay shifted to his other knee and picked it up. He held it out to her but Kallista ignored it, so he set it on the chest. "You're too tired for words. Not breathing'll do that to you. Come to sleep."

She was tired. Tired of strangeness and impossibilities and mysteries she couldn't comprehend. She wanted her life back the way it had been before the Tibran invasion, but she feared that was one of the impossible things, and it frightened her.

Torchay lay down and turned his back to her, waiting for her to set hers against it. Careful in her weariness, Kallista stretched out on her own pallet. Rather than turning her back, she tucked herself in behind him and wrapped her arm around his waist. He startled, then lay still. Too still, as if afraid to move, to breathe.

"I need to hold on to something tonight," Kallista said. "Let me hold you."

He didn't reply, but the tension slid out of him. She snuggled closer, the tip of her nose just touching the top of his spine. This was against regulations, rules she had carefully kept for years. The rules had a purpose, one she agreed with. But right now, tonight, she didn't care. She needed to hold on to something that was real, that was flesh, blood, bone, against the dreams coming again.

Aisse lay in her hiding place for a day, a night and another day. She crawled out only for water. By the second night, though every inch of her body ached, she could stand, and even walk without too much dizziness.

The noise of the camp—animals bellowing, men shouting, warriors marching—sounded much too near. Now that she could walk, she needed to move farther away, to a hiding place where they couldn't find her no matter how hard they searched.

She crawled back beneath the tree and gathered her few pitiful belongings, then she returned to the riverbank. Aisse looked downstream, toward the camp. That way lay death. She turned her face upstream and began to walk. This direction might not hold life, but as sure as the sun rose every morning, she knew it at least held hope.

Three days later, Kallista had finished all ten of her damned notification letters and delivered them to headquarters, to be included with the next set of dispatches to the capital. River traffic had returned almost to normal. The Tibrans no longer had enough manpower to interdict travel by boat along the Taolind, and they'd never had enough boat power. The river was the best means of travel to the interior, to Arikon far to the west, and regular dispatches were getting through again.

But now, Kallista had nothing to do. She had no younger naitani to train in their magic. She had no call on her own magic once she chased the cannon from closing on the river gate. Her paperwork, the bane of her existence, was complete. She'd even had time to experiment on her hair with Torchay, settling on simply tying back her front hair in a small horsetail on the back of her head, and leaving that behind her ears to fall free over her neck. She was bored.

Boredom and curiosity had her taking the long way from her billet to the Mother Temple's library by way of the breach in the western wall. Repairs had begun already and Kallista wanted to see how they were going.

Torchay stalked at her side like some bright avenger, scowling at anyone who came close. He didn't like all the gossip about the "scythe of death" as the dark magic she'd done was beginning to be called. He took the epithet personally, unable to shrug it off as well as Kallista could, which wasn't all that well. She tried to tell him it was useless to resent people for their ignorance, but he didn't seem to hear.

The streets grew thicker with people as they neared the breach. Kallista could see the two walls of mortared stone that formed the inner and outer surfaces of the city wall, and some of the rubble filling the wide gap between the two walls that provided much of its strength. Civilians and a few companies of infantry conscripts swarmed the breach now, clearing away the broken and fallen stones so the walls could be repaired.

She frowned, squinting against the sun's fierce brightness. The scene seemed familiar, as if she had been here before. A woman dressed in darkest blue straightened, beckoned to the child carrying the water bucket. And there—two men used iron bars as levers to pry up a larger stone. And the brown-haired woman in red lifted the shoulder yoke holding two filled baskets and staggered toward the dump. Kallista clutched Torchay's arm as terror froze her in place.

"What's wrong?" Torchay looked outward, hunting the threat.

She couldn't answer. This was her dream. She had dreamed it four nights in a row, always the same. Now, the man in the white tunic would call his daughter down from the pile of rock. He did. Her eyes snapped to the southern edge of the broken wall. The thin trickle of sand poured from the mortared interior.

"Get back!" she shouted, throwing herself forward. "Get away from the wall! It's going to fall!"

Unlike her dream, heads turned. People heard her. They started to move, slowly at first, uncertainly. But when the trickle of sand became a stream of gravel, they ran.

"Hurry!" Kallista snatched up the disobedient girl and thrust her into her father's hands. "Run! That way!"

Torchay grabbed Kallista and shoved her into the shelter of a deep doorway just as the first of the dressed stone fell from the top of the mortared wall to shatter on the street's cobbles. He held her there, shielding her with his body until the thunder of falling rock ended and he allowed her to push him away.

Fine dust clouded the air. Kallista coughed as she peered into the collapse, trying to see broken limbs, crushed bodies.

"This was your dream." Torchay's voice held no doubt.

"Yes." There should be casualties. A child's body there, beneath that largest stone—but no, Kallista had given that child to her father. And the woman who should be moaning, trapped over there with her face bloodied—Kallista had seen her run into an alley two houses over.

As the air cleared, people began to emerge from the cover they had taken, staring about them from frightened eyes in dust-whitened faces.

"Who's hurt?" Kallista shouted. "Is anyone missing?"

"My sedil, Vann," a man called.

"No," another answered. "I'm here. Not hurt."

The workers milled about, shouting an occasional name, but in the end, all were accounted for. The cuts on Torchay's legs and back where the shattered rock had struck him were the worst injuries. He and Kallista had been closest to the collapse.

"But how did you know?" the mason in charge of repairs asked. "How did you know it would fall? Even I had no warning."

Anxious to get Torchay to the temple for healing, Kallista did not want to take time to answer. Torchay hung back. "Do you not see the blue of her tunic? She is a North naitan. She can read the earth and the things carved from it. Not often. But sometimes. When there is danger."

"Ah." The mason nodded in understanding as Kallista urged Torchay on.

"Your back is still bleeding badly," she scolded. "We do not have time for these delays."

"Better to give them an explanation they can swallow than leave them to wonder and invent something even more outlandish than the truth."

"Fine, fine. It's done." Kallista lifted her hand from the deepest cut to find it still bleeding. She put it back, but it wasn't easy to maintain sufficient pressure as they walked. "Just don't bleed to death before we reach the temple."

Torchay chuckled. "Such tender concern for your underling."

She pressed harder, knowing it hurt him, but wanting the bleeding to stop. "Hush."

For a while he did, but she knew it was too good to last. "While they're tending my back," he said, "I want you to talk to Mother Edyne. Tell her about the dreams. Tell her everything."

Kallista scowled. She didn't want to. If anyone else knew, it would somehow become more real. "I'll consider it."

"*Tell* her, Kallista. You must. It's no' normal, what's happenin' to you. What if you stop breathin' again and I can't bring you back? I didn't last time."

"Yes, you did." They hadn't talked about what happened, though they'd slept back-to-back every night since then. She didn't want to talk about it now, but it appeared Torchay was of a different mind. "You called me back."

"Back from where?" He stopped at the temple door and gripped her arms, the light, clear blue of his eyes blazing almost white as he glared at her. "Where were you? It wasn't a dream, was it? You don't know what's happening to you. I certainly don't. You need to find someone who does."

"You think that's Mother Edyne?"

"I don't know. Neither will you until you tell her." His hands tightened, digging in till it almost hurt. "Promise me you'll do it."

She dragged her gaze away, stubbornly silent. She couldn't make that promise. She just couldn't.

"Pah!" Torchay pushed away and strode into the temple.

Kallista scrambled to catch up, rushing down the long corridor after him. "Dammit, Torchay, you're bleeding again."

"Let it." He rounded on her again, just outside the entrance to the sanctuary, bending down until his nose almost brushed hers. "At least I have sense enough to be going to get it mended, unlike some too-stubborn-for-her-own-damn-good naitan I know." He whirled and stalked across the worship hall.

"Torchay—" Kallista called after him, but he only gave one of his disgusted growls. Better to let him go. Maybe he'd be in a better temper later.

She wandered toward the center of the worship hall, her hand drifting to the ring in her pocket, the one she could not possibly possess. The ring given to her in a dream. She had yet to put it on a finger, but neither had she been able to leave it behind, lying on the chest in her room. She'd carried it in a pocket the last three days.

Kallista drew the ring from her pocket. The rose on its crest was identical to the one inlaid in the center of the temple floor, the faint reddish hue derived from the wax left behind when it had been used as a seal. What did it mean? How had she come to possess it? She had far too many questions and far too few answers.

Perhaps she *should* consult Mother Edyne. But what could an East magic prelate of a provincial temple know about mysteries such as these? Kallista started to put the ring back in her pocket and almost dropped it.

She caught it again, gripped it tight in her hand, heart pounding. She couldn't lose the ring, no matter how little she wanted it. Somehow, she was certain that it was a key to many of the answers she wanted. She didn't understand how an inanimate object could answer questions, but the certainty would not leave her. Perhaps she was meant to look the ring up in some archive or other. However the answers were to be had, she could not lose the thing. And the safest place for it…

Kallista sighed, resigned to the inevitable. She removed her right glove and slid the ring onto her forefinger where the dream Belandra had worn it. But it would not fit over her knuckle. Her hands were apparently bigger than the dream woman's. The ring went on the third finger of her right hand. It looked good there.

"It's about time." The woman's voice behind her brought Kallista spinning around so fast, she lost her balance. *It could not be.*

But it was. Belandra lounged carelessly against the wall not far from the western corridor. She looked younger than she had in Kallista's dream, her hair a brighter red, her body more slender, but still a decade older than Kallista.

"Who *are* you?" Kallista wavered between backing away in horror and drawing near with curiosity. "How did you come to this place?"

"I told you. I am Belandra of Arikon. As for how I came here— you brought me." She gave a mocking smile as she waved her hands in a flourish. "You have questions? I have the answers. Unfortunately, I am not allowed to give you all of them."

"Why not?"

"Because some things you must learn for yourself."

Kallista shook her head, trying to clear it. That wasn't what she wanted to know. She tried to sort the questions crowding her mind, to find those most urgently needing answers. "How did I get this? What is it?"

"A ring." Belandra rolled her eyes, seeming to mock Kallista for asking something with such an obvious answer. "And I gave it to you back before I died."

"A thousand years ago." Kallista let her doubt show.

"Give or take a few dozen, about that."

"That's not possible."

"For the One, all things are possible. Obviously it did happen, because I am here talking to you. You had to have something of mine in your possession before I could come to you. And here I am, at your service." Belandra pushed herself off the wall and bowed, as much a mockery as most things she'd done.

"You're a ghost." Kallista didn't believe in ghosts. Or thousand-year-old dream rings. But the one on her finger had come from somewhere.

"Something like that, but not exactly." Belandra shrugged. "Oresta who came before me explained it, but I never quite understood. Does it really matter? I'm here now. And I probably ought to tell you before you use them all up that you're only allowed six questions each time I am allowed to come to you."

"Allo—" Kallista cut herself off, trying to count up how many questions she'd already asked. She couldn't remember. "Who allows it? When will you come back? What questions *may* you answer? What are the rules? Are you truly dead?"

Belandra waggled an admonishing finger. "That's five. You only had two left. Which means I can answer the first two, but the others will have to wait until next time, provided you still want to ask them again. Though I already answered the fifth, if you will consider. Unless you believe I could still live after a thousand years."

"I'm not sure I believe you ever lived at all."

"Believe what you like. Your belief doesn't alter the truth. Do you want me to answer your questions?"

"Please." Kallista gestured for her to continue.

"It is, of course, the One who allows me to appear here before you, and at least one Hopeday must past before you next summon me."

"I didn't summon you this time."

"Did you not? You put on the ring. You desired answers. I am here." She gave Kallista a sardonic grin. "My first year, I summoned Oresta every chance I got."

"Your first year of what?" Kallista demanded. Belandra's answers only created more questions.

"Apologies, my lady Kallista." The grin on the woman's face didn't look very apologetic. "But you are out of questions."

"Who are you talking to?" Torchay's voice brought Kallista's head around to see him walking across the worship hall as if he thought his steps might fracture the tiles beneath his feet. His expression held barely disguised fear. Behind him came Mother Edyne, whose expression was more guarded.

"To her. Belandra." Kallista waved a hand in the other woman's direction.

"Naitan," he said, voice as careful as she had ever heard it. "There is no one there."

Kallista turned, looked, and Torchay was right. "She must have gone."

Torchay reached her, moved between her and the place where Belandra had been. "I have been here listening and watching for some time. Since you asked whether—she?…were dead. You spoke. You listened. You spoke again. And I saw no one. Who was it?"

She let out a long breath, looking past Torchay's worried face to Mother Edyne's curious one. "The woman who gave me this." She held up her ungloved right hand, showing the ring. Mother Edyne, to her credit, did not flinch at the sight of the naked hand. "Belandra of Arikon."

CHAPTER SIX

Safely behind the closed doors of Mother Edyne's chamber, Kallista told her the rest of the story while the prelate tended Torchay's
cuts with her healing East magic. She sat with head bowed while
Mother Edyne examined the mark Kallista had never herself seen.
Finally, the older woman let the hair fall and sank into her chair with
a sigh.

"Well?" Kallista hoped Mother Edyne had more answers than
Belandra had proved willing to share. Provided Belandra had been
anything more than a flicker from a fevered mind.

Edyne shook her head, hand over her mouth. After another moment, she removed it. "I fear that I have neither the knowledge
nor the wisdom to deal with such mysteries."

Kallista hid her instinctive wince at the word. *Mystery* was of
the West. "Then what should I do?"

"Ask the Reinine. The oldest records in Adara are in Arikon.

What the Reinine does not know, she will be able to learn. Most important, she should know that this happened."

"I'm a soldier, I cannot go here or there or to Arikon on my own whim."

"I will speak to the general. It will be arranged." Mother Edyne rose, the other two with her.

"Do you not have a—a *guess* as to what all this means?" Kallista didn't want to beg but couldn't seem to help it.

The prelate opened her mouth as if to speak, then shook her head. "Better not to guess. You will know soon enough. The Reinine will know."

Kallista nodded. "Come, Torchay. Seems we should pack."

They sailed upriver with the dawn.

"What's wrong with you?" Someone had hold of Stone's hair, shaking his head as if it were a sackful of kittens to be drowned.

His mind felt full of kittens, crying and yowling and crawling over each other. His head hurt. And his hands. He was shocked to see his fingers raw and bleeding. "What did you do to me?" His voice croaked like a frog's.

"What have *we* done?" The fat guard gave Stone's head another shake. "You've done it to yourself, you barmy idiot. Clawin' at the walls, bangin' your head on it. We should've give you back to your side. Let them keep you from killin' yourself." He grabbed an arm and hauled Stone to his feet. "Come on."

"Where are you taking me?"

"Not that it matters—whatcha goin' ta'do? Not come?" The fat man laughed at his feeble joke. "But you're getting' a cleanup. General wants you. Told 'er you were barmy, but she don't care. You're the only one we found alive. She wants to see you."

Stone's knees sagged at the reminder. Fox was dead. They were all dead. Save him.

He submitted tamely to the humiliation of his bath. They

stripped away the stained remnants of his uniform and stood him in a courtyard with a drain in one corner, his hands fastened before him in finely wrought steel shackles. He'd never seen such expert workmanship wasted on a prisoner. The fat guard pulled a lever and cold water poured down on Stone from a pipe over his head.

He was scrubbed from head to toe with a rough brush, drowned again in the water and dressed in an Adaran-style tunic and trousers of unbleached cotton. Again the quality of the cloth was much higher than he would have expected. If this was their poor stuff, no wonder the king wished to rule here.

With the clothing sticking to his wet skin, Stone was marched into a second room where his hands were bandaged and his hair was taken down from the tangled top knot tied there days ago by Fox. Stone didn't protest. He wanted the memory gone. Remembering caused pain.

The fat guard waited while another man combed the knots from Stone's hair and began to braid it into one of the tight pigtails worn by Adaran warriors. No, not warriors, soldiers. They were not born to their trade. His hair was too short in the front and kept falling away, but the rest was caught tight.

"Perhaps your birthmark is the reason you survived the dark scythe," the hairdresser said as he tied off the tail of hair.

"What birthmark?" Stone had one on his hip, round and small, but it was covered.

"This one." The man ran a finger over the nape of Stone's neck. "Shaped like a rose. Maybe the One protected you, since you bear His symbol."

"I don't have a birthmark there." He'd never seen the back of his neck, but Fox would have teased him mercilessly about any flower-shaped mark.

"Of course you do."

"Let me see." The guard lumbered closer and shoved Stone's

head forward to expose his nape. After a few seconds, he made a sound through his nose and backed away. "You're clean enough. Time to go."

The guard kept his distance as he escorted Stone out of the prison and through a square to a squat, imposing building, prodding him with the heel of his pike to indicate direction. He'd used his hands on Stone before, dragging and shoving him. Before he'd seen the rose supposedly marking Stone's neck. Did he fear the mark? What did it mean?

Stone walked through corridors and antechambers filled with Adaran soldiers clad in dun and gray, their tunics decorated with bold devices like those on divisional banners in the Tibran army—green trees, gold lions, red stags. Most soldiers had ribbons in white, yellow or red tacked to the shoulders of the sleeveless tunics, left to fall free front and back. Stone's skin crawled when he realized that the majority of the people wearing the uniforms were female. Why did the gods not punish them for their blasphemy?

Then the guard was opening a door, ushering him into a large room faced with maps and charts. A soldier stood at the window beyond the wide, paper-cluttered desk, back to him, shoulders sprouting a veritable fringe of red ribbon. The guard came to attention, snapped the heel of his pike against the floor and held it at ready. "General Uskenda. Sergeant Borril reporting with the Tibran prisoner as ordered."

The gray-haired general turned around. Stone staggered and would have fallen except for the guard catching his arm. The *commander* of Adaran forces was also a woman. How could this be? The defenses should have fallen the first day. Everyone knew women had no war skills, no war sense. Of course, they had won through magic, not in a fair fight. That had to explain it.

"So." Uskenda walked toward him, around him, as if conducting an inspection. "You are the one who lived."

Stone stared straight ahead, refusing to speak to any woman who did not know a woman's place.

"What is your name?"

He remained silent.

The general sighed and moved away a few paces, clasping her hands behind her back. "You would do well to answer of your own will."

Stone's eyes flickered toward the guard. He let his contempt show. Nothing they could do would change his mind.

"Oh, I know physical persuasion will do no good." Uskenda lifted a sheet of paper, perused it briefly. "That's why we rarely use it. We have no need. Corporal!"

The door behind Stone opened and a man spoke. "Yes, General?"

"Tell the naitan I have need of her."

"Yes, General." The door closed again.

Naitan. The word Adarans used to name their witches. Cold rushed from Stone's heart into his outermost parts, and the hair along his spine rose.

"Do you understand me?" Uskenda leaned against the desk. She somehow looked like a warrior with her stern face and close-cropped gray hair, despite her femaleness. How was it possible? "I think you do. I think you understand every word I say."

The guard came to clashing attention again and spoke when Uskenda looked his way. "General, the prisoner speaks perfect Adaran."

"Thank you, Sergeant." She crossed her arms and studied Stone. "How did you come to learn it?"

How indeed? And when? Stone had picked up a word or two of the local language in the week after landing, but no more than that. He hadn't realized he *was* speaking Adaran until this moment. His mind had been too filled with...what? Grief? Must have been. His thoughts were so fogged by grief that he scarcely knew how much time had passed since his capture. That was likely how he'd learned the language without realizing it, listening to his captors.

"What is wrong with his head, Sergeant?"

"General. The prisoner injured himself by striking his head against the wall, General."

She tapped a forefinger against her mouth. "And why did you do that? I wonder." She studied Stone a moment longer, then moved behind the desk and sat in the high-backed chair. "Ah well, no matter. We will know soon enough."

They waited. Stone and the guard stared straight ahead. General Uskenda reviewed papers on her desk. The door opened once more and the general looked up.

"Ah, good." She smiled. "Thank you for your promptness, naitan. Please, come in."

Uskenda came forward to greet a tall, slender woman. The naitan was dressed in a pale blue robe open over a tunic and trousers much the same color as those Stone wore, but of an even finer quality. Her brown hair fell past her shoulders in a froth of curls. She looked much like any woman found in any women's quarters. Until she turned her eyes on him. They were the same blue as his own. Stone shuddered, suddenly understanding how uncanny they seemed to others.

"I will allow you one more chance to give your own answers," the general said to Stone. "The naitan holds North magic. She is Ukiny's far-speaker, speaking mind to mind with others of her gift. Do you understand what I am saying?"

Stone tried to hold his gaze steady, to focus only on the window in the far wall, but his eyes rolled toward the blue-eyed witch again before he could jerk them away.

"She can touch minds. There is a kind of North magic that can reach into your mind and see what is there. You do not have to say anything at all. A naitan can simply take what we wish to know from you." Uskenda pursed her lips. "Of course, sometimes it isn't easy to find what we are looking for. Who knows what havoc might be worked upon your mind?"

In his peripheral vision, Stone could see the witch looking most unhappy. Did the process perhaps cause her discomfort too?

"General, I don't—" the witch broke off when the general raised a hand.

"Naitan, does this sort of magic do all that I have said?"

"Well, yes, but—"

"*And,*" Uskenda interrupted, "does it not on occasion leave those who are mind-searched…altered?"

"Yes, it might, but I—"

"Do not bother to explain the techniques. This Tibran would not understand. His kind have no magic. Is this not true, Tibran?"

Stone tightened his jaw and stiffened his spine yet again. He feared no man. Nor did he fear any woman. Any ordinary woman. But this witch and her magic…how could he not fear a thing that could go crashing about in his thoughts, shredding them to bits, stealing away whatever seemed interesting?

Long moments slid away while Uskenda watched Stone and Stone watched the far wall.

"Shall we start again, warrior?" The general's gentle voice reminded him of ease, of soft comfort in women's quarters. "What is your name? A simple thing, your name."

Simple, yes. But the first word spoken, the first truth told would change everything. Would the gods forgive him for failing to punish this woman's sacrilege? Would they count his blasphemy against him for following her orders? The warrior god was a harsh one, demanding much and forgiving little. But surely he would understand about the magic.

Uskenda sighed. "Naitan—"

"Stone." The sound of his own voice startled him. "Stone, Warrior vo'Tsekrish."

Uskenda came to attention and saluted him. "Warrior." She

nodded at the witch. "I believe we will not be needing your services after all, naitan. But please hold yourself in readiness in case our Tibran friend changes his mind."

The witch smiled, bowed and left the room. Stone sagged in relief, but only for a second.

"Stone, Warrior vo'Tsekrish." Uskenda paced the floor before him. "You are a long way from home, are you not?"

"Yes, General." He hoped all his answers would be so guilt free, but the hope was small.

"How *did* you learn our language, warrior?"

"I...do not know. I—after the assault, when I was taken prisoner, the soldiers spoke to me, and I understood."

"This was after the—" She checked a paper on her desk. "After the dark scythe, the magic, was it not?"

"Yes, General."

"You were captured in the breach?"

"Yes, General."

"And you never advanced into the city. Is that correct?"

"No, General."

Her head came up and she stared. "No?"

"Fox—my partner and I were in the First and Finest, those leading the assault. We took the breach, held it for the next wave, then advanced into the city." Talking about the past, things that had already happened would surely hurt nothing.

"How far into the city?" She spread a map on the desk, obviously expecting him to come look. Stone spared a glance for his guard who grunted and prodded him forward with the pike.

Uskenda indicated the position of the breach and the high-spired temple with its colored windows. Stone pointed to a street a quarter of the way between, his shackles rattling. "Here."

"Are you sure?" She held his gaze, the light gray of her eyes almost as unsettling as the blue of the witch's. "Every other Tibran within the city walls was found dead."

Stone studied the map again, letting the shivers take him. He was among witches now. He had to live with the fear. "It might have been here." He pointed at a place a few streets to the south. "My memory isn't good, not for those minutes—but I know we were inside the city."

"Then how is it you were found in the breach? Alive?"

He met her gaze, held it, willed her to believe him. He did not want her to call the witch back when he was telling the truth. "I do not know. I remember the world coming to an end. And then I remember waking up in the breach. Nothing else."

They stared eye into eye for a long moment more, until Uskenda broke contact, looking down again at the map. The guard crashing to attention startled both of them. "General," he rapped out.

"What is it, Sergeant?"

"There is a mark on his neck."

The general's eyes widened and her eyes flicked from one man to the other. "What kind of mark? Show me."

The guard seized Stone by the scruff of his neck, forcing him to his knees, shoving his head forward. He raked the pigtail out of the way. Uskenda's gasp as she touched a finger lightly to the nape of Stone's neck sent a thrill of terror shooting through him yet again. What was this mark? What did it mean?

The guard released Stone's head, but held him on his knees with a foot on the chain connecting wrist shackles to leg irons. Uskenda shuffled through the papers on her desk. She found the one for which she searched and scanned it quickly.

"You say this man has been behaving strangely?" she asked the guard.

"He beats his head on the wall and claws at the stones. You see the bandages. His hands are much worse than his forehead."

"Does he know he is doing this?"

The guard shrugged. "Who can say? All Tibrans are barmy, you ask me."

"Are you aware?" Uskenda asked Stone. "When you do these things?"

He didn't want to answer. But more, he didn't want magic mucking through his mind, making things worse than they already were. "No."

Uskenda touched the back of his head and he bent it obediently forward. She moved the pigtail aside but made no attempt to touch him again. Then she released him and stepped back, her boot heels a brisk clap against the polished wooden floor. "Make ready to take the prisoner to Arikon." Her orders snapped out with spine-chilling authority, the corporal appearing again to take them. "I wish I had seen him earlier so I might have sent him with Captain Varyl, but no matter. He will go on the next boat, at dawn tomorrow. Inform your captain. I want him escorted by an officer and a quarto of her best soldiers."

Once more, the guard stiffened to attention. He hauled Stone to his feet and hustled him out of the building and back to his prison. What would befall him next in this cursed land?

Torchay spent the first day of the week's journey upriver fighting sleep. Since the night his naitan had suddenly stopped breathing, he'd scarcely slept at all, dozing off and jerking awake seconds later, afraid it had happened again. It hadn't, but that didn't mean it wouldn't. The riverboat hadn't enough room for him to keep moving and every time he stilled, sleep tried to claim him.

He studied the boat, hoping the mental activity would help. Typical of its class, the *Taolind Runner* was long and narrow with a shallow draft to keep it running when the water level dropped in late summer. The exposed wood of the decks gleamed with varnish, but the exterior hull had been stained inky black with tar before it was sealed and proofed by South magic. The single triangular sail was set well forward in the crew section, its lack of wear evidence of more South magic. A pair of North naitani wind-callers took turns keeping the blue-and-gold-striped sail filled, moving it briskly against the current.

All the magic that had gone into this boat gave evidence to the prosperity of the owner who captained the ship and served as one of the wind naitani. The four elegantly furnished passenger cabins near the ship's stern attested to the same. On this leg of the journey, only two cabins were taken. Torchay would have expected some of the wealthier citizens of Ukiny to take advantage of the opportunity to escape the city, but the general had apparently forbidden it.

His head bobbled and he jerked his eyes open, blinking rapidly in an attempt to convince them to stay that way.

"Go ahead and sleep," his captain said from the chair beside him under the blue-and-gold-striped awning stretched over the passenger area at the stern.

Confinement area, to speak truth. The crew did not want passengers wandering indiscriminately about the ship. Torchay had been sent politely but firmly back to the "passenger section" several times already. "I need to be alert, watch for threats." He scanned the bank to either side, peering into the scattered trees for human shapes.

"You can't be alert if you don't get some sleep," she said, sounding far too reasonable. "No one can function without sleep, and I know you're not sleeping at night. Sleep now. I'll watch."

"It's against regulations. My duty is to—"

"How can you do your duty if you're asleep on your feet? We've been on this boat all day. We're beyond the Tibran lines. There are no bandits or river pirates between Ukiny and Turysh. We took care of the last band ourselves two years ago, remember? Sleep. I'm tempted to sleep myself."

He didn't want to admit it, but she was right. He needed to sleep. "We should go to the cabin." They would have more protection there.

"It's too hot. If you're that worried about my breathing, ask Uskenda's courier to keep an eye out."

"Excellent thought." He could tell by her expression when he stood that she hadn't expected him to take her suggestion seriously and was none too pleased that he had. But he would take no chances with his naitan.

The courier, an amiable young man, seemed surprised and not a little nervous at Torchay's approach. Those in bodyguard's black often evoked that reaction. Still, the courier willingly agreed with a little puffing out of his chest to move his chair closer and keep watch.

Torchay stretched out on the long wooden chair, arranged the cushions behind his back, stuffed one under his head and closed his eyes. But now that he had the opportunity to sleep, it eluded him.

Sounds intruded—the slap of water along the boat's sides, the creak of the sail's rigging, the murmur of voices as the boatmen talked and laughed among themselves. He could feel the hum of magic over his skin as the naitan on shift directed the pocket of winds pushing them against the current. He opened his eyes a slit to be sure his own naitan hadn't moved. Their chairs sat side by side, wooden flanks touching, but too far for him to sense her continued presence.

"Oh for—" She took his hand, laced her fingers through his. "There. Now you'll know if I decide to run away."

Content, he closed his eyes again. The sounds swelled then faded away as he categorized and dismissed them. Without their distraction, his mind began to buzz. He was seriously worried. The not-breathing business was only a small part of it. Though she tried to pretend otherwise, something more had happened to Kallista when that dark and deadly magic swept through her.

She dreamed things that came true. She saw people who weren't there and talked to them. Dead people, by her own words. Torchay felt a faint chill slide down his spine. West magic was as much a gift of the One as any other. He believed that. But it still unnerved him by its very nature. Not that it mattered. His place was by her side.

She could manifest magic from all four cardinal directions at once and his place would not change. He was her bodyguard. Her welfare, her life was in his charge. And that was why he worried. That, and the fact that he loved her, had loved her for years.

He'd loved her since she took the blame for the fiasco he'd caused, almost getting them both killed in their first year together, in his first combat. He'd been wounded, nearly gutted, spent months with the healers recovering. She'd visited nearly every day. And when he came out, she insisted he be reinstated as her bodyguard. How could he not love a woman like that?

There had been a great deal of hero worship about it at first, but after nine years at her side, he loved her for her flaws as well as her virtues. He would never inflict his emotions on her. She didn't want it. Her highly disciplined, carefully controlled, duty-bound life had no room for anything as messy as love. But he could pour his devotion out on her without having to speak the words. It had taken nine years to gather the courage to speak of friendship. That was enough.

Shouts from the front of the ship brought Torchay bolt upright out of a sound sleep he didn't remember falling into. The lanterns on the very back of the ship held back the night's darkness. He had been asleep for quite some time. He still held Kallista's hand clasped in his.

Torchay stood, releasing her hand. "I had better go see what that is. Go back to the room and wait for me."

She gave him her "think again, Sergeant" look and followed him down the narrow walkway beside the passenger cabins.

Just past the cabin area where a passageway cut from one side of the ship to the other, half a dozen crew members were standing over a huddled figure crouched on the deck, arms folded protectively around its head.

"What's happening?" Torchay asked.

Kallista leaned over the boat's rail to look around him, trying for a better sight of the situation. Torchay elbowed her back upright with a snarl to stay hidden. She crouched to peer beneath his elbow. His protectiveness could be so annoying.

"We found a stowaway. A Tibran spy." One of the sailors kicked at their find.

"Don't hurt me. Please don't!" the stowaway cried in the high-pitched voice of a child or woman. "I mean no harm. I'm no one. I'm not a spy."

Kallista tried to squeeze past Torchay. She should have known better. The man could give lessons in immovable to mountains. "What are you, then?" she called past the barricade of his body.

"A woman. Only a woman." The stowaway shuffled around on her knees to face Kallista's direction as much as she could. She wore a torn and dirt-stained tunic. Her hair was chopped raggedly short, matted with more dirt, and her thin arms were dirtier yet.

All the crew members had stopped their abuse to stare at Kallista. Even Torchay looked over his shoulder at her until he recalled his duty and swung around to face front.

"Tibran?" Kallista said. "Are you Tibran?"

"No longer. I was born in Haav, over the sea, but I have left Tibre. I am here and here I wish to stay." Still curled into a ball, the woman stretched her hands along the deck, reaching toward Kallista in supplication.

"Why? Why abandon your home?"

"It has never been my home." The woman's bitterness startled Kallista.

"Do you understand her, naitan?" one of the crew members asked. Kallista thought he was a boat's officer since he wore a tunic rather than going about bare-chested like most of the other males in the crew.

"Yes." She almost continued with a question but thought better of it. Setting her hand against Torchay's taut back, she leaned forward and murmured in his ear, "Please tell me you understand what she's saying."

CHAPTER SEVEN

Torchay turned his head slightly to reply. "No, Captain. I cannot. Is it—could you be speaking Tibran?"

Kallista sighed, letting her forehead come to rest on his shoulder. She was so very tired of waking up every day to discover some new peculiarity about herself, some new magic that had made its home inside her. She wanted it to stop. "I suppose it must be," she said. "She says she's from Haav. Isn't that one of their ports?"

"I believe so, naitan."

"She also says she's left Tibre. She wants to be Adaran now."

"Oh, she *does,* does she?"

Kallista could feel the suspicion bristling from Torchay like some prickly cloak.

"Naitan." The tunic-clad officer spoke again. "Captain's compliments, and would you come to the foredeck and assist in interrogating this stowaway?"

"Yes, sir, I would be happy to." Kallista straightened.

Torchay held his position while the stowaway was hauled to her feet and hustled up the gangway to the high foredeck at the prow of the boat. Only when the party was a certain prescribed distance ahead did he follow, always keeping himself interposed between Kallista and the Tibran.

"I doubt that poor child is much of a threat." Kallista stalked slowly behind Torchay's broad back.

"As do I. But anything is possible, and I will not be careless of your life."

As she rolled her eyes, he spoke again. "And do no' roll your eyes at me."

Mouth open in surprise, Kallista halted two steps down from the high deck. "How do you know—"

He turned and held out his hand to escort her the rest of the way. A smile lurked in his eyes and nowhere else on his solemn face. "Because you always do when I say such things."

She shook her head, smiling despite herself as she took the hand he offered. "I think you have been my bodyguard far too long."

The stowaway stood before the stout, stern-faced captain, shivering in the night's warmth. Obviously a woman, now her delicate build and surprisingly full breasts could be seen, she hugged herself, head down, eyes on the deck beneath her bare filthy feet.

Kallista greeted the riverboat captain, one of a prominent trading family based in Turysh. Kallista had known a number of her children in school before the lightning came.

"Who is she and what is she doing on my boat?" The captain clasped her hands behind her back and rocked on her heels waiting for Kallista to translate.

Hiding a sigh, she summoned military posture and took a step past Torchay to see the woman she was to interrogate. "Stand up straight," she said, disturbed by the woman's abject demeanor. "Have you no pride?"

The stowaway flinched as if under attack, and huddled tighter.

Torchay leaned close and murmured in Kallista's ear. "That was Adaran. Maybe if you tried speaking Tibran...?"

She glared at him. She hadn't known she was speaking Tibran in the first place. How was she supposed to know which language she spoke when they sounded the same to her?

Abruptly, the stowaway threw herself to the deck again, so swiftly that Torchay had a blade out and poised to strike before holding his blow. The woman curled onto her knees, arms once more stretched toward Kallista.

"Please, please," she said. "Allow me to stay. I will do anything you ask. I will cook your food and wash your clothes. I will rub your feet. I will even service your man—" There came a little pause in the woman's babbling before she went on. "Though, if I could *choose,* I do not think I would choose to, because he looks large and would probably hurt me, and he is rather ugly, but if you wish it, great lady, I will do it."

Kallista could hide neither her shock nor a quick amused look at Torchay.

"What?" he muttered, flipping the naked blade in his hand. It was a good-size one, narrow and long enough to come out the back if he thrust it in the woman's throat.

"What? What is she saying?" the captain echoed.

"She wishes to stay. She is offering herself as my servant." Kallista turned to Torchay and lowered her voice, letting her amusement out. "And she offered to 'service' you, though she'd really rather not, since she thinks you're ugly and probably too big." She finished with a significant glance below her bodyguard's waist, expecting a snort and a roll of the eyes. She got it, along with a blush she didn't expect.

Puzzled, she swung back to the prostrate stowaway. Was Torchay attracted to the woman? Was that where the blush came from? She'd thought he had better taste.

"How did she get on board?" the captain said.

Kallista finally repeated all the questions.

"I am Aisse, woman of Haav, assigned to Warrior caste. I climbed onto the ship from the water, during the night, when the watch was on the far side." The woman did not move from her submissive posture. "I beg of you, great lady, if you will not let me stay, allow me death rather than sending me back."

"Why?" Kallista asked before translating for the captain.

"I will face death anyway, but theirs will not be a gentle one. It is so for anyone who rebels against his lot in life, but it is worse for a woman." The Tibran, Aisse, looked up then, finally exposing her face to the lanterns' light.

Kallista recoiled, shock exploding in gasps from throats around her. This Aisse might have been beautiful, might be beautiful again. At this moment, it was impossible to tell, given the swollen discoloration of bruises covering her face.

"What—" Kallista reached for the woman's hand, beckoning when she did not seem to know what was wanted. "Stand up. Stand up straight and look me in the eye."

Aisse did as she was told, slowly straightening from her hunched defensive attitude until she stood in a smaller echo of Kallista's. Her eyes were a dark, rich brown, rarely seen in Adara. The smudges on her arms were more bruises, not dirt.

"What happened to you?" Kallista asked. "Who did this?"

"One of the Farmer caste." Aisse shifted a shoulder. "I did not know him. He caught me as I was escaping. The morning the warriors died."

The day of the dark magic. Kallista stifled her shudder as she translated, sensing Torchay's impatience. He did not respond well to a lack of information.

"When they died," Aisse went on, "I got away."

That sent another chill through Kallista. Did she sense the hand of the One in this? "You were already running away, before this beating?"

"Yes. One beating is much like another, just as one man is like another. They are a woman's lot, men and beatings. But I wish to *choose*. I want a life that is *mine*."

The sincerity in her voice rang clear to Kallista's soul. She too had wished for more choices than she'd been given, though she'd had more than Aisse. "Neither men nor beatings are a woman's lot in Adara."

"That is why I want to stay."

Kallista nodded, her mind made up. "Will you renounce Tibre and swear loyalty to me as representative of Adara's Reinine?"

Aisse started back to her knees again, joy shining through the bruises on her face, but halted at Kallista's upraised hand and the sight of Torchay's glittering blade.

"What are you doing, Captain?" Torchay asked through gritted teeth.

Kallista shifted her upraised hand to halt him as well. "Slowly," she said in Tibran. "Kneel. Swear on the One, the Mother and Father of all, that you renounce all ties and loyalty to Tibre."

"I worship Ulilianeth, great lady," Aisse said as she knelt, eyeing Torchay's blade all the way down.

"A beautiful aspect of the One, but only a small part of Her glory. Do you swear?" Step by step, Kallista led her through the oath, cobbling it together on the spot from other vows she had heard and sworn over the years.

"Naitan." Torchay stepped close, bending to growl in her ear, "Kallista, *what are you doing?*"

"This woman has renounced her Tibran birth and begged citizenship in Adara," Kallista said in Adaran as she gestured Aisse to her feet. This time it did not take so long for her to stand straight.

"And you gave it?" Torchay demanded.

"I will take responsibility for her as my servant, until we reach Arikon and the Reinine can decide whether to grant her request," she said to the riverboat captain, "and of course I will pay her passage to Turysh."

"And you're sure she's not a saboteur or spy?" The captain studied Kallista's new servant with doubt.

"I'm sure." Though her certainty bothered her. How was she so sure?

"How?" Torchay asked, voice ringing through the foredeck. "How can you know she speaks the truth?"

I just do. But that wouldn't convince them. "My magic is of the North." Her blue tunic would have told them so already, but truthsayers were also of the North. It wouldn't convince Torchay, but it might the others. Probably.

He retreated first, however, giving her a hard look that faded to worry, then stoic acceptance. He bowed. "As you say, naitan."

His acquiescence convinced the others. The captain nodded, dismissing the crew still standing guard.

"If I could beg a bath for my servant Aisse?" Kallista said.

The male officer, in charge of passengers and cargo, if she remembered right, bowed. "I will see to it, naitan."

"I will be watching your new 'servant' with careful eyes, naitan," Torchay murmured as he gestured for Aisse to follow the other man.

"I expect nothing less." Kallista gave him a wicked grin. "That's why I'm putting her in your charge. See that she has what she needs—new clothes and a pair of shoes to start with. Probably food. And then, teach her Adaran."

"I'm no scholar."

"No." She patted his shoulder. "Which means your teaching will be eminently practical. Just try not to teach her too many curse words."

"Here! What are you doing? Are you mad?" A hand caught Stone's arm, jerked him back.

Stone was standing at the prow of a boat, trying to climb onto the railing. The shackles he wore on his ankles and wrists wouldn't allow it.

"Of course you're mad," the voice attached to the hand muttered. "What was I thinking?" It was male, belonging to the officer in charge of the soldiers escorting Stone up the river to the Adaran capital.

"Sergeant!" He shouted back down the length of the boat, and the fat guard from the prison came clattering up the stairs to the high foredeck.

"Sir!" The sergeant came to attention, obviously missing the presence of his pike. He had nothing to pound on the deck.

"Who, Sergeant, is supposed to be guarding the prisoner this watch?" The icy fury in the lieutenant's voice made even Stone shiver with fear.

"I am, sir. Me and Dyrney. The Tibran's asleep." The guard's voice faltered as he realized just who his superior held by the elbow. "Or he *was*. How'd he get out?"

"Precisely what I would like to know."

So would he. Stone had lost time. Hours, if not days. He did not remember boarding this boat.

Stone tried his voice, swallowed and tried again. "How long—" His voice crackled, as if he'd either not been using it, or been using it too much.

"I dunno, sir," the sergeant answered the lieutenant. "I swear we was watchin' him. He couldn't've got out the door."

"Then perhaps he left by the window, hmm?" The officer turned to Stone, impaling him on the glare from his uncanny blue eyes. Save for those eyes, this man looked like a proper officer. His brown hair was pulled smoothly back from a high forehead into that tight Adaran queue, his face set and hard with an attitude of command. His rank was marked by a single white ribbon on either shoulder of his dun-colored tunic.

"How long?" He repeated Stone's question. "Are you with us, warrior?"

Stone cleared his throat. "How long have we been traveling?"

The man leaned closer, peering into Stone's face. "Yes, I believe you are here. Welcome back. Do you recall who I am?"

It took some effort, but Stone finally dredged up the information. "Lieutenant Joh...I don't remember your other name. Twenty-first Infantry."

"Joh Suteny, but that doesn't matter." He continued staring.

"How long?" Stone asked again.

"Oh. Yes. We have been on the river almost one full day." He gestured at the lowering sun, then at the stairway. "Shall we go down?"

Surprised by the courtesy—it was seldom offered to prisoners in shackles—Stone shuffled toward the steps. The sergeant moved as if to take Stone's arm, but the lieutenant got there first.

"*I* will secure the prisoner," he said, his voice all ice and iron. "Since it seems your incompetence knows no bounds."

"Yessir. Nossir." The fat guard bobbed his head, backed away.

The lieutenant had to hold Stone upright during the descent down the steep gangway. The shackles made it almost impossible to maintain his balance.

"However did you get up there?" Suteny asked in a mild conversational tone as they made their slow way down the walkway to the cabin that was his prison during the river journey.

"Up is easier than down."

"When you leave us—" Suteny opened the cabin door and ushered him inside, then followed to lean against the closed door "—where do you go?"

Stone shuffled to the bunk and sat down. How *had* he got out of the cabin? He would have sworn his shoulders could never fit through that porthole.

"Warrior?" The Adaran spoke.

Oh yes. He'd asked a question, hadn't he? Stone fought through the fog clouding his mind. He didn't have the brains Fox had, but he'd never had trouble thinking. What was wrong with him? *Was* he mad? "I don't know," he said. "I—the time is just…gone. I don't—"

But he did remember something. An urgency. A pull. A need to— "I have to go…somewhere. I'm—I'm looking for something. I don't know what it is. But I must find it. I *must*. Or…" He shook his head again. "I don't know. I don't know what will happen if I don't find it. Bad things, I think."

"I see." The lieutenant looked down, seeming to think. "I am afraid we are going to have to add to your burden. I have been ordered to treat you with courtesy, as far as I might. But when you do not yourself know what you are doing…

"I will make the chain a long one so that you may move about the cabin, and you may take the air on deck with an escort, as the journey is several more days. But—for your own safety—I must chain you in place. Do you understand?"

Stone nodded, hiding the relief that ebbed through him. A chain would hold him. Even if he injured himself fighting the chain, which he feared was likely, at least he could not plunge to his death over the side of the boat.

"You seem a reasonable man, warrior—Stone, is it?" Suteny waited for an answer. Stone nodded and the other man went on. "When you are here with us, that is. Do you know what triggers these…little spells of time?" The lieutenant put his head outside the door and spoke in a voice of quiet authority before closing it again and turning back to Stone.

Hunching his shoulders, Stone shook his head. He wished he knew. He wanted to be rid of it, his madness or whatever it might be.

"Would you allow me to try calling you back?"

Stone stared at the pale-skinned Adaran. "You wish to do this?"

Suteny seemed surprised by Stone's surprise. "It would make my job easier, would it not? If you could retain better possession of your senses."

"True." Stone shrugged. "I see no reason why not. Try."

"Very well. We are agreed."

A knock sounded at the door and the lieutenant opened it to admit one of the other guards, young, with a dogged determination that made up for his lack of experience. He proceeded to attach a long chain to Stone's ankle bonds and to the bolts holding the cabin's bunk to the floor.

"Is there anything else I can provide for your comfort?" Lieutenant Suteny asked. "Some reading material perhaps?"

Stone shook his head, testing the chain's length. "I can speak Adaran, but I can't read it." He'd tried to read the words on the general's map.

"Oh?" A single eyebrow arched high on Suteny's forehead. "Pity."

Stone shrugged. He'd never been much for reading anyway. Not like Fox.

Suteny watched him another long moment. It made Stone uneasy. As if the man was studying him. Preparing a report. He probably was. When they reached Arikon, he would likely be called upon to report to his superiors everything observed about their Tibran prisoner and whether he was too mad to be of any use. Stone would like to know the answer to that himself.

Aisse was sitting in complete idleness on the back of the boat a short space apart from her mistress and the man. It was the second afternoon from the time she had been discovered and Aisse still did not understand what sort of service was expected of her. She didn't understand much of anything in her new country.

Kallista was the captain, but it did not seem to mean the same as it would in Tibre. She did not own the man. Nor did he own her. He protected her. He served her, carrying out duties Aisse had thought would be hers.

When the man came that first night, while she was in her bath, Aisse had feared his purpose. But he had ignored her naked self to empty her bag on the floor and search it, then carried her clothing away. Aisse had been confused, then amused when she realized the man had been searching for weapons, things that could harm the captain. Then she remembered that in this place, women were indeed as dangerous as the men, if not more so.

The man brought her new clothes, a tunic much like the old one and trousers to cover her legs, all the way to her waist. Aisse liked trousers. The man brought her to the cabin, gave her a blanket and a corner for sleeping. He gave her food and the words for food and blanket, for cup, bowl and spoon. But when she tried to begin her duties by putting away the captain's things, he had growled and sent her away.

He would not allow Aisse to touch anything belonging to either the captain or himself. He did not allow her to collect their food from the boat's kitchen. He did not trust her. It was a strange feeling for Aisse, to be considered important enough for suspicion, worthy of distrust.

She rested her head on her knees and wrapped her arms around her folded legs as she watched the captain and her man. She did not understand relations between men and women in this new country either. She had thought women ruled here—and they did, but not in a way Aisse could comprehend. She did not have words for the things she saw.

The man argued with the captain. They did not shout, but spoke quietly through clenched teeth and glared lightning bolts at each other. It amazed Aisse that he would dare to argue, but dare he did and without any apparent fear of punishment. She did not understand. But that was not all that confused her.

Aisse had thought the man did not make any demands for sex because he belonged to the captain. And he did in some way, but she did not know what it was. They slept side by side, their bodies touching, and they did not have sex. The man did not touch the captain save for when they slept and when he tied up her hair. He did not grope, squeeze, fondle, or anything at all.

The captain touched him sometimes, on the hand or arm, or perhaps laid a hand on his shoulder. But not often. It didn't make sense. Did she want the man or not? Did he want her? If he did, maybe Aisse could stop worrying over having to do sex.

She was trying to puzzle the matter out when one of the boatmen approached her, the one who had ordered the others to bring her bath. He sat in the chair beside her, speaking his pretty language. She shrank into a smaller ball, struggling to pick out a word or two. She could not remember what she had learned. He was too close. He frightened her.

"He means no harm," the captain said. "He's only saying how sorry he is you were hurt and that you must be very beautiful indeed, for even now you are beautiful."

Aisse made a face. Much good beauty had ever done her. Captain Varyl laughed. The boatman spoke again and she translated. "He says if there is any service he might do for you, you have only to ask."

"I want him to go away," Aisse said, surprising herself with her bravado. "I will not do sex with him. But I want to say it myself. What are the words?"

The captain had to have her man give the words to Aisse. The boatman did not look angry or frustrated when she said them, merely sad as he rose to do what she ordered.

"He was not looking for sex," the captain said. "He's one of the boat captain's iliasti. Didn't you see his anklets?"

Aisse looked as the boatman climbed the stairs to the foredeck and saw a pair of narrow gold bangles encircling one ankle, and three more shining from the other. "They mean he belongs to the captain?"

"And she belongs to him and both of them to the rest of their ilian."

That word was in Adaran, like the other strange words she used. "What is that? Ilian?"

"It means they are—are mates. Oathsworn to each other in the temple, joined by love in a family to raise their children. They all belong to each other."

Aisse shook her head. She was confused by more words than just *ilian*. Love was what a person owed the Rulers. How could love join someone? Family—that had to do with children, she thought. Aisse had no children, would never have them, so she wasn't sure of that term. She understood swearing an oath and belonging. But one person belonged to another and the one who was owned could not then own the one who owned her. Could she?

She frowned. "The boatman and the boat captain...love?"

"Yes. And their ilian. It has six members. Didn't you see? He wore five anklets, three on the right and two on the left. Three women and two other men. The captain wears five bracelets, two on the right and three on the left. They belong to their ilian and do not—don't have sex with anyone else."

"Your man does not have an anklet."

The captain sighed. "Torchay is my bodyguard. Not my ilias. We are not bound in that way."

"Then who does he do sex with?" Should she worry after all?

"Whoever he wishes, I suppose." The captain's face turned pink, but Aisse did not understand the reason for the blush. "And if she wishes it as well. Sex must be agreed to by all involved."

Aisse nodded. She could like that rule.

The captain's blush faded and she turned thoughtful. "He's never taken a lover though, not for more than a night or two."

"Have you? Taken lovers?" Aisse needed to understand.

"Yes." The captain's face was pink again. "And I believe this conversation has ended."

Aisse rested her cheek on her knees as the captain walked away, followed by the man. She had more than enough to think through.

Kallista set aside her reading when Torchay returned with the evening meal. He'd taken Aisse with him this time, allowed her to bring her own food, grudgingly admitting before they left that she might not be a secret weapon aimed by Tibre at Adara's naitani. Kallista moved over as he set her meal on the room's narrow table, took his own from the tray and sat down opposite. Stew made from last night's roast chicken. She sampled it. Not bad. Better than field rations.

"Today is Graceday," Torchay said as he tore off a piece of brown bread and dunked it in his stew.

"I know."

"Means tomorrow is Hopeday. Have you decided the questions to ask this Belandra person?"

Kallista sighed. "No. I'm hoping she doesn't come back."

"If she's got answers, seems you'd hope she does. Will you ask about the breathing?"

"Yes, I'll ask about the damn breathing." In her opinion, Torchay was far too interested in the movement of her chest.

"What?" he said. "What will you ask?"

"Can you tell me why—no, if I ask it that way, she'll likely say, 'Yes, I can tell you,' and then not tell me because that wasn't the question."

"Say 'Why did I stop breathing before and will it—is it likely to happen again?'"

"All right, fine."

"Maybe you should write it down."

"Enough, Torchay," she snapped. "I've had enough of your hovering."

He went still, spoon halfway to his mouth. Then with great dignity he stood, picked up his bowl and retreated to the corner where Aisse sat eating. He lowered himself to the floor beside her, never once saying a word.

"Oh for—I didn't mean it like that." Now she felt guilty. He hadn't used to be so touchy. Had he? This friendship business was damn complicated.

He just sat in the corner and ate his stew.

Appetite ruined, Kallista threw her spoon on the table and stood. "I need some air."

Torchay rose to follow, ostentatiously shoveling the last bites of stew into his mouth to make her feel more guilty for not allowing him even to eat his meal in peace.

"No, stay." She waved him back. He ignored her, of course. "Where am I going to go on this boat that you can't hear me? That you can't see me for the One's sake. Give me a little space. For once."

He just stood there, waiting for her to go out the door so he could follow. *Damn him and his duty.* Sometimes—times like this one—she wished she could... She wanted to call up a tiny spark and shock him with it, just a little one.

With the thought, she felt the spark gather. It grew, started skipping from finger to bare finger. She hadn't put her gloves on yet, they still were tucked in Torchay's belt. Now it was too late. The spark refused to be called back, refused any control. It danced around her hand, sending little pieces of itself in all directions as it tried to escape.

Kallista brought her other hand up, let the spark leap the gap. She couldn't let it free inside the cabin or anywhere on this wooden boat, but she couldn't let it jump back and forth between her hands indefinitely. As out of control as it was, each time it leaped from one hand to the other, it would gain in power. "Open the door, *quick*."

CHAPTER EIGHT

Torchay scrambled to obey, thrusting the door wide and shouting for everyone to stand clear.

"Which side is nearest the riverbank?" She strode calmly out, fighting to keep the spark contained. She couldn't let it strike the water either. She'd learned that lesson early and had the scars to prove it.

"The closest bank?" Torchay called to one of the crew. She pointed. It was on their side of the boat, thank the One.

Kallista strode to the railing, holding the spark between her two hands now. It crackled blue between them, building strength, and this time, she let it. She would need the power to fling it all the way to the shore without touching water.

She scanned the darkened riverbank, hunting a rock or a bare spot where the foliage wouldn't catch fire. It was early spring yet, not dry as it would get later in summer, but fire was still a risk.

"There." Torchay pointed upstream. "The farmer has plowed but not yet planted."

The field stretched dark and fallow into the night for a good distance along the bank. The boat had turned and was making for it, closing the gap quickly.

"Not too close," Torchay shouted to the captain. "You want to keep some distance."

The angle of approach softened. Kallista held the spark, concentrating her magic and her will, begging the One for aid to control it. She hadn't lost control and called lightning like this in years. Almost twenty of them.

They neared the field. Kallista calculated her distance and trajectory. She had to clear the reeds springing up at the water's edge. She focused her intention, pressed her hands together, squeezing the spark, then flung it forth.

It leaped in a high, blue-lit arc from her hands to almost the center of the field. The boom of thunder that accompanied it rattled the boat's rigging and the shutters over the windows.

Torchay had her gloves ready, holding the right—her lead hand—open for her. She thrust her hand in with a single motion and held the left ready for the few seconds it took him to open the other glove. Without her control, she shouldn't be able to call sparks that would escape the leather. When she was safely gloved, her knees sagged. Torchay caught her elbow for support, holding himself back.

Kallista wanted to rest her head on his shoulder but she refused herself that small comfort. His stiff manner said he wouldn't welcome it. He was still sulking.

"What happened?" Torchay asked as the boat captain came charging down the companionway to ask the same thing.

"An accident." Kallista used her best civilian-soothing voice. She had plenty of practice with it, but generally on behalf of the young naitani under her command, not herself. "I had ungloved in private. I will not do so again." She tugged at the cuffs of her gloves, seating them more securely. "It won't happen again." She hoped.

The captain scowled at her. "You're old enough you should have better control of your magic. I remember when you were a girl, shocking and blasting things all over Turysh. But you're no longer a girl."

"No, Captain." Kallista's face burned at the reprimand. "Something...*happened* in Ukiny. It interfered with my magic. That's why I'm going to Arikon."

"See that it doesn't happen again on my boat."

Kallista bowed deep in apology. The captain retreated to her quarters and the rest of the crew backed away. Even General Uskenda's courier looked uneasy. She sighed. Nothing new there.

"What happened?" Torchay asked again, through clenched teeth.

"I don't know, all right?" She jerked away from him and stalked toward the stern, ignoring the wide, rolling eyes of the watchman posted there. She was sick of this. Sick of frightening civilians, of not knowing what might leap next from her hands, of all of it, everything that had been dumped on her since—since birth.

"I've never seen you lose control like that." Torchay had followed her. Of course. She couldn't get rid of him.

She wanted him there. And she wanted him gone. Somewhere else. Not bothering her. Not reminding her of things she'd rather forget. "It's been years," she said, wrapping her leather-clad fingers tight around the stern railing. "Since before you and I ever met." She leaned on the railing, letting it hold her up. "But then, you never saw me kill tens of thousands of men in one sweep before either, did you?"

"You think it's connected?"

Kallista gave him a disbelieving look. "You think it's *not?*" She kept her voice quiet but couldn't stop the emotion that hummed in it. "How could it not be connected? For fifteen years—more—

I am in perfect control of my magic. One moment on a city wall and everything's changed. I cast magic that cuts warriors down like they were so much harvested wheat. I talk to people who aren't there. I dream dreams that come true. What else am I to think when suddenly I generate a spark I had no intention of making and I can't call it back?"

"You must ask Belandra when she comes."

"Ask her *what?* How to control magic I've controlled for years? What could she tell me that I don't already know? Stop nagging me, Torchay. Give me a little peace. A little space without you picking at me." She felt him recoil as the ugly words left her mouth, and she wished them back. Except…she did need space and peace. She wanted to lean against him and soak up that prickly comfort of his, but she couldn't. He was her friend. Her bodyguard. He could be nothing more.

"As my captain wishes." Torchay retreated as far as the open doorway to the cabin.

She heard him order Aisse to return the dishes to the galley in the pidgin Adaran he'd been teaching her, then nothing. She resisted the urge to turn around, see where he was. He would be close, watching over her at a distance, tending to his own affairs at the same time. They had quarreled like this before. Not often, but enough it had a pattern they both recognized.

Kallista leaned against the railing, letting the night seep in through her skin. She ought to work on questions for Belandra, but not now. Now she needed calm, needed to soothe her jangled nerves and lose some of her worry. She watched the water swirl up from beneath the boat, disturbed by its wind-fed passage.

The lanterns on either corner of the stern reflected off the muddy green surface, illuminating only the first layer of the Taolind's depths. Three more days from here, at Turysh, the water would be cleaner, clearer. The river picked up dirt and debris on its path, carrying it to rest in the delta near the coast. Kallista pitched her worries into the water, let the river carry them away. They would be back tomorrow, but for tonight, the Taolind had them.

Gradually her mind quieted. Her body refused to do the same, holding on to its restlessness. The naitan-directed wind blew across her skin like a caress. She rubbed her arms, craving touch. *I dream dreams that come true.* But how did she know which ones were true visions and which ordinary dreams?

The collapsed wall had been a true vision. She had dreamed exactly the same thing for nights. Belandra, she still had her doubts about. But she had also dreamed of men, of lovers. Just thinking of those dreams sent heat spreading through her body, pooling in her breasts and lower, making demands. How long had it been since she'd taken a lover?

Months. Since before the posting to Ukiny. She often went months between lovers. That was nothing new. Except she'd been looking lately. It had never taken her so long to find a partner, not once she went looking for one. But none of them had appealed. They were too young. Too needy. They would all require too much effort. So she'd done without and she'd missed it. Missed the kisses, the feel of hard male flesh against her own, missed the passion and fierce delight.

And then the Tibrans had invaded and her mind was on that rather than potential lovers.

The conversation with Aisse this afternoon hadn't helped. It made her wonder about Torchay and his lovers. The lovers he didn't have. He wasn't abstemious by any stretch. But he never stayed with one lover, not for months like Kallista did. He had a well-deserved reputation as a flirt, sharing a night or two with a woman before moving on.

Perhaps his way was better. He never seemed faced with any tearful scenes of farewell when it was time to move on. Maybe she would try it sometime. *Now* seemed like an excellent time.

Only a few of the boat's male crew members wore ilian anklets. Maybe one of them...

She turned to stroll forward, toward the place designated for crew washing. She'd already spent several pleasant moments watching men stripped to the waist, water sluicing past muscle as they washed away the day's sweat and grime.

A man was there now, washing hurriedly though no one waited for the bucket or sponge. His shoulder-length wet hair trickled water along a deep-set spine, muscle rising to either side in a tantalizing sweep. His broad shoulders narrowed to a slender waist above taut round buttocks displayed by his tight trousers. He raised his arms to squeeze excess water from his hair, and Kallista's breath caught at the flexing and bunching of muscle beneath his skin, pale in the moonlight, like the milk-white marble of Arikon. He gave another brisk pass of the sponge beneath his arms and reached for the piece of rough toweling on the nearby hook to dry himself.

Kallista took a step forward, her bait phrase ready, her seduction planned. He turned, toweling his face, and the lantern light struck his hair, calling red from its depths. She froze. There was a crewman with red hair, but his was cropped short, and not such a dark intense red as this.

He tossed the towel back at the hook and picked up his tunic. Now she saw the chevrons tattooed on his arm, saw his familiar hook-nosed face. *Torchay?* When had he become so beautiful? Or had he always been and she never saw it?

Before she could back away he turned, pulling the tunic down over his head to cover that sculpted chest and abdomen, and saw her. "Captain?" He approached, squeezing water from his hair one more time. "You have need of me?"

Kallista had to close her eyes and put her hands behind her back before she could respond. Sex between a naitan and her bodyguard ruined their working relationship. She'd seen it happen again and again. She would not let it happen to them.

"I wanted to apologize, Sergeant Torchay." She opened her eyes. It hadn't helped much. She could still smell him. She locked her hands together to keep them where they were.

He shook his head. "No need."

"There is need. My foul mood is not your fault. I can beat you with my temper and you are still there filling the need, doing what must be done. But I cannot shout at you simply because I know you will let me. I was wrong, and I apologize."

He watched her for an endless moment, as if searching for something—whether his own response or something in her, Kallista didn't know. He spoke finally. "You've never apologized before."

"I should have." Despite the grip she had on them, one of her hands got free, reached out. "Friends?"

Torchay clasped it in his. "Always. You know that."

"I do. And I shouldn't take advantage of it." She pulled her hand back, long before she wanted to. She wanted to set it free, without the prison of gloves, let it wander across the marble-white landscape of his body, and it could never happen.

"It's late," he said. "Tomorrow is Hopeday, and we've left that Tibran pet of yours alone in quarters long enough."

Kallista sighed and let him direct her back down the walkway. "You don't still believe she's a spy, do you? Or an assassin?"

"I don't know what she is, other than Tibran." He opened the cabin door, scanning it quickly before allowing her inside. Aisse was in her corner, already wrapped in her blanket.

Torchay turned down the coverlet on the wide bunk and began divesting himself of the majority of his blades, readying himself for sleep.

Her palms itched, wanting to touch. She should have looked for another, once she realized it was Torchay she saw washing. But she couldn't drag him out after her again, and after the incident with the spark earlier, she doubted any of the crew would be willing to let her get close.

"Are you sleeping in your boots?" He was sitting on the bed, pulling his off already. Torchay went down on one knee, ready to help her with her tighter boots.

Kallista sat and let him do it. "Perhaps I should take the bed alone tonight."

He gave her a sharp look but said nothing as he rose and set their boots between the chests holding their belongings.

"It's been almost a week with no dreams, no problems," she said. "I should—"

"No."

"But—"

"*No.*"

"Aisse can share with me, keep watch, if you still think it's needful." Kallista didn't think she could bear lying next to him, touching him, without doing something she shouldn't.

"No!" Torchay turned a ferocious scowl on her. "I will not have that Tibran near you while you sleep. I will not have you sleeping alone. Is it suddenly so distasteful, sharing with me? Are we not friends?"

"We are. It's not that. It's not—" She couldn't explain it to him, couldn't expose her sudden weakness. "Not right. It's—you're my bodyguard."

"And that means I'm the one who decides about this. It's your safety here. No battles. No armies. Not even any bandits. It's my say, and this is how it will be." He held his hand out for her gloves.

"I'll keep them on." She tugged the cuffs higher on her wrists.

"You know how your hands peel when you sleep in the gloves." He beckoned with his fingers, demanding the gloves. "Give them over. You don't call magic in your sleep."

But she could be tempted to touch, knowing she could feel it. Feel him.

"Give." He crooked his fingers again.

With a sigh, Kallista stripped off her gloves and handed them over. She pulled off her tunic and crawled into bed in her chemise and trousers.

"It's hot," Torchay said as he removed his tunic, then the sheath holding the big blade he wore beneath it. Kallista squeezed her eyes tight shut and turned her back so she couldn't see him. "Are you sure you want to wear your trews to bed?"

"If I get too hot, I'll take them off," she lied. The more clothing she wore, the better. If the crewmen were too afraid of her lightning now, she would hook a man when they reached Turysh. It had been too long. That was all.

Torchay lay down beside her, the bare skin of his back singeing her through her chemise as he set it against hers. He faced the door, ready to defend against anything that might come through. But he couldn't protect her from herself. She would never fall asleep like this.

"Kallista?"

"What?" She hoped she kept from snapping at him, but it was a faint hope.

"Are you—holding your breath?"

Oh. She was. Stupid thing to do with him so focused on her breathing. "No."

"It was an accident. It won't happen again, now you're on guard against it."

He thought she was worried about the stray spark. And she was. Yes, certainly she was. She was worried to death about it. "I know it won't."

"Good. Then go to sleep."

"Yes, General." Kallista tucked her hands beneath her arms and did her best to obey his order.

"That's supreme high generalissimo to you," he said.

Torchay shifted position, rubbing his naked back against her. She bit her lip, trying very hard to keep breathing slowly and evenly. She was never going to sleep again.

* * *

The next morning, on Hopeday, the riverboat captain read a brief service on the boat's foredeck for any who wished to attend. Kallista was there, with Torchay and Aisse trailing behind. She felt the need to draw closer to the One who had given her so much she didn't want. It didn't seem to help. It felt as if there were a stone wall just above her head. Lack of sleep, undoubtedly.

She must have her skin on inside out, the way the slightest breeze, the least brush of Torchay's arm or leg or hand against her made her shiver all the way through. She'd slept in fits and starts, waking up twined around Torchay and backing off to try again to sleep. If he weren't so determined to maintain some sort of contact between them, it might have been easier.

No. It wouldn't.

Kallista managed to doze a few hours on the passenger deck, which left her feeling groggy and cranky the rest of the day. She tried playing queens-and-castles with the courier, but couldn't concentrate. Then the day was over and it was time to attempt sleep again with Torchay snuggled in beside her. Sheer tempting torture.

Peaceday dawned with Kallista lying balanced on the edge of the bed, staring at the ceiling. The list of questions for Belandra sat on the table, but Kallista didn't need it. She had them memorized. They'd decided she would stay in the cabin until Belandra appeared, to keep from spooking the crew. Kallista wasn't looking forward to the confinement.

How did one summon a ghost? Or whatever it was that Belandra was supposed to be? Like one summoned magic? She started the pull, then remembered her control problems and closed her hands into fists. She elbowed Torchay. "Wake up. I need my gloves."

He fumbled on the table, taking so long to find them she knew he hadn't opened his eyes. Torchay wasn't fond of morning.

"Oh, just get out of my way." She reached across him.

He blocked her. "I've got them. Here." He thrust the brown leather gloves at her and collapsed back onto the bed, his eyes still closed. "What's your hurry?"

"I don't want to try calling Belandra without them." Kallista tugged the gloves into place. It felt strange to be still lying in bed wearing them. Like going to sleep in boots. "In case I call something else without meaning to."

Torchay's eyes opened and he stared at her in alarm. "Like what?"

"Lightning, you idiot. Not demons." She smacked him lightly on the head, then paused. What if she did call something else? Could she? The One only knew. Literally, given the freakish way her magic was behaving. She would have to try very hard not to call anything but Belandra and hope it worked.

"Wait." Torchay scrambled out of bed. He pulled on his tunic and back sheath at the same time. Quickly he returned his many knives to where they belonged, the longblade sliding into the back sheath first, as always.

Kallista watched him, amused. "Do you think your blades will have any effect on a ghost, even if you could see her?"

Knives hidden, Torchay grabbed a comb and started putting his hair in order. "No. But if she truly is Belandra of Arikon, I want her to see a proper bodyguard at your side."

While Kallista resembled a dockside slattern, lounging half dressed in the crumpled bedclothes. She wasn't sure she cared, but Torchay obviously did. "Come here. I'll braid your hair for you."

He sat and presented his back to her. "Take off your gloves. You'll never get it tight enough if you leave them on."

"All right, but if you get shocked, it's your own fault." She pulled them off as she stood, taking the comb he handed her.

She'd done this hundreds of times, not as often as Torchay had done her hair, but often. Had his hair always felt so silky? Had the natural waves he hated always curled around her fingers like that? Refusing to allow herself to linger over the task, Kallista divided his hair and set to work, pulling it tight as she twisted the red, red locks over each other. Briskly she tied it off and stepped back, taking up her gloves again.

She climbed back into bed, sitting cross-legged in the middle, and closed her eyes. Concentration would be difficult enough without having to look at Torchay. She focused on Belandra as she had last seen her, filling her mind with the image of the red-haired woman. When the details were complete, Kallista called. Magic grew, filling the air with crackling power. Then it fell into an endless depth, and vanished.

CHAPTER NINE

Kallista reached, shouting for Belandra. Nothing. No answer. Not even an echo of her call from the void.

"Is she here?" Torchay's question brought her eyes open.

Maybe she just missed the answer. But the room lay empty of anyone but Torchay, Aisse and herself. "No."

"But I felt the magic—"

"Did you?" She gave him a sharp look. He'd said before that he could tell when she called magic. "Most people can't, people without their own magic. Have you always been able to tell?"

"Not always. Try again." He held his hand out. "Without the gloves. Maybe they interfered."

"When did you start, when did you first feel it?" Kallista pulled the gloves off again and handed them over. Good thing the leather was so soft or her hands would be abraded raw by now with all the putting-on and taking-off.

"After I got out of healer's hall, that time I was gutted. Try it now."

"So, if there's any magic floating around, you can sense it?" She dried her sweaty hands on the sheet and settled again.

"Not any magic. Just yours."

"That's strange."

Torchay shrugged. "Maybe so. Try it. Call her."

Giving in to his persistence, Kallista closed her eyes and went through the whole process again. And again nothing happened. The magic dropped away into emptiness.

"Well?"

Kallista sprang off the bed, snatching her gloves from his belt. She reminded herself that it wasn't his fault she couldn't do it right. "Nothing. It's not working. It's—the magic just…vanishes."

"What happened before, when she came before?" Torchay found the tunic she hunted and gave it to her. "What did you do then?"

"Nothing." She pulled the tunic on over the chemise. "I didn't do anything. She was just there."

"Are you sure? Think."

"Of course I'm sure." She snatched up the comb and dragged it once through her hair before Torchay took it away from her. She bowed her head to give him access. "We'd been quarreling, remember? I…" She searched her memory. "I got the ring out of my pocket, put it on, and she was there."

Kallista pulled off her glove, removed the rose signet ring from her finger and shoved it back on, looking expectantly around the cabin. Torchay paused, holding her hair in one hand. "Nothing," she said yet again.

"Damn." He tied it off, combing the lower layer of hair down over the mark on her neck. "What could be wrong?"

She held on to her temper with both hands, stepping away from him. "Don't you think I'd be doing it if I knew?"

"Yes, of course you would. I'm just trying to think."

She *hated* this. Her new awareness of Torchay, added to all the rest that had gone wrong, would make her crazed. "Sorry. I just—I didn't sleep well and—"

"Why not? Trouble breathing?"

"No, nothing like that. I—kept waking up. And I'm hungry."

He grinned. "That always makes you short-tempered. *Aisse*."

The quickness of the Tibran woman's response said she'd been feigning sleep. She bowed and lifted her eyes to his—a feat that had taken several days' instruction.

"Clean up," he said slowly, indicating the cabin. "I'm going for food. Make ready."

Kallista raised an eyebrow. "You're trusting her with me?"

"You're awake." He made a show of studying their disparate heights, Kallista almost a head taller than the tiny Tibran woman. "I think you can take her if she attacks. Your blade is as sharp as mine."

Because he'd sharpened it for her. He'd also drilled her in its use. She would never be as proficient as he, but she could hold her own against any but a bodyguard, and such a battle would never happen. Not outside practice.

Belandra didn't appear before Torchay returned with the meal. Nor did she turn up all during the morning. Or in the afternoon. Or evening.

"I don't understand," Kallista complained late that night as she stripped off her gloves, boots and tunic, handing them one by one to Torchay. "She said I had *summoned* her. She said I could do it again after Hopeday had passed. But the newt-eating daughter of a goat didn't tell me *how* I could do it."

"You can try again tomorrow." Torchay arranged her belongings to suit him and pulled off his own tunic.

"I can't bear being stuck in this cabin again all day tomorrow. No." She climbed onto the bed, trying her best not to look at Torchay and failing miserably. Goddess, he was lovely. "No, I'm not calling her again. I've called. If she wants to answer, fine. If not–I don't need her. We're doing just fine on our own."

"Are we?" He sounded skeptical, and doubtless looked more so, but she turned her face resolutely to the wall.

"Well enough," she said. "What else can we do?"

Torchay sighed as he lay down and settled his back against hers. "I wish I knew."

Two days later, at dawn on Seconday, the *Taolind Runner* pulled into dock at Turysh. Kallista left the boat around noon. She'd done most of her sleeping lately after Torchay rose, not nearly enough of it. He'd doubtless sharpened all his knives to slivers waiting for her to wake. Served him right. But they were in Turysh now and she could work this itch out of her system.

Kallista took a shallow dockside breath. Same familiar reek of new tar and old fish. She turned, surveying the long stretch of docks on both banks, boats bobbing alongside in all sizes, from the big downriver boats like the *Runner* and the smaller upriver boats like the one that would take them on to Boren, to the rowboats for individual use. People, men and women both, thronged the piers, loading and unloading, bargaining for goods, arguing, laughing. Living. Save for the bubble of space around her own small party.

With a sigh, Kallista motioned Torchay into the lead. Aisse carried their overnight bags, trailing behind them. Porters would deliver their trunks to the upriver boat once passage was arranged. She stopped at the shipping office to take care of that matter first. Then she headed toward the barracks.

The local military presence was situated near the river, since that was where most of the trouble in Turysh arose. Of course, a great deal of that trouble was created by the passions, tempers and pranks of the several hundred high-spirited young men garrisoned there while fulfilling their mandatory military service.

Kallista entered the inn that catered to barracks traffic and bespoke a large room, one of those reserved for naitani. She sent Aisse up to deliver the bags and approve its suitability, mostly because she didn't want to climb stairs and Torchay wouldn't go without her. While they waited, Kallista rubbed her temples. Her head ached.

"You all right?" Torchay steered her into a chair in the inn's spacious public room.

"Tired is all." She propped her elbows on the table in front of her. "And Turysh always gives me a headache. I need to visit my parents while I'm here and that just fills my heart with joy." Her voice sounded as joyous as a funeral dirge.

"You always enjoy seeing Dardra."

"That's true. Because my fifth mother always seems happy to see me. The twins should have finished their training by now. Maybe someone will have word of them. But let's eat here first. We'll go visit right after and escape before dinner."

The twins were sedili born to Kallista's birth mother when Kallista was twelve. She'd been one of the girls' caretakers and when Karyl's North magic had awakened, they'd become closer.

"Your choice. They're your family." Torchay signaled the waiter and pointed at the tabletop.

"Why haven't we ever visited your family?"

"Because my family doesn't live in a convenient spot like Turysh, but away north in the Devil's Tooth Mountains, as you well know. Besides, I haven't quite as much family as you. I only have four parents, not twelve. Do you even know how many sedili you have?"

Kallista shrugged. "I quit counting when I left for the academy. Temple families are different, though. You know that. The temple has to be staffed, so there's always somebody new marrying in when somebody leaves for whatever reason. I could probably count two dozen parents if I wanted to."

Aisse returned and looked around as if hunting a spot where she could hide. She worried Kallista sometimes with her timidity. Torchay stood, getting her attention, and Aisse, relief on her face, made her way to their table.

"That was a nice thing to do for a spy." Kallista leaned back watching him.

"You've taken responsibility for her. That makes her my responsibility as well. She doesn't speak enough Adaran to be left alone here. Especially since she's afraid of men."

"True." Kallista took note of all the male eyes following Aisse across the room. Her bruises had faded enough that she was well worth following. A gratifying number of glances flicked Kallista's way as well and she couldn't help smiling. She would have no trouble at all hooking a man to scratch her itch.

They ate their lunch—fish cakes, fried potatoes and some kind of greens that smelled awful and tasted worse—then headed through town to the Riverside Temple. Turysh boasted six temples to serve the population. Riverside was the oldest, but the Mother Temple had been moved years ago to the city's center, away from the noise and turbulence near the docks. Kallista had grown up in the midst of it.

Her visit went about as she expected. Her birth parents forced smiles and asked politely after her welfare, managing never to touch their eldest child. North magic disturbed Kallista's mother. She seemed to believe the inanimate things North magic dealt with might corrupt her own East magic healing talent. Yet both her children with magic were of the North.

Only Kallista's fifth mother, the temple administrator, seemed truly glad to see her, enveloping Kallista in a plump, fragrant hug and asking when she was going to make an honest man of Torchay. The joke fell a little flat this time, mostly because Kallista felt a tiny twinge of envy as Dardra gave Torchay his hug. Kallista vowed to begin trolling her line as soon as they got back to the inn. She needed a man badly if the sight of her fifth mother hugging her bodyguard disturbed her.

Aisse's presence was remarked upon. She got a hug too, but was left to her privacy as Dardra caught Kallista up on all the family news. The twins were indeed through with their education and would soon return to Turysh to set up their business. Karyl was a far-speaker and Kami would manage the business end of things. They had met a pair of sedili, men who had just finished their military duty. The wedding was to be in three months. Kallista was expected to attend.

With promises to move heaven, earth and Tibrans if necessary, in order to be there, Kallista managed to escape before the rest of the current family gathered for dinner.

"That wasn't so bad, now, was it?" Torchay said as they walked back to the inn.

"No, not so bad. It was good to see Dardra. But now it's done and I intend to play tonight."

Torchay rolled his eyes, as he always did when Kallista slipped out of harness. Aisse looked from one to the other. "What is play?" she said in hesitant Adaran.

"Children play." Kallista grinned and picked up her pace. "And sometimes grown-ups play as well."

"It means," Torchay said, "that the captain hunts—you understand hunts?"

Aisse nodded, eyes wide as she scurried along.

"She hunts for a man tonight."

"Maybe two." Kallista winked at Torchay just to watch him roll his eyes again.

"Two?" Aisse said. "What great-captain do with two men?" She still had trouble remembering that Kallista preferred "captain" to "great lady." But she stuck to Adaran. Not that Kallista could tell, save by the occasional missing word.

"The same thing I would do with one." Her grin felt predatory. "Play with them. Have fun."

"Not have sex?"

Kallista lost a step before she burst out laughing. Even Torchay had to hide a smile. "Yes, Aisse. I will have sex with them. Him. Whoever I find. To me, that is play. Fun."

Aisse made a face. Obviously she didn't agree, and Kallista's laughter faded. "It is fun, Aisse, but only if everyone wants to play, and only if it's done right. If everybody isn't having fun, then it's not right."

The Tibran woman still looked skeptical. Kallista glanced at Torchay, wondering if he was at all interested in convincing Aisse otherwise. How would she feel if he did? Kallista squirmed.

She didn't want him for herself. Not really. She had just gone too long without, and she'd discovered a new appreciation for his finely honed physique. He was an attractive man with all that rich, wavy flame-red hair. His nose fit his narrow, bony, familiar face. And if he wanted Aisse, or any woman, he should have what he wanted.

"How?" Aisse asked. "How you hunt for man?"

This time Torchay laughed, a short bark of laughter. "She doesn't have to actually hunt. She just walks through the room, trailing perfume and sex, and they line up behind her with their tongues hanging out. Then she just picks the one she wants."

"When did that ever happen?" Kallista demanded. "Maybe when I was younger, but not lately. Not for a long time."

"You don't see the way they look at you." He mimicked a cross-eyed moonling. "It's a wonder they don't fall over their own tongues."

"You think you are so funny, don't you?" She shoved him and he swayed slightly, laughing at her.

"Watch," Torchay said to Aisse, tipping his head in Kallista's direction. "Watch and learn."

She went up to the room, where she washed and changed out of her uniform into a long red dress tunic made to be worn without trousers. It laced up the sides to fit her shape snugly. The slits up the side seams were there for ease in movement and to show off her legs. Kallista had nice legs, or so she'd been told by more than one lover.

She changed her gloves for a pair of red kid-leather ones that climbed to her elbows, and hung a pale blue faceted stone the size of her thumb set in silver around her neck. Torchay pulled her boots off for her and she slipped on a pair of high-heeled shoes, red to match dress and gloves. She'd have to be careful. She hadn't worn the heels in months. But a woman never forgot how to walk in heels. She brushed her hair, letting it fall free to her shoulders. She dabbed on the perfume Torchay had given her for a New Year's gift ages ago, used a bit of red on her cheeks and lips, and she was ready.

Torchay and Aisse followed her back down to the public room, Torchay because it was his duty, and Aisse because he insisted she come for the lesson. At least he'd consented to change out of his bodyguard's black into the brown tunic that flattered him more and made him less noticeable. Aisse wore her same baggy un-bleached cotton and looked virtually invisible.

Kallista hadn't reached the bar before a crowd of soldiers invited her to join their table. While she looked them over, another table issued an invitation. When did the soldiers get to be so young? They all looked younger than eighteen, but she knew they didn't leave the remote camps for the first two years. They had to be at least eighteen. She finally sat with the first boys who asked. They looked a little older than the others, a little closer to the end of their service.

They were all lovely with their fair Adaran skin, light eyes and hair in all shades of yellow, brown and red. Kallista couldn't choose among them so she let them sort themselves out, laughing at the games of arm wrestling and dart throwing that determined who would sit next to her as she ate. Until the end of the next competition. One young man with soft brown hair and deep green eyes seemed to win more than his share of the games. As the evening wore on, she touched him and allowed his touch in return, until he opened his mouth close to her ear and murmured, "Will you come upstairs with me?"

Amused by his boldness, Kallista smiled. She stood, trailing a hand over his broad shoulders, then took his hand to lead him away while his comrades shouted out good-natured advice and abuse. Torchay would follow, of course. He'd be in the next room, but she could pretend he wasn't. They'd learned how to make this work long ago. She stopped with her young soldier on the stairs' landing out of sight of the public room to share a kiss. It was more sweet than hot, but Kallista let it go. There would be time for heat.

He was so young, his body not yet filled out to the promise of his broad frame. Outside the room, Kallista stopped again. She ran her hands down his back to cup his buttocks and he seized her face between his hands for another kiss. Again, it held light without heat. She opened the door. Inside the room, he stripped away his tunic before wrapping his arms around her, grinding his erection into her stomach.

"Easy, soldier." She slowed him with her hands on his face, his chest. "Plenty of time. No hurry."

"You sure?" He gasped for breath. "I feel like I'm going to explode."

"Not yet, if you please." She trailed a hand down to find the drift of fine hair descending from his navel.

He stopped breathing. She almost made a joke of it before she remembered he wouldn't understand. He didn't have Torchay's obsession with breathing.

That thought spoiled her mood and she reached for it, wanting it back. She leaned close to breathe in the musky male scent of his skin. He found the side lacings of her dress and began to loosen them, running his open mouth along the side of her neck from shoulder to jawline. Kallista shivered. That was it. This was what she wanted.

She let a finger dip into the waistband of his trousers. He froze for a second before drawing her earlobe into his mouth and sucking on it. She whimpered, turned her head to the side to give him better access. She needed this.

"Tell me," he whispered into her ear.

"Tell you what? Tell you you're sexy? Tell you I want you? You are. I do."

He gave a breathy little chuckle. "Yes, that. But—is it true? Did you slay a thousand Tibrans with a single word?"

Kallista went cold from the inside out. Was this the attraction? Was this what had him here panting over her like a rutting stag? "Who told you such a thing?"

She wanted to hurt him, to punish him for the gossip, but he wasn't to blame for anything more than listening.

He nuzzled her neck. "The courier," he said. "It's all over barracks. How the enemy battered down the wall in Ukiny and were coming through. Until you spoke the word."

"Is that why you're here with me?" She backed away, her voice cold as the winter inside her. "To see what I might do? Is it the fear that excites you?" Kallista began drawing off one of her gloves, watched his eyes go wide with fear. She wouldn't call magic, wouldn't actually remove the glove, shouldn't tease him at all, but the cold made her cruel.

He shook his head, swallowed hard, cupped his hands together over his groin.

"No?" Kallista tugged the glove back into place, denying the temptation. "What then? Knowing I killed so many? It wasn't a thousand, you know. More like ten. Ten thousand. Though not all of them died. Nor did I speak. Not a word."

She lifted her hands high like a theatrical charlatan pretending to call power. True calling required nothing so showy. "I merely—" She threw her hands wide as she had cast the magic, and the boy stumbled back, fell onto the bed. Terror showed in every line of his young face and it shamed her.

"*Goddess.*" She turned away, smoothing her gloves down. "I'm sorry." She rubbed a hand over her face. "I'm so sorry."

What right did she have to anger? Her motives tonight were no purer than his. Less so. He at least wanted something of her. She wanted someone else. She was just using him in a stupid attempt to satisfy that want. She should know by now it wouldn't work. She'd have to simply endure it till it wore off.

"I—it's the power," he said, voice shaking. "All that magic. A woman with so much—it's—"

Kallista nodded. That was a more pleasant thought than the alternatives she'd come up with. She picked up his tunic and tossed it at him. She yanked her laces tight again, but didn't bother to tie them.

"Can't we still—" He balled up the tunic in his hands.

She shook her head. "I'm sorry. I shouldn't have led you on. I'm—there's someone else."

"Someone you can't have." He sounded far wiser than his years.

"You'd better just go." She couldn't bear looking at him any longer, couldn't face any more guilt.

"But—my friends. They'll think—"

"The truth?" Kallista shook her head. "No. I'm—" She would not apologize again, though she should. "This isn't your fault. Stay. I'll go. You can tell them…whatever you like. Except that I raised power for you. I didn't."

"You *didn't?*"

Kallista held up her still-gloved hands and turned them this way and that to remind him they'd never been uncovered.

"Oh." He walked with her to the door. "Are you sure you won't—"

She put two red-gloved fingers over his mouth, then kissed his cheek. "I hope you find your naitan," she said. "But love *her* as well as her magic."

He swallowed, nodded, and she left him.

Torchay and Aisse were already in the room next door. Aisse was bundled in her blanket in the cot near the door, asleep or pretending to be. Torchay had changed out of his finery into old trousers, his tunic off against the heat as he worked through his bodyguard exercises.

"Don't you usually do that earlier in the day?" Kallista tossed her pendant on the table beside the big bed and kicked off her shoes.

"I did." He finished the flowing form he was doing and stopped. The faint sheen of sweat over his lean musculature tempted her eyes to look, to drink their fill. "I felt like doing it again. I didn't expect to see you before dawn."

"Yes, well…" She tugged her fingers free of the thin snug leather and pulled her gloves off, flexing her sweaty hands in the slightly cooler air. "Didn't work out."

Torchay walked toward the table. Kallista backed off. She couldn't bear being so close to him. Not now. He poured water from the pitcher into a cup and drank it, then poured the rest into the basin and splashed it on his face. Kallista watched his every move.

When he had dried his face with the flimsy towel, he turned and saw Kallista watching. "Can I ask you somethi— No." He shook his head. "Never mind." He hung the towel up and reached for his hair to release his queue.

"What?" Kallista loosened the laces of her dress tunic. "If you have a question, ask it. You know you can ask me anything."

"Can I?"

She looked up and saw his gaze focused on her. The candlelight reflecting from his eyes made them glow with blue flame. She lost herself in them for a moment before she recalled he'd asked her a question. "Yes, of course. Anything."

Once more he hesitated, seeming to look for something as he gazed at her, but what, Kallista didn't know.

"All right," he said finally. "I will." He ran his fingers through his unbound hair and it fell in waves around his face, crimson in the candlelight. "When you have gone out hunting all these years—" He paused for a deep breath, looking away only an instant. "When you have hunted a man, why did you never choose me?"

CHAPTER TEN

Kallista swayed, Torchay's question touching unseen things deep inside her, drawing her tight, opening her up. Her nipples beaded beneath the brocade weave of her dress and she tucked her hands beneath her arms, more as a guard against unwanted magic than an attempt to hide her body's reaction. Why did he have to ask her that question now? Now when she wanted him so much it made her mouth dry and other places all too wet?

"I— It's not that—" Goddess, what could she say that wouldn't either insult him or encourage him?

Torchay waited, his face an impassive mask, candlelight licking over his sculpted form, tempting her to do the same. She curled her hands into fists against the urge to touch.

"You're my bodyguard, Torchay." She winced at resorting to that old excuse yet again. He deserved more than that. "Goddess knows you're an attractive man. But I have seen so many solid, working relationships ruined when a naitan gets involved with her bodyguard. It's not so much his protectiveness—you're all so protective to begin with you're paranoid. But *she* becomes protective of *him*.

"She starts avoiding her duty because it might get him hurt, or doing—doing stupid things that wind up getting him killed anyway. And jealousy? You've seen it too, how crazy they can get. We've talked about it, how sex messes up a perfectly good partnership. We have a good one. I don't want to ruin that just for a few nights of horizontal hide-and-seek."

His smile flickered. "I'm good for a few nights, eh?"

Kallista raised an eyebrow. *Honestly.* Men and their self-esteem. "Okay, a week."

The smile flashed again and faded away. "I didn't die." The intensity in his gaze made her look away. "You're talking about your first bodyguard, aren't you? The one who was killed."

The army had no secrets, but gossip wasn't always accurate. "My first bodyguard retired to the coast to sell beer and tall tales." She took a deep breath. "It was the second who died."

"Did you love him?"

Did she? She'd thought so at the time. But she'd learned since then that sex and love tended to get tangled no matter how hard one tried to keep them separate. That was why she never took a lover for more than a few months, preferably one near the end of his enlistment. Simpler that way. "It was a long time ago. I don't remember."

He nodded. His hair fell forward, hiding his face as he looked down, fingers fidgeting with the edge of the table.

"Is that what you wanted to know?"

He shrugged, nodded again, picking at the rough wood, creating splinters.

Kallista sighed. Why couldn't a man be more like a woman? "Torchay, it isn't that I didn't *want* to choose you..." He looked up and she met his eyes briefly before letting her gaze trail down over his breathtaking body, letting him see just how much she appreciated it, how much she wanted him. Goddess, he was as aroused as she.

She spun around, clamping her hands securely in place, fighting for breath. "I can't do this. It's too much." She heard him move, coming toward her, and she flinched away. "No. Don't touch me. *Don't.* If you do—"

"I wouldn't mind."

Her laughter sounded more like a sob. "I would. Sex would ruin everything, Torchay. What we have is too important to me to risk that. I won't. Please don't ask it of me."

"It doesn't have to ruin things." He stood so close behind her she could feel the heat radiating from his body.

"It would. You know it would. Even though we've been friends for ages, saying it out loud has changed things already." She ought to move away, put more space between them, but it was all she could do to stand upright without swaying back into him.

"For the worse?" His voice sounded flat, the way it did when he locked himself away inside.

Kallista fought the urge to turn into his arms and bring him back. She hated hurting him. *Hated* it. "No, of course not. How could it be worse? But it *is* different. We haven't adjusted to that much change. More could be disastrous."

Torchay backed away now. From the corner of her eye, Kallista saw him cross to the open window and turned to watch him. He leaned on the sill to stare out into the raucous barrackside night. The old threadbare trousers he'd changed into stretched across his buttocks and had her catching her breath all over again.

"I thought it would be easier if I knew," he said without turning. "If I knew for certain you've never fancied me. I was sure that was why…" His hands tightened on the wooden sill until Kallista feared it would crack. He lifted his face to the night sky, his hair sliding back with a crimson caress. Kallista wanted to touch it, to run her naked hands through it and watch the way it twined around her fingers.

"I'm sorry," she said.

He shook his head, his hair sweeping his shoulders. "I shouldn't have asked."

"Probably not." When she had indulged herself enough with his hair, she wanted to slide her hands over those shoulders. She took a deep breath and squeezed her fists tight. "But we'll manage. Somehow."

"Aye. Somehow." Torchay gave her a quick glance over his shoulder. "You should go on to bed. The upriver boat leaves early tomorrow. I'll join you after I finish my Fan Dai." He gave the intricate graceful exercise of the bodyguards its proper name.

"You still mean to…?" Kallista gestured at the bed. She shuddered at the thought of sharing it with him after tonight's conversation.

"Are you still dreaming?"

Goddess, yes. Every night. But nothing she could share with Torchay. She dreamed of men. Sleek, hard bodies, golden and pale and brown, caressing her in turn, arousing her, driving her relentlessly toward tonight's disaster. The dreams were erotic, though. Not prophetic.

Torchay took her silence as answer. "Then my place is there." He took a deep breath, hands tightening on the sill again. "We can bear it because we have no other choice."

He was right. They had no choice. Not one they were willing to make. She refused to ask for another bodyguard. She prayed he would not request reassignment. Kallista found her bag and drew out a chemise. She'd left it off when she dressed for her abortive hunt. Quickly she changed, laying her dress tunic over a chair to let it air before she packed it again.

She crawled into the bed, moving to the side against the wall to give Torchay his space. He waited until she stopped rustling around then stepped back into the center of the room. He stood for a moment, head down, motionless. Then he poured himself into the proper position. Another second of stillness and his body flowed from one action to the next, pure masculine grace in motion.

Kallista let her eyes slide half-shut as she lay there in the bed. The damp breeze from the river wafting over her bare legs did nothing to cool her as she watched him and wanted him. She drifted off to sleep with his image burned into her brain.

The next morning as they headed up the docks to the shallow berths where the upriver boats were docked, they passed some sort of uproar near the downriver boats. Someone was shouting, almost screaming, as soldiers rushed to bring the man under control. Kallista caught a glimpse of him as his eyes rolled back in his head and he began to convulse, poor soul.

She felt magic stir around her, seeking entry, and she shut it out. The East naitan trying to calm him wouldn't welcome Kallista taking what wasn't hers. Torchay caught her arm and hurried her past. She could do nothing to help.

The journey up the Alira, which joined the Taolind there at Turysh, was slow due to spring runoff from the mountains. The boat's single naitan could not maintain a constant wind pocket strong enough to fill the sails against the current, so they anchored at night. They didn't reach Boran until Sixthday, and in all that time, Belandra failed to appear. Kallista began to doubt she ever would. At least she hoped it.

In Boran they hired horses and attached themselves to a caravan whose merchants were so delighted to have a military naitan with them, they waived any fee. Kallista hadn't heard that bandits were preying on the Arikon passes again, but one never knew.

Late on the second day out of Boran, the caravan emerged from Highroad Pass into the broad Veryas Valley and Kallista saw Arikon the Blessed rising from the slopes and cliffs beyond. The gray stone spires glowed warm and welcoming in the golden light of the setting sun. The new copper roof of the Mother Temple of all Adara gleamed as it towered high above the city. The massive blackwood gates in the high south wall stood open, admitting any who cared to enter. Here, Kallista felt as if the city reached out to welcome her, unlike Turysh, which barely tolerated her presence. Here, she had been trained in the North Academy. Here, she had found her place.

A chill gripped her as a cloud cut off the sun. In the lower fringes of the Shieldback Mountains, it was cooler than down in Adara's flat plain. But she wouldn't lie, even to herself. The chill was fear. She feared what would happen when she passed through those gates. Would she lose the place she had made? Would she lose herself? She wanted to run away, pretend nothing had happened. But she couldn't. Duty required she report to the Reinine. If she didn't have her duty, she had nothing.

This time Stone came to himself in a bed that didn't move. Sunlight filtered through closed shutters into a room stifling with humid heat, worse than that in camp at the Adaran city because the air did not move. He sat up, moving slowly against aches worse than any hangover he'd ever known. The rattle of chains reminded him where and what he was. A prisoner of the Adarans en route to their capital for questioning.

Khralsh, he hurt. Every muscle in his body, down to his smallest toes had been wrenched out of place, twisted mercilessly and put back wrong. He was thirsty. Squinting through the dim light, he saw a pitcher, a basin and a cup of heavy stoneware sitting on the square table beside the bed. Stone summoned his strength and reached for the pitcher.

"Thirsty?"

The voice startled him, almost knocking him flat on the bed again. Stone rubbed his eyes and gradually brought the lieutenant into focus. Joh Suteny. In command of Stone's escort.

"Do you want water?" The lieutenant reached for the pitcher and cup. "Will you drink?"

Stone nodded. He rubbed his eyes again, trying to rub away the ache without success, then swung his feet carefully to the floor. He wouldn't try standing yet, not until his thigh muscles stopped twitching. His mouth felt sand-scoured and he reached eagerly for the water Suteny handed him.

He drank deep before attempting to speak. "How long?"

"Do you remember disembarking in Turysh?"

Stone nodded, drank again and handed the cup back for more. Suteny filled it. "That was two days ago."

"What happened? Who beat me?" Stone tried a smile to show he was joking. *Gods,* even that hurt.

"No one." Suteny didn't seem to have much of a sense of humor. "You were walking along the dock, and out of nowhere you went into some sort of screaming fit. Convulsions. Are you prone to convulsions?"

"No. I've never had one before. Wouldn't be a warrior if I did. I'd lose my caste."

"Oh?" Suteny's eyebrow went up, asking without actually asking.

Stone didn't speak. No one liked to speak of that, of what happened to a casteless male, and he was no exception. Especially since, as a prisoner, he had lost caste already. He didn't even want to think about it. When the silence stretched, he shrugged, hoping that would distract the Adaran, and drank his water.

"Are you hungry?" The lieutenant stood. "Do you think you can manage meat?"

Even his teeth ached. The thought of chewing tough beef made them ache more. "I feel half-starved. I could eat something soft. Fish, maybe. We are on a river, aren't we?"

"I think that can be arranged." Suteny studied Stone in the dim light. "Do you feel ready to travel?"

"Walking?" He couldn't manage that.

"Not for a few days more. Another short journey by boat."

Stone nodded. He could sit on a boat.

"Good." The lieutenant nodded in a brusque salute and vanished.

By the time they left the boat in the next town a few days later, the aches had left Stone. He had no trouble mounting his horse once the leg shackles were unfastened. Of course, his hands were bound and a soldier held the chain attached to his wrists as well as the lead rein to his horse. He was still a prisoner. A valuable one, apparently, for Suteny had a soldier ride to either side of him whenever there was room on the trail in case he had another fit. They were supposed to keep him from falling. Stone just wanted it all to be over.

They reached Arikon, a city as impressive as any in Tibre and far more beautiful, though if they'd asked him, he'd have denied it. Stone was sent to a guest chamber in the company of his escort, rather than to a dungeon cell. It surprised him, even though the chamber was small and modestly appointed. And in relative comfort, they waited.

Joh held on to his temper as he strode through the web of corridors that made up the Arikon palace complex. It was far past midnight, he was tired after spending all day on horseback and he had never had much patience with secrets and intrigue. He did, however, have extended experience at holding his temper. As one of only ten men promoted to officer rank in the Adaran army, he'd had to learn that long ago.

He thought he'd left the Summerglen Palace two corridors

and a courtyard back, which should put him in Winterhold Palace if he hadn't taken a wrong turn somewhere. He ought to be coming up on his goal, a neglected chapel. The next corner brought him to a doorway.

Carved and painted black briars twined up the pillars on either side of the pale gray door and tangled together on the pediment above. The sight of them broke Joh's stride, forcing him into a stutter step to maintain his balance. It was a chapel to the mysterious Western face of the One. No wonder the place was deserted.

And no wonder the Barinirab Master had chosen it for a meeting. Joh had been told that the Master had a fine and sardonic sense of humor. Drawing the white hood of his cloak farther down over his face, Joh entered the chapel.

He scarcely had time to look around himself before a tall figure wrapped in a black cloak stepped from the shadows cast by the candles flickering on the white marble altar. Someone still cared for this place, unless the Master Barb had lit them himself.

"Give your report, Renunciate." The man's voice was a raspy croak, disguising itself against identification.

Joh bowed low. "Master. The Tibran appears to have no magic whatsoever, whether of the West or any other compass point. He may be mad, or simply ill."

"But the mark—does he have the mark?"

"He has *a* mark. Whether it is a godmark, I do not know. It's on the back of his neck, red, like a birthmark or a scar."

"In the shape of a rose?"

"I could not say." Joh had studied the thing endlessly, trying to decide. "It's round. A circle. It could be seen as a rose—or most anything else that shape. Truly, Master, the man is—he's no more than any other poor unfortunate who cannot control his own mind."

The black hood moved as if the head inside nodded agreement.

Joh could not see even the shadow of a face inside it, and it made his skin crawl.

"Very well," the cowled figure said. "I accept your report, Renunciate."

"Master." He bowed again and turned to go.

"Wait. One more matter. It is believed by the High Council of the Order of Barinirab that you are ready to become an Initiate. Do you agree with this assessment?"

Once more Joh bowed, deeper than before. Many members of the Order never advanced beyond Renunciate. He felt the honor deeply, though he wondered whether he deserved it. His belief seemed shallow compared to the few other Barbs he'd met.

He had joined because the Order was one of the few organizations admitting men and he thought it might help his advancement. But the Order's teaching about West magic made sense to him. How could death be anything but evil? And the teaching fed his almost insatiable desire to learn. The more he learned, the more he wanted to know. If he became an Initiate, what new things might he learn?

The Master apparently took Joh's silence as agreement. "You will be contacted."

Recognizing dismissal, Joh departed gratefully. He had a long trek back through the palaces to his charge and his bed. He would be contacted. Sometime before then, he needed to decide what his answer would be.

"Five days." Kallista paced the confines of the small guest chamber in the palace complex where they'd been lodged, feeling like a caged wolf. If she did not escape soon, she might just bite something. "They've kept us waiting five days while they *consult.* Who knows what that means? Who are they consulting? Seems the logical person to consult would be me, wouldn't it? After all, I am the person these things have happened to. I'm the one who cut down all those Tibrans. But no..."

She waggled her hips and her fingers, mocking the one courtier who'd condescended to tell them anything and pitched her voice into its soprano range. "The Reinine is a busy woman."

She dropped it back to normal. "I know she's busy. We don't have to talk to the Reinine. A general would be fine. Or a colonel. A prelate. No, better yet, a scholar. Someone who's studied things like this and knows what's going on.

"It's Fourthday already. If they don't see us tomorrow or Sixthday, it will be the week's end again and we'll have to wait three more days before anyone will do anything."

Torchay stopped sharpening his blade, the big blade this time, so big it probably qualified as a short sword. "What do you expect me to do about it? I can't very well march down to the high steward's office, hold a point to his throat and demand an appointment, can I?"

"No." Kallista flopped back onto the bed, spreading her arms wide in a careless sprawl. Five days of waiting after the rush to get here had Torchay's temper as sore as hers. "All I expect of you is to listen while I complain."

"I'm like to go deaf with it," he grumbled.

She laughed. "If you go deaf you won't have to listen to me anymore." She twisted on the bed until she could poke him in the arm with her unshod toe.

Torchay froze motionless. "Kallista, don't."

She jerked her foot back and rolled to put her back to him. The wait had restored much of the ease between them, but not all of it. Not when she was forbidden the least teasing touch. Torchay was right, though. The least touch could hurt.

"How is Aisse doing on her Adaran?" Kallista still had to be careful to concentrate on the person to whom she intended to speak to be sure she spoke in the right language.

"Aisse speaks much Adaran," the servant said from her corner. She tended to crouch there when Kallista started pacing.

"Yes, you do. You speak very much Adaran. Good for you." Kallista rolled onto her stomach and beamed at her.

"I have a good teacher." Aisse ducked her head to look at Torchay through her lashes. "He angers—gets angry, but he not—he does not..." She paused and switched to Tibran to ask, "What is hit? Beat?"

Kallista had to ask Torchay, who had to tell Aisse the words. It was awkward to teach a language when she never knew which language she was speaking. They both sounded the same.

They were advancing to more abstract concepts like kindness and cruelty, when a knock sounded at the door. Aisse answered it to reveal a palace functionary dressed in a vivid green calf-length tunic with short puffed sleeves slashed to show gold and blue satin beneath. Formfitting tights—one leg blue, the other gold—flashed from the thigh-high slits in the tunic. Kallista forced herself to smile at the woman without shielding her eyes against such brilliance.

"Captain Kallista Varyl?" The courtier's long brown hair was all loops and whorls swooping dizzily around her head.

"I am Captain Varyl."

The courtier put her blue-clad leg forward and swept in a deep bow, complete with hand flourishes. "Naitan. I am Erunde Nonnald, fourth undersecretary in the Reinine's Staff Command, directly serving under High Steward Huryl Kovallyk."

Feeling grubby and unkempt in her wrinkled duty-tunic and flyaway hair, Kallista made a leg and an equally elegant bow. "The pleasure is mine, Undersecretary," she lied. She'd never cared much for bureaucratic types.

"If the naitan pleases, Her Holiest Majesty, Serysta, Reinine of all Adara, awaits your presence and that of your escort, on the hour."

"On the—" Kallista blinked and glanced toward the window. The Summerglen tower clock could be seen from it, the bells marking the hours clearly heard. "On the *next* hour?"

Erunde looked vaguely distressed as she gave a slightly smaller bow. "That is so, naitan. You have, I believe, half an hour to ready yourselves."

"*Goddess,*" Kallista swore. "Wait, you said 'my escort'—does that mean my bodyguard alone, or both of them?"

"I..." The courtier seemed to notice Aisse for the first time. "I do not know, naitan. However, on the side of caution, you might—"

"Right. I'll bring them both. If Aisse isn't wanted, she can wait outside." Kallista turned to Torchay who already had the wardrobe open, pulling out their dress uniforms. Fortunately, they'd been cleaned and pressed days ago in anticipation of this moment.

"By your leave, naitan." Erunde's voice startled Kallista. She wasn't gone already? Kallista dismissed the woman with a slap-dash salute and continued with her business. It was Aisse who shut the door again.

Twenty minutes later, Kallista and Torchay strode through the palace corridors at a brisk ground-eating pace that had Aisse jogging to keep up. Kallista tugged at her tunic. The heavy embroidery depicting the tree-and-crown of her home prinsipality made the front of the thing want to bunch up. The red-and-gold stag on Torchay's black tunic gleamed in the late-afternoon sun. The honors and service awards attached to their gold-colored chain belts jingled madly as they walked. They had medallions recognizing service in every campaign they'd taken part in, and over the past nine years, they'd taken part in almost all of them.

Kallista caught a glimpse of Aisse in the mirrors lining the wall opposite the tall windows. She still wore the same clothes she'd worn during their journey. They should have considered that the Reinine would want to inspect a Tibran and acquired better clothes for her, or at least trimmed the hacked-off hair into some sort of shape. But they'd left it too late.

Kallista's queue felt strange after only two weeks of going

without, but it looked better this way. Much more tidy. Kallista approved her own reflection and Torchay's. His muscular arms, bare in the sleeveless summer uniform, almost glowed against the black of his tunic.

They reached the crowded anteroom just as the clocks in all the towers began chiming in chorus. Torchay had to push a passage through to the front, for once needing force. Most times, people tended to melt away when they saw his bodyguard's black-with-blue. They reached the doorkeeper's post just as the echo of the last chime faded away.

The doorkeeper frowned, her chins quivering in disapproval. "You should have been here at least a quarter hour ago."

"I only received word a half hour ago that my presence was required at this time." Kallista refused to be bullied. She tugged at her black dress gloves.

The doorkeeper hmmphed, but said only, "Did you bring the Tibran?"

Torchay stepped aside and tugged Aisse forward. The doorkeeper's chins quivered alarmingly as she looked the small woman over. "Very well."

They still had to stand waiting until after the clocks chimed the next quarter hour before the reception-room door opened and a brace of perfumed and bejeweled prinsipi swept out. From Gadrene, Ukiny's prinsipality, according to the white-and-blue ship emblazoned far too frequently on their clothing.

A man in a gray robe that did nothing to subdue the brilliance of the scarlet and sky-blue tunic and tights he wore beneath stood in the doorway as if guarding it. His eyes were surrounded with creases that said they'd seen it all and hadn't been impressed with much of it. His mouth was set in straight lines of dissatisfaction. He had to be the doorkeeper's superior, High Steward Huryl.

Kallista had never met the man. She didn't run in such powerful, expensive circles, but she'd heard tales of his astonishing rise.

A man rarely received such an important governmental post, overseeing the palace staff and managing access to the Reinine. The task gave him monumental power. He had done it through efficiency and assiduous devotion to duty.

She admired that in anyone, but it was particularly impressive in a man. Male passions tended to distract them—though they never had Torchay. But Torchay was a special case. She had never heard that Huryl abused his power either. He neither accepted nor demanded bribes to grant appointments.

But seeing him now, Kallista didn't think she could ever like the man, no matter how admirable his morals might be. He looked too sour to ever be good company.

"Is the captain here with her party?" Huryl spoke to the door-keeper while his eyes roved the packed antechamber.

Kallista's eyes narrowed. Huryl seemed to be hoping they hadn't come. Why? He could have no reason to dislike her without ever having met her, and she could be no possible threat to his power. She had to be imagining it.

"Yes, High Steward." The doorkeeper gestured. Kallista stepped forward, Torchay just behind her left shoulder, Aisse trying to keep out of sight behind both of them.

Huryl looked them over with the same dissatisfied expression he'd done everything with so far. "Very well." He backed away, holding the door wide. "Come."

Kallista felt her queue as she approached the door, checking for neatness.

"Stop fussing," Torchay muttered. "You look fine."

She glanced at him, flashing a quick grin. "So do you."

And they were inside, proceeding down the length of a high, wide, endless chamber between two rows of white marble columns. The floor was an inlaid mosaic—stone, not tile—of green and gold twining cheerfully around and through the black-and-white marble geometrics.

When they drew close enough, Kallista saw that the golden throne sat empty, a red velvet throw tossed carelessly over the arms. Huryl led them past the throne on its dais to a door hidden behind a tapestry depicting hunters flying hawks. Beyond it, they were ushered into a room like many Kallista had known, with maps and papers tossed onto tabletops, books crowding shelves, chairs scattered everywhere. It was a working headquarters. The furnishings were of more luxurious materials than Kallista was accustomed to, and the inhabitants smelled rather better, but the familiar scene relaxed the tension between her shoulders.

The breeze coming through the open windows stirred the clutter on the wide desk. A slender white arm emerged from the cluster of fringe-shouldered generals, picked up a gem-crusted silver goblet and used it as a paperweight.

Huryl cleared his throat. "Your Majesty."

CHAPTER ELEVEN

The generals parted and Kallista caught a glimpse of the Reinine before sweeping into a bow so low her forehead nearly touched her knee. "Majesty."

"Rise, Captain. All of you," the Reinine added when Torchay and Aisse didn't move as Kallista straightened.

The ruler of the twenty-seven prinsipalities of Adara held out her hand. Startled by this gesture of extreme honor, Kallista took it and bent to kiss the ring she wore—a ring that could be the twin of the one on her own finger. The Reinine's ring showed centuries of wear that Kallista's did not, and it made her stifle a shudder. She could see Huryl frowning from the corner of her eye. What did he have against her? Or was she imagining his animosity?

"Come." The Reinine gestured toward the window and Kallista followed as she drew aside.

Only now could Kallista take in details of the woman to whom she had sworn allegiance. The Reinine was a small woman, not as tiny as Aisse, but half a head shorter than Kallista. Her blond hair was streaked with gray, dressed simply in a coronet of braids atop her head. Her blue eyes held an ageless wisdom, and a warmth that had Kallista wanting to wrap herself in it.

"So," Serysta Reinine said. "Tell me what has happened to you, my naitan."

Kallista found herself pouring out the tale. It took some time in the telling, with the Reinine's frequent interruptions for questions. There was a quarrel with the Reinine's pair of bodyguards over whether Kallista would remove her glove to show the ring she had received in her dream. The Reinine won.

The glove was removed, Torchay standing close by to hold the glove and return it when the inspection of the ring was completed. When Kallista's tale was done, Torchay was called to the window to tell his tale, and after him, Aisse.

The clocks had told several hours by the time they finished. "Do you know what this means, Majesty?" Kallista asked when she and Torchay were bid to join Aisse.

"No, naitan, I am afraid I do not. I have suspicions, but—"

Kallista wanted to demand explanations but could not. Not of the Reinine. Instead, she inclined her head in obedience. "I await your pleasure, Your Majesty."

"I have not seen you at dinner, have I, naitan?" Serysta Reinine said.

"Er—no, Your Majesty." The question startled Kallista. "We've been eating in our chamber."

"I was not aware you wished the captain to be included in court activities," Huryl said smoothly. "I will see to it at once."

Kallista didn't know whether to resent Huryl's subtle insult in using her military rank rather than her title as naitan, or the Reinine's unexpected generosity. She didn't think she wanted inclusion. Court was expensive, and as a temple child, she did not have an independent income. Nor did she particularly like the thought of putting on her best clothes and best manners every third night. But it was kind of the Reinine. "Thank you, Your Majesty."

The Reinine smiled. "Do not feel that you *must* come, naitan. Only if you wish."

"Thank you, Your Majesty." This time a smile accompanied Kallista's words. She should have known the Reinine would read the truth. It was her magic, after all, truth-saying.

"We will speak again, when I have consulted with my scholars and meditated on the matter."

Kallista bowed low and left the room with her companions. The Reinine, her guards and the generals followed her out, but stopped at the dais. Kallista decided the next appointment must be designated for the throne room. Someone they needed to impress. Huryl escorted them down the length of the room, not quite so endless now they were departing, and opened the door.

The waiting crowd swayed forward as they emerged. Huryl had turned to the doorkeeper, Kallista and her party already forgotten. Torchay stepped forward to force a passage from the antechamber, when a hoarse shout echoed through the room.

"Chosen One! Chosen of the One!" a man's voice cried out.

Kallista turned, her attention caught like that of everyone else in the room, and saw a hand reach through the press of bodies toward her. Steel encircled the wrist, led to another hand, led to a man in shackles, his eyes wild as he struggled to free himself from the soldiers who held him.

She could see Torchay caught by the curious crowd, fighting to reach her, heard him bellow her name, but the prisoner held all her attention, somehow keeping her in place. Despite the tight queue it was bound into, the bright yellow of his hair and golden hue of his skin declared him another Tibran.

Where had he come from? Why was he in Arikon? What was

he doing? He threw himself forward and his outstretched hand latched itself around Kallista's wrist.

Power slammed into her with the force of a storm-driven wave and she screamed as it tumbled her head over heels in its wake. The Tibran shouted in chorus with her, convulsing as the magic reverberated between their bodies with ever-increasing speed and strength.

She could feel him inside her skin, or perhaps she was inside his. They slid through each other, touching things that were never meant to be touched, a fiery caress of souls that made her scream again with the pleasure of it. The magic exploded, fountaining up through the room in a pyrotechnic shower of invisible color. She could not hold it, neither the pleasure nor the magic, and she screamed one more time as she collapsed on the anteroom floor, bringing the Tibran down with her.

The magic faded, folding in on itself. She felt stretched, somehow made larger. Slowly the magic ebbed out of her, not into the air around them or the marble beneath them. It flowed into the Tibran lying with his face in her lap. His shackled hands clutched her knees as he shivered and twitched on the floor.

"No." The Reinine's voice carried from the doorway over all the noise. "Don't touch them. Don't separate them."

Kallista could see Torchay's hand held motionless, inches away from her, other hands stopped as they reached for the Tibran. She gasped for air, trying to comprehend what had just happened.

"Well," the Reinine said as she entered the suddenly vacant anteroom. "It seems you have made your presence known to the court in an interesting way, my naitan."

"Wh—" Kallista had to stop and make her lips cease trembling before she could try again. "What was that?"

"Other than enough magic to move mountains, I am not sure." The Reinine pushed between her bodyguards to come closer. "What do you think it was?"

Kallista shook her head. She felt hollowed out, empty, perhaps because she had been so full.

"You're petting him," Torchay said quietly from his place on one knee beside her.

So she was. Without her realizing it, her hand was stroking over the Tibran's head, smoothing down the hair that rebelled against its confinement by fluffing out wherever it could. She stopped the motion, but could not seem to remove her hand. It…comforted her somehow, though she couldn't feel much through her glove.

"Who is this man?" the Reinine asked of those remaining in the room.

"Reinine." An officer in infantry dun bowed low. One pair of ribbons, white. A lieutenant.

A man, Kallista realized, when he straightened. No wonder the voice had seemed so unusually low-pitched. She'd heard there was a male officer in Ukiny's garrison, but had been too busy to seek him out, to see what such a creature might be like. Was this the same man or one of the few others?

"This man is a prisoner from the battle at Ukiny," the lieutenant said. He was old for a lieutenant, almost Kallista's age, she judged, and she was old for a captain. But then he was male. His medium-brown hair was combed straight back from a forehead as high as Torchay's into a tight queue three times as long as most, falling forward over his shoulder. From her vantage on the floor, Kallista could see the crossed swords of Filorne prinsipality, just to the north of Turysh, embroidered on his dun tunic in silver and black. "Stone, Warrior vo'Tsekrish," he continued. "He is the only Tibran inside the city to survive—"

The lieutenant seemed to realize then just who held his prisoner's head in her lap. Without altering his low bow, he looked at her, the bright blue of his eyes meeting her own. "To survive the—the magic that ended the assault."

"I was told no one lived. No Tibran." Kallista had to still her hand again. It wanted to stroke him.

"As was I." The Reinine's amused voice startled Kallista. She had forgotten her ruler's presence. "Rise, Lieutenant. Suteny, isn't it?"

He looked as if he would sweep into another bow, but confined himself to a deep nod instead. "Yes, Your Majesty. Joh Suteny."

"Of Filorne. They raise fine horses in Filorne. And fine men. Congratulations on your accomplishments."

The praise made him blush. He inclined his head again. "Thank you, Your Majesty."

The man in Kallista's lap went stiff with tension, his trembling ceased. Kallista removed her hand from his head. What had the lieutenant said his name was? "Stone."

The Tibran threw himself back, scrabbling along the floor in a clatter of chains until he fetched up against the wall, his eyes white and rolling with terror. Torchay moved when Stone did, interposing his body between Kallista and the bound man.

"Aisse," Kallista called to her servant. "Speak to him. Tell him he's safe." She feared she would pick the wrong language to try on the prisoner.

The small woman spoke from her position crouched behind Kallista, relaying the message. Stone looked wildly from one woman to the other.

"He speaks Adaran." Suteny moved toward the huddled Tibran. "Perfect Adaran." He went down on one knee, speaking quietly to Stone, but the chained man's eyes never left Kallista.

He had blue eyes too, strange in a Tibran's golden-skinned face. He was a handsome man with a finely carved straight nose and sensitive mouth. He looked as if he was a man who smiled often, or had been once. Now his face showed only fear.

"Warrior," Serysta Reinine said, but he did not look away.

His tongue crept out, traveled across dry, shaking lips. "What have you done to me, witch?"

Kallista used Torchay's shoulder to get back to her feet. "The proper title is naitan, and I should ask you the same. What did you do to me?"

He shook his head. Suteny stood and lifted the Tibran to his feet. "Nothing," Stone said. "I did—I don't—I remember nothing until—" He blushed and Kallista knew he recalled the sensuous rush of the magic pounding through them both. She had felt it with him, felt what he felt and knew now that he had received her reactions in turn. It disturbed her, yet she thought it should disturb her more.

"Are you marked, warrior?" the Reinine asked.

Marked? Kallista shot her Reinine a sharp look. What hadn't she been told?

Suteny took the prisoner by the shoulder and turned him so his back was to the Reinine, then tipped his head forward and moved aside the stubby queue. Kallista shivered in a sudden chill. Serysta glided forward, her feet invisible beneath her wide-skirted robes. The Tibran had to bend lower before the Reinine could look at the back of the warrior's neck. Then she turned and beckoned to Kallista. "Come and see."

Shaking her head no, Kallista came as she was bid, Torchay hard by her side. She looked.

There on the Tibran's nape, rising almost into his hairline, was a round, mottled red mark. The shading, red into pale into red again, made it look very much like a...rose. Kallista's hand lifted, touched it. Stone twitched as he might have if she'd shocked him with a spark, but she was gloved. The sparks couldn't escape until her control improved. Nor could she feel his mark's texture. She wanted to, needed to, but couldn't remove her glove here.

"Does it look like—" She glanced at the Reinine first, who didn't notice her, or didn't wish to, then at Torchay.

He nodded. "Like yours, without the compass." His eyes were liquid with compassion. She wanted to step into his arms, use them to ease the yearning ache the magic had created.

"Show him," Serysta Reinine said.

Now Kallista turned, lowered her head, moved aside the queue. She could feel Torchay's tension vibrating the air as the prisoner turned, his cascade of chains rattling. She could feel his gaze on her neck, or imagined she could. The chains rattled again and Torchay moved, lightning quick as only he could, catching the prisoner's wrist.

"Let him touch, bodyguard," Serysta said. "You may stop him if he tries anything else."

Kallista tightened her muscles, awaiting it, but his touch was feather light. Nothing more than a fingertip brushing over her skin. It made her want more. More touching. More— She reached a hand toward Torchay. He caught and held it tight.

"You have both been marked." The Reinine's voice cut through the uncomfortable silence. Kallista looked up, moved away from Stone nearer Torchay, still gripping his hand.

"That much is obvious," Serysta went on. "But what it means— No one believed those old stories could be literally true. We must delve into palace archives, learn what we can."

She turned to the lieutenant. "Suteny, I am placing you and your quarto under Captain Varyl's command. You and your prisoner will be quartered with her party."

"Erm—" Kallista began, then began again. "We haven't room for so many in our chamber, Majesty. We can barely fit ourselves—"

"Huryl, provide the naitan and her party—her expanded party—with suitable quarters."

The sour look disappeared so quickly from the high steward's face, Kallista could not be sure she had seen it. "Yes, Majesty," he said.

"Noonday Suite should do, in Daybright Tower. I want them close at hand."

Huryl bowed lower. "Yes, Majesty."

Serysta Reinine nodded, so regal that Kallista found herself bowing again. When she rose, the Reinine and her escorts had vanished, the throne-room door just closing behind her. Kallista looked around at her new command.

"Lieutenant." She received his salute, returned it, then extended her hand. After a moment's startled hesitation, he exchanged the clasped-wrist greeting of officer to officer.

"I am Kallista Varyl. I don't believe we've met before." She folded her hands behind her back, assuming an attitude of friendly authority. He might be male, but she would treat him no differently from any other lieutenant in her command. Though she rarely dealt with other officers. Her commands were usually too small. Often only herself and Torchay.

"No, Captain." He gave a slight bow. "May I present my men?"

The quarto of soldiers came to clattering attention. They were well drilled at least, their uniforms neat and in order, though the tunic stretched alarmingly across the fat sergeant's paunch. When the brief inspection ended, Kallista accepted and returned their salute.

"My bodyguard." She waved a hand in Torchay's direction as he snapped off a crisp salute. "Torchay Omvir. And my servant, Aisse vo'Haav."

The Tibran male's head jerked up at Aisse's name. "Vo'Haav," he croaked in his rusty voice. "Tibran? She was speaking Tibran at me?"

"Yes." Kallista's eyes narrowed. "Did you not understand?"

He shook his head. "I didn't even know what language it was. *Gods,* what did you do to me?"

"Nothing." Kallista waited till he met her gaze, held it. "Whatever was done, was done to me as well. You know that."

Stone looked away, flushing red beneath his golden skin.

"If you're ready, Captain?" Huryl insinuated himself into the group, again making a faint insult of her rank.

"Thank you, High Steward." Kallista inclined her head, refusing to give his rank any more recognition than that. She was who she was, a captain and a naitan in the Reinine's army, defending Adara's safety. If he did not like it, too bad.

Huryl led her from the antechamber, the others following, and through the corridor beyond, now crowded with all the people who'd been banished when the magic had erupted. At the end of it, he lifted a hand, summoning the green-gowned undersecretary Erunde, and turned them over to her.

The Noonday Suite was indeed close at hand. It took them only a few moments to reach Daybright Tower, situated in a cluster of towers with similarly poetic names. After they climbed two flights of stairs and walked down a short corridor, Erunde threw open the ornate double doors with a flourish as if awaiting gasps of amazement. The enormous sitting room, done all in shades of white, yellow and gold, deserved amazement, but Kallista was too tired for gasping.

Now that the meeting with the Reinine was over and the magic was gone, she felt utterly drained. She wandered through the long chamber, past sofas and chairs upholstered in silk, velvet and brocade set in charming little groups with carved, marquetry-topped tables holding graceful candelabras, and she wondered where they were expected to sleep. Dimly she was aware of Torchay requesting that Erunde have their belongings gathered and sent up, and of Erunde bowing her way out of the room. Then she heard the other sergeant start in on Torchay, blustering on about something. Kallista headed back to take matters in hand, but before she could reach them, Joh Suteny spoke.

"Sergeant Borril." His voice snapped with an authority Kallista would not have believed had she not heard it.

The sergeant snapped to attention. "Lieutenant."

"What color is the tunic Sergeant Omvir is wearing, Borril?" Joh's voice quieted but still held that authority.

"Black, Lieutenant."

"And who wears a black tunic, Sergeant?"

"The bodyguard of a naitan, Lieutenant."

"And who holds the higher rank *at all times* between a naitan's bodyguard and a regular soldier of similar rank?"

"The bodyguard, Lieutenant."

"You're sure?"

"Yes, Lieutenant. I'm sure."

"Then why, Sergeant, did I hear this…whining about length of service and time in rank from you?"

Sergeant Borril flushed red with anger and embarrassment, shooting a glare at Torchay, who watched with passive face and arms folded across his chest. "No reason, Lieutenant."

"Good. I trust that it will not happen again. See to your prisoner." Joh turned from dressing down the sergeant. His eyes widened briefly in surprise when he found Kallista standing so closely behind him. He inclined his head. "Naitan."

"You handled that well." She smiled. "I'd likely have made a mess of things. I'm used to dealing with sergeants who are all bodyguards, some with dozens of years of service. It's like walking through sleeping wildcats to deal with them."

Joh returned a hesitant smile, as if he wasn't quite sure smiling was safe.

Torchay called from across the room where he was exploring. "The bedrooms are behind these doors."

"Choose one for us then," Kallista called back, then spoke to Joh. "I'll leave it to you to assign quarters for your men and your prisoner."

"As far from the naitan as possible, if you please, Lieutenant," Torchay said, returning. "We'll take the south room farthest from the door."

"I don't want Stone hard by the exit, but the next one over on the north side will do," Joh said. "My men will take the rooms nearest the door."

"Where will you be?" Torchay asked.

"With the prisoner."

Kallista let her surprise show. "Really?"

"I can keep a better watch on him that way. He…wanders."

"Wanders?" Torchay's head came up in alarm. "What about chains?"

Joh waved a hand, wiping away his words. "Wanders in his mind. Whatever happened to him…disarranged his thoughts. He wanders physically as well, but the chains are effective. He's had to be chained since he tried to leap off the boat on the journey here." He gave the Tibran warrior standing passively a few paces off a pitying look. "He's more likely to harm himself, I believe, than someone else."

"Guarantee that, can you?" Torchay asked, eyeing the Tibran.

"No, but I believe it."

"Has he—" Kallista stopped. She was too tired to stand for long and this promised to be a long conversation. She beckoned Joh and Torchay toward one of the seating arrangements. "Stone too. We should talk."

The Tibran shuffled forward, the shackles limiting his motion, and perched gingerly on a delicate chair upholstered in pale yellow silk. The fat sergeant took up a post directly behind his prisoner. Torchay held the chair at the opposite end and frowned when Kallista sat on the white-and-gold brocade sofa instead. It looked more comfortable. She waved Torchay down on the end nearest Stone. Joh took the sofa opposite.

"Has he ever—" Again she stopped and addressed her question to Stone. He was the one with the mark. "Have you ever had that happen before? What happened just now?"

He shook his head, then paused, looking to Joh. "Not exactly like that. I don't remember—"

"You went into convulsions back in Turysh," the lieutenant said. "But you're right. It wasn't the same."

"Wait." Kallista put up a hand as more cold chills danced through her. "In Turysh? On...Thirdday last week? On the docks?"

Joh nodded, looking as uneasy as Kallista felt. "Yes. Why?"

She looked at Stone, tried to picture the man she had seen. "I saw you," she said. "I think. Your hair was loose—wild..."

Stone stared back at her, horror in his eyes. "I don't remember."

"Do you think—" Joh began hesitantly.

"What?" Kallista didn't bother hiding her impatience.

"Could it be possible that—that your presence triggered these fits?"

"How?" She didn't want to believe it, but it had a feeling of rightness about it.

"I don't know. I'm no naitan. I know nothing of magic and this..." Joh paused for breath. "This reeks of it."

"The Hand of the One," Sergeant Borril said.

"But I'm perfectly all right now." Stone's chains rattled as he shifted position.

"Maybe it's ended." Kallista didn't like the idea of throwing people into bellowing fits.

"Maybe it requires touch," Joh said.

Torchay skewered him with a glare. He did not want them touching. Kallista didn't have to read his mind to know.

"If a touch is going to throw us into another one of those episodes, we need to know it," she said.

Grudgingly, Torchay nodded and stood, moving out of the way. Kallista extended her hand. Stone stared at it, seeming to shrink away without actually moving.

"Take my hand, Stone," she said. "It can't be any worse than before."

"Are you sure?" But he lifted his manacled hands and folded one of them around hers.

Nothing happened.

"Is that how you were touching before?" Joh studied their clasped hands. "It doesn't look right."

"No. Stone, you had hold of my arm. Here." She indicated her bare forearm above the glove.

"Skin to skin," Joh said.

The words made Kallista shudder with want and memory.

"Touch her arm, Stone." Joh's intense scrutiny didn't change.

"You're enjoying this," Torchay accused the lieutenant. "You like experimenting with my naitan's safety."

"It's important to know."

"The lieutenant is right." Kallista untangled her hand from Stone's and pulled off her gloves, handing them to Torchay. Joh swallowed hard at the sight of her bare hands and some of the guardsmen backed away.

Kallista sighed a quick breath. "I don't often wear gloves in private. If any of you has trouble with that, perhaps he ought to request reassignment."

"I'm fine." Joh looked back at the soldiers. They straightened to attention and remained at their posts to either side of the door, though one young man's eyes were white with nerves and another kept swallowing.

"My magic—the magic I was born with," she corrected, "is lightning. I would normally tell you that my control is excellent, but since—well, nothing is as it was. I will do my best—and Torchay will help—to be sure no one is harmed."

"There are six tower spires just outside the window," Torchay said, "if they are needed."

Good, he had checked for safe targets for the lightning. And perhaps the spires would make safe targets for any other magic that might come strolling through her. They were as ready for what might happen as they could be without knowing what would actually happen.

Kallista turned back to Stone and held out her bared hand, leaving it up to him to decide. He met her gaze, blue eyes to blue, and his chin came up, answering her unspoken challenge. With a rattle of chains, he raised his hands and clasped hers.

Magic stirred, inside Stone, not Kallista. It lifted, as if asking what she required, waiting for her command. She touched it, felt it answer, felt Stone's gasp, and backed away. She could call it. But this was not the place to experiment. She had no desire to destroy the Reinine's delicate furniture with who-knew-what-sort of stray magic crashing around.

Stone shuddered when she released his hand. As did Torchay. "You called magic," her bodyguard said, going down to one knee beside the sofa. It brought him closer to her.

"Yes." She nodded, taking her turn to shudder. "No. I touched magic. Inside Stone. I didn't call it. This isn't the place or the time. Not when we don't know what it will do."

"No." Stone shook his head, huddling inside his chains. "No. I am no witch. I have no magic. Impossible."

Kallista looked at him—it was no hardship. He was a beautiful young man. "You have never called magic? Never done something you should not have been able to do? Or done something very much better than everyone else?"

"I am fastest at reloading my musket, fastest with a bayonet, but that's skill, not magic."

Aisse fidgeted in her chosen place near Kallista, drawing attention to herself for the first time. Attention she didn't want, by her demeanor. "Magic not—*is* not liked in Tibre. Those with magic are punished. Lose caste, lose magic or—made dead."

"Killed," Torchay corrected automatically. Aisse repeated the word while Kallista thought.

"Perhaps," she said slowly, "the magic is not there for your use, since you are no naitan. I do not call magic from inside myself but from—from the air around me, from the sky, from the One. I ask Her gift and She gives it. Could it be there for me to call?"

The sound of hands clapping brought Kallista's head up. Belandra stood behind the sofa where Joh sat, clapping her hands in sardonic applause. "Congratulations, you discovered something on your own."

CHAPTER TWELVE

Kallista's mouth opened to demand where Belandra had been, and her eyes fell on Joh, his face filled with overdone curiosity. "Out," she said instead. She did not want outside witnesses to this conversation. "Everyone out."

She retreated a few paces toward the window, holding her hands up so they might believe she held magic. She pointed an elbow at the guards nearest the door. "You two, outside the door. Don't let anyone enter until you're told otherwise. The rest of you, in your rooms. *Now.* Torchay, with me."

Joh picked Stone up from his chair, knocking it over, and hurled him toward the chosen bedroom. The rest of the soldiers vanished in a flurry of action as Kallista moved a few steps more toward the window.

"You too, Aisse," she said when the small woman stood frozen in a panic of indecision.

"I help," Aisse protested, despite her trembling.

"Torchay's enough. You *go*." Kallista threw out her hand to point at the bedroom door and both Aisse and Torchay flinched. Aisse hesitated a moment more, then ran to do as she was told.

When the room was empty, Kallista lowered her hands and took a deep breath, looking back at Belandra, who appeared highly amused by all the activity.

"I feel magic," Torchay said, moving close to Kallista as he searched for danger. "But it's not yours. It's *like* yours, but it isn't yours...Belandra?"

Kallista nodded. "She's here."

Belandra left her position and walked toward them, circling to inspect Torchay. Kallista circled too, keeping herself between her bodyguard and the long-dead woman.

"Why didn't you come before now?" Kallista demanded. "Two Hopedays have passed."

"I thought the redhead here was godmarked. Your marked companion. But he's not, is he?"

"No, he's not marked. And that doesn't answer my question."

"Who's the little blonde?" Belandra strolled toward the door where Joh and Stone had disappeared, but didn't enter.

"Answer my question." Kallista forced the words through gritted teeth.

"I could not come because you had not yet found *him*." Belandra pointed through the closed door. "You had not joined with any marked companion."

"Well, why— No." Kallista waved her hands, wiping out the question before she got it asked. She didn't want to waste any of the six allowed, and she'd already asked one. She thought over the things Belandra had already said. "You didn't tell me because you thought this 'marked companion' was Torchay. My bodyguard."

"Exactly." Belandra wandered toward the window and looked

Gail Dayton

out, then swung around, shock in her expression. "This place is Arikon."

Kallista nodded. "Arikon the Blessed. It's the capital of all Adara."

"It's——" She turned to look again, leaning on the windowsill. "I recognize nothing but the mountains."

"Look there." Kallista joined her at the window, Torchay at her back, and pointed down and to the left. "Beyond that dome-topped tower. That's Sanda's Hall. It's all that's left from your time. Most of the old palace was destroyed in the Plains Rebellion about six hundred years ago, and what wasn't, tumbled down on its own a hundred years later. It's been a thousand years. You should have expected as much."

Belandra shook her head. "I didn't think. I don't—a thousand years. For a thousand years, the people have been safe?"

Kallista blinked. She hadn't thought of it that way. But wasn't that what she had demanded of the One? To keep the people safe? "Not…perfectly safe, but yes, safe enough."

She put her hand up to keep Belandra from speaking again. "It's my turn. There are things I need to know. My bodyguard says that the night you gave me the ring, I stopped breathing. I almost died. He wants to know—I am asking— If it happens again, what must he do to keep me alive?"

"You stopped——" Belandra actually appeared worried. She turned around and leaned against the windowsill, folding her arms. "It must have been because you had to travel so far. You had to come to me the first time, to receive the ring. You must have something of mine in your possession so I can come to you. It will not happen again. I come to you now. Tell your bodyguard to stop worrying." She frowned. "Why do you have a bodyguard?"

"For protection, of course." Stupid question.

"Can you not defend yourself?" Belandra's retort was scornful.

"Of course. But not during battle when I am calling magic. Very few naitani can keep track of their immediate surroundings when they call magic, and in a battle with bandits—or opposing armies—that can be deadly. The bodyguard watches for us. A naitan and her bodyguard work in tandem."

"What danger faces Adara—"

"My turn," Kallista interrupted.

Belandra swelled up with temper, then seemed to think better of it and subsided.

"What has happened to me? What is all this?" She cursed herself when she realized she'd asked two questions, using up four of her precious six.

"Do you not know already?"

"I don't know anything except that my magic is tangled like an old fishing net and I'm afraid to call it because I don't know what it will do next. I speak perfect Tibran as well as Adaran, but I can't tell which one I'm speaking when it's coming out of my mouth. I killed tens of thousands of the enemy in one sweep of magic from these hands." Kallista held them up, then quickly tightened them into fists to stop their shaking.

Torchay touched her shoulder and this time she let herself lean back into his support. He stiffened for a second, then relaxed, his chest against her back. He stroked his hand down her arm. He must have decided this was duty, not pleasure.

"You've been godstruck," Belandra said. "Chosen to join with those who've been marked as your companions to protect the people of the One. The marked ones carry the magic. You use it. You are the naitan. The focus."

"Use it how? And—"

This time Belandra put up her hand. "Don't ask your last question. Not yet. I have to leave soon after it's asked and there is much I want to know. As for how you use the magic—it varies. It depends on what sort of danger, what need you face. You are given what you need. When you killed all those enemies, were you alone?"

"Torchay was with me."

Belandra frowned. "But he is not marked. The magic—was it like a dark mist? Spreading in all directions with you at its center?"

Kallista nodded, clamping her teeth tight together to keep the questions inside. Had Belandra used that particular bit of magic herself?

"The dark veil requires a tremendous amount of power. Even the most powerful naitan working alone can rarely create a circle of more than twenty paces around her. And yet you—how big was the circle?"

Kallista looked back at Torchay. "The dark scythe—how far did it travel? How far would you say the Tibran camp was?"

"At least two hundred paces. Maybe a little more. The scythe didn't travel quite the whole distance."

"Goddess," Belandra swore. "There had to have been someone else to channel all that power. There had to have been. And you're sure this one's not marked?"

"Bend your head down." Kallista moved away from Torchay so he could do as she asked. She pushed aside his thick queue and the few curls that had escaped it to expose his pale, unmarked nape. "Both I and the Tibran are marked here."

Her mouth dropped open as she realized what she had said, as Torchay straightened. "The *Tibran*. Stone was in the battle. On the other side. The only one of the invaders inside the city who lived. Could he have— *Goddess,* one of the enemy?"

"Stone is the one who is marked? The good-looking blonde?"

"Yes." Kallista realized something else. "The questions—I wasn't asking *you*. I was just—"

"Just wondering." Belandra gave one of her crooked, sardonic smiles. "I know. Sometimes they count, sometimes they don't. I think it depends on intent. If you 'just wonder,' hoping to get around the six-question limit, it counts. And the One does not care which side of battle her people are on. What matters is surrender. That man—"

She pointed at the door behind which Stone had vanished. "He surrendered himself to the will of the One. That is why he still lives. That is why he bears the mark."

"Goddess." Kallista sagged against Torchay once more.

"For even one companion to carry so much power as you describe is unusual. There's bound to be another out there. Maybe two."

"How do I find them?" Kallista asked, and then swore. She hadn't meant that as her last question.

Belandra grinned, a wicked grin if ever there was one. "They'll find you. The marks draw them. Wait. They will come."

"How many?" Kallista cried. "How will I know them?"

But the red-haired woman was gone. Vanished between one breath and the next. Kallista swore again. A limit on questions was stupid. How would she ever learn what she needed to know?

"She's gone?" Torchay backed away, putting space between them.

"Yes." Kallista spent the next few minutes telling Torchay the few things she had learned. Important things they needed to know, but not enough. Not nearly enough.

When she was done, she took a deep breath. "I suppose you can let the others out of their rooms and tell the two standing guard they can admit visitors again. Someone's supposed to be bringing our trunks, aren't they?"

Torchay nodded and went to take care of matters. Kallista turned to look out the window again, trying to soak up the beauty of the palace and surrounding city, rather than find safe points for her lightning.

"Naitan!" Torchay's alarmed shout brought Kallista running to the room where her supposed godmarked companion had retreated.

Stone lay on the bed, limp and breathing hard, as if he'd been running a race. Joh looked up from beside him, accusation in his eyes. "What did you do? He went into convulsions not long after I closed the door."

"I—nothing." How could she explain without admitting she spoke to ghosts? The Reinine knew, but she'd kept the words between them quiet. None of the others in the room could have heard, and Kallista wanted it kept that way. West magic, if that was indeed what they were dealing with, disturbed too many people. "I went to the window to—take care of things. A false alarm, I'm afraid. That's all."

"He seems all right now," Torchay said, checking the man's pulse, his eyes, his heart.

"*Khralsh.*" Stone groaned, sitting up. "Whatever you did, woman, don't do it again. I feel as if every muscle in my body has been wrenched apart."

"She is a naitan," Torchay snarled, "and a captain in the Adaran army. You will address her as *naitan* and speak to her with respect."

Kallista waited for Stone to respond to Torchay's reprimand. She understood Stone's attitude—he was Tibran, after all, and had been through much—but he needed to learn that things worked differently in Adara. He would have to adapt.

Stone glared at Torchay, then looked at Kallista. After a moment, he nodded. "Naitan," he said. "Pardon my rudeness."

"Granted. Now, we need to discover what happened so we can prevent it happening again."

Torchay stood. "You seem fine now. Your heart is beating a little fast, but slowing."

"You're a healer?" Stone asked with more respect than he had accorded Kallista.

"I'm a bodyguard," he said, as if that explained everything.

Which it did, but perhaps not to a Tibran. Torchay crossed to Kallista, drawing closer than she expected. She held her breath as he lowered his face toward hers, then realized his intent and tilted her head so he could speak quietly into her ear. "Could Belandra have caused his fit?"

It was a tempting theory. The problem with it was— "Belandra was in the room before I sent everyone away. He was fine then." Kallista offered Stone her hand. After a moment's hesitation, he took it—no magic stirred—and she pulled him to his feet. Joh stepped in to provide needed support.

They moved into the parlor for more room and sat Stone on a sofa in the middle of the chamber just outside the bedroom door, facing the window. One step at a time, carefully watching the Tibran's every reaction, Kallista backed toward the window. She'd taken perhaps a dozen steps when Stone's eyes rolled back in his head and he went limp. Joh kept him from hitting his head on the serving table as Kallista hurriedly took a step forward. Stone's eyes fluttered open and he struggled to sit up.

"Well," she said, "that settles that. Torchay, send Aisse to find someone to have dinner brought up. We won't be joining the court tonight." She gauged the distance between herself and the godmarked man. Maybe ten paces. Half the length of the narrow central chamber.

"Why not?" Joh watched her as she closed the distance.

"Because I can't go farther than ten paces from Stone without sending him into convulsions and I'm not taking him along to dine in the great hall loaded down with chains. He's a Tibran prisoner, but he's also a soldier. I won't put him on display for the court's amusement like some trained monkey."

She'd seen monkeys. Southron traders sometimes brought them through Turysh on their way to become a spoiled rich man's pet.

Joh inclined his head, his face holding an expression Kallista did not know how to interpret. Wonder? Surprise? Respect?

"Besides," she went on, looking over Stone's grimy prisoner's garb. "His wardrobe needs some improvement before he's fit for such surroundings."

"He can't sleep in that room," Joh said as Torchay returned. "Not if you're in the opposite end."

Torchay sighed. "Take the next chamber. Move the beds against the shared wall. The rooms aren't large, but even if they were, that would serve. Aisse can move across the way."

That reminded Kallista of something. "Lieutenant, inform your troops not to bother my servant. Young ones sometimes have trouble recognizing when their attentions aren't wanted. And you, Tibran—" She fastened her glare on the yellow-haired man. "If you don't understand it already, I'll explain it to you now. This is Adara. Not Tibre. Women are off limits to you. No sex, understand? Unless someone approaches you, you'll do without."

"I must—" Stone seemed to struggle for words. "Provide service to them?"

"Only if you wish." Kallista should have expected his misunderstanding. According to what Aisse had told her, anyone with power could demand any service from one without. And Stone had no power here. "If one asks, you may say yes or no. But *you* may not ask. And you will not demand. This includes my servant."

"Make demands in these?" He held up the chains, rattling them at her. "I hadn't intended to."

"Good." Kallista looked yearningly at the doorway to the room Torchay had chosen as theirs. She was tired. She could rest until dinner came. But she would drag Stone behind her on an invisible ten-pace chain.

"Let's have those off." She gestured at the steel shackles Stone wore.

"Is that wise?" Joh asked before Torchay could.

"He's obviously not going anywhere. Ten paces from me and he collapses."

Stone scowled at her as Joh got out his key. Was it the thought of the magical tether he didn't like, or her? Did it matter?

"And if he takes you prisoner?" Torchay said in a low angry voice, quiet so only she could hear, as if afraid of giving Stone ideas. "If he takes you along on his escape attempt?"

Kallista patted Torchay's shoulder. "That's what I have you for. Besides, where is he going to go? We're days from the coast and other Tibrans. Weeks, if he travels on foot."

"I don't like it."

She sighed. "Fine. You're in charge of safety. But at least let him be rid of some of them."

Torchay left him in the manacles, with a short chain leading from his wrists to the one around his waist, limiting his reach. The leg irons came off.

Dinner came and went, better food than even the wonderful meals they'd had in their previous quarters. Servants brought their belongings, then moved furniture under Torchay's direction. After that, Kallista retreated to her room and collapsed in the bed. She woke sometime in the night to the sound of the tower clocks chiming. Something was strange, someone moving around.

"Torchay?"

"I'm here," he replied from beside the door. "I heard Joh checking on his troops. Go back to sleep."

"Are you—"

"I'm taking the cot. Your breathing is fine."

Belandra had said so. Kallista was glad Torchay slept across the room now. She *was*. But she missed him lying next to her. Missed his warmth. Missed his presence. She put her hand over her mouth to keep from telling him so. Things were hard enough as they were. She turned over and told herself to go back to sleep. But it was a long time before she dozed.

It was nearing noon before Joh managed to go back to the little Black Briar Chapel in Winterhold Palace. The black-robed figure awaited him, seeming to quiver with suppressed anger.

"You're late," he growled in his disguised voice. "I summoned you last night and you send excuses. I summon you today and you are late. This is unacceptable, Renunciate."

"I have my duties, Master." Joh tried not to sound as if he resented the reprimand, though he did. "And I am quartered now with a naitan. Her bodyguard wakes at the slightest sound. I cannot slip away in the night. The best I can do is to stretch errands, and even now I haven't much time. What is it you require of me?"

"You are to watch this naitan in addition to your previous assignment. There is disturbing talk coming out of Ukiny. This is the woman who cast the dark magic?"

"Yes, Master Barb."

"West magic indeed, though she masquerades as North naitan. We must know more. We must know everything. Tell me what happened after you retired with her yesterday."

"I haven't enough time," Joh protested.

"Then write it down. You're producing reports for the army, are you not? Write one for the Order as well. A simple thing."

"Yes, Honorable One." The writing would help him sort his thoughts, understand what was happening. He could decide later how much to share with the Order. The thought made him feel disloyal, but he had other loyalties.

"Good, then we are agreed." A black sleeve waved in dismissal and Joh took his chance, slipping away from the eerie place.

The captain's magic made him nervous, especially the prisoner's fits every time he got too far from her. Despite it all, Joh liked her. She treated him like an officer, not merely a man. She even showed respect for the Tibran, something few would do. He just wished she would keep her gloves on.

The Reinine sent for Kallista in the late afternoon of the next day. Because she couldn't leave Stone behind, the summons became a major expedition, only Aisse remaining behind in the suite. Erunde, acting as escort again today, led them not to the throne room, but to Evening Glow Tower, not far from Daybright Tower where they were quartered. Kallista was glad they'd left the leg irons off Stone. The four flights of stairs would have been endless with him shackled.

High Steward Huryl met them outside a set of doors set with copper and silver, carved with scenes from Adara's history. He refused to admit anyone besides Kallista and Torchay, whereupon Kallista requested he relay a message to the Reinine. Huryl refused to do that as well. The "discussion" had deteriorated to a staredown when one of the Reinine's bodyguards put his head out the door.

"What's keeping the—oh, you're here." He opened the door wide. "Come in, then. She's waiting."

"She wants to bring the Tibran inside," Huryl interjected, his voice an ugly hiss.

The guard's eyes narrowed. "Why?"

"Because he convulses if he gets more than ten paces from me," Kallista said, holding tight to her patience.

The bodyguard's expression didn't change.

Patience evaporated. "Can you endure a demonstration?" she asked Stone.

He sighed and nodded. Joh took hold of his arms as Kallista turned and walked away. She'd reached the stairwell, a pace or two farther than yesterday, before Stone collapsed in Joh's grip. She hesitated there a moment, then returned.

"I'll inform the Reinine." The guard disappeared inside the

room, reappeared a moment later and beckoned, ordering the quarto of soldiers to remain outside.

Torchay, Stone and Joh were left with a bodyguard near the door while the other escorted Kallista to the Reinine who was sitting at a large desk near the window. Stone collapsed again when she got halfway and had to be moved farther into the room as Kallista advanced.

"Interesting," Serysta Reinine said when Kallista had bowed. She stood and came from behind the desk, gesturing Kallista into one of a pair of comfortable-looking high-backed chairs as she took the other. Kallista felt strange, sitting in her Reinine's presence, but she did as she was bid.

"According to every record I have been able to trace," Serysta Reinine said without preamble, "it is virtually certain that you and the Tibran are godmarked. You have been chosen by the One to fulfill a task protecting Adara, or Adara's people."

Kallista allowed the Reinine to tell her the things Belandra had already shared, half listening.

"Therefore, since it is evident that it is to Adara's benefit to assist you in your task, whatever it is, I am placing our resources at your disposal. I would like to have the wedding as soon as possible."

"Weddi—wait, *what* wedding?" Kallista had missed something.

The Reinine smiled. "I wondered whether you were listening to everything I said. The records state a number of times over that the godstruck and her companions are joined in an ilian. Therefore, the warrior Stone will become your ilias. He will marry *di pentivas.*" She used the ancient term for a male captured in war and claimed as a prize.

"The laws allowing this have never been repealed though no one practices the ritual anymore. They will prove useful in this. And I thought, to make up a proper ilian, your bodyguard and the Tibran woman might be willing to join with you. They are not marked, but I believe they have been called by the One to serve. You may decide regarding them, whether to offer them the choice. But I want you and the Tibran married within the week."

Kallista stared at her ruler, stunned at the outrageousness of the idea. In centuries past, the Reinine had often ordered strangers to wed, usually to end quarrels between prinsipalities, occasionally for other reasons. But society had progressed beyond that. She forced herself to think. "But...why *marry*? Why an ilian?"

"The records were not perfectly clear, but I believe it is because the marked ones must join so closely together. They must be bound closer than an ordinary working relationship, as close as iliasti. They must care for each other."

"How can strangers—"

"The One can do whatever we allow. We are His hands in this world."

Kallista had to clear her mind and think this through, understand what was ordered without the little voice cheering in the background at the thought of claiming Torchay as ilias. She was a soldier, sworn to obey her Reinine, but this went far beyond anything she'd ever expected. "You truly believe this is the best course of action?" She risked the question.

"I do. I realize this comes as something of a shock to you. I will allow you to inform your future mates. But do not take too long. I am receiving reports daily from the coast that alarm me." Serysta Reinine stood and Kallista scrambled quickly to her own feet. "Today is Fifthday. I would like to have the wedding by next Thirdday."

Kallista gathered up the men with a glance as she passed on the way out of the Reinine's private chamber. The quarto fell in outside the doorway, Erunde waiting to guide them back to their suite. Kallista didn't speak. She couldn't, didn't know what to say, and none of the others spoke either.

Back in Noonday Suite, Kallista walked straight through the

parlor to the window, followed by the three men who'd come with her. "Give me some space, Torchay," she said quietly, hands clasped tight behind her back as she stared out at the towers and court-yards of the palace complex. "I need room to think. If you could move everyone back five paces or so?"

"What happened in there?" Torchay stood too close, head bent to speak privately to her. "What upset you?"

"Let me think first." She smiled at him, let herself touch his arm. "I swear I will tell you. But I need to sort it out in my mind first."

CHAPTER THIRTEEN

Torchay nodded and moved away, taking Stone and Joh with him. And for the rest of the evening, Kallista paced and thought. Or tried to think.

When dinner came, she joined the others for the meal, insisting that Aisse join Torchay, Stone and Joh at her table while the other ranks ate together near the door. Kallista contributed nothing to the minimal dinner conversation. She was too busy thinking. Afterward, she retreated to the window again.

She had always wanted an ilian, a normal life, but this scarcely qualified as normal. Despite Mother Dardra's teasing, she'd never allowed herself to think of making Torchay her ilias. Such a truncated, half-formed ilian with only the two of them would have emphasized how pathetic the attempt was, and finding additional mates had always been impossible. Until recently, she'd never believed Torchay willing. He might not be willing now.

Ilias was not the same as lover. He would have to give up his flirtations. But the thought of her band around his ankle was the only appealing one in this whole mess.

The Reinine had ordered her to marry a Tibran. She wanted her to marry *two* Tibrans. Wouldn't Torchay just love that? Aisse scarcely counted as Tibran, given how much she hated the country and customs of her birth, but Stone was a warrior and a prisoner of war. One of the enemy. He was also godmarked.

His mark, so nearly matching her own, meant they were bound already. Bound closer than iliasti. Did that mean they had to *become* iliasti? For any reason other than the Reinine's order, that is? Was she actually considering defying it? Refusing to marry? Would it change the reality of the magic if she did? And who else would suffer the consequences?

Torchay watched his naitan stare out the window. She'd been tearing herself apart all evening over whatever the Reinine had said, and it was all he could do to leave her to it. She knew he would help her in any way he could, but apparently, he could not help with this.

The clocks chimed again and yet again, and still his captain stared out the window. Aisse retired to the room she had claimed. The guards set their watch at the door, those not on duty closed in their rooms. The lieutenant yawned over a castle board, attempting to teach the prisoner to play queens-and-castles. But the Tibran seemed even more tired than his keeper, his head propped on shackled hands. Torchay realized then that the Tibran's assigned bedroom was too far from Kallista's position at the window. He would collapse before he reached it.

Kallista had given up her occasional pacing more than an hour ago to sit in one of the overdecorated chairs and stare at the darkened courtyards below, and she showed no signs of moving. She would fall asleep there if no one acted, and it was Torchay's duty to act.

He crossed the room and sat in a chair facing her. "It's late." He pitched his voice low to keep from startling her. "You should sleep. The problem will still be there in the morning."

She turned slowly toward him, her expression blank, almost as if her face had become granite. "I am to marry, Torchay."

His heart froze inside him. Who? When? What place would be left for him?

A tear spilled over and slid down her expressionless cheek. "She has my iliasti all picked out." More tears followed the first, breaking Torchay's heart.

He used his thumb to wipe them away. He knew she hated tears. "Who?" He asked the question beating at him.

"Stone."

"The *Tibran?*" He kept his voice quiet despite the shock.

"He's marked. The archives claim the godmarked always form an ilian." She captured his hand as he pulled it back.

"Who else?"

"He's the only one I'm ordered to marry." She swiped at her face with the back of her free hand. "But if I wish——"

"What?" He resisted the urge to turn his hand, twine his fingers with hers, but he allowed her hold on him.

"The Reinine says Aisse has obviously been called by the One. She could join with us."

"No one else?"

Her gaze locked onto his and she smiled, a flicker of brightness in the tears. "You. I can have you, if I wish."

"Kallista——" He didn't know what to say, had never known since the night he offered himself to her and she turned him away. She said then that it wasn't because she didn't want him. He'd seen the desire in her eyes that night. But he hadn't seen it since, and he began to doubt what he'd seen. "What did you tell her?"

"That I had to think. I don't know what to do. She's my Reinine, it's my duty to obey. I—I wanted to marry, once. But to have it forced on me…"

"Don't let her force you, Kallista. The man is Tibran, an enemy. This is beyond duty. It could be your life." He clasped her hand in both of his and rested his mouth against it. He would give an eye to be her ilias, but not if she didn't want it too.

"It could be your life too, Torchay." She brushed a strand of his hair, fallen loose after the long day, behind his ear. He resisted the urge to turn into her caress. "If I asked you, what would you say?"

Torchay gave up his resistance and rubbed his cheek over her hand. "When you decide, ask me, and I'll tell you."

She stared at him, mouth open in surprise, then she laughed. Torchay's heart started beating again. Kallista stood, using their clasped hands to pull him to his feet.

"My apologies, Lieutenant, for keeping you up so late," she said, retreating toward her room. "Put your prisoner to bed."

Joh stood, bowed his head, and nudged the dozing Stone awake. Torchay waited until the lieutenant had closed the door before entering the room he shared with his naitan. At least he did not have to share her bed any longer. Sleeping beside her without making love had become almost unbearable.

She was already in the big bed, her eyes closed. Possibly asleep, but Torchay did not think so. He readied himself for sleep, loosing his hair, removing his blades. He drew the big blade from its scabbard at his back and placed it under his pillow.

Perhaps he should ask to join her ilian, if she did not ask him. He could not think of her bound to the Tibran without him at her side as well. But if she did not want him… Torchay banished the thought from his mind. He would consider it later. For now he had to focus on his duty, on protecting her.

Kallista dreamed. She recognized the misty landscapes and fought to leave them. She didn't want more visions, didn't care to meet any more ghosts, but the dream pulled her on, relentless in its flow. She sped over Adara's northern coast, saw Ukiny with its wall half restored, saw Kishkim in its swamp with the cannon arrayed around it on individual rafts half sunk in the mud. Then she was over the ocean, speeding farther north.

In moments she crossed another coast, flew across plains, past massive cliffs marked with sparkling waterfalls to a high, broad plateau from which a city rose, its once-white stone stained with gray. She had no time to see more as she was swept into the city's heart, into a sumptuously but crudely furnished room. The room itself felt *wrong* somehow, but she didn't have time to puzzle it out.

Kallista saw three men. Their golden hair had faded with age, but the golden cast of their skin proclaimed them as Tibran as Stone. One of the men, tall and stern-faced, his hair cropped short, wore a red jacket like the jackets worn by the warriors out-side Ukiny, but with a double row of brass buttons down its front. The other two wore purple, and one of them bore a gold circlet on his head. Could this be the Tibran king's chamber? Was this a vision of things to come, or did it happen now?

The crowned man yawned. "But the invasion progresses, does it not, General?"

The man in red clicked his boot heels together and bowed low. "It does, my king. The setback in Ukiny is serious. We lost most of an army and over fifty ships, but the cannon are untouched. We can shift them to one of the other cities and—"

"We *need* Ukiny," the third man interrupted. "It sits at the mouth of the Taolind River, which will take us straight into the heart of that witch-ruled place."

As Kallista watched them argue strategy, she became aware that she was not the only unseen presence in the room. An aura of pure malevolence hung over the crowned man.

She narrowed her eyes, concentrating her focus, and a black

thing slowly coalesced. It crouched on the king's shoulders, a hideous misshapen thing of claws and teeth that slid into and out of the king. Kallista shuddered, unable to fathom what evil it might be. Then it lifted its pulsing head, turned red, glowing eyes on her, and hissed.

She stumbled back and fell through the floor and completely out of the building. The thing had *seen* her.

Then the dream had her in its grip again, whirling her through colored fogs until she fell to her knees in a dirty, tumble-down building, stars shining through a hole in its roof.

"Naitan," Aisse cried, crouching over something on the floor, tears streaming down her face. "Hurry! You must do something. You *must*."

Gripped by sudden panic, Kallista scurried forward on all fours to see Torchay lying on a pallet made of old, mounded canvas, his pale skin gone pasty white. His eyes met hers and he opened his mouth to speak, but only a bubble of bright red blood emerged.

"Torchay! Oh, Goddess, *Torchay*." Kallista looked down, saw his hands clutching his stomach, saw blood staining them, saturating his clothes, dripping onto the canvas beneath him. "Goddess, *no. No!*"

The word ripped from her throat in a scream and she was sitting up in bed in the night darkness of Daybright Tower in Summerglen Palace in Arikon, with Torchay's arms around her.

"I'm here." He rocked her in his arms, face tight against hers, speaking in her ear. "It was a dream. Only a dream."

The door opened, bumped against the cot Torchay had pulled across it. "What's wrong?" Joh shouted through the opening, pushing harder.

"Nothing. Get out." Torchay shouted back, curving his body around Kallista as she clung to him.

Joh kept coming. "Naitan, are you all right?"

"I'm fine, Lieutenant." She pulled herself together enough to tell him. She didn't want anyone else to see her like this. "I'm fine. Leave us."

He stopped pushing against the door but didn't leave. "Are you certain? What happened?"

"Nothing. A dream." Pray the One it was nothing more. Kallista shuddered in memory. "That's all. Please. Go."

"Yes, Captain." Joh shut the door.

Kallista could hear him speaking to the others, sending them back to bed or to their posts. She put her arms around Torchay and held on tight until she stopped shaking.

Then she pulled back enough to grip his face between her hands and inspect it. She checked him over carefully, touching where the tiny disk of the moon through the window did not provide sufficient light for her to see. She ran her hand across his stomach, searching for wounds, and found none. As expected. When she was satisfied he was whole, she put her arms around his waist and laid her head on his shoulder.

He was whole. For now. But what sort of dream had it been? She had the impression that the meeting of the Tibran king with his advisers under the malevolent glare of the shadow being had been taking place now, at the same time she dreamed it. But Torchay was obviously not bleeding his life away in some derelict building. Was that his fate?

Her arms tightened around him and she choked back a sob. He stroked a hand over her hair and murmured something, his mouth pressed to her forehead, making nonsense of his words. She had prevented injuries when the wall collapsed in Ukiny because she had been forewarned. Could she do the same for Torchay?

"I need to send a message to the Reinine," she said, her voice muffled slightly. "Now. Right away."

"It's three hours till dawn." He drew back, but stopped when Kallista tightened her hold. She wasn't ready to let him go yet. "The Reinine will be asleep."

"I don't care. She said to send word soon. This is soon."

"Send word about what? What did you dream?"

Kallista locked her hands together behind his back. "Marry me, Torchay. Will you marry me? I need you with me. I can't do this without you."

"If you need me, I will be there."

It took her a moment to understand what he said. She drew back to look at him, search his face in the faint moonlight. "Is that yes? You will marry us?"

He captured her hand and pressed a kiss to her fingers where they curled around his. "Yes. I would be honored to be your ilias."

"Stone too? I have to marry him too. Will you also?"

His expression soured, but he nodded. "I would not leave you alone in this. Yes, I will join your ilian, whoever it holds."

Kallista seized him by the back of his neck and pulled him in for a kiss. She could resist no longer. Torchay opened his mouth under hers, rising high on his knees to bring her whole body tight against his. He felt so good to her, so right. She melted under his sweetness. She wanted this, wanted him. The vision of Torchay broken and bleeding slashed into her mind and she fought it back. He was alive. Goddess willing, she would keep him that way.

She broke the kiss, backed away breathing hard. Message. She had to send word to the Reinine. With Torchay as her ilias, surely she could keep him safe. "Light," she said. "I need light."

"Kallista—"

Ignoring Torchay's protest, she called a tiny spark to light the candles in the stand on the bedside table and carried them to the desk beneath the window.

"Kallista, this can wait till morning."

"No, it can't." She couldn't wait. Something might happen. The Reinine wouldn't mind. She hoped. She found paper, quill and ink and scratched out a quick note, then folded it and used the candle wax to seal it. "Have one of the guards on watch deliver this to the Reinine."

Torchay crawled off the bed, scratching his chest. "You're mad, you know. And when I get back, you're going to tell me what you dreamed."

She would. Part of it anyway. The part about the men and the dark thing. She needed him to help her understand it. But not the rest. Kallista handed him the note. "Just go."

The morning after the Adaran witch woke everyone with her screaming in the night, Stone couldn't contain his restlessness. He paced the fussy parlor from one end of his magical leash to the other, waiting for the witch to wake.

Why did they not take him for questioning? Why was he held here in this luxurious suite in the—the ruler's palace? A woman as king made his skin crawl, but he shoved the feeling aside. What did they want him for? He did not hold magic inside himself. He could not, it was not possible. He was no witch. He was a warrior. Or he had been one. He was a prisoner now. Without caste.

That fact had soaked in during his long journey to this place. He was theirs to do with as they willed. He just wished they would hurry up and do it.

Despite his attempts to settle, Stone fretted over the matter until the witch ordered him to join her and the bodyguard at the end of the room near the window. The red-haired man had skills Stone could respect. Too bad he wasted them in defense of a witch. Stone did not understand these people and every day among them confused and unnerved him more.

When they were gathered, including the useless woman who served the witch, the red-haired man spoke. "My naitan has called you together this morning because the Reinine has ordered the binding together of an ilian between the captain and the warrior,

Stone. I will also be a part. Aisse, it is your choice as to whether you join as well."

Stone didn't see any point in acknowledging. He didn't understand the meaning of anything that was said, nor did it appear he had any choice in the matter. Why speak?

"Ilian," the small woman said. "The naitan talked about this on the boat. Ilian partners—"

"Iliasti," the bodyguard corrected. "One ilias, many iliasti."

"The iliasti—" she used the word carefully "—belong to each other. They are—family? This is right?"

"Family, yes," the witch said.

A woman and her infants were important to a ruler, Stone supposed, because the males would eventually join their caste and the females would breed more sons. But potential value was not the same as real value. He must have made a noise, because the black-haired witch frowned at him.

"This is Adara," she said. "In Adara, family—ilian—is important. After the One, ilian comes first."

"In Tibre," the serving woman said, "family is not important, because family has no caste. Family is a woman and her children before the males are old enough to join caste."

"This is not Tibre." The witch looked at Stone with her disturbing blue eyes, somehow preventing him from looking away. "Here, caste is not important. There is no caste. In Adara, there is only family. Ilian."

Stone struggled to understand. Caste created order. It gave a man his place in the world. Without caste... But Adara was not filled with chaos. He hadn't seen much of it, but no society without order could create the kind of things he had seen on his journey. "Ilian...takes the place of caste?"

The witch considered. "Perhaps. What is caste?" She looked at the small woman and spoke the gibberish that made Stone's gut churn because he knew he should understand it.

"Caste is order," he interrupted. The bodyguard scowled, but didn't reprimand him, so Stone went on. "A man is born to his caste. He enters it when he is six years old. It gives him his place in the world. It tells him who he is, what his value is, what his purpose is in life."

"What if he wishes a different purpose?" the witch said.

"What if he is stupid," the bodyguard said, "and born to a caste that requires intelligence?"

Stone had known stupid Rulers. He had no answer for that.

"There is no caste here." The witch's voice gentled. "Yes, ilian takes the place of caste. It tells us who we are and that our value is infinite. It anchors who we become. As the ilian's children go out into the world, the new iliani they create do honor to that from which they have come."

Stone sat up straight, frowning. Ilian was not the same as caste, he didn't understand it. But it seemed to serve the same purpose. It gave its members a place to belong. As prisoner, he was as casteless as a woman. He was anyone's meat. As…ilias, would that still be true?

"Do you understand, Aisse?" the bodyguard—Torchay—said. "The four of us would be bound together into a family, a new ilian. We would swear to the One to put each other first, to care for each other and any children we might have. It is more than caste."

"I cannot do children," Aisse said, her voice flat. "When I was young, before I old enough for Woman's Service, a Ruler did sex with me. He hurt me so I never bear children. They choose me for Adara, to serve the Warriors, because I not slow them down with a child."

The emotionless tone of her voice as she told of the thing that had happened to her sent chills rippling through Stone. A man was taught that there was an order and a season to all things, and though women—and children—had no caste of their own, they were to be protected as bearers of the future. And yet… A man had the right to make demands of those in castes below his own. He had the right to do as he saw fit with those who had no caste. If a Ruler had done this thing, he must have had reason. Surely.

"It does not matter." Torchay crouched beside her as the witch took the woman's hand. He seemed to speak for his captain. "Ilian is not for the purpose of creating children, but if they come, all the members protect them, raise and teach them. Ilian is a partnership, a joining together."

"You said—" The woman pulled her hand back and the witch allowed it. "You said iliasti do sex only with each other."

So... Stone focused his attention. This could be a benefit of a caste—or whatever this ilian thing was—with women. Would the witch's rules change? He missed sex.

"Yes, that's right," the bodyguard said.

"I do not want sex. I never do sex again."

Khralsh, what a waste. The woman was built for sex, small, soft, cuddly. With hips made to cradle a man and—Stone jerked his eyes away to stare out the window. He would only make it worse if he thought about it. With the chains he wore, he could not even ease himself without announcing the fact to everyone in hearing distance. Lieutenant Joh would say nothing, Stone was sure, but he would know.

The witch said something to the woman, then cut herself off and spoke in an undertone to the guard.

"You will not be forced to do anything you do not wish," Torchay said when she stopped, apparently translating. "Even if you join us, you do not have to have sex. You bring other things to the ilian."

"What?" Stone's frustration sent the word exploding out of him and once begun he might as well continue. They could punish him only once. "What else can she contribute? What can she do?"

"I do plenty, stupid warrior." The woman sprang to her feet, throwing a cushion at him. He couldn't raise his hands high enough to keep it from hitting him in the face. "You ever feed youself, warrior? Ever clean you own clothes? Ever clean you barracks? Why you think they bring so many women? For sex? Ha! To cook you food so stupid warriors not starve to death before they get theyself killed on battleplace."

The bodyguard was laughing so hard, he'd tipped onto his backside on the floor. Even the witch was smiling. Laughing at Stone. "You look as if a kitten suddenly turned into a tiger in front of your eyes," she said.

"I not—I am not a kitten. I never was a kitten. Always tiger," the woman said, then scowled down at herself. "A small tiger."

Torchay draped his arms over his knees and grinned up at her, his face more open than Stone had seen it. "I could teach you a few tigerish things," he said. "If you like. Things that even small tigers would find useful, that would give you teeth."

The woman smiled at him, her delight transforming a pretty face into beauty. "Teach me to fight?"

He nodded.

"I like, yes." She looked at the witch. "I not—I do not have to do sex?"

The witch shook her head, her face solemn again. Stone frowned. That meant the witch would be his only chance for sex. He studied her. She was tall, only a bit shorter than he, and slender, but she possessed a woman's curves. Her hips flared wide from a small waist, her breasts just the size to fill a man's hand. Her near-black hair and pale skin gave her an exotic look. But those uncanny blue eyes… Still, if she was willing, Stone was sure he could get past the eyes.

"Then I agree. I join." The small woman sat back in her chair.

"Your rules don't change, Tibran." The red-haired man loomed over Stone's chair, scowling down at him. He must have seen Stone looking at the witch and got to his feet to appear more threatening. "You'll do without, unless you're asked." He glanced at his captain. "And who knows when that will happen, if ever."

Stone looked at the witch again, at those pale eyes too much like his own. "Why do you want me in this ilian? I'm a prisoner. An enemy. Why not just lock me up?"

"Because of your mark." She touched the back of her neck where she bore a mark similar to his, or so they told him. He hadn't seen his own. "You and I have already been bound by the One. This is only a formality."

Stone suppressed a shudder. He didn't like to be reminded of the thing lurking inside him, this magic she claimed he carried for her. The mere thought of it cramped his gut. He was trapped. Changed. Ruined. He had no hope of returning home even if he thought he could regain his caste. He couldn't even understand the language anymore. "Am I condemned to this—this chain forever?"

"When I can trust you, the last chains come off," Torchay said.

"I don't know," the witch said. She understood what he meant. "I wish I did. I have been told that we bear these marks because we have—you and I—surrendered our wills to the One, who has a task for us. Perhaps when the task is done, we will be released from it. But I do not know."

"This One is your God?"

The witch nodded. "There is only One God."

"I serve Khralsh, the Warrior God."

"Which is one of the many faces of the One God. By focusing on only one face, you miss the many gifts the One has in store for you."

"Gifts like this magic?" Stone sounded sour even to himself.

The witch's smile was crooked. "Sometimes the good is hard for our limited vision to see. It can be very hard to trust in the One's wisdom. But what else can we do? We have it. We cannot give it back. We can only do what lies next before us."

"This ilian business."

"Yes."

"I still do not understand—" He did not even know what to ask. "What is ilian? What are the rules? Who is in charge?"

The witch and the red-haired man exchanged a look Stone didn't know how to interpret. She was the one who spoke this time. "I don't know how to explain when we have no reference points in common. Was there never anyone you—you cared for?"

"Warrior pairs," Aisse said. "Did you have pair partner?"

Stone felt his face shut down. "My partner died. I found his body in the breach."

"But you—he was important to you?" The witch's words poked at him. "His death caused you pain?"

"My pain is my own." He ground the words out between his teeth. "It is not for your amusement."

"*That* is ilian," she said, triumphant. "Iliasti care for each other. They watch each other's backs. They share. Whatever they have belongs to all. When one is hurt, all feel the pain. The ilian comes first—that is the only rule."

Stone refused to care for anyone else the way he had for Fox. How could he? Impossible to care for a woman like that, or an enemy. "But who decides? Who is in charge?"

"Normally, decisions are made together, and the one in charge is the one who knows most about a particular thing." The witch slowed her speech as she thought. "Which I suppose means that as the naitan, I am in charge because I know about magic. That is, as far as our—our task is concerned. Torchay would be in charge of security and health, Aisse in charge of supplies—food and such—and you…"

She looked at Stone and shrugged. "Well, I'm sure we could find something for you besides 'magic-bearer.'"

"When is the wedding?" Torchay asked.

"The Reinine would like it within the hour, I'm sure." The

witch looked at her bodyguard and smiled, a smile that spoke of long knowledge, as if they made up a warrior pair. Not possible. The captain was a witch and a woman. "But I have certain conditions. It will probably be on Hopeday to give time for those conditions to be met."

"When is Hopeday?" Aisse asked.

"Today is Sixthday, which makes tomorrow Graceday," the bodyguard explained. "Then Hopeday and Peaceday, and after the week's end, Firstday again."

The witch looked at Stone, the blue of her eyes pinning him to his chair. "You will be swearing oaths to the One who is your God and mine. You will swear to put the ilian above all others, to owe them your love and loyalty. If you can do this in truth, I will ask the Reinine's permission to remove the guard from our quarters."

"Kallista—" Torchay began.

She held up her hand, halting his protest. "If we are to be a true ilian, we do not need extras poking themselves into what should be between us. The Reinine has truthsaying magic. She will know if Stone swears in truth or if he lies in his oath. If we do not even attempt to treat him as a true ilias, why should he bother to become one?"

The red-haired man stared at Stone as if he could read his heart. Finally he nodded. "If he swears in truth, then I'll allow it."

Stone was confused again. "The witch is—"

"Naitan," the bodyguard interrupted. "Or Kallista. Iliasti give each other respect. 'Witch' is not respectful."

"Pardon." His head felt stuffed full. For a thing with only one rule, ilian seemed to have a great number of them. "The—naitan is also the captain, is she not? And the bodyguard, you are a sergeant, under her command?"

They both nodded.

"Then how can the sergeant 'allow' something the captain has commanded?"

Now they both smiled, indulgently, as if at a foolish child who could not understand. Exactly the way Stone felt.

"A naitan and her bodyguard are similar to an ilian in one way," the wi—Kallista said. "In matters of magic or duty, the naitan is in charge. At other times, in matters regarding the naitan's safety, the bodyguard has final say."

Stone thought he saw the sense in that. Maybe.

"Now—" the naitan clapped her hands together and rubbed them briskly "—it is time for Aisse to show her skills in securing supplies. She will accompany Erunde Undersecretary to the tailor's street and—" She went off into the nonsense that was supposed to be Tibran.

Stone looked at the bodyguard who looked back at him and shrugged. It was a moment of perfect male understanding. Stone jerked his gaze away. He did not need or want another partner. He'd had one, and Fox was dead. No worm-pale, blood-haired Adaran could take his place.

"Stone. Warrior." The wi—naitan was calling him. "What color do you prefer?"

"Red," was his instant reply. Red was the Warrior's color. He might be changing from caste to ilian, but he was still a warrior. Could he turn those skills against his people? Would he be asked to? What would he do if he was? Khralsh help him, he did not know.

CHAPTER FOURTEEN

Kallista stood on the edge of the red stone mosaic rose in the center of the sanctuary at the center of Arikon's Mother Temple and looked around her in satisfaction. For all its hurry, this would be a proper wedding. Aisse had outdone herself in the matter of clothes. Kallista smoothed down the blue silk of her sleeveless dress tunic. She'd consented to the parti-colored tights in blue and green, but had refused to submit any further to the extremes of current fashion. Though her elbow-length gloves were in two colors as well.

She looked beyond Aisse, who was wearing a vivid yellow dress tunic that enhanced her golden coloring, to the Reinine, robed today in black over pale blue tunic and tights. Serysta Reinine would be performing the ceremony herself in her role of High Prelate of Adara. An ilian could have no more auspicious beginning.

Kallista even had family present. Karyl and Kami had been found, still in Arikon for one week more before their journey home to Turysh. They would act as witnesses and attendants for Kallista and Aisse. Their iliasti-to-be had offered to provide the same service for the men and been accepted, since it would take weeks for any of Torchay's kinsmen to reach Arikon even with far speakers sending invitations. The Reinine refused to wait so long. His parents had sent their blessing through Karyl's magic. And the young men would be kinsmen soon enough through ties of ilian.

The only other witness was the lieutenant, Joh Suteny. Torchay had not wanted to do away with the entire guard escort before any oaths were sworn, and when Stone indicated that Joh had become something of a friend, Kallista acquiesced. Stone had lost everything else familiar, even his language. What harm could it do?

The sound of the gong shivered through the high sanctuary. Kallista turned to face the eastern entrance through which she and Aisse had recently come. Torchay led the way, his hair loose glowing waves of flame brushing his shoulders. His tunic was a green so dark it was almost black and yet still green, suiting him far better than his blacks ever did. It fit him superbly, displaying his masculine perfection with mouth-drying clarity. Kallista swallowed hard.

Then Stone appeared in the doorway and she had to swallow again. His cotton-soft yellow hair seemed to float around his shoulders. And what shoulders they were. The baggy prisoner's clothing had not done him justice. The red of his tunic was dark, almost a brick red, and looked well with his coloring, as gold as Aisse, his hair shades brighter. *These* were to be her iliasti?

How would she ever keep her vow? Kallista could not at this moment remember why she had made it. Why would any sane woman swear not to have sex with men such as these? Her contraceptive spell was in place. She quested inward to check one more time to be certain. Yes. If there were no children, they would be free to separate when they had completed this task of theirs, whatever it was. How could they do what was needed with the complication of children? She could have—

The rattle of chains against the tile floor broke her train of thought. Stone wore chains again, part of the *di pentivas* ceremony. Kallista had requested that he be allowed to marry without them, but the Reinine had insisted, even though no one had married *di pentivas* in hundreds of years, save perhaps in the most remote prinsipalities. Stone would have no escape from this marriage.

That was why she had made the vow. Because he had no choice. She feared that she had coerced Torchay into consenting to marry as well. She had been so hysterical that night, after the dream. How could he have done anything else, being who he was? He would not mind having sex with her. But that wasn't the same as wanting it, was it? She would not use these men as playthings, either of them.

The men took their places between the compass points, the four of them spaced evenly around the rose with the Reinine in the center, their witnesses a few paces back. The Reinine had Kallista remove her gloves, and began to speak.

Kallista made her vows first as the oldest female in the ilian. She was more than ten years older than Stone, and Aisse was even younger. It made Kallista feel ancient. Protective. She took the bracelet from her blood sister and crossed the rose to Aisse, fastening it about her wrist, repeating the promises, and exchanged a brief kiss.

She went back across the rose to Karyl and took the gold anklet. Kneeling before Torchay as she fastened the band around his right ankle, she repeated the promises to him, looking up into his eyes. She stood and kissed him, her eyes filling with unwanted tears. Why should she weep? This was what she wanted.

Once more she made the trip across the tile rose to collect the final anklet from her attendant. This one was gold like the others, but it had a fine silver chain hanging from it in loops. A *di pentivas* anklet. The chain was not mere decoration. It had been spelled long ago by a North magic metalworker to be stronger— much stronger—than it looked. The anklet and its chains had last been used centuries ago, when Tamonda Reinine had married four sedili from Korbin prinsipality—Torchay's home—and brought Korbin into the unity of Adara.

Kallista fastened the band around Stone's ankle, once more repeating the vows. She stood and leaned toward him for the kiss and he flinched away. Kallista cupped his head with her hand, murmuring under her breath, "It is part of the ceremony."

He swallowed, his nervousness screaming at her. "I know. I just—could you—would you mind closing your eyes?"

"Why?"

"They're blue."

What did that have to do with anything? This Tibran—this man made no sense to her. "Your eyes are blue."

"But I don't have to look at my own. I—brown eyes are normal. Blue—any light color is...uncanny. Disturbing. I—it would be—please?"

Kallista sighed. She could feel the others watching, wondering what the delay was. If closing her eyes would help him get through this, she would close her eyes. Still cupping his face, she kissed him, fumbling a moment before finding his lips. They were dry, a bit chapped, and the instant she kissed him, the magic inside him stirred, responding to her touch.

Stone gasped, his quiver matching hers. Kallista *reached,* soothing the magic, laying it back down, and it obeyed. She could sense its eagerness, how it strained at the leash. Quickly, she ended the kiss, her body shaking in reaction, and she strode back to her place on the rose.

Aisse went next, moving from one to the other, repeating the vows, fastening on bracelet and anklets. Again, there was a moment of hesitation before she exchanged the kiss with Stone, on her side this time. But in the end, it was done, and it was Torchay's turn.

He held Kallista's gaze as he spoke the vows that completed their joining, fastening a silver bracelet around her left wrist. Silver rather than gold was used in the mountains of his home because the strength of pure silver represented the strength and purity of their vows. He explained it to her as he bound them together. As their lips touched in this second kiss, she felt tears gather again at its pure sweetness. He was hers as she was his. But she would let him go in the end.

Finally it was Stone's turn to take the bands from his attendant. Rather than crossing the rose to the others, he waited in place and they came to him one by one, first Kallista, then Aisse, then Torchay. Afterward, Kallista attached the chains to his anklets, turning his ilian bands into shackles, and fastened the bracelets around his wrists. The *di pentivas* bracelets weren't like hers. They could be hooked together in an instant to immobilize him. He had no choice. Neither did she.

As soon as the last kiss between Stone and Torchay was exchanged—very quickly—Kallista relaxed. It was done. The ilian was complete.

The Reinine looked around at them as she spoke. "Prelates are often asked by young priests why black robes are worn for weddings. Why not green for beginnings and a fertile union? Or yellow for hearth and home? Why the color of the West? Of endings and death?"

Kallista had wondered that herself. At the few weddings she'd attended, the priests had never said why.

"And the answer is always the same. A wedding is an ending as well as a beginning, just as death is both beginning and ending. The old life has ended. You are no longer four solitary souls, but an ilian. And that is the deeper reason for the color of the West, because the bonds of ilian are a mystery. Who in this world can understand how four souls, or six or twelve, can be many, and at the same time one? Yet we know it is so. It is the mystery of the One."

The Reinine beckoned, calling them into the center for the final moments of the ceremony. As they joined hands, Kallista to Torchay, Torchay to Aisse, Aisse to Stone, Serysta Reinine moved out of the center of their circle, taking Kallista's hand and Stone's in hers.

"As you have each vowed today in truth," she said, "giving and receiving these bands in pledge and in symbol of the vows you have made, as the High Prelate of all Adara, I recognize this ilian. May the One bless you with love, with loyalty, with grace, hope and peace."

"May it be so," everyone said in unison.

The Reinine stepped back and placed Stone's hand in Kallista's. The magic didn't wait for her call. It leaped across their clasped hands, slamming into her with as much force as the first time. She barely had time to gasp before the magic jumped again, into Torchay, beyond him into Aisse and back home again to Stone. It bound the four of them with threads of magic that felt like nothing so much as sweet hot passion.

Kallista could feel the threads spinning out from her, sensed Torchay and Aisse beyond a veil, felt Stone swimming through her skin. The magic flowed, thrummed, crested, and she cried out as it broke over her, Stone's cry echoing with hers.

She staggered and would have fallen had Torchay not caught her as the magic drained back into Stone, teasing them with a last quiver. Stone swayed and Torchay caught him too, Aisse finally lending support to keep them all upright.

"Is that going to happen every time we touch?" Stone gasped, leaning hard against the other three.

"What was that?" Torchay shuddered. "Is that what happened when you—"

"I think—" Kallista took a deep breath, reaching for control.

"I think you felt only an echo of what we did. You're iliasti, you and Aisse. But you're not marked."

"If it does happen every time—" Stone pulled back, stood on his own wobbly legs "—I don't think I will mind overmuch if I don't get sex."

"That was not like sex," Aisse protested. "It felt good. Nice."

"Sex done right feels a lot like that." Kallista found her own feet.

"Are you all right?" Karyl rushed in, her twin close behind her. "What happened?"

"I think," the Reinine said, her voice carrying in the perfect acoustics of the room, "that we have all just witnessed something very special. The creation of the bonds of ilian as they were meant to be."

"I sensed magic," Karyl said, looking puzzled.

"West magic?" Joh Suteny drew attention his way, looking uncomfortable with it.

"Perhaps." The Reinine ignored Kallista's wince. She didn't want her peculiarities gossiped about the palace. "Whatever sort of magic, it was a sign of the One's blessing on this ilian." She smiled, spreading her arms wide in her own blessing. "Come. This is cause for celebration indeed."

The wedding party was swept along in the Reinine's wake. Kallista had managed to persuade her not to show any special favors. She was a soldier, not a courtier, and did not want to deal with the jealousy such favoritism would inevitably cause. She didn't want any functionary worried about her job when there was no threat. Whatever the task before her, Kallista knew it was not at court. She had the uneasy feeling it had to do with that thing she had seen in her vision.

However, the Reinine would not hear of a quiet celebration in their quarters. The party was escorted to the great hall to mingle with the courtiers while the Reinine retired to change from prelate's robes into ruler's finery before dinner. Fortunately, the

Reinine hosted a state dinner every Hopeday, so no particular notice would be drawn to the new ilian. Now Kallista's only worry was negotiating the evening without getting separated from Stone or tripping over palace politics.

By remaining in the background, refusing to jostle for table position and avoiding conversation with anyone who hadn't been present at the ceremony, Kallista and her ilian made it through the meal without problems. Trouble arose when the tables were cleared away for dancing.

Before Kallista could herd her family out the doors, a courtier approached. The young woman wore the shortened tunic and cropped hair of a brava, the omnipresent sword of that swarm of reckless aristocrats at her side. A sense of doom settled over Kallista as the courtier bowed low before Stone. "Your beauty has dazzled me. Grant me the gift of a dance."

Stone backed away, his eyes rolling side to side as he looked for rescue. "I don't—I can't…dance."

Kallista could not push through to his side quickly enough.

The woman trailed a finger down his sleeve. "I cannot believe such a sweet morsel as yourself would not—"

"He is claimed." Kallista shoved one of the brava's crowd aside and stepped in beside Stone, taking his arm. "And he speaks truth. My ilias does not dance."

The courtier's eyes sparkled with mischief and her lips twitched in a mocking smile as she bowed again, this time to Kallista. "My pardon, aila, if I have made too free with what is not mine. May I present myself? I am Prinsipella Viyelle Torvyl of Shaluine."

Wonderful. The spoiled offspring of a prinsep. Kallista returned the bow without all the hand flourishes. "Kallista Varyl, captain naitan of the Third Detachment, Reinine's Own."

"A military person, eh?" The prinsipella smirked. "I wonder that you have wed, given all the perquisites of military life. Do introduce me to your ilias."

Kallista's smile went tight, but the brat hadn't yet been overly insulting. Just subtly so, implying that Stone was her only ilias. Kallista would mind her own manners. "My iliasti." She gestured to them behind her, and started with Aisse because the prinsipella wasn't interested in her. "Aisse vo'Haav, Torchay Omvir and Stone, Warrior vo'Tsekrish"

"Vo'Haav, vo'Tsekrish—unusual names."

"Yes." Kallista didn't respond to the woman's hint for more information. "They are."

Viyelle ignored the nonresponse as if it were never spoken. "Surely you would not begrudge me a dance, just one dance with your lovely war prize?"

The prinsipella already knew Stone's origin? But why wouldn't she? Their meeting had been spectacular enough to have all of Adara gossiping, not just all of Arikon. Without waiting for Kallista to consent to the request, Viyelle swept Stone off into the rollicking, stomping country dance.

Kallista hesitated. Should she go after him? Stone's seizure could discourage other flirtations. But a seizure would draw unwanted attention, especially since they were already subjects of gossip. And the seizures were painful.

She got Torchay's attention with a touch and a look, asking silently what he saw from his greater height. He pointed and Kallista pushed her way through the dancers in that direction, but a hoarse cry told her she'd left it too late.

Quickly, Kallista motioned Torchay ahead of her. She didn't want anyone connecting Stone's sudden, miraculous recovery with her approach. She moved forward at a slightly more deliberate pace, forcing her way through the collected crowd to find a woozy but upright Stone leaning on Torchay. Lieutenant Suteny hovered nearby.

"My ilias is not well," she said to the alarmed prinsipella, and to the crowd at large. "Too much excitement is not good for him."

Kallista took Stone's other arm, though with his usual rapid recovery, he didn't need the support. He pretended to, however, as they left the hall. Kallista's sedili met them at the great double doors, filled with concern for Stone.

"Stay." Kallista waved them back. "This is your chance to mingle at court. Enjoy it. Stone will be fine once we reach the quiet of our rooms."

"And it is your wedding night after all," Kami teased. "I think you can be forgiven for cutting your evening short."

Her smile crooked, Kallista bid her sisters a good evening. Sweet heaven, it was her wedding night. How would they get through it? What would happen next?

Each ilian handled sex in its own way. In some, the iliasti paired up two and two. In others, everyone crawled into the same oversize bed and participated in whatever seemed most enjoyable at the moment. Yet others—Kallista didn't know, but she assumed there were as many patterns as there were iliani.

Aisse didn't want sex. She'd made that clear. Stone obviously had hopes but no expectations. Torchay, though… Torchay would have expectations. Even if he were more resigned than eager, he would expect more than a kiss and a cuddle, and his fragile male esteem would suffer if he didn't get it. But her own esteem would suffer if she felt only duty from him in their coming together. She had intended to avoid sex altogether, but could she?

At the door to their suite, Joh made as if to follow them inside. Kallista blocked his way, sending the others in ahead of her. "You're quartered out here now, Lieutenant. You and your quarto. Stone is ilias now, and as such, we will care for him."

Joh's face was blank as he saluted, fist over heart. Kallista sensed undercurrents beneath his bland exterior. Something was going on in that curious, watchful head of his, but she didn't have time to work it out now. Joh was under her command, not in her ilian, and at this moment, her new-wed mates came first. She returned his salute and retreated inside.

Noonday Suite was designed to house the largest of iliani with its private bedrooms down each side of the long central parlor, seven on one side, five on the other. The center bedroom next to Stone's was double the size of the other eleven and contained little more than an enormous sleeping platform, in case the entire ilian wanted to sleep all cuddled together. Their ilian had not reached that point, and odds were good that it never would.

Aisse was already closed in her room across the parlor from Kallista's. Stone and Torchay were waiting together just inside the main door, Torchay's face as carefully blank as Joh's had been. Kallista sighed, pulling off her long gloves. She had a good idea what lay behind that expressionless face. Torchay didn't know who or what she would choose tonight, and Kallista couldn't reassure him. She didn't know herself.

"Go to bed." She kissed Torchay's cheek, and because Stone was ilias too, she kissed his. "It's been a long day. I'm sure you're both tired." She looped an arm through each of theirs and walked the length of the parlor with them.

"Your day's been just as long," Torchay said. "Aren't you tired?"

"Too tired to sleep." Her smile flickered and faded. "I'm...restless. Maybe if I pace a while..." Maybe she could decide what she ought to do.

"Don't pace too far," Stone said, his first spontaneous remark since the end of the wedding. He obviously didn't want another seizure tonight.

"I won't." She patted his hand as they stopped outside his bedroom door. "That chair, that chaise longue, that table." She pointed at each in turn. "And no farther."

Stone nodded and retreated behind his door.

"Torchay—"

"Kallista, I—" They spoke at the same time.

"Go on," she urged as she walked him to the next room.

He shook his head. "I don't remember what I wanted to say."

She wasn't sure she believed him, but let it go. They stopped at the bedroom door and stood there, awkward together, unable to look each other in the eye. The possibility—the probability of sex had landed between them like an enormous boulder and nothing was the same. All the ease between them was gone. They couldn't even talk anymore. She had been right all along. Sex ruined everything.

But how could she disappoint him? How could she let him think she didn't find him attractive, so attractive her mouth went dry just looking at him? Goddess, she didn't know what to do. So she kissed him. Not quite on the mouth, but almost.

"I'll be along soon," she said before he could turn his head, make it a true kiss.

Torchay lifted his hand as if to touch her cheek, but she looked away deliberately and he didn't. "Kallista—" He paused. "All right. If you go to him, be careful."

Her eyes snapped to meet his. Was he sending her to Stone or warning her away? "Stone *is* ilias. You heard the Reinine. He swore his vows in truth."

"I know." The vivid blue of his eyes seemed to have depths she'd never seen. "But he's still Tibran. He doesn't understand yet all that ilian is. Just—be careful."

"I don't have any plans to go to any—to do that—to—" Goddess, could she put her foot in it any worse? "With Stone." There, that should clarify. "Not tonight. Or—" She couldn't say ever. She didn't plan to, but plans sometimes changed.

Torchay nodded, carefully not looking at her now. He backed into the bedroom. "I'll be waiting." And he shut the door.

Kallista wanted to bang her head against the wall, but that would only bring Torchay back out to see what was wrong. She wanted him. She wanted to pull the lacings from his tunic and lick her tongue across each fraction of skin exposed. She wanted to pull the tunic off and run her hands over every bit of his shoulders and back and chest and stomach, lingering in those spots where he responded with gasps or groans. She wanted to take him deep inside her and ride his strength till they both screamed. And she knew if she did what she wanted she would destroy what she had.

She started pacing along the wall, down to the chair past Stone's door and back to the table just past her own. Her mind whirled, thinking about everything and nothing, circling again and again past the same contradictory arguments. She could no longer make sense of anything. *Please, Goddess, just let me know what to do.*

Joh paced the confines of the guardroom office where he had been summarily relegated tonight. His mind sorted through what he knew, what he had learned and what he suspected. When he understood, he would know what steps to take.

The magic he had seen—the strange connection between his Tibran prisoner and the naitan—was disturbing enough in itself. The Reinine had hinted that this magic could be of the West. It certainly possessed enough mystery for this to be true, but he did not know it for fact.

The Tibran had been joined to the other three by the ancient rites *di pentivas.* That was a fact. Joh's reaction to it was pure emotion.

It made him angry. Ragingly, blindingly furious. He wanted to smash something. Men had fought for many years for the right to choose, to be treated as individuals, as persons worthy of equal respect. A man was not a piece of property to be handed off to any woman who could keep him. Joh did not know what the captain had said to have the Tibran given to her, but whatever it was, it was not reason enough. The man was an enemy, yes, a prisoner. But he was still a man like any other.

The captain seemed sincere in her claims, that she would treat him as any other ilias. But as long as Stone wore the bracelets and the chain-looped anklets of *di pentivas,* he was not like other iliasti. Still, perhaps she did mean it. Joh decided to reserve judgment for another few days. Until he knew from which direction this new magic came.

Already Joh had received a terse note inquiring when a report might be expected. Joh sat down at the desk, squeezed between the cot and the weapons rack, to write down what he had learned. Best to be ready when his decision was made.

CHAPTER FIFTEEN

Kallista found herself standing at the edge of a bed, staring down at the man sleeping in it, without knowing how she came to be there. She didn't much care, and in a far distant corner of her mind, she wondered why she didn't. But the corner was far, far distant, and the man was right here before her. His cotton-soft hair, almost silver in the moonlight, lay spread on the pillow beneath him. The urge to touch it became more than she could bear and she crawled onto the bed.

"Stone." She breathed the word out, quieter than a whisper, fingers stroking across the softness of his hair, moving toward his face.

The sandpaper roughness of his cheeks fascinated her and she cupped them in her hands, sinking into him. The magic stirred, welcoming her, flowing into her body and curling round like a cat stropping itself across her senses. She shuddered.

Stone's eyes opened. "Captain?"

"Kallista," she corrected. She stroked her hands down his neck and across his shoulders, shaping her hands to their strength. He was bare-chested. Was he perhaps bare all over?

At that thought, the magic flared, searing her senses and leaving them both awake and quivering. The brush of silk was too much against her skin and she sat up to rid herself of her tunic. Stone sat up with her, yanking away her chemise beneath so he could wrap his arms around her and bring her bare breasts against his naked chest. He rubbed himself against her too-sensitive skin and she cried out with the pleasure of it.

The magic had her in its grip now, driving her. That distant part of her held an awareness that this wasn't right, that she shouldn't use him so, that she hadn't intended this, but the passion rode her, refusing to let her go. Almost frenzied, she pushed him back down on the bed and dragged the coverlet off him. He was naked beneath it.

For a moment, Kallista paused to look her fill. Stone was beautiful in the moonlight, broad-shouldered, slim-hipped. The disks of his nipples were dark against his hairless chest. A line of hair began below the dip of his navel and ran down to join the brown nest from which his erection rose, thick and powerful. Kallista's whole body tightened. She wrapped her hand around the base of his shaft and his hips bucked.

He tried to roll, to bring her beneath him, but the magic helped her push him back. She fought against the surge of power, wanting to draw the pleasure out, to linger over her fine dish of Stone, but the magic was so strong. It wanted completion.

Kallista relaxed her muscles, collapsing on top of him. She could hear, could feel the thunder of his heart against her jaw. If she tipped her head just a little, her tongue could touch his nipple, so she did it. Stone jerked beneath her.

"For the god's sake, Captain, put me out of my agony." He groaned the words out, his body writhing. "I want—I need—"

"Shh." She covered his mouth with hers, kissing away his power of speech. Stone conveyed his want and need in his openmouthed kiss instead, drinking her in, giving back what he took.

Kallista wanted. She needed, and with every touch of his mouth, hands, body against hers, the power of that desire increased, like lightning bouncing between her hands. She would not be able to control it much longer.

"Say it." She tore herself gasping from the kiss to press her cheek tight to his, her lips brushing his ear. "We are ilian together. I am your ilias. I want to hear you say it."

Stone's hips bucked, his tip just nudging her entrance, and they both hissed with the feel of it. "What? What do you want me to say? That we are ilian?"

"My name, ilias. Say my name." She couldn't keep from rubbing herself against his slick broad tip, but she wouldn't let him inside. Not yet. She had that much control. For this instant. Who knew what the next would hold?

"Say mine." His hips rose off the bed, lifting her with them as he sought entry. He was making this a competition, a challenge to see who would win and who would lose. He didn't understand that in an ilian, no one lost.

She bit his earlobe, licked her tongue over it and murmured, "Stone, Warrior vo'Tsekrish. Ilias. Now, Stone, you."

He fought against it, turning his face away, pressing his lips tight. He raised his hands overhead and clutched at his pillows as if he could resist more easily if he didn't touch her. Kallista knew better. She sat up, fitting his length in the slick heat of her channel, his tip against her sensitive bud, and rocked. He cried out.

"I'm not your enemy, Stone. Not anymore." Kallista teased him, rocking again and again until her eyes threatened to cross.

Magic rushed between them, blocking her senses from everything but where they touched. She felt him thick inside her and realized what the magic had pushed her into doing: exactly what she wanted. It was impossible to stop, to back away. Her body wouldn't let her. The magic wouldn't let her.

"Kallista—" He moaned her name as she came fully down over him and ground her hips against his. Once more he lifted her in the air, straining against her.

"Again," she whispered. "Say it again." She set her hands on his chest, her fingers over his nipples, rising off him to plunge back down.

"Kallista!" he cried.

They strove together without rhythm or pace, slick and sweating, crying out the other's name at every beat. They rolled and slid, clutching at each other until Stone lay over her, the force of his thrusts threatening to drive her across the bed. He would have if not for the equal force of her hips lunging to meet him.

"Stone, Stone, Stone—" She could scarcely breathe, the pleasure had dragged her so deep into its grip.

"Kallista, Kallista—" He echoed her, giving a little extra twist of his hips at the end of each thrust that made her squeak.

Magic and passion mingled together, dancing through them both until Kallista scarce knew which skin she wore, building higher and tighter until it burst. She screamed again and again until Stone shouted and plunged shuddering into her one last time. The magic exploded in a fiery shower that would have blinded them both had it been visible to the eye.

She didn't know how much time had passed before she came to herself once more. The round disk of the moon was visible through the west-facing window, so it had to have been hours. She thought. Kallista sat up, pushing her hair out of her eyes. Blessed One, what had she done here?

She looked down at the man beside her. Stone. He sprawled naked on his back, his body marked by her hands and—dear

Goddess—her teeth. Her own body shuddered with remembered pleasure.

Horrified, she scrambled off the bed so fast she landed on her backside on the floor. She didn't know how this had happened. Well, she knew *that,* the mechanics involved. But how she'd decided on it, what had brought her into his room—she couldn't... Even the first touch was a blur in her memory. Nothing was clear until she was naked in his arms and after that, everything was colored with the haze of passion. *What had happened?*

Kallista scrambled for the door, rising to her feet only when she reached it. She had to get out, get away. The door stood ajar—when had she come through it? Had she left it open? Why couldn't she remember? She wouldn't have left a door open during such an intimate encounter. Would she? It creaked when she opened it wider to slip through.

"K'lista?" Stone mumbled her name.

"Go back to sleep," she said gently. It wasn't his fault she'd done what she had. But she needn't have spoken. He slept again before she did.

How could she face him in the light of day? What would he expect from her? Sweet words? Kisses and cuddles? More of the same? She wasn't the cuddling sort and more would only compound the error. Dear Goddess, how had this happened?

She was inside her bedroom halfway to the bed when she realized where she had come and why. Not to her room for privacy, but to Torchay for...for comfort. She couldn't cry on one man over mistakenly giving in to sex with another. Even she knew that wasn't wise. Kallista turned to leave.

Torchay sat up in the bed. "Kallista? Where are you going?"

Damnation. She should have remembered how he woke at the slightest noise. He'd probably been awake since she entered the room. Since she left Stone.

"I—" she began, then lost every thought that had ever been in her head when Torchay got out of bed and came toward her.

He was naked. As naked as Stone. As naked as she.

He put his arms around her and laid his cheek on the top of her head. "What's wrong? Are you hurt?"

She shook her head. Physically—her body ached, and it hummed with pleasure. She slid her arms around his waist and moved closer, until she could feel the touch of his skin all along hers, the press of his arousal against her stomach. Her heart ached. Her mind struggled with what she had done. "I didn't mean to—"

"Perhaps you needed to." Torchay lifted her in his arms and carried her to the bed. He set her in the center and got in with her, pulling her into his embrace again.

Of course, he knew what she was referring to. She'd left the door open. She'd screamed. "Why would I need to? He's a stranger. I haven't known him for a week. And I've gone longer without. If I needed it that much, I have you."

His mouth curved into a smile against her forehead. "You're such a romantic. But that's not what I meant. I think the marks...make things happen."

"Isn't it enough we're ilian?" She squirmed closer, needing to feel more of him.

He froze motionless a moment before taking a deep breath and resting his chin atop her head. "Perhaps not."

She shifted position again, settling her bottom between his thighs.

Torchay tightened his hold on her. "Kallista, don't. Be still."

"Why?" She looked up at him.

"Because you don't..." His voice trailed off as he returned her gaze.

"I don't—what?"

"You don't want—don't..." He squeezed his eyes tight shut and let his head fall back. She kissed the tip of his chin, rough with the day's beard. He jerked away. "Goddess, Kallista, I can't—"

"You can." She took his face between her hands and held him in place while she kissed his mouth, sipping him like a delicate wine. He shivered, his fingers twitching faintly where they rested on her shoulder and hip. She kissed him again, deeper, more insistently, and he opened his mouth to admit her tongue. She wanted him, wanted this, wanted something real and true, though she feared the magic still drove her.

Her skin thrummed with the need to be touched, alive to every whisper along it. Had it always been so sensitive? She didn't know, couldn't recall.

Torchay's passive response began to erode. His tongue brushed against hers, flicked past her teeth, slid into her mouth. The kiss deepened yet again. Kallista rose onto her knees as they kissed and kissed. He had to want this too. He couldn't hide the obvious, didn't try to, and she was grateful. The magic might ride her, but it didn't ride him. He *did* want her.

Kallista straddled his lap, wrapping her legs behind his back as she lowered herself onto him. Torchay gasped, breaking the endless kiss. He looked at her, shock and wonder in his face. He didn't say anything, just watched while she took him inside herself, using her heels against his back to bring him closer. The incredible intimacy of it, staring into his eyes while he filled her clear to her heart, was almost more than she could bear.

"Torchay," she said. Nothing more. She needed nothing more. Only this. Only him.

With a groan, he curled forward, laying his head on her shoulder, his breath skittering warm down her breast. Kallista shivered and arched her back, offering her breasts up to him. His strong arms moved to support her as he kissed his way down the slope from her shoulders in little soft, moist kisses that made her skin scream for more. The pointed tip of his tongue slipped out for a quick taste and she jerked. He chuckled, wickedly, laying a kiss in the hollow between her breasts.

She swayed, moving him in minute increments inside her. His arms tightened and the kisses stopped for a brief second. Then he rocked back, not actually moving within her, but increasing the pressure against something incredibly sweet. Her hands thrust themselves into his hair, her fingers combed through the waves and moved down across his muscled back. His tongue flicked out again in concert with another rocking motion and she gasped.

Slowly they rocked together, touching and withdrawing, gripping and releasing. Torchay worked his way across her breasts one tiny kiss at a time. Kallista wanted to scream out her frustration at his slow, slow pace, and she wanted him to go on kissing her like that all night, forever. When his tongue finally licked over the peak of her breast, she gave a violent shudder as the long-anticipated delight shot through her. He opened his mouth and drew her in, teasing her nipple with his tongue as he suckled. Her shuddering continued.

He moved to the other breast and his hand came up to console the abandoned one. Kallista wrapped her arms around his head, cradling it to her, and bent down to press her lips against his hair. It was too much, more than she could bear, and she whispered his name. "Torchay."

She let him go when he pulled back, until his gaze met hers and held it, without ever ceasing his slow, seductive rocking inside her. "I'm here," he said. "Always. You know that."

She couldn't answer, unable to trust her voice. She just lost herself in the intimacy of his lightning-touched gaze and the passion he built inside her with everything he did.

This was worlds apart from the frenzied violence of the episode with Stone. The only magic here was the sort created between two people who knew each other well and liked what they knew. The pleasure wasn't any less. In a way, it was more because it was real. True.

Her lips curved in a smile and after a moment, he answered with one of his own.

"Kallista," he said. "Ilias. I—"

But whatever he intended to say was lost in the sudden onrush of her climax. It rose out of nowhere, sweeping over her in a flash, forcing a faint cry from her as she throbbed around him. Torchay cried out, his arms whipping around to hold her tight, and his climax answered her own.

For a brief moment, as his seed pulsed into her, Kallista regretted her contraceptive spell. A child—her child—was one of the dreams she'd put behind her when she found herself sentenced to the military. She was old now, thirty-four, and past dreaming. She had to give Torchay—and the others—their chance at freedom once this mysterious quest was ended.

She didn't want to think about it now. She had to move her legs from behind Torchay as he lay back, still holding her tight against him. "Sleep," he said, refusing to release her when she would have moved off him to one side. "It's been a long day."

Daylight shining through the high open window woke her. That and the weight of Torchay's leg across her middle making it hard to breathe. He stirred when she slipped out from beneath it. "No, stay," she murmured, setting her hand on his shoulder. "Sleep. I'm only visiting the necessary."

He mumbled something and pushed his face back into the pillow, taking her at her word. Grateful for the respite, Kallista collected fresh clothing and escaped. When she returned to the parlor, washed, dressed and feeling wrung out, she still had it to herself. Hopeday had passed. Could she summon Belandra again?

Kallista looked down at the ring on her ungloved finger and idly pulled a thread of magic from the air, weaving it into her desire to speak to the ghost woman.

"I'm here, I'm here. You can stop." Belandra seemed to walk

through a door of nothingness into the parlor. "What is it this time?"

She hadn't prepared any questions beforehand, Kallista realized. "I'm not sure how to phrase my question to get the answers I want."

"Why didn't you do that before you called me?" Belandra looked the younger woman up and down. "You look like—" She seemed to have second thoughts and broke off. "As if you had a rough night," she said instead. "What do you want to know?"

"I got married yesterday."

"Obviously. Should I congratulate you?" Belandra raised an eyebrow in question.

Kallista took a deep breath and let it out slowly. "I think so. It's difficult to tell. Have the godmarked always married? Is it necessary?"

"What do they teach children these days? Don't you know anything? Iliani began a thousand years before my time with the first godstruck naitan. Powlas married her three marked companions. Why do you think an ilian always has at least four iliasti?" Belandra paused. "How can you have half an ilias?"

"There are four of us." Kallista shook her bracelets at Belandra. "But I want to know about the necessity of it."

Belandra counted off her own bracelets, five on each wrist. "Your bracelets say otherwise."

"Aisse." Kallista lifted her right arm, showing the band her female ilias had given her, then lifted her left. "Torchay. Stone. Three iliasti."

"They give you only one band?"

"That's the custom. About necessity..." She had to work to keep from asking the question again. She didn't want Belandra—or whoever was counting—to count the same question twice.

"My iliasti gave me a pair each." Belandra made them chime against each other.

"Twelve bracelets on each arm get heavy. And expensive." Kallista ground the words out between her teeth, stifling the urge to scream. She did not want to wake the others. "You have not answered my question."

"I don't know if it's precisely *necessary* for the marked ones to marry," Belandra said. A quirk of her lips told Kallista she'd been avoiding the question for her own amusement. Could one strike a ghost?

"The marks draw you together," Belandra went on. "They bind you into an ilian whether you go through a ceremony or not. It's more that the ceremony recognizes what already exists."

"Two of my iliasti aren't marked."

Belandra shrugged. "There's no rule you have to marry only your marked companions."

Kallista recalled her most important question. "You said we've been marked because the One has a task for us. How will I know what it is?"

"You will be shown."

This time the frustration got out, strangled down to an odd noise. "Dammit, Belandra, stop trying to be so mysterious and obscure. Just tell me."

"Some things you must learn for yourself, naitan." Belandra snapped the words out. "You will be shown your task. In visions. You will see the problem."

"I've already saved people from a collapsing wall that I saw in a vision."

Belandra shook her head. "Too small. Not enough for the kind of power you've mentioned. Is that your only vision?"

Kallista went still, remembering the horror. "I saw my ilias injured, bleeding his life away and no healer to stop it." Then she recalled the other vision, the one that had preceded it. "And I saw men talking. Tibran Rulers. And a...a thing sitting on the shoulders of the man wearing the gold coronet on his head."

"A thing? What sort of thing?"

"Darkness. Just…shapeless darkness at first, with eyes. But as I watched, it took on form and shape. It…looked at me. It saw me. In the vision."

"Goddess." Belandra wiped both hands down her face, wiping away her horrified expression. "Could it be?"

This seemed worth a question. "What?"

"Demons were described thus. But they were locked away during the Demon Wars long before Powlas was ever chosen."

Kallista counted her questions. She had two left. How best to apportion them? "It seems then that defeating the demon would be my—*our* assigned task."

Belandra pushed off the back of the sofa where she'd been leaning to pace, worry in every line of her body. "It would be reasonable to assume. Tibrans are the ones you killed? The enemy facing Adara? Yes, you said that. And if the demon is behind this attack…"

She stopped her pacing and met Kallista's gaze. "Very few records survived to my time from before Powlas. Scraps of stories that told of the demons' defeat, but not how it was done. I wish I could tell you more. But I will tell you this—Do not go after this demon until you have gathered all of your marked companions.

"They are—every one of them—necessary to succeed in your quest. You must have what each one carries."

"Goddess." Kallista slumped against the wall. "How many more? I can barely deal with the ones I have now. I had not expected ever to marry."

"At least one. Possibly—*probably* one more beyond that. At the very least. A demon— Four of the marked does not seem enough. There were six of us and we had mere humans to deal with. I would honestly expect you to need more than that." Belandra frowned. "What do you mean, you can barely deal with them?"

"It's complicated. By more than just magic. And it's personal."

"I am the only other godstruck person you can discuss it with. Who else is there? What do you mean, complicated?"

Kallista shook her head. "I don't want to talk ab——" And yet Belandra was right. Who else would understand? "I just——I think I made a huge mistake last night. Two of them. I... Can the magic push me into having sex when I don't want to? It seemed——" She broke off at a noise behind her.

The awful clutching feeling in her gut told her it was bad. Worse than bad. Kallista turned and saw Torchay standing fully dressed in the open doorway of the bedroom they shared, his face completely blank. The clutching twisted into knots.

"Don't worry," he said. "You'll not be forced into any mistakes again. Not by me." He stalked the length of the parlor toward the double doors.

"Oops." Belandra actually looked sympathetic. Amused, but sympathetic.

"Oh, Goddess," Kallista groaned. She'd hurt him and she didn't know how to fix it. Because she did believe that she should never have given into the temptation last night. This morning's fiasco proved it. Sex ruined perfectly good relationships. But she had to do something.

She started after Torchay, then remembered Belandra was still there and turned back.

The copper-haired woman laughed. "I'm sorry. It's cruel of me, but to watch you dance between me and your ilias——I can't help laughing. And if you fight it, the magic will fight back. I find it very difficult to believe that you didn't want to make love to a man such as that. Or the blonde. Did——you said *two* mistakes. Both of them? At once?"

"Not at once." Kallista's face burned, though it had no reason to. They were both her iliasti.

"Why would you want to deny yourself?"

"Stone is *di pentivas*. I thought to give him time. And Torchay—" Kallista frowned at the other woman. "I thought you had to leave shortly after my last question was asked."

"Shortly after I *answer*. And the answer is this—The magic cannot make you do anything against your nature. It cannot force you to—to murder, for instance, if you are not a murderer. But if the magic needs a thing, and it is within your nature—despite your denial of that fact—then it will get what it needs."

"Why would it need me to—" she began, but Belandra was gone. She couldn't help wondering why the magic would need her to have sex. It didn't make sense, and she didn't want to compound the existing mess by doing it again. With Torchay angry at her, resisting his temptation would be easier. But somehow she had to mend things so they could at least work together again, even if their friendship was shattered beyond mending by the stupidity of sex.

It would have to wait for his return. Until Stone was awake and mobile, she was stuck here while Torchay talked with the guard lieutenant at the far end of the parlor, just inside the door. How long had Lieutenant Suteny been there? Had he seen her talking to Belandra? She wanted to like the man, but his constant watchfulness unnerved her.

Kallista opened Stone's door and stopped just inside. She wanted to wake the man, not his magic. "Stone," she called. "I've things to be doing and I need you with me."

He lifted his face from the pillow where it was buried, and looked at her through his manic hair. "Kallis...ta..." He seemed bemused by his ready use of her name. He pushed his hair back and looked at her without its veil, his eyes losing their drowsiness. "Did I dream it or was it real? You with me—"

"Real enough. It won't be happening again. Get dressed. We have work."

As she left the room, she heard him mutter, "Didn't expect it this time, don't know why she thinks I'd expect it again."

* * *

As Joh talked with the naitan's bodyguard, he could only hope that his words made sense. His mind was reeling with what he had heard and seen. Or rather *not* seen.

He had been up early as usual, but reasoned that the ilian would not have slept much on their wedding night and thus would not yet be astir. When he heard voices, he had knocked. He hadn't knocked very loud, true, mindful of his intention to understand the naitan's purpose and motivations. But he had knocked. And when he opened the door, he had seen the naitan talking and listening intently to no one at all.

No one visible to Joh, at any rate. With the hair rising on the nape of his neck at this blatant display of West magic, he left the door ajar and listened. The naitan spoke of demons and magic and forced sex, and with every word, Joh's neck prickled more until he could have sworn his triple-length queue had to be pointing straight out behind him. This wasn't right. It could not be the hand of the One.

But before he could retreat and add this information to his report, he heard the bodyguard sergeant speak, heard his boot heels sound between the rugs as he approached the door. Omvir would notice that it stood ajar. He was too good a bodyguard not to notice, naitan's ilias or no. So Joh pulled the door open and stepped in, greeting him with the felicitations owed a newlywed male. And they had talked, but Joh could not have told what either had said.

"Lieutenant." The naitan approached, Joh's former prisoner trailing behind her. Stone didn't look too much the worse for wear under casual inspection. In truth, he looked rather...cat in the cream.

Joh came to strict attention and saluted. "Captain, how may I serve?"

"We need a space, preferably away from population I think, where we can practice."

"If I might inquire——" He did not want to offer insult, not to a naitan with her strange magic. "What do you intend to practice? So I know what sort of space you need."

"Magic," she said.

"And combat," the sergeant added. "I would know my iliasti's skills."

Joh touched his overlong queue. It was lying flat against his neck, despite his unease. "I am not familiar with the...practice of magic. Do you require——"

"Much the same sort of space as for practicing combat." The naitan's impatient words made Joh's heart pound. "But with fewer people. Preferably none." She made a face. "And it should be as nonflammable as possible. This...mark has mucked with my magic and I'm not so sure of my control as I once was."

"I will see what I can do." Joh bowed and departed as quickly as he could. He would carry out the captain's orders, but first he would deliver his report for the Master Barb to the briar-painted chapel.

CHAPTER SIXTEEN

When palace servants came bringing breakfast, Torchay made a point of sitting between Aisse and Stone at the table. It was petty perhaps, but he felt petty just now. He should never have allowed himself to hope that being ilias rather than mere bodyguard might have changed things between them. If he hadn't had hope, it might not have hurt so much to hear Kallista call the incredible, intimate passion they'd shared a mistake, to understand that if the magic had not forced her, she might never have made love with him.

He focused his attention on his other iliasti, making sure Aisse had the crisp bacon she preferred and Stone's cup was kept filled with the palace's excellent cider. Aisse caught on quickly to how the game was played and did the same courtesies for the iliasti seated to either side of her. Torchay didn't think the other two noticed anything.

When the meal was ended, Torchay stood and offered his hand

to assist Aisse. It appeared to startle her, but she was nothing if not adaptable, and she slid her small hand into his. She stretched toward him onto her toes and Torchay bent to see what she wanted.

Lips near his ear, she murmured, "I still not do sex with you."

His chuckle felt bleak. "Just now, that sounds perfect," he murmured back. He kissed her cheek as he straightened, playing the part, and Aisse bustled away to tend to something.

"Torchay." Kallista touched his arm.

He pulled it back, blanking his face save for a faint questioning expression.

"We should talk." She shook back the darkness of her unbound hair, the hair that had brushed like silk across his naked skin in the night.

"I don't know what we have to be talking about." Torchay knew she was right, but he couldn't face discussing it now, especially with Stone as an audience. On the other hand, maybe it was better he was here.

"Dammit, Torchay!" she exploded quietly, her words hissing as she spoke. "This is exactly what I was afraid of. Perfectly good relationships ruined because feelings got hurt over sex."

"It wasn't the sex that ruined it," he retorted, temper flaring. Anger helped burn away the hurt. "It was knowing you think of me—of both of us—as mistakes." He waved a hand toward Stone who appeared to be trying very hard to avoid notice.

"*You* aren't a mistake. Neither of you is. I would never think that. Goddess." Kallista looked up at the ornately painted ceiling with its scenes of picnics and hunting. Her eyes blinked rapidly. "I don't know how to do this. I'm a soldier. I'm barely capable of managing friendship. I don't know why I thought I could cope with an ilian."

Was she blinking back tears? Kallista Varyl, captain naitan of the Third Detachment, Reinine's Own? Surely not.

Except...Torchay had always known there were more depths

to her than the devotion to duty she let everyone see. Now he resented her for the faint niggling of guilt she instilled in him. "Perhaps you should have thought of that before you married us," he
said, and immediately wished he hadn't when she winced at the
spoken blow.

"I did," she whispered. "But you know I had no choice."

Torchay took a deep breath and let it out, seeking calm. He
hated this sort of emotional turmoil. "Goddess."

Kallista looked absolutely miserable. The way he felt. Stone
looked as if he wished he were anyplace but where he was. It was
bad all round. Torchay couldn't force Kallista to feel something
she didn't. He couldn't make her want him. He was fighting
against the river's flood if he thought otherwise.

He took another deep breath. "Sniping at each other isn't getting us anywhere. We have to deal with what is. And that is this
poor, misbegotten, magic-riddled ilian of ours."

"I suppose you have suggestions?" Kallista's tone sniped at them
once more.

Torchay scolded her with his expression. "I *suggest* that we at
least treat each other as iliasti should. As if we are in this by
choice, not duty." He had chosen. He should act like it. Just because his choice had not lived up to his dreams was no reason to
whine about it now. His hurt was unimportant compared to the
vows he'd made.

"I had no choice." Stone took this moment to speak up after
maintaining silence for so long.

"Pretend," Torchay said, giving him a level look.

The other man shrugged and nodded, and Torchay looked at
Kallista.

She bit her lip, obviously worried. "I don't think sex should be
part of this."

"Fine. Whatever. I think you're foolish to rule it out entirely,
but if you can't bring yourself to want either of us—"

"It's not that I don't want you—" she interrupted him, then broke off when Torchay held up his hand.

"Don't. I believed you when you told me that before, but—" This time he stopped himself, shaking his head. "It doesn't matter. It's just—perhaps if we act as if we are a normal ilian—except for sex," he said with a tip of his head toward Kallista, "we can *become* a normal ilian."

"I don't think—" she began again.

"Then don't. Don't think." Torchay had had enough. "Thinking's never been your greatest strength. *Act*. You're good at that. We're an ilian. Act like it." He wanted to walk away, but that wouldn't be the behavior of a good ilias. Once more he had to take a calming breath. They didn't seem to be very calming this morning.

"My apologies," he said. "I'm not doing very well at following my own advice."

Kallista waved his words aside. "No need to apologize when you're right. I'm better at acting than thinking. It's why I'm always saying such appalling things. I never meant to hurt you, Torchay. I'm sorry."

But she still thought their incredible lovemaking was a mistake. She didn't want him as ilias, not truly. She didn't seem to want any of them.

"I'll get over it," he said finally. "Will you answer me a question, though?"

She nodded, though she didn't look any too certain.

"Why *did* you marry us—Aisse and me? Do you even know?"

"I—It—" Kallista stammered to a halt then tried again. "It seemed the best thing to do."

A poor answer, but it would have to do. It was all he had. "Perhaps I should see if I can assist Lieutenant Suteny in finding a practice room."

"Torchay, I truly am sorry."

He nodded. "I know."

"Are we—all right?"

Eventually that calming breath ought to work. But not yet. "Yes," he said. "Or we will be. I am not a good enough actor to pretend nothing happened, but I am still your bodyguard and your ilias. That won't change. Just—I'm flaming furious with you right now and it's going to take some time to burn down. If you don't want me takin' your head off, I suggest you keep your distance for a bit of a while. Leave me to myself, a'right?"

It wasn't until Firstday afternoon that Joh reported back. He'd found a Winterhold Palace courtyard, deserted this time of year, that would serve their purposes admirably. The courtyard was paved with flagstone, surrounded by stone walls, and adjacent to a large reception room behind a wall of glass windows. The parquet floor in that room would work better for Torchay's instruction and could be padded to prevent bruising.

Kallista wanted to move their quarters into Winterhold, closer to the practice area, but the Reinine wouldn't hear of it. It would take them too far from court and be inconvenient for the servants. The Reinine added in her note that once their Firstweek as a new ilian was over, they would be expected to attend the regular court dinners with everyone else residing in the palace.

So it was on Seconday morning that Kallista's ilian trooped through two palaces on their way to their private practice yard. Torchay intended to teach Aisse ways to protect herself, and Kallista needed to learn what she could do with the magic Stone carried. They couldn't afford to waste any time while waiting for the other marked iliasti Belandra was so sure would appear.

"Naitan." Torchay stopped them all in the entrance to the courtyard and turned to Kallista. "I accept your gloves."

The formality jarred her. It brought her back to earth, stopped her mind from fretting over what she could have done differently, how she could have prevented this fiasco their ilian had become. Torchay slept outside her door now, not inside it. But it wasn't important now.

This was important, what they were about to do here. She needed her mind on her magic, not her men.

"Thank you, Torchay." She drew off her short-cuffed brown uniform gloves and handed them to him, smiling as she did so. Of a wonder, she got a smile back. A rather bleak, wintry smile, but a smile nonetheless. It made her grin at him outright.

His smile twisted, became more true, though she could see his reluctance to give in to it. "Go on with you, then." He tipped his head toward the courtyard. "You've magic to get sorted. And I've a small tiger to sort, myself."

Aisse grinned at him, fairly dancing in place with her eagerness to begin. Torchay grinned back, pointing toward the door on the far side of the courtyard. "In there, Tiger Aila."

Kallista was glad they got along so well. The pang she felt was merely that she wished the same ease between herself and Torchay. But then, she'd had sex with him. Aisse had not.

"So?" Stone paced a circle around her at the limit of his magical leash. The chains on his anklets rattled with every step. "The gloves are off. What happens next?"

She held her hand out to him, palm up, as if inviting him to dance. "Shall we find out?"

Stone stopped motionless near the center of the courtyard, making no move to approach. Kallista circled toward him, almost stalking him. He wore red again. A brighter shade today, in a tunic of everyday wear that looked far better on him than the clumsy prisoner's clothing. Her ilias was a beautiful man with his golden hair and skin and his finely honed body. She could almost wish he were less so. He would be less of a temptation.

She came to a halt directly in front of him, holding her hand up at chest height, daring him with her eyes to take it. He swallowed visibly. They had not touched, not skin to skin, since the night they had come together. She truly had no idea what would happen now.

It frightened him. She could sense it. She would swear before the One that magic was the only thing in existence he did fear.

His hand rose, coming toward hers. It was one of the bravest things she'd ever seen. "Courage," she whispered when he hesitated.

"Kallista." His gaze locked onto hers. "Ilias."

She nodded. "Ilias, Stone." She knew what he asked and reassured him. She would not let him be lost inside the magic, would not let it have him, no matter the risk to herself. She was the naitan. He was in her care.

Kallista could sense Torchay and Aisse watching beyond the bank of windows. Torchay had wanted to remain in the courtyard, but she had insisted otherwise. She wanted to motion them farther from the glass but could not let her concentration waver. She shook her right hand to keep it loose and held the left up, waiting on Stone.

He took a deep breath, let it out and clasped her hand in his.

The magic woke. Instantly alert and eager, it rushed for the point where they joined to cross over into Kallista.

"No." She spoke aloud to reinforce her mental command for it to halt, to stay where it was.

It paid her no attention whatsoever, leaping from Stone into her. It bounced about, stirring things up that needed no stirring, running through both their bodies with exquisite skill. Stone's head went back and he shouted, not in pain.

"Stop."

But it didn't. Kallista did the only thing she knew how to do. She fisted her free hand and brought it in to her chest. Then she flung it wide again, letting her fingers fly open as she wrenched the magic out of her and forced it into lightning.

A huge jagged bolt flashed from her hand, blackening the flagstones all the way across the courtyard to the leaden gutter pipe. It crackled up the length of the pipe to the roof where it broke a gargoyle from its place, which crashed to the ground at their feet.

"Khralsh!" Stone pulled his arm from where he'd wrapped it over his head and looked at her, his eyes showing white all the way around. "Is that likely to happen again?"

Kallista shook her tingling fingers. The lightning had shocked her. That had never happened before. It had burned her a time or two, but never shocked. "I'm afraid it's more than just likely." She looked down at their still-linked hands. "You didn't let go."

"I was afraid to. I thought if I held on, the lightning might think I was part of you and leave me alone."

Kallista grinned at him. "Smart man."

"That's not what Fox says. I've the brains of a tent flap, according to—" His speech faltered and his face shut down, all the wry humor gone. He tried to pull his hand away but Kallista held on tight.

"Fox—your partner who died?" She wanted to comfort him but didn't know how. Didn't know why. She'd barely known him a week. But he was ilias. That was why enough.

He nodded once, refusing to look at her.

"I'm sorry, Stone. I truly am sorry for your loss." Especially since she was the one who'd caused it.

Stone remained silent another moment, then seemed to give himself a mental shake. "He was a warrior. We knew it would happen sooner or later to one of us." He looked at her and hefted their clasped hands. "What now?"

But the *way* he had died wasn't a warrior's death. "You shouldn't be afraid to talk about him. He was your friend and you loved him. Remembering honors his memory."

This time Stone managed to twist his hand free. "Don't tell me how to mourn my *brodir*," he snarled. "You keep me bound close with witchery and flaunt my status with pretty jewelry that's nothing more than dressed-up shackles. You crawl inside my mind and make me want you so I can think of nothing but the pleasure we have together. You own my food, my clothing— There is *nothing* I have, not even myself, that you do not possess, except *this*. It is mine and mine alone and I will not share it. Do you understand me? *I will not share.*"

He stood in the center of the courtyard, magnificent in his anger, his eyes wild, nostrils flaring, mouth set. Kallista saluted him with her fist over her heart and bowed. When she rose, she saw Torchay beyond Stone's shoulder, hesitating in the open doorway, and she sent him away with a look.

"My apologies," she said, "for intruding." She considered saying more, that she'd forgotten he was Tibran, forgotten his status, but decided he wouldn't appreciate it at this moment.

He nodded once, brusquely, accepting her apology.

"Do you wish to be finished for today?" She had learned virtually nothing so far this morning, but if Stone could not face more...

He shook his head. "No. I can take it, if you can." The sly grin on his face startled her. He could smile again already? "Just warn me before you set any more lightning off." Stone held his hand out to her, the challenge in his eyes this time.

Kallista had to smile. "Torchay does not forgive so easily."

"Torchay cares more. You were partners first." He grinned again, wickedness in it. "Besides, who says I have forgiven?"

She laughed outright at that. She was still smiling when she gathered her concentration and slid her hand into his.

The magic was there and awake, but calmer. More willing to listen and—perhaps—obey. When nothing untoward happened for a moment or two, Stone began to relax and the magic calmed more.

"Good," Kallista murmured. "That's good."

"What is?" His tension ratcheted up again, the magic with it.

"No, relax. Can you feel it?"

"I feel your hand in mine."

"That's all?" She lifted her free hand, wanting to take both his hands but afraid of what might result if the circle closed.

"I…don't know. It's not like the other times, when you ran the magic through me."

"That was the magic on its own, running through both of us." Kallista's mouth twisted. "I had no control over it. It was controlling me. Controlling us. That's why we're here now, to learn to do something a bit more useful with it, and I hope, how to make it behave."

Stone gave her another of his mischievous grins. "I wouldn't object if you let it run through me every now and again."

Kallista shook her head, smiling in spite of herself. "You are a wicked man." She flexed her free hand, trying to decide on a next step. "It does feel good, doesn't it?"

"My one compensation." But he still smiled as he said it.

"Let me try something. Tell me what you can sense." Kallista called a thread of magic from him.

It shot out so quickly she almost didn't catch it. She raised her right hand, willing the sparks to dance, but the magic felt skittish, hard to shape. She let it slide back into Stone, her fingers tingling again. She rubbed them against each other. "What did you feel?"

"Did you do something?"

"Very little." She pulled her left hand free of his. "I want to try something else."

Kallista strode a few paces from him, motioning him back when he would have moved with her. She stopped at the farthest point she could get from him, opened herself and called the lightning.

A tiny spark crackled blue from her fingertip. She set it dancing from one finger to the next, laughing out loud when it obeyed.

She called a spark to her other hand and bade them pirouette in unison. She brought her hands toward each other in front of her and the sparks leaped the gap, crackling as they joined forces, stretching bright and blue between her ten fingers.

She gathered the lightning into one hand, compressing it into a compact spark, then threw it to the other hand. Back and forth she tossed it, from hand to hand, letting it build in power until it was a blazing, spitting ball larger than her head. Finally she caught and held it, feeling her unbound hair stand out straight from her head with its force. Then bit by bit, she let it bleed safely away into the ground below her feet until all that remained was a single, tiny spark on the tip of her right forefinger. With a flip of her hand, she extinguished it and let the satisfaction fill her up.

The sound of hands clapping brought her attention back to Stone. "I stand in awe," he said, walking toward her, still applauding. "If you can do all that, why do you need me?"

"That's what we must discover." Kallista sought words to explain what she had just learned. "The magic you carry—I can't do with it what I just did. It—if I must, I can force it into lightning, but I could never—"

"Make it dance?"

"Yes, exactly." She reached for his hand, asking silent permission with her eyes before she touched. Stone gave it by taking her hand in his. "This magic of yours is shaped for something else."

He grinned and raised a salacious eyebrow.

Kallista felt the blush burn. "I doubt *that* is its only purpose," she scolded. Or tried to. Stone seemed impervious to scolding.

"What other things can you do with magic?"

She blew out a breath. "Once I would have said nothing, but now…"

Stone raised the other eyebrow, inquiring.

"Now, I am afraid of what I might do."

"That's probably a good thing." He tightened his grip on her hand, their palms beginning to sweat where they touched. "At least you'll proceed with care."

Could she call that dark scythe again? Dark veil, Belandra had called it. Kallista could see Torchay and Aisse dimly through the window, reflected in the mirrors on the far side of the room. Torchay had survived the magic the first time she'd called it, but had Aisse? Or had she simply been out of range?

Kallista was beginning to like the little Tibran, beyond the pity she'd originally felt. And she was ilias now. Kallista didn't want to risk hurting any of them. She would wait for another time, when she and Stone were alone, to risk calling the dark magic.

What else could she do? She could see things far off, things that hadn't yet happened. She could talk to Belandra a thousand years dead. Could she talk to other ghosts?

She pulled another small thread of magic from Stone. He gasped.

"I felt that. Like your hand inside me." He stroked the back of her hand down his cheek. "A touch no more than that. What did you do?"

"I drew out a bit of magic. I'm going to—" Did she want him to know she talked to ghosts? Would it disturb him more than the magic alone already did? "Try something," she ended.

"What?" His breath came a bit quicker and his grip tightened.

She had better tell him. Not knowing made him nervous. Knowing might make him more so, but he wouldn't like being kept in ignorance. She understood that much about the man. "To call a ghost," she said. "I can talk to one ghost. I thought I'd see whether I could call others."

"What earthly use could that be?"

"I don't know. I won't until I try. Be still."

Stone went absolutely motionless.

The magic seemed a bit easier to shape this time, though it

jumped about like quicksilver, leaking through her control before she could grasp it all. Finally she caught hold of what she could and sent it questing for ghosts.

For a long moment nothing happened. Or nothing she could see. Then a flickering of pale mist blocked the sun's light. Kallista shivered at a sudden chill. A man rushed through the solid stone wall, stark fear in his face. "My children," he said. "Have you seen my children? Four of them. They went climbing today, but they should be back—"

Kallista's entire body went cold. The Searching Father had been a story told for years, how he wandered Arikon in search of his missing children after he fell to his death trying to reach them where they were trapped on the cliffs below the city.

More mist floated through the courtyard, some thick enough for faces to appear, or arms, hands grasping. Screams shivered in the air, cries for mercy, for aid, for justice. Just how many ghosts had she raised?

"Here now!" A plump prelate bustled into the courtyard. "What do you think you're doing? I've only just got him settled and here you go stirring him up again!"

"I'm sorry—stirring who? Who are you?"

"Per Ostra, of course. Who did you think I meant? He's only been bashing everything in the palace for the last two hundred years."

Kallista frowned. "Who? I am sorry, Mother Per, but I—"

"*I'm* not Per, you idiot. I'm Domnia Varyl. I've been trying to lay the man for—"

"Grandmother." Kallista bowed low, trying to hide her shock. Domnia Varyl was the many-times-great-grandmother who'd founded the Varyl line some twelve generations back.

"Grand—" The ghost stopped in her tirade to peer at Kallista. "I don't know you."

"No, Grandmother. I am Kallista Varyl, daughter of Irysta

Varyl who is the daughter of Sinda Varyl, the daughter of—" She recited her grandmothers as she had learned them in childhood, the blood of her line, ending with "—Domnia Varyl who ruled the Mother Temple in Arikon."

"Oh my." The ghost fluttered her hands. "Has it been so long? My child—" She beamed at Kallista in a way that might have been maternal.

"My ilias, Stone." She presented him and he bowed, without taking his eyes off Domnia.

"Ah, newlyweds. How nice. Congratulations."

Kallista thought to ask how she knew, but a violent crash sounded as all the windows surrounding the courtyard exploded into a glitter of shards. Kallista snatched magic from Stone and threw it outward in a frantic attempt to catch the glass before it impaled either of them. The magic eluded perfect control, flaring and sliding in all directions, but it stopped the biggest shards, grinding them into a sharp dust that rained down on them.

"Are you all right?" Kallista shouted, dragging Stone with her as she ran toward the now-windowless room where Torchay and Aisse had been working.

"Are you?" Torchay caught her in a hug, then shoved her back to arm's length to inspect her for damage. He brushed at the glass dust coating her face and scraped off a layer of skin.

"Careful, it's glass." She pulled out of reach, spitting out more glass.

"What happened?" Torchay pulled Aisse from behind him into the circle. "You've never done that with windows before."

"That was Per Ostra," Domnia the ghost announced. "You raised him, now you have to lay him again."

CHAPTER SEVENTEEN

"How do I do that?" Kallista demanded.

Torchay took a step backward. "Belandra? But Hopeday hasn't passed again."

"Not Belandra. My twelve-times-great-grandmother." Kallista introduced her iliasti to her grandmother's ghost, even if they couldn't see her.

"If you don't know how to lay him, what are you doing raising him?" Domnia demanded. "Don't you know better than to be mucking about with magic you don't understand?"

"I'm trying to learn," Kallista retorted.

"Without a teacher? You're more a fool than I thought."

"Who is there to teach me? There's not been a godstruck naitan in a thousand years. She can only answer six questions at a time. I scarcely learn anything and she's gone."

"The godmarked are a myth." Domnia's mouth turned down in semitransparent scorn.

Stone gave a short bark of laughter. "Is this a myth?" He lifted his flyaway hair and bowed his neck. "Is the magic I carry inside me a myth?"

When he straightened, Torchay leaned close and muttered, "You can see her?"

"You can't?" Stone's glance showed his increasing unease.

Kallista squeezed his hand, hoping he would find it reassuring. "Just tell me how to lay this ghost, the one who broke the windows. I'll deal with the rest of them later."

"The trick isn't so much laying him as it is finding him," Domnia said. "He's wicked fast and he's angry. Give me a weeping ghost anytime over one who feels his grief as anger. Per Ostra's lover was killed in battle during the pacification of the northern coast. He was brought to Arikon to be married *di pentivas* because he was a handsome man. The night of the wedding, he killed his ilias and himself, and he's been taking out his anger on Arikon's palace ever since."

"Until you laid him to rest," Kallista said.

"Well, yes, I suppose." Domnia's satisfaction was short-lived. "Until you woke him again." She folded her arms across her ample chest. "I suppose I'll have to wait here for months while you find him."

Stone shivered as Kallista scooped a bit of magic from him. "Did you feel it when I blocked the glass?" she asked.

"Yes. What are you doing now?"

"Hunting a ghost." She tacked a name onto the summons, fighting to keep hold of the slippery magic, and sent it out, willing it to return with the missing Per Ostra. It spun out into the distance, connected to her by a thin filament she struggled to maintain. Distantly, she felt it strike, sweeping the raging ghost back toward her.

"All right," she said, her attention focused on the poorly controlled magic. "I've found him. He's on his way back here."

"How——" Domnia shook her head. "Never mind that. You've done it. To lay him, you must soothe his anger. He must want to sleep. Remind him that his lover waits. They will be reunited in the arms of the One. A little *push* in that direction won't hurt."

The ghost of Per Ostra was little more than pulsing, formless rage when she reeled it in. Kallista pulled more magic from Stone to control it, but thought she might be having more trouble controlling the magic than the ghost. They both had their own ideas about what they wished to do.

Eventually the ghost took on shape as the anger faded, becoming more like the man it once was, and Kallista was able to use persuasion. By the time he dissolved completely away, she was bathed in sweat, her muscles quivering with exhaustion, and she sagged against a hard male body. Torchay's, she discovered when she looked. Stone didn't appear in too much better shape than she was.

"We are finished for today," Torchay said firmly, encircling her waist with an arm. He took Stone's arm to provide support and after a second's hesitation, Aisse let Stone drape his other arm across her shoulders. They made a disreputable-looking crew as they trudged back through two palaces to their suite.

Lieutenant Suteny came out of his office chamber as they approached, and Kallista dragged the others to a halt.

"Lieutenant." She summoned enough energy to return his salute. "You might see that someone is sent to sweep up glass from our practice yard. But don't bother having the windows replaced just yet. In case."

He inclined his head and saluted again, suspiciously blank-faced. "Naitan."

She was too tired to worry about the lieutenant now. Kallista let Torchay propel her on into the suite.

"Baths." Aisse turned back at the door. "Send servant for baths."

Over the next several weeks, Kallista struggled to master Stone's magic. It defied her control, slipping through the tiniest cracks to go racketing around inside her until she thought she would either scream, or take Stone up against the courtyard wall like some bitch in heat. The paving wasn't safe. Shattered glass still lay all over the flagstones.

Joh assured her that he had given the message to have it cleared, but it had obviously got lost somewhere in channels. Just as well. The glass gave Kallista something to practice her magic on.

Torchay would leave Aisse with her exercises and come through the window to toss glass at Kallista for her to deflect. Sometimes she could stop and hold it in midair for brief moments. Sometimes she could only bat it away. Sometimes the best she could do was shatter it into mostly harmless bits. But she'd never been able to do any sort of defensive magic before.

She was better at defending Stone than herself—she wasn't sure why. Perhaps because he held the magic. Or perhaps simply because he was her ilias and that was what one did. Kallista had small cuts all over her right hand and arm from the bits that got through. Stone got one on his shoulder the first day, and none thereafter.

Ghosts kept appearing and following Kallista through the palace complex, asking her questions she didn't know the answers to. Mostly she ignored them, since no one else seemed able to see or hear them. A few she managed to soothe and lay to rest. Her however-many-times-great-grandmother wasn't one of them.

Domnia always appeared at the least convenient moments. Save for that, Kallista didn't mind her presence so much. Domnia knew a great deal about ghosts and visions and didn't mind imparting her knowledge to her descendant. The fact that Domnia had been a West naitan had been suppressed by some family archivist in the last several generations. No one wanted to admit having West magic in the bloodline.

Domnia was herself horrified to hear that the West magic academy had been shuttered for almost fifty years because no child had been born with West magic in much longer than that. She spent a great deal of time pacing the palace halls muttering about imbalance and sacrilege.

Belandra came when summoned. Most of the time. Kallista didn't yet understand what rule attached to summoning, beyond the passing of Hopeday, though there had to be one. Nor did she flatter herself that she'd gotten any better at asking her questions, though she learned more with every encounter. It was still not nearly enough.

Kallista was careful not to be seen talking to, or even noticing, the ghosts, but whispers about West magic began to float through the palace nonetheless. Whispers linked to Kallista and her ilian. The rumors were so pervasive that when they returned to the court dinners as ordered by the Reinine, they were avoided and isolated.

It didn't bother Kallista particularly, nor did she think it bothered any of the others. They weren't in Arikon for political advancement or for playing social games. They had a task lying before them—once she understood what it might be.

She did worry when it seemed that the rumors began to interfere with that task. The failure to clean the glass from the practice yard was only the beginning.

Kallista's and Torchay's army pay packets, thin as they were, went astray. Servants answered summonses only after extended delay and sometimes not at all. And when they did answer, they responded to orders with either sullen disrespect or eye-rolling skittishness. These were small, annoying things, but they did not bode well for the future. And they had Torchay turning himself inside out trying to watch for danger.

He nearly exploded the morning halfway through Katenda, the first summer month, when Kallista announced that she and Stone would go to the practice yard alone. She had researched the dark veil magic as much as she could, given the archives' scarcity of West magic records. It was time for her to try it. But she didn't want Torchay, Aisse or anyone else anywhere in the vicinity of her experiment.

"No." Torchay stood in front of the suite's double doors, arms folded across his chest. "Absolutely not. I forbid it."

"This is magic, Torchay. Not your authority. It's too risky for you to be there." Kallista glared back at him, her stubborn stance echoing his.

"I survived the last time."

"I'm not taking that chance. Stone will be with me. You've honed his skills yourself. He's almost as good as you are."

"He's still a Tibran." Torchay's glare shifted past Kallista's shoulder to Stone, standing just behind her. "Who knows if he'll bother to defend you?"

"Who knows if I'd survive her death?" Stone said cheerfully. Sometimes Kallista did not understand the man. "I certainly don't. Better to keep her alive."

Torchay growled and Kallista had to hide a smile. "See? He's not going to let me get killed and he's obviously not going to kill me himself. If he wanted to, he could have done it the night after our wedding. He didn't do it then and he won't do it now."

"Especially since she can bring me to my knees just by touching me." Stone shivered elaborately. "Please, ilias?"

Kallista thumped his arm, bare in the sleeveless summer tunic. "Stop goading him."

"Do that again. With your gloves off."

She smacked him lightly on the back of his head and he laughed.

Stone could make them all laugh. Even Torchay when he wasn't being stubborn and Stone wasn't being deliberately provoking.

"Come along as far as the end of Summerglen." Kallista gave in as planned, offering the compromise she hoped Torchay would accept. "But not into Winterhold. Stone and I go on alone."

"You can have the mark if you like, Torchay," Stone offered, "and I'll stay behind."

Torchay made a disgusted noise in the back of his throat and stepped from in front of the door. "Are you coming, Aisse?"

The bond between Aisse and Torchay had grown even closer during the past weeks of instruction. Kallista comforted herself with the thought that he treated her like a younger sibling, a sedil related by ilian rather than blood, then scolded herself for feeling comfort. They were all in this ilian. And she'd mucked things up with Torchay all on her own.

"No. I practice here." Aisse had on the baggy muslin she wore for working out.

"Don't go out alone," Torchay warned as they left.

He spent the whole of the walk through Summerglen Palace trying to change Kallista's mind, but she remained adamant. She would not allow him anywhere near while she attempted this dark and deadly magic.

At the narrow service corridor where one palace melted into the next, Kallista sent Torchay to the suite. He could return in an hour to escort them back. She didn't know if he would go, but at least he stopped there. Without too much argument.

In the practice yard, Stone surprised her. He turned and gave her the small, formal bow of the military, then held out his hand. "Naitan," he said. "I accept your gloves."

Did he understand what the little ritual did for her? How it helped to center her and focus her attention on the test ahead? Kallista returned his solemn gaze as she pulled her gloves from her hands and placed them in his. Perhaps he did. He tucked the gloves in his belt, just as Torchay always did, and extended his hand. She clasped it in hers.

The magic inside him quivered with eagerness, but it didn't go rushing uncontrollably about. They'd learned that if they made this connection at least once every day and Kallista used the magic for something—anything—she was better able to control it the next time they touched. She didn't know whether it was a matter of keeping the magic "in training" or whether it simply had to be bled off daily to avoid an uncontrollable buildup. Why didn't matter.

Stone complained on occasion because the mind-shaking surges of pleasure came less often, but Kallista thought the attitude was mostly for show. Her control wasn't yet *that* good.

"I'm going to pull as much magic as I can," Kallista warned him.

Stone took a deep breath and nodded.

Praying for control, she drew the magic from him as fast as she could until there was nothing left to draw. Magic swam behind her eyes, roared in her ears, stoppered her nose, and yet it still wasn't as much as she'd held on that first day. Perhaps it wouldn't escape the courtyard.

She focused on the veil itself rather than what she wanted it to do. The crumbling records had seemed to hint that the naitan's intention had an effect on the deadliness of the veiling mist, that it didn't always kill.

The magic seemed to understand what was wanted, but that didn't help in controlling it. The power built, shaping itself. Before she could finish, the magic burst from her grasp in a lopsided glitter of pale blue that dissolved the remnants of broken glass halfway across one side of the courtyard.

"Was that what you were trying to do?" Stone eyed the shiny new surface on the exposed flagstone.

"I don't think so."

"Useful, though. You might want to remember that one."

"At least it did something." Kallista heaved a sigh. "I've never had so much trouble controlling magic as I do with the stuff you carry. It got away from me before I was ready."

"Try again."

She wasn't sure the spell would work any better a second time. To put it off, she brought up something that worried her, something she should probably have spoken of long before now. "Does it bother you, working this magic that—that defeated your army?" *That killed your partner.* She didn't dare say it aloud.

"I'm here, aren't I? Try it again." Stone wiggled the hand he held.

"But I'm the one who kill—"

"Not alone." He cut her off. "You didn't do it alone. Do you think I don't know that? That you couldn't have done what you did without this thrice-damned magic I carry? I know. I know you need to discover how to do it again. And I know I can't go back."

Stone's hand tightened on hers almost to pain. "I am dead to Tibre. I can't even speak the language anymore. My old life is ended, as dead as Fox. *This* is my life now." He lifted their clasped hands and shook them at her. "*This.* I can't be looking back all the time. I don't want to. The past is past. Let it stay there."

Kallista absorbed his impassioned speech with a blink. She rather wished Torchay could have heard it, but then he didn't like trusting her safety to anyone but himself. And she rather doubted Stone was quite as reconciled to his fate as he claimed. "So you're ready to try again?"

"Ages ago."

She pulled magic again, more than she expected but less than before. It escaped again before she could complete the forming, this time a bit more evenly shaped, but red and foul-smelling.

"Khralsh!" Stone pinched his nose shut. "I suppose you could stink the enemy to death…"

"Oh, be quiet. Let's go again." Kallista reached for his magic and again it poured out, a seemingly inexhaustible supply.

But the naitan calling it was all too exhaustible. The struggle to control and shape the magic into such a powerful spell eroded her energy far quicker than she expected. The hour was not yet up when Stone pulled his hand from her grasp and handed back her gloves.

"Torchay will have my thumbs if I let you continue," he said. "Besides, I'd rather not carry you back to our rooms. One more time, and I would have to."

Kallista gave him a crooked smile as she tugged the leather over her hands. "It *is* a long way back."

"And you're no lightweight."

They had crossed out of Winterhold and were walking along the endless corridors toward the tower that held their suite, when their way was blocked by a cluster of courtiers idling in the narrow gallery. Their short-cropped hair and extreme clothing style, as well as the short sword carried at each one's waist, male or female, marked them as part of the reckless, fashionable set. Six of them, laughing and roughhousing together, they took up the whole of the walkway.

"Excuse me, aili. Could we pass?" Kallista bowed politely, all too conscious of her sweaty, disheveled condition.

"Excuse you?" The Shaluine prinsipella who had dragged Stone into a seizure on their wedding night turned to face her, only now showing her face. "I don't believe I will. There is no excuse for you."

Kallista sighed. She was much too tired for this. "I wear no sword, aila. I have no quarrel with you."

"Perhaps I have one with you." Viyelle Prinsipella advanced, hand on the hilt of her sword. The other bravos spread out around her, their bright capes swirling about their hips.

Stone moved up close behind Kallista. "There are six of them," he murmured.

She didn't reply. This could still, possibly, end without a fight.

"And what quarrel might that be, principella?" Kallista made her voice calm and soothing while loosening the glove on her left hand. "If I have given offense, tell me how, so that I can make amends."

"Your existence offends me. Your ilias offends me——"

"Because he is Tibran, or because I married him?" Kallista's interruption didn't help matters, but at this point, she didn't believe anything would. The principella seemed determined to fight. "I am afraid, aila, that I cannot alter the fact of my existence."

"You could die." Viyelle still had not drawn her sword, but it was only a matter of time. And perhaps of form? Kallista did not know the court rules.

She held her hands up and out, keeping the loosened glove on her hand with widespread fingers. "I am not familiar with courtiers' games. We are soldiers, I and my ilias. Warriors." She let her voice go hard. "We don't play games with rules. We kill. Stone has killed dozens."

"Hundreds," he said, his voice light and pleasant, almost eager. "At least. And Kallista has killed ten times that. Thousands."

Some of the bravos backing the principella began to look uneasy, but her expression did not change. "You can't call magic here."

"No?" Kallista shook her glove to the floor and raised her bare hand.

One of the courtiers flinched. "Viyelle, maybe——"

"No. She would not dare kill a principella of Shaluine."

Kallista's fraying temper snapped. "And yet you would dare attack the godmarked? Warriors called and marked by the One for Her purpose? You would set yourself up against the God's will?"

Viyelle laughed. "You think old stories for children will protect you?" Her short sword snicked from its sheath. She held it carelessly, overconfident in Kallista's apparent lack of weapons.

A sound behind her had Kallista glancing over her shoulder to see Stone with a naked blade in his hand and a fierce grin on his face.

"There *are* six." She drew her oversized knife from its sheath along her spine.

"Good." His grin filled with a warlike glee. "I wouldn't want to outnumber them too badly."

Viyelle motioned for her cohorts to surround them. Kallista allowed it, Stone folding back to set his back against hers as the courtiers edged down the windowed wall past them.

"Try not to kill them if you possibly can." Kallista kept her eyes on the leader as she called a spark to her naked hand.

"Ah." Stone's grin sounded in his voice. "A challenge. I like challenges."

The prinsipella was too arrogant to see the danger she was in. Had she been allowed to win at everything because of her rank? Kallista respected rank. But not enough to let her ilias—or herself—be killed.

With a scream calculated to alarm, Viyelle attacked. Kallista sidestepped, Stone moving with her in perfect unison. "You've fought this way before," she said, letting the spark fly to sting the courtier beyond Viyelle.

"Torchay taught me Adaran methods."

Kallista parried a thrust with her shorter blade and shocked the prinsipella with another small spark. Someone came at her from the side. Kallista ducked and Stone sent him reeling back with blood pouring from a slice along his arm.

"Is that all you can do with your magic?" Viyelle jeered. "Shocks no worse than a wool carpet in winter? Oh dear. I'm shivering with fear of the deadly naitan."

"I'm trying *not* to kill you." Kallista kept her voice pleasant, but her teeth were showing. Not in a smile.

At some invisible signal, all six courtiers attacked at once. Kallista found herself hard-pressed to keep from killing them without allowing herself to be killed or badly injured. Stone was a blur of motion behind her as he protected her back. Kallista reached and found magic, despite the lack of skin-to-skin touch. She whispered to it as she drew it carefully out, trying to keep from distracting Stone.

"Protect yourself!" Stone cried, just in time for Kallista to raise magic and blade. Two short swords slid aside. "Don't get lost in the magic, woman. Stay with me. I need you here."

She had to let the magic go, unable to both control it and stay in the fight. It slid back into Stone as she shoved Viyelle into a companion, tangling them together enough to move a few paces ahead. She was tired. Too tired to be careful. Someone was going to get killed, and it wouldn't be her or Stone.

Kallista called a bigger spark, knowing she couldn't gauge how much would stop hearts. This had to end.

A familiar bellow of rage echoed down the gallery. Kallista glanced up to see Torchay, sword in hand, charging toward them. She'd never seen anything more welcome.

First one, then two, then all the courtiers broke and ran, even the prinsipella. Torchay and Stone chased after them, but Kallista hadn't the energy to join them, so the men broke off and returned to her side.

"I knew it." Torchay dredged up some choice oaths from his early days in the army. "I knew I shouldn't have let you come alone."

"I wasn't alone." Kallista picked her glove up off the floor and put it back on. "Stone was with me." She brushed his golden flyaway hair from his face and kissed his cheek.

Stone grinned, turned his head and pointed to the other cheek. With a chuckle, she kissed that one too.

"And you arrived right on time." Kallista looped her arm through Torchay's and stretched up to kiss his cheek.

"I might not have," he grumbled, starting back to their suite. "You could have been hurt."

"But we weren't, and we didn't have to kill any of them." She beckoned Stone closer to loop her other arm through his. "There was something very odd about this little encounter."

"Other than the fact you pulled magic from me without touching?" Stone said.

"That could be helpful." Torchay perked up. "Give us another blade while she does her spells."

"Besides that." Kallista tugged at their arms, bringing their attention her way. "There was something odd about the prinsipella. I noticed when I pulled the magic, but I couldn't quite see it before I had to let it go."

"You can look tonight," Torchay said. "At dinner."

Kallista made a face. She hated the court dinners, dressing up and parading around to entertain the idiots. Something occurred to her. "D'you suppose we'll get in trouble for brawling in the palace? Maybe the Reinine will banish us from dinner. Maybe for the rest of the time we're here."

Torchay laughed. "No harm in hope, but more likely she'll require *more* attendance at court events, in hope their manners might rub off on you."

"I have manners. Very good manners. Better than theirs." She tipped her head back toward the gallery where they'd fought. She knew she sounded like a petulant child but didn't much care. She hated those dinners.

"True. But you're not a prinsipella, so you have to behave better."

Kallista sighed. She did not look forward to tonight.

The sun was setting as the caravan approached Arikon. The trader resisted the urge to push faster. Caution was required. He did not know the territory, had never considered that his destiny might lie across the Mother Range, in the Northern Outlands. Other traders ventured past the mountainous barricade to journey through these strange lands. He had never been one of their number, had never heard any of their tales. Only this year had he left the cloistered existence of his former life to take up his new life as a trader, gathering up all he had won. And now he was here, unable to resist the call of his God.

He'd pushed them all relentlessly to reach this place in so little time, not stopping to trade—or even rest—in any of the tiny villages they had passed. The beasts were exhausted. The pull was strong, so strong that surely he would soon hold his dream in his hands, possibly this very night. After waiting so many years, he could wait a few more hours. With effort.

He looked back at the caravan stretched out behind him, heard the jingle of harness and bells, the creak of leather. He had fifty mules piled high with fine goods from all the corners of the world; twenty horses from his homeland, the best in existence; all the wealth he could collect and carry at the speed he had needed to travel. Surely with all he had to offer, his bride would not reject him. Impatience gripped him. Again, he fought back the urge to hurry, but it was difficult. He was anxious to meet the one to whom his life had been tied.

Kallista leaned against a pillar in the great hall of Summerglen Palace, surrounded by her ilian and a small circle of space. Lieutenant Suteny moved in and out of the space, caught between duty and discomfort at being too close. She and Torchay wore their dress uniforms yet again, complete with the gold chain belts and the honors and service medallions dangling from them. They clinked more than Stone with his *di pentivas* chains.

Kallista didn't much like wearing the belt. It was heavy. But it seemed to impress the locals, and the Reinine had asked where it was after the first dinner. Too bad the emblems weren't real gold or they could have pawned them when their pay packets had gone missing.

"When do you think they'll bring out the food?" Stone asked. "I'm hollow." He was in warrior's red again, his wedding tunic.

He and Aisse both needed more changes of clothing if they were to keep up this palace existence, but Kallista didn't know how it could be managed without money. She didn't want to go begging to the Reinine—but she'd be forced to if their pay didn't catch up with them soon.

"They've brought out the tables to set up," Torchay commented.

"There. The prinsipella who danced with Stone." Aisse pointed into the mingling company at Viyelle of Shaluine.

"Good eyes, ilias." Kallista touched the small woman's arm in acknowledgment. "Stone, I'm going to draw, just a little."

He nodded, moving closer to touch his bare elbow to hers. Kallista would have liked to try drawing magic again without touching him, but many courtiers and even more of the bureaucrats were naitani and might sense the magic. She was mostly sure she could do it this way without acquiring unwanted attention.

Kallista called the smallest possible tendril of magic from Stone, his faint quiver telling her he felt it. Her gloved hands made it almost impossible to control the skittish magic, so she tucked one hand into Stone's elbow and pulled it free of the glove. She left the glove in place on his arm, hiding her bared hand between their bodies. Carefully she cast the magic toward Viyelle Prinsipella, willing it to "see" her.

A faint, red, pulsing vapor appeared around the prinsipella's head. Kallista frowned, but as she wondered what the stuff was, the magic told her. "She's been bespelled," she murmured.

"The prinsipella?" Torchay sounded shocked.

"I told you something seemed odd. I didn't see her as so quarrelsome at that first meeting. Reckless, yes. Dramatic and foolish. But harmless. This anger has been forced on her."

"Can you do anything?" Stone asked.

"Shouldn't you tell someone?" Aisse looked toward the Reinine's throne.

Kallista looked too. A herald was handing the Reinine a small scroll. As she took it, she looked out over the crowd, directly at Kallista and held her gaze a moment, before turning to speak to the herald again, assenting to something.

"Later," Kallista said. "She's busy now. I think I ought to...do something. Before the prinsipella causes more trouble."

"What, exactly do you plan to do?" Torchay said.

"I'm going to see if I can undo the spell. Pulling more, Stone."

"Have you tried anything like this before?" Torchay pushed off the pillar where he'd been leaning and stood straight.

"No, but I think I can do it." Ignoring his protests, Kallista drew another tiny thread from Stone and sent it after the first. It attacked the red vapor like a terrier on a rat, ripping it into shreds that faded into nothing.

The prinsipella looked a bit bewildered as the scowl left her face. Then one of her companions spoke and she joined in the laughter. Kallista let Stone's magic dissipate with the vanished spell.

"Done." Kallista drew one more tendril of magic, using it to see whether anyone else in the chamber had been bespelled. "Do you think anyone's noticed?"

Torchay scanned the room. "I noticed."

"You always do. I meant anyone else."

"What are you doing now?" He scowled at her, resting a hand on the hilt of the blade he wore at his hip. The blades at his wrists were worn just as openly but didn't look as threatening as his stance.

"Looking for more trouble. Other spells."

"If you're not careful, you'll make trouble."

"No one is watching us more than before," Aisse said. "No

trouble." She spoke almost exclusively in Adaran now. Kallista still couldn't tell which language she spoke herself, but the men asked for translation less often, so she thought she spoke Adaran to Aisse as much as Tibran.

Kallista found a bit of loose magic floating around hunting someone to latch on to and appropriated it into her own spell. As it was a love charm rather than more of the anger magic, she didn't bother seeking its source. She was about to continue when a commotion among the gathered courtiers distracted her.

The disturbance seemed to be moving from the grand entry doors directly toward Kallista's ilian. Quickly she pushed her hand back into the glove propped on Stone's arm. Torchay stepped forward to block whoever approached and Stone instantly moved up beside him, stretching the magical link, but not breaking it. Aisse took his other side, forming a wall of her iliasti between Kallista and whatever approached.

Annoyed, Kallista stepped behind Aisse. She could at least see over the smaller woman. Courtiers parted, revealing a man.

Taller than Torchay, he had hair black as the West briar, skin browned by a hotter sun than Adara's and eyes as dark and sweet as a night's pleasures. His hair curled slightly as it brushed broad shoulders, framing a face that haunted Kallista's dreams. She had kissed that mouth with its short upper lip and full, sensuous lower one. She had smoothed her thumbs over the tattoos marking those high, sharp cheekbones. She had gazed deep into the dark seduction of those eyes.

Who in heaven was he?

CHAPTER EIGHTEEN

His loose white clothing flowed around him as he walked to Torchay, where he halted and bowed. "I asked permission of your queen to meet the Chosen One. I failed to consider that I might have to present myself to others who are as I am."

"Who are you and what do you want with us?" Torchay's expression didn't change.

"I am Obed im-Shakiri." He bowed again from the waist, a straightforward motion devoid of the hand flourishes of the courtiers. "I have traveled from the South, far beyond the Mother Range. I am a vessel of the One. I come to join with you. To serve."

A vessel? Kallista stepped forward, wanting desperately to remove her glove again. Could this be one of the others Belandra had mentioned? She let her arm rest against Stone's, strengthening the link between them as she let go of the magic she'd called. She pushed at Torchay so she could draw as near to the stranger as he would allow. "Are you marked, Obed im-Shakiri? Marked by the One?"

"I—marked?" He looked puzzled.

Torchay folded his arms. "Why don't you come back later, in the morning perhaps, when we have time for a chat."

"Wait, please. I brought gifts." Obed rummaged in his robes, but apparently couldn't find what he sought. He gestured toward the doors. "I have a caravan, at the inn. Fifty mules, laden down. Horses. Garments. Blades of the finest steel."

"You think to buy her favor?" Torchay took a step forward, crowding the stranger.

"No. My apologies." He bowed again. "Do not send me away. I beg you. I cannot—it—please."

Everything in the hall had stopped, even the setting up of tables for the meal, while every person present watched the drama. All this attention could not be good. Kallista touched Torchay's arm, stretched up to murmur in his ear. "We should move this elsewhere."

He nodded, gestured toward the door. "If you would—" But he got no farther.

"I've been traveling for a year," Obed cried. "Coming to this place. To you. To *her*. I cannot—" He reached toward Kallista.

Stone intercepted him, grasping Obed's bare wrist in his naked hand. The magic roared.

It raced screaming through Stone to crash over Kallista like storm waves over rock. The scream poured from three throats. She sensed something inside Obed wrench to one side and he shouted again, this time in pain. Then he was there with them, sliding through Stone, through Kallista, as she went sliding through each of them. The faint echo of pain vanished in rushing pleasure and Kallista reached for Obed.

Her glove was in the way. She couldn't take it off, not here, but she needed his touch. "Take my arm," she gasped. "Past the glove. Now."

Torchay stepped out of the way, eyes on the gaping courtiers rather than his iliasti and this new man. Kallista was aware of that much before the magic stole her senses. Obed caught her arm and the touch of his bare skin to hers nearly sent them all to their knees as the magic erupted into more pyrotechnics. The human body wasn't made to hold so much pleasure, not without coming apart.

She screamed and the magic seemed to take that as its signal. It quieted, flowing swiftly back into the bodies of the two men.

"Get me out of here," Kallista gasped when she could form words. "All of us. Out. Home."

Torchay commandeered Lieutenant Suteny to help support the weak-kneed Stone. Joh didn't seem so averse to touching the Tibran. Torchay got a shoulder under Obed's, leaving Aisse to hold up Kallista. They stumbled from the hall, the entire Adaran court gaping after them. Suteny's soldiers fell in behind them outside the heavy carved doors.

"Trouble." Kallista tried not to lean too hard on Aisse, afraid they'd both go down if she did. "Not my fault."

"No, not your fault." Torchay hauled the stranger down the corridor at a quicker pace.

Thank goodness Daybright Tower and their suite wasn't far from the great hall's entrance. "Not his fault either," Kallista said. "He had no way of knowing what would happen." They reached the stairs and started up.

"Do not send me away." Obed still gasped for breath. "Do not, I beg—"

"We're not sending you anywhere, you stupid git." Stone shook himself free of the lieutenant and opened the door to their suite.

"Thank you, Lieutenant." Kallista smiled at the man but didn't offer her hand. He'd become one of those unwilling to take it. "We'll be fine from here."

"Captain." He stepped back and saluted as the ilian disappeared into their rooms with the stranger.

Kallista crossed the bare stretch of the parlor where they'd removed the furniture to have room to practice Torchay's Fan Dai instruction. Aisse turned back to the door for a moment, joining the others in the seating area a moment later.

"I asked Lieutenant to send for food," she said as they watched her sit in the corner of the sofa she favored. "No one has eaten yet. You say I am in charge of supplies, so I get food."

"Good." Kallista smiled at her. "I'm glad someone's making sure we get fed."

Stone swept low in a credible imitation of a courtier's bow, despite the wobble at the end. "I thank you, dear ilias, and my stomach thanks you."

Aisse scowled, tucking her feet beneath her on the sofa. "I still don't do sex with you."

Stone laughed and threw himself down on the opposite end of her sofa. "After what just happened, who cares? Stop obsessing about sex, dearest Aisse. You're the only one who is."

Obed watched the exchange with an air of bewilderment, still leaning on Torchay. "I do not under—you are not sending me away?"

"Just try and leave." Stone propped a foot on the delicate serving table in front of him. "I doubt you'd get twenty paces."

"Stop it, Stone." Kallista pulled her eyes from the sight of the two men, dark and bright, and moved to the center of the furnished parlor area. "He's confused enough. Please, Obed, sit." She indicated the chair between the sofas at one end of the seating area. Its position made it look a bit like an inquisitorial chair from a judgment hall, but she couldn't help that.

He did as she asked, his eyes trained on her, like a dog awaiting instruction from its owner. As if he wanted only a command to obey. The notion disturbed her.

Kallista moved behind him, elbowing Torchay out of her way as she pulled off her gloves. "I'm going to touch you. The magic should be quiet now, but I don't know for certain."

Obed's hands tightened on the arms of the chair, but he gave no other reaction. Kallista laid her hand on the black silk of his hair to tip his head forward, struggling to ignore its sleek warmth. She brushed his hair aside, exposing the nape of his neck, and there was the mark.

"Well?" Stone propped his other foot on the table.

"It's there."

"Did you have any doubt? After what happened?"

"No." She sighed. "Come show him yours."

He cocked an eyebrow at her. "Show him my *what?*"

"Your mark. What did you think I meant?"

He winked as he levered himself off the sofa and sauntered toward her. "I don't know, do I, ilias? That's why I asked. Why don't you just show him yours?"

"Because mine is different. Yours and his are alike."

Stone stopped and looked from Obed to Kallista, then down at himself. "I should think that would be obvious."

Her face burned hot as she finally caught on to his innuendo. She should never try talking to the man when she was this tired. "Just get over here and show him your neck before I throw something at you. Like a lightning bolt."

He made a great show of mock fear, dropping to his knees and bowing. When had he learned he could tease like this without reprisal?

Aisse giggled. Torchay's cough covered a laugh. Kallista couldn't help smiling, though she truly wanted to smack him with something. Stone slid toward Obed. Once there, he bowed his neck and pulled his hair aside, showing the rose-shaped mark to the dark man.

"You see?" Kallista leaned over Obed's shoulder to trace her finger over Stone's red-stained skin. "You bear the same mark, just like this one."

"You bear one as well?"

With a sigh, Kallista went to one knee beside his chair and pulled her hair aside. The touch of Obed's finger as he traced the compass points of her mark called up shivers from deep inside her. Had she dreamed him because of his mark? Torchay wasn't marked and he inhabited her dreams as much as Stone or this man. But he was also her ilias.

"Have you seen enough?" Kallista asked.

"I—yes." Obed folded his hands in his lap.

She moved to the sofa opposite Aisse, then scooted down as Torchay squeezed himself between her and the new man. Stone sat on the floor where he was, arms loosely wrapped around upthrust knees. Kallista didn't quite know where to begin.

Awed by what he had seen and felt, Obed stared at the backs of his hands, tattooed with ideograms similar to those on his face, then held them up to display the marks. "I marked myself to show my devotion to the One God. Never did I dream that She would mark me with Her own hand."

"You have other tattoos," the Chosen One said. "Nine of them in all, the number of perfection completed."

"Yes." He stared at her, eyes wide with wonder. Truly she had been touched by the One. "How do you know this?"

"I dreamed them."

The red-haired man gave her a sharp look. "You never told me about any dream like that." He was possessive as well as protective, the leader of the group after the Chosen. Was he her mate?

She turned a delicate shade of pink and Obed's heart shuddered. She was not beautiful, exactly. She had a strong face—thin, angular, with high cheekbones and a wide mouth, pale-skinned beneath hair almost as dark as his own. She was magnificent. "The dreams were all mixed up. I didn't think they were real."

"Were they?" The man looked at Obed again, a challenge in his eyes. "Where are they then, these other tattoos?"

"Two on his face, two more on his hands." She told them off. "Two on his feet."

Obed shivered deep inside where she had touched him, moving quickly to unlatch his shoes and kick them off. He displayed the dark blue marking above the arch on each foot.

"Two on his chest, high." The Chosen touched her own chest a short distance below either shoulder, where his tattoos lay. "Here."

Obed stood and removed his outer robe, then untied the neck of his long, loose tunic. He had never exposed his body, other than hands, face and feet, outside the most private intimate moments. But whatever the Chosen required of him, he would give, up to and including his life. Removing his clothing to display the devotion written on his body was nothing.

"And the ninth circles his navel," she said as he pulled the tunic up and over his head to show the last tattoos exactly where she said they were. Where she had dreamed them.

The red-haired man stared at Obed's tattoos, then turned to stare at the Chosen. "What else have you dreamed that you have no' told me about?"

Again her cheeks pinkened. "I'll tell you later."

Would he still be here? Obed sat in his chair again. What would he do now? What should he do? He cursed his ignorance of the outside world. He had come to be the mate, the helpmeet of the Chosen One, but it seemed she already had one.

"When I came here," he found himself saying, "I had intended to offer—I had hoped to find the Chosen One free to—that is…" He stumbled to a halt, feeling seven kinds of a fool. He couldn't propose marriage to a woman already married.

"Oh, heaven." She called his attention from his self-castigation. "We haven't told you our names, have we? I am Kallista. My iliasti—Aisse, Torchay, Stone."

He'd heard the woman's name, and the yellow-haired man's. Now he knew the others. He wondered what iliasti were, but tucked the word away to ask about later. He watched the Chosen—Kallista—and she watched him in return. He couldn't bear not knowing, had never been patient.

"If you do not intend to send me away, what *will* you do with me?" Obed suppressed a shiver. The room was cool for a man half-unclothed. Especially one from a Southron clime, used to far warmer air. But he saw the way her eyes strayed down over his body and considered himself content. "I offer myself for whatever service you might require."

Kallista gave a sigh, looking briefly at the others for a moment before she again captured his gaze. "Will you marry me, Obed? Marry us?"

"But—" His mind had difficulty comprehending the question. "Are you not already married?"

"Yes, the four of us are an ilian. We want you to join us." She looked again at the other three, more slowly this time, waiting for a reaction. Stone shrugged and nodded. Torchay scowled and nodded. Aisse just shrugged.

Obed struggled to get his mind around the concept. "They are all married to you?"

"We are married to each other, each of us to the other three." She gave him a gentle smile and his heart turned over.

He wanted to belong to her, desperately needed to belong to something or someone, but...*this?* His heart's desire was there for the taking—love, a life with true purpose, everything he'd ever dreamed of—but only if he could share. Though, as she went on to explain the institution of ilian and their particular practice of it, it seemed there was no sharing of any sort occurring at the moment.

Could he do it?

The One had brought him to this place, this person, this point.

Obed had followed where he was led, out of his Southron home-land, through plain and desert, over high mountains, mile upon mile into a new land. How could he balk when the One proposed to lead him into a new territory of the heart and mind? But could he marry four at once?

He eyed the two men, uncomfortable with the thought of mar-riage to them. But as she explained it, their relationship would be like that of sworn brothers, since none of them was apparently inclined to…more. That bit of information eased his mind. Then he cast all his thoughts aside.

Obed had been called to serve the Chosen One. Nothing else mattered. Not the numbers bound with him in that ser-vice. Certainly not his own comfort level. He would get used to it. He would make no other choice. It was his own will to do this.

"When?" he said.

Kallista looked at the others. "Tomorrow? Will that give us enough time?"

The red-haired man, Torchay, sighed. "Should we be stocking up on anklets? How many *more* will the One be bringing us?"

"Do you think I know? Even Belandra doesn't." She tipped her head onto his shoulder. Obed wanted that closeness for himself. She went on. "It might not be a bad idea to get more than one. He'll need anklets and bracelets for us as well."

Jewelry? At last, something Obed could understand. And offer. "I have gifts. I am not a poor man."

"No?" Her smile twisted. "Good. It's a good thing one of us isn't. Torchay and I are overdue on our pay and the other two came to us very nearly in their skins. But we're marrying you for your mark, not your gifts."

"And I give them from my heart, not in hope of return." Obed left his chair, going down to one knee, one eye on her pro-tector in case he thought to object. He took her hand and curled down to press his forehead against it, shivering again at the stirring deep inside him. "I am yours," he said. "I gave myself to the One years ago, and now the One has given me to you. Everything that I own, everything that I am is yours to do with as you will."

"Oh," she said. "My."

Aisse stood in the vast worship chamber on the edge of the red stone rose set into the floor, her ilian spaced evenly around it. The concept was taking some getting used to. The *men* were taking even more. And now the captain—it was still hard to remember to call her Kallista—now she was adding yet another man.

Although so far, it hadn't been so bad. Aisse had never thought it possible to even *like* a man, much less trust one. But she did. Torchay would never strike her, never force her to do anything she didn't want. Like sex. He taught her ways to defend herself, to strike back. He could even make her laugh. She liked him. Stone was another matter.

She couldn't trust him, knowing his Tibran nature. Mostly she ignored him, and since he ignored her in return, things seemed to be working out.

This new man threw something different into the mix and it worried her. How would the dynamics change? What would he expect? What sort of man was he?

Aisse took the anklet from the witness—a priestess of the temple this time, since Kallista's sisters had gone home—and fastened it around the dark man's ankle, repeating the words she had spoken three times already. Could she truly put his welfare and that of all those bound to her above everything? Aisse glanced at Kallista and at Torchay. They expected it of her. They had brought her safely out of the hell of her previous existence and made her equal with themselves. How could she not live up to their expectations?

* * *

Kallista could feel the magic stir as Obed began his part of the ceremony that would bind her to yet another stranger. She couldn't stop the whisper in the back of her mind, saying, "I didn't want this, not this way," any more than she could stop the one that murmured, "Just *look* at him, and he's *mine*."

Magnificent, beautiful as he was, Obed was still a stranger. Marked by the One, yes. Kallista trusted that judgment. She needed his magic. But she didn't know him. She wanted an ilian of her own choosing, not one thrust at her. And yet—could she choose any better?

She shook her left wrist slightly, so that the new bangle chimed faintly against the other two. Their new ilias seemed to be wealthy indeed, if the quality of the bands he'd produced was any indication. Obed fastened the last anklet on Stone, stood and spoke the words, then was led to his place in the circle. Kallista tensed. Would the magic rise again with the addition of this new magic bearer, the way it had before?

The Reinine, taking time out from her busy day to perform this ritual as well, spoke her blessing and joined Kallista's hand to Obed's. The magic woke, shooting between the three marked ones, touching the other two, binding them tight together. Five now, rather than four.

Gradually, the magic subsided, leaving Kallista shivering alone inside her own skin. She wanted. Needed. The last time, she'd found herself in Stone's bed, almost driven there. She could not let it happen again. But could she prevent it, or would the magic drive her where it was best she did not go?

Smiling, accepting the well-wishes of the temple attendants, Kallista searched inside herself, checking her contraceptive spell in case she once more proved too weak. It was gone.

Sometime in the past month, it had expired without her noticing. Thank the One that she had been holding apart from her iliasti or the complications could be unfathomable. Tomorrow, she would have the spell restored.

No, today. It had to be done today. She couldn't take the risk that the magic would be stronger than she. Again.

"How may I help you, naitan?" The healer, a tall, voluptuous woman of about Kallista's age who had introduced herself as Merinda, closed the door on the gaggle of men beyond and turned to smile at Kallista. "What could be so important that you must come see me immediately after your wedding?"

Torchay had asked the same question when she had announced her intention to visit a healer. Kallista told this woman what she had told him. "I need my contraception spell renewed."

Merinda's eyes twinkled and her amusement—obvious from the moment Kallista appeared with her train of iliasti—expanded. "Ah. I can see where that would have some urgency."

She gestured toward the couch set across the room. "Come then. Let's have a look at you."

Kallista measured the distance and shook her head. "Look at me here."

The healer raised a curious eyebrow but Kallista returned her gaze without changing expression. Enough people knew their secrets. Finally Merinda shrugged.

She raised her hands, holding them a few inches to either side of Kallista's face. Kallista felt the stir when Merinda called magic—she'd never been able to feel it before. She waited without much patience while the other woman moved her hands slowly down Kallista's body, stopping to hover just over her lower abdomen. Several moments later, Merinda pulled her hands back and stepped away.

"Is it done?" Kallista remembered it taking longer before.

"No." The healer rubbed her hands along the textured green fabric of her overtunic. "You hum with magic."

"Is that a problem? You can still do the spell, can't you?" Kallista kept herself from tumbling over the edge of panic, but barely.

Merinda looked up into her eyes. "No, I cannot. But not because of your magic."

"Then why?" She clung to that edge with mental fingernails.

"Because you are already with child."

The words hit Kallista like one of the Tibrans' cannonballs. She stared at the healer, trying to take it in, then her head went fuzzy and she found herself held upright as Merinda helped her across the room to the backless couch.

"No." Kallista pulled away, or tried to. When had she become so feeble? "No. My men—the magic—I can't be so far from them."

"You need to sit before you fall."

"Then I'll sit here." She let herself down to the floor in the center of the chamber, leaving Merinda looking down at her in ... exasperation? Amusement? Something of the kind. Didn't matter. What mattered was— "How can I be pregnant?"

Merinda merely lifted that mobile eyebrow as she sat on the floor in front of her.

Kallista hated to blush. "All right, yes. I know *how*. But—my spell was intact. I checked it. And—I haven't been sick. Not once. I haven't even missed my courses."

"No?" That blasted eyebrow stayed up.

"They're a little late, but that's nothing new. All this magic rumbling around would interfere with anyone's system." Kallista groaned. "Heaven help me—you think that's what happened? The magic negated the spell? Are you *sure* I'm pregnant?"

Merinda nodded, her face solemn. "I am sure. About three weeks along."

Kallista scrubbed her hands over her face, then smoothed them back over her bound hair. "Three weeks plus a day—twenty-eight days, exactly." She knew when it had happened. Could probably name the chime of the clock.

"Is it such unwelcome news?" The healer's voice was gentle, soothing.

Was it? "I have a task before me. A quest, set by the One. How can I fulfill it if I am waddling like a sow?"

And yet—*a child.* She had given up hope of a child of her own when she had given up hope of an ilian, telling herself she would make a terrible mother. Likely she would, but her arms ached to hold a child—*this* child. Her own. She loved it already, her heart burning, stretching, overflowing with seconds-old emotion.

"It will be some while before you waddle." Merinda smiled.

Kallista smiled back, her vision blurred with sudden tears, sudden worry. "What about the magic? There is so much of it, and—"

She hesitated to tell everything. But healers swore an oath to keep to the grave all that was told in confidence. "And I cannot control it. The magic escapes my grasp and goes blasting around doing whatever it likes. And now I have *two* marked companions filled with magic I cannot command. Could it…harm the baby? Cause some deformity?"

Now the healer frowned and Kallista's stomach twisted. "I don't know," Merinda said. "Pregnant naitani gradually lose their magic-calling abilities over the course of the pregnancy, until birth, when it is completely gone. And it does not recover for some time afterward. It is possible that this happens because the magic is somehow harmful to the child. But it is also possible that calling magic is not good for the mother. That added to the stress of childbearing, it would be too much strain. That is the more likely reason, I believe."

Kallista dropped her face in her hands. "I don't know what to do," she said quietly. Could she condemn her baby to the half life of a cripple? Would the magic do anything at all to it? What about this task before her? And what about her vow to give the others their freedom when it was done? A child would change that.

"You still have time to decide." Merinda stood and held both hands out to Kallista. "You might want to consider this, though. You have been chosen and marked by the One for Her purposes. Couldn't it be possible this child is part of that purpose?"

Those few words were all she needed to become a great, pulsing mass of guilt and confusion. She wanted a child, but not like this. Just as she'd wanted an ilian, but not this way. She felt hunted. Trapped. Kallista took Merinda's hands and let her haul her to her feet.

"Is there anything I should be doing, or not doing? Until I decide." Kallista straightened her long dress tunic, dusted off the seat.

"As long as you are feeling well, there's no reason for your activity to change. If you feel tired, rest. If you're hungry, eat. If you do have some morning sickness, eat something bland. Tea and toast can work wonders." Merinda twinkled. "And if all those men of yours get to hovering too much, send for me and I'll sort them."

Kallista's laugh felt weak. Tell them? The world would end before she told. It would definitely end if she did. Torchay would wrap her up in cotton padding and put her in a box until the baby was born. The others—who knew how they would react? She scarcely knew them.

She gathered up the men and walked with them back to their rooms. Aisse had already returned to check on the celebration meal. Thank the One they did not have to face another state dinner tonight. Last night's performance had been quite enough.

A baby. She was going to have a baby. Her own child. Hers and—her ilian's. It often happened that a woman didn't know which of her iliasti sired her children until the infant was born and its bloodline read. Stone or Torchay—the child belonged to both of them. To all of them, even Obed, now that he was ilias.

She couldn't give it up. Some women did because they were

too old or too young or too ill, returning the life to the One before the child was born. But she couldn't do it. She had tried to
smother the longing, but hadn't succeeded in killing it. She wanted
this baby. But what did that mean for their task?

Kallista ate the meal Aisse had ordered, sitting between Obed
and Stone. She thought she managed to behave normally. Torchay
didn't give her more than one of two piercing looks, so perhaps
she did. She was too distracted to play well when Stone pulled out
the queens-and-castles board, losing quickly and giving up the
game.

Her magic would fade as her child grew inside her. She would
need both magic and agility to carry out this assignment of theirs.
She had seen the demon again in her dreams. At least she thought
it was the demon.

Something malevolent seemed to haunt the dreamscape when
she skittered through it on the few occasions when her nights
weren't filled with dreams of erotic sensuality. She'd seen Tibran
Rulers and Warrior chiefs, seen smoke-colored shadow hovering in the rooms where they met and plotted. It kept her from
hearing their plots, obscured her view of their plans. She could
not stop the invasion of Adara from this distance. She had to go
to Tibre, meet the demon-ridden king face-to-face and set him
free. But when?

CHAPTER NINETEEN

Kallista watched Stone and Torchay at their queens-and-castles game, Aisse in the open space beyond working through the Fan Dai exercises Torchay had taught her. Because she could move farther than Stone's and Obed's magical chains allowed, she often did. Kallista sometimes wondered if she did it to taunt the Tibran male, but as long as there was no open hostility, she let it slide.

Tired beyond words, she retreated to her room and stretched out on her bed. One by one, her muscles began to relax, and as her body eased, her mind began to clear.

They couldn't wait until after this child was born to sail for Tibre. Adara's danger was too great. The reports coming in from the northern coast told of towns and villages burned, people slaughtered. No cities had yet fallen, but it was only a matter of time. Ukiny would have fallen already if not for the dark magic she'd called.

They had to accomplish what was given them to do before her magic left her, whenever that might be, before her pregnancy slowed her down. Before it began to show. Because if Torchay knew she was pregnant, he would never allow them to go anywhere, not until the baby was born. Therefore, he couldn't know. And if she couldn't tell Torchay, she couldn't tell anyone.

The sun was barely over the palace walls when Kallista woke to odd sounds and came stumbling from her bedroom to see workers piling crates and trunks and bales of goods in the center of the parlor. Torchay watched them, feet planted wide apart, arms folded across his chest, a bemused expression on his face. Obed and Stone stood at the entrance to the room they now shared, and as Kallista moved farther into the parlor, pulling a dressing robe over her chemise, Aisse appeared across the way.

"What is this?" Kallista stopped next to Torchay to tie the sash of her robe.

"I believe someone has decided to deliver our new ilias's luggage." Torchay slanted an eye toward the other men.

Obed approached, rubbing sleep from his eyes. He wore only those long, loose white trousers of his, exposing all of his tattoos. Kallista couldn't help staring.

"Did you order this?" She jerked her gaze from Obed back to the rising piles on the once-empty floor.

He shook his head. "I told them to wait for instructions. I suppose they got tired of waiting."

"What *is* all of this?" Kallista had never seen so much…stuff all in one place.

"It is yours." Obed stepped forward and threw open a hinged crate, revealing racked swords with the distinctive black scabbards of the Heldring forge. The best swords in existence, birthed of folded steel and blue-hot North magic, taking a year or more to complete each one—and the crate held ten of them.

"Khralsh——" Stone breathed the word. He moved toward the swords as if drawn by chains and reached into the crate.

"Not that one." Kallista spoke before she realized she had.

Stone jerked his hand back, stepped away, eyeing Torchay as if he feared punishment. Kallista paid little attention. He would learn. These swords had magic hammered into every folded layer of steel. The sword must be carefully matched to its bearer before that person touched it. A poor match could be disastrous.

She wrapped a length of silk spilled from one of the bundles around her hand—she didn't want to go back for her gloves—and studied the swords in the crate. Kallista didn't have to call magic. She knew Stone. He echoed through her now, without need for a touch.

"This one." Kallista picked the sword up by the scabbard, the black surface chased with an ornate red geometric design, both hands wrapped in the blue silk. "You should have this one."

Kallista turned, held the sword out hilt first to Stone. He stared at it, hunger in his eyes, then looked up at her. "Me?"

She could sense his confusion through that echo inside her. "You have already fought for me, with me. You're not Tibran anymore, Stone. You're ilias."

With a swift glance back at Torchay, Stone stretched out his hand and grasped the hilt of the sword. Kallista felt no magic stirring, but Stone smiled. He drew the sword from its scabbard and tested the balance, moving away from the others to make a few experimental swings. It was double-edged, straight and long, a mountain sword, suited for thrusting as well as cutting.

Kallista turned back to the rough crate. There. That sword was meant for Obed. A sabre, slightly curved, edged only along the outer curve with a black-on-black scabbard. And there—twin short swords in a double sheath chased with twining green coils— they belonged to Torchay. There was a sword for Kallista, its scabbard slashed with jagged blue streaks, and one for Aisse, subtly striped with bronze, smaller than the others to suit her smaller build, but equally fine.

"How did you know?" Kallista gave Obed his sword.

He drew it without taking his eyes from her. "You are sword master as well?"

"How did you know which swords to bring?" She offered Torchay the blades made for him. He drew them both in a smooth cross-hand motion.

"I did not. I bought all they were willing to sell me, hoping you might find use for them." Obed slid his sabre back into its sheath. As close as he stood to her, she could feel his desire for her mixed with awe and a sense of...worship? Why?

She stepped away from him to give Aisse her sword, then took up the one that called to her, finally shedding the silk coverings on her hands. Kallista drew it from the scabbard, a rapier, narrow and sharp, lightweight, perfect for the training Torchay had given her. It felt good in her hand, secure, confident. Was it her own confidence, or the sword's?

"There are four left," Torchay said. "Does that mean we wait for four marked companions—four more iliasti yet to come?"

Four *more?* She couldn't deal with the four she had now. "You heard Obed. He bought as many as they would sell him."

"But there was a blade to match each of us. Folk are turned away from Heldring every day because no sword will match them."

"And it took ten blades to find one—or two—to match each of us." She didn't have time to wait for any more iliasti to turn up. They had to move quickly. It was time to tell them.

Kallista took breath to call her ilian together and choked on it. At the opposite end of the long parlor, Stone parried a thrust, fighting invisible enemies with his new sword. Far beyond the ten paces he had been confined to for so long.

"Stone." She returned her blade to its home, backing a few steps farther.

He whipped the sword in an intricate pattern, spinning to a halt facing her. His eyes widened as he saw the distance between them. "I am—"

"Still upright, yes." Kallista took another step back, and another, until she bumped against the wall.

Obed collapsed, but Torchay caught him before he hit the floor. Kallista took several quick steps forward until the dark man began to recover.

So Stone backed away. Was it real? Had he been released from his magical confinement? He had counted on the dizziness that hit just before he passed the boundary to tell him when he'd moved too far from Kallista, as he had these last weeks. But there had been no dizziness.

Again, he measured the distance between them. At least twice what he'd been allowed before. He laughed out loud in sheer joy. Could he go farther? Did he still have limits? Stone opened the door to the suite and stepped outside.

Nothing. Not even dizziness. He moved farther, past the guards' quarters to the top of the stairs. Still nothing. He headed down the stairs. Lieutenant Suteny followed, but Stone paid him no attention. Joh followed everywhere he went.

Stone picked up speed as he descended, clattering faster and faster down the stairs until he was taking them two at a time. People scattered when he burst into the wide gallery at the end of the stairwell. Stone laughed again, spreading his arms wide and spinning in a circle. *He was free.*

He could go anywhere he wanted. Do anything he pleased. And he wouldn't fall down in a faint. He grinned at the courtiers eyeing him warily and swept into a low bow. And Kallista's touch shimmered through him.

Even here, as far from her as he stood, they were linked. She touched things inside him never meant to be touched, spearing him through with delight. Could he go far enough away to escape that? Did he want to? And if he did, where could he go? What place out there was better than where he was?

"Warrior. Stone." Joh was talking to him.

"What?" Stone couldn't prevent the irritation in his voice. He shouldn't want to go back to Kallista. He didn't want to want it. And again, her touch stroked sweetly along his soul.

"Put away the blade, warrior." The steel in Joh's voice brought Stone back to his surroundings.

The lieutenant and his guards encircled Stone, separating him from the few frightened-looking courtiers who still lingered in the gallery, and he suddenly realized how this looked. A wild-eyed Tibran dashing through the Adaran palace with a naked sword in his hand, laughing like a madman—it would alarm anyone.

Stone rotated the sword's hilt in his hand, preparing to hand it over, and the sword...protested? Accepting it as yet one more magical improbability to deal with, Stone considered his alternatives. He'd left the scabbard above in the parlor, so he couldn't put it away. "Move out of my way so I can go home."

He started for the stairwell as if he expected the guards to move out of his way, and they did. *Home,* he'd said. Was it? Not the suite. But the people inside were as close as he was likely to get, now Fox was gone. He belonged with them. It would never be like it was with Fox. He didn't want it to be. But they were all he had. He would be stupid to throw them away.

Halfway up the stairs, Stone paused and looked over his shoulder at the guards herding him back. Torchay wasn't among them. Nor was he waiting at the top of the stairs. Then again, Stone had been running, sword in hand, *away* from Torchay's charge. The bodyguard probably hoped Stone wouldn't return. Despite the fight with the prinsipella and her gang of rowdies, Stone knew Torchay still didn't quite trust him.

But they were all of them sitting around breakfast, listening to

Kallista as they ate. She looked up and smiled. "I'm glad to see you return on your own feet. Did you find the limit?"

Stone picked up the red-chased scabbard and slid his new sword inside. "I'm not sure there is one." Her smile made him feel strange and he didn't like it. She was just a woman, despite her magic. "Why didn't you come after me?"

"Should I have?" She watched him approach. They all did, but her eyes touched him. "Would you have felt as free?"

The truth hit him and he would have staggered save for his grip on the chair. She had known every step he took. He pulled it out and sat, watching her as she did him. The others might have been shadows for all the attention he gave them. "But I'm *not* free, am I?"

"No more than I." She held his gaze, her eyes as blue and bright as the lightning she threw. "You at least are bound only to me. I'm bound twice over."

He didn't want to think about that. His own troubles were burden enough. He wanted to blame her for them, and didn't like feeling it might not be fair to do so.

"I'll give you all the freedom I can." She handed him a plate filled with sausages and sweet buns, all the things he particularly liked. "You returned just in time. I was about to tell everyone what I believe the One has destined for us."

"And what is that?" Torchay entered the conversation, already sounding as if he disapproved.

"We must travel to Tibre and rid their king of the demon that rides him."

"What? *No.*" Stone slammed his eating knife down on the table. He wouldn't go back to Tibre. He couldn't. His life as a Tibran warrior was no more, but his heart was still Tibran. How could they expect him to fight and kill his own people?

"Stone, we must."

"I will not take part in any plot to kill my king."

"He's no' your king any longer." Torchay watched him, obviously ready for any threatening move.

"With any luck, we won't have to kill him." Kallista laid a hand on his arm and Stone resisted the urge to throw it off. "There is a demon riding his shoulders. *That* is our enemy. I've seen it in visions. It whispers in his ear. 'What does it matter how many warriors you lose? Breed more. Who will mourn them when they die? Their mothers forgot them. Their fathers don't know them. Take the land. Take the cities. Take their wealth for your own.' I've heard it, Stone."

Her words turned his blood to ice. "Do you tell me this...*demon* is the cause of the wars?"

"I believe it, yes. I have seen it. Who knows how long it has ridden Tibre's kings?"

Stone opened his mouth to deny the existence of demons and found that he could not. He had seen, had felt too many impossible things since he woke up in that breach in the walls of Ukiny. How could he not accept the possibility of a demon? If this demon were stripped from the king...might not some of the warriors have a chance to know those things Fox had longed for on the night before he died? Perhaps they would be able to go home and soak in the baths, sleep in a bed and dally with a woman who had all her teeth.

He cut his eyes toward Aisse as if she could hear what he was thinking. He'd learned to be wary of her sharp tongue cutting up his peace. Not warrior's behavior, but she had him thinking things that weren't warrior's thoughts. Like—what if the woman didn't *want* to be dallied with?

"When do we go?" Obed's question called Stone back from his errant thoughts.

"As soon as we can be ready." Kallista pushed back her plate, half the food still remaining on it. "We'll need supplies, horses, that sort of thing. Aisse, you go through all of this—" She waved her hand at the goods half filling the long parlor. "See if any of it might be useful, then find somewhere to store the rest of it. Or send it to my sisters and let them take care of it. Torchay, help her. You'll know what we need."

"What about us?" Obed asked.

"We will be practicing magic, you and I and Stone." She sighed. "If we are to face a demon, I had better know what I am doing with what you two carry."

Joh stalked through palace halls seething with emotion. Anger, disgust and loathing roiled in his stomach, made worse by generous dollops of guilt and shame, though he had done nothing worthy of either one. If he could just leave this place, get out of this damn poisonous atmosphere. He hated sneaking about. He wasn't a spy, he was a soldier.

He pushed his fist hard against the pain in his gut, shooting a glance over his shoulder. Goddess, he hated it all. He hated the way the captain looked at him at the times when she would have once offered her hand but didn't any longer, as if he had disappointed her somehow. He hated the fear that crawled through him then, wondering just what dark magics she held in her ungloved hands, whether she could read his thoughts, his fear. He wanted out.

Joh pressed his lips together, quelling the need to vent his frustrations in a more physical way. He could go to the training yard later and take them out on some hapless sparring partner. His request for transfer to a forward unit had been turned down. Again. Maybe they were hoping after four requests, he would give up and resign himself to his useless post. He wouldn't. But he'd wait a bit before presenting the next request. Just now, he'd been summoned back to the little Briar Chapel in the bowels of Winterhold Palace.

Joh strode down the aisle, finding the expected hooded figure in the shadows.

The Master Barb glided forward. "The Barinirab Order requires your service."

The jab of pain through Joh's burning gut was scarcely noticeable past the dread. "What is it?" He dipped his head slightly, Renunciate to Rejuvenate, unable to keep all the resentment from his voice.

"West magic is an abomination before the One." The master's voice deepened, crackled with fervor. "It is death and destruction, permeated with darkness. It is a perversion of everything that is good."

Joh listened, though he'd heard it before. No one was comfortable with West magic or its dark connections. He least of all.

"This naitan has disrupted the government. She has set the court on end with her wild magic and her evil intent."

"Well—" Joh wouldn't go so far as to call her evil, exactly. She made him uneasy—truthfully, she frightened him. Because he didn't know what she could do. Or would do. But evil?

"West magic is insidious," the rasping voice went on. "It steals away a person's will, tempting them with knowledge, with dark powers never meant for mere humanity. It twists the one it possesses, changing them, leading them deep into its dark web."

That made sense. "What service does the order ask of its Renunciate?"

"We must stop them."

Joh recoiled. "How?" He wanted to stop the magic, but certain things he would not do. Murder was one of them. He killed, yes, but the enemy in the battlefield, face-to-face, not his soldier sedili with a knife in the back.

"You reported that the naitan goes daily to practice her magic."

"Yes, that's right. With her ilian. They all go together. What do you plan to do?"

The Master Barb moved out of his corner, revealing a small keg in the deeper dark. "We have a naitan, an East magic healer, who can block the West magic with the help of this medicinal powder."

"You want me to mix it in their drinks? Sprinkle it in their food?" There was a tremendous amount of powder in the keg for that, but Joh couldn't think how else it could be used.

The master's laugh sounded like stone scraping on stone. "It must be burned, so it becomes a vapor to be breathed. But not in their suite. In the yard where they practice, so the vapors can dissipate when the healer's spell is finished. You must burn it without the captain naitan knowing it. The West magic grips her hard, it will not want to let her go."

"There may be a drain where I can pour it."

"No. It must remain inside the cask. Will the whole of it fit inside the drain?"

Joh frowned, taking a visual measurement of the container. "I don't know. I'll have to look. How am I to start it burning without the naitan seeing me?"

"Simply pour a small trail from where you hide the cask to where you hide yourself. The spark will travel along the line of powder."

"Won't the naitan see the spark burning?"

"You will have to ensure that she doesn't." The master's voice crackled with anger. "And if you take the cask directly to this practice yard when you leave here, no one will see you transport it."

It was late, the ilian closed tight in their suite, and Winterhold Palace abandoned for the summer months. "This spell will free the naitan from the West magic?" Joh asked for verification.

The Master Barb inclined his head. "It is the only way."

Joh lifted the keg to his shoulder. "I hope this works."

"As do I, Renunciate." The cowled figure bowed again and disappeared into the shadows. "The healer will be at the courtyard at ten strikes of the clock tomorrow morning."

* * *

By the light of a silver moon, Joh scoured the practice yard for a place to hide the keg. It had to be close by, so the vapors would permeate the entire courtyard as well as the windowless chamber adjoining. He contemplated sinking it into the central drain. It was large enough to hold it, but he feared a powder trail leading to it would be both too noticeable and too easily scuffed away, whether by accident or purpose.

He finally settled for concealing the keg partially inside the broken-off gargoyle lying in a corner near the adjoining chamber. He wrestled the keg back out and poured a generous trail of powder along the edge of the wall, into the empty chamber, down a corridor and around a corner. He studied the harmless-looking stuff. Would a spark truly burn along all that distance?

Joh set the keg down and pulled out his flint and steel. The powder caught at the first spark, flashing into a spitting flame that sped back along the trail so fast he had to run to keep up with it. The acrid black smoke it gave off smelled foul enough to work some sort of magic. He only hoped the naitan or one of her iliasti did not notice the scorch marks on the parquet floor. They would likely notice the spark, but as swiftly as it flashed down the powder line, they would not have time to act before it reached its goal.

He went back to where he'd left the little keg and poured out another trail of gritty black powder, making a pool of it beneath the gargoyle. He tucked the keg in on top of it, upside down so that the spark could ignite the powder through the bunghole opening. In the morning, he would follow when they came to practice. When the tower clocks struck ten and they were focused on their activities, he would light his powder trail and with luck, the captain naitan would notice nothing until the healer naitan had her spell under way. It would work. It had to.

* * *

"How, exactly does this practice of magic work?" Obed asked the next morning as he, Kallista and Stone wound their way through the palace complex.

Kallista answered something, hardly thinking about what she said. Torchay hadn't even blinked when she left him behind with Aisse to organize their new riches. They'd explored them all day yesterday, draping each other with silks and velvets, trying on dancing slippers and riding boots, necklaces and coronets. Today was for business. She just wished she knew whether Torchay's easy acquiescence meant he trusted the other two men, or he didn't particularly care anymore.

Trust. Had to be that. Because even if he didn't care, he would never, ever shirk his duty.

"And here we are in our charming work space." Stone bowed them into the barren courtyard. "Mind the glass. Kallista's powdered most of it to dust by now, but there's still the odd shard or two."

"And now, how do we proceed?" Obed walked into the courtyard ahead of Kallista, looking curiously about him. He wore Adaran tunic and trousers today, black like Torchay's uniform, but without the blue trim or military cut. He looked even more exotic in ordinary dress, with his black hair curling over his shoulders and the tattoos marking his face and hands.

"Naitan." Stone's voice cut through Kallista's distraction. "I accept your gloves."

CHAPTER TWENTY

The tower clocks began to chime as she drew the gloves off, finger by finger. She had called magic from each of them yesterday to keep it from building too high, but she'd done it one at a time. She hadn't touched both of them at once since the ceremony that had bound Obed to them. She still couldn't control the magic Stone carried. Would Obed's make it easier? Or worse? The only way to know was to try.

The chiming stopped and she held a bare hand out to each man. Stone closed his hand around her left one. "You've always used your right hand to cast the magic," he said. "How will you do it if you're holding his with it?"

"That's what we're here to find out." Kallista held her hand out to the dark man, challenge in her gaze.

Obed smiled. He took her hand in his and as the magic stirred, responding to her touch, he raised her hand to his mouth and kissed it. "All I am is yours."

Shaking her head—did he have no sense of self-preservation?—Kallista called magic, pulling it from both men, stirring it together inside her. It bubbled up, escaping her faster than it ever had. She grabbed for it, but it eluded her grasp, twirling away to do Goddess knew what mischief.

"That's new," she said, utterly disgusted.

She could feel Obed's heart pounding, his eyes watching her. "You worked magic?" he whispered.

"I didn't work anything. It got away from me before I could do anything at all with it."

"She *called* magic." Stone grinned. "Told you it felt good."

Obed rubbed a hand down his face. "Saints and all the sinners, I will be laid low before the morning is out."

"Be glad it doesn't hurt." Kallista glared at Stone.

"Believe me, I am." His grin widened. "I'm very glad."

"We're here to work, not play." Her scowl made no impression whatsoever on Stone, so she snatched magic, making him gasp. "Work."

"As you will, my ilias." His words came rough, through gasping breath. "I—"

"Work," she repeated in an attempt to cut him off. May as well have tried to stop the wind.

"A man could grow to like your discipline."

It wasn't so much the last word Stone had to have, as the chance to tease he could never resist. Kallista had found nothing yet that would stop him.

So she ignored him and went to work. She tried calling the magic with Obed holding Stone's hand, which made Stone scream as both magics poured through him. When Stone held Obed's hand, the magic drove their new ilias to his knees. She tried it while holding Obed's hand with neither of them touching Stone and that worked a bit better, but she still could not wrestle the magic into anything resembling a spell.

The clocks were chiming again when Kallista released Obed's hand and took a step back.

"It's not going well, is it?"

She tensed when Obed set his hand on her shoulder, then relaxed as he began to knead her muscles, thumbs pressing in hard in a way that hurt and felt wonderful at the same instant. "No," she said. "Not well at all. There is twice as much power, and I have less than half as much control over it."

Stone drifted closer, eyes intent on Obed's activity. "What is that you're doing?"

"It's a technique I learned in my land called massage. For relaxing tight muscles, easing the pain. I'll teach you if you like."

"I would."

Kallista opened an eye. This massage was seductive—and she had no doubt that was why Stone wanted to learn it. "You just want to put your hands on me."

"Of course I do. Haven't you been listeni—" Stone broke his words in half, his head jerking up as his nostrils flared. He sniffed the air. "I smell gunpowder. How—"

She saw the spark hissing furiously along the courtyard wall at the same time as Stone, but he was the one who acted.

"Down!" He tackled her, knocking Obed down with her. "Get down!"

They hit the pavement as it moved up to meet them. A blast greater than any lightning Kallista had ever thrown exploded through the courtyard. She grabbed magic, frantic to protect them, willing it into a shield wall. The blast shook them, burst an eardrum—she couldn't tell whose. She was too busy with her struggle to hold the magic. It writhed in her grasp as stones, shaken loose by the explosion, rained down upon them. But she wouldn't let it go, couldn't. Their lives were at stake.

"Kallista—" Stone stirred, wrapped his hand around her wrist.

The magic curdled, but held. Something weighed them down, pressing against them, making it hard to breathe. Blackness hovered at the edges of her vision, but she couldn't let go. Magic kept them alive. Her magic. *Their* magic.

She pushed at it, shaped it, slapped it when it wouldn't behave. She forced it to harden, willing it to hold despite their fading consciousness. Someone would come. Such a blast could not fail to be noticed. Pray the Goddess they came soon.

"Eighteen silver cups." Torchay repeated the count Aisse gave him as he wrote it down. His hand was beginning to cramp. Next ilias they acquired ought to be a scholar. This kind of work was not for him, though Aisse seemed to be enjoying herself. He'd have to teach her Adaran script, then she could do this part and he could rummage around in the trunks and crates.

Obed's goods weren't all useless luxuries. Besides the swords—Torchay's hand rose to touch the hilt of the twin sword rising over his shoulder—they had found a crate of carefully racked daggers and knives, one of light, shimmering mail and another containing what appeared to be three matching pairs of delicately constructed miniature cannon no longer than his forearm.

Torchay had gone out at dawn with Obed's directions and a letter of introduction to look at the horses and mules their new ilias had brought. He had never seen such magnificent beasts save at a distance as Adara's prinsipi went riding by. Kallista's kin in Turysh wouldn't know how to treat them. His own people now...he could send to his parents, have his sedili come down to collect them. The high pastures of Korbin would suit the animals far better than cramped stables in a city. Tomorrow, he would go back, choose mounts and pack animals for their journey, then—

The floor vibrated beneath his feet, rattling the gemstones

piled on the table before him, and a boom like nearby thunder echoed through the window. A window open to a cloudless sky.

Torchay threw his quill down, overturning the chair as he dashed for the door. He could hear Aisse call to him, but her words didn't matter. Only reaching Kallista did. His iliasti could not protect her against something that sounded like that.

Courtiers crowded the corridors, asking questions no one could answer. They grabbed at him, trying to stop him, asking.

"I don't know. I don't *know*, dammit." He threw off their hands. "I must get to my naitan."

Some of them followed him, curious, or perhaps because he had purpose and they needed one. A few of them stayed with him all the way into Winterhold.

Dust and smoke floated in the air of the corridors leading to the practice yard, an odor he'd last smelled on the battlefield at Ukiny. His heart shattered like Ukiny's walls and he stumbled.

"Goddess, *no*." Torchay found his feet again and ran on, terror speeding his steps.

The courtyard door was gone, rubble blocking the way. He picked up a stone and threw it behind him, almost striking Aisse with it. He grabbed the next and dragged it aside.

The courtiers and guardsmen still with him moved forward to help. Aisse stopped one of them. "Go back," she said. "Tell others—someone important. Get more help. Healers—send healers."

Yes, healers. Please, Goddess, let the healers be needed. Torchay clawed at the stones, desperate to get through. He was glad Aisse could still think sensibly. Sense was an impossibility with this terror gnawing at his soul.

The gap in the rubble finally opened large enough for Torchay to wriggle through. He brought dust and gravel down as he did, but no more large stones. Shaking the dirt from his eyes, Torchay looked, terrified of what he might see.

White with dust, Joh Suteny worked frantically to move fallen stones from a mound near the center. Torchay saw a shoe, a long delicate foot protruding from beneath the stones, and slithered down the piled-up rubble. "Keep working," he shouted to those behind him. "So help can get through when it arrives."

Joh looked up but didn't pause in his digging. "*Hurry.* I can't lift them by myself."

Massive stones from the collapsed walls lay atop Torchay's iliasti. Were they dead? He couldn't reach them to find out. He fought down his panic, trying to see which boulder should be moved first.

"This one." Joh tapped a broad slab leaning at an angle. "It's holding everything else down."

Torchay seized the stone and pulled. Joh joined him a second later. He couldn't get under it to push without stepping on his iliasti. Aisse appeared, somehow wriggling between Torchay and the heavy stone to set her back against it and push up with her legs. A few moments later, another man joined them, and then another, and finally the thing began to rise. Higher they pushed it, until it teetered on end. Everyone jumped back as it slammed down the other direction and snapped in two.

"This one now." Joh directed the rescue workers to the next stone.

Torchay moved smaller rocks out of the way, reaching through the crevices until he touched...something. Not hard stone or warm flesh. It gave as he probed it, spongy, becoming less resistant by the second.

"*Magic.*" The word emerged on his breath and he took another. "She's shielded them with magic, but it's fading. I doubt it will hold much longer. *Hurry.*" He seized a stone and lifted as he stood, other hands coming to help.

"They're alive," he said. They couldn't be otherwise. This kind of magic died with its maker, and it was tied to all three of them. "Get them out of there. Now."

He prayed with every breath that the magic had held against the crushing weight of the stones, that it would hold long enough. He prayed that the fading shield didn't mean fading life. She complained about poor control, that the magic didn't do what she willed it. He prayed that was the problem now.

With a mighty groan and eight pairs of hands, the last of the big stones was lifted free. Aisse was already clawing away the smaller rubble, carefully brushing dust and grit from their faces.

"Don't move them," Torchay ordered when the others would have done it. "Let me check them first. I've got the training. I'm her bodyguard."

Then why weren't you here? He could hear them thinking the question, though none of them said it aloud.

Stone lay sprawled atop Kallista, Obed beneath both of them. No remnant of the magic shield lingered as Torchay quickly checked pulses and breathing. All normal, thank the One.

He inspected Stone for injuries first, wishing he were conscious so Torchay could ask him to move hands and feet. He found no obvious breaks, no bleeding wounds, and only one lump on the man's hard skull.

"Stone. Warrior." Torchay tapped his ilias's cheek and he stirred, moaning. "Can you move? Are you awake?"

"Think so," came the muttered reply. Torchay didn't want to acknowledge his relief but it was there. Stone lifted himself far enough to roll off Kallista and lost consciousness again.

"It's safe to move him." Torchay directed the bearers to a cleared spot against the single wall still standing.

Kallista's shallow breathing alarmed him, but at least she *was* breathing. He found no breaks, bruises or bumps. Between the two men, she'd have been shielded from the worst, but her pallor disturbed him, as did her failure to respond to his attempts to wake her. Finally he let the others move her beside Stone. It would take a healer with more skills than his to determine the problem.

Obed had a lump on the back of his head that nearly doubled its size, but Torchay could find nothing worse. A rise in the level of noise behind him made him turn and sag with relief at the sight of the green-robed naitani scrambling over the rubble leading back into the palace.

He stood, met them as they approached. "She shielded them with magic. The harm seems minor, given what it could have been, but I cannot see what might lie beneath the surface."

"We'll just make sure then, shall we?" The healer, an older woman with a gentle face, patted his arm once before she began to direct her staff in caring for the injured.

Torchay stepped back and found himself next to the guard lieutenant. Joh looked shattered. Sweat and blood from minor cuts washed dark paths through the dust caked on his skin.

"You got here quickly." Torchay wiped dust and sweat into mud on his own forehead. "I'm grateful."

Joh mumbled something, the words indistinct. Did he mean them to be heard? Torchay glanced at him, then looked again, seeing something more than worry in the other man's face.

"What did you say?" Horror sank its insidious fingers into Torchay's heart.

"I didn't know." Joh turned unseeing eyes on Torchay, his voice barely above a whisper. "I swear to the One, I didn't know. It was a vapor, a healing vapor. I didn't know it would—"

The instant understanding struck, Torchay was on him, his hands around the murderer's throat. Joh closed his eyes, surrendering to Torchay's rage without a struggle.

"Sergeant! Release him at once."

He heard the order but it didn't penetrate the violence gripping him until hands laid hold and dragged him away. The lieutenant collapsed to his knees, coughing and gasping as air returned.

"What is the meaning of this?" Serysta Reinine demanded an answer.

Torchay snapped to attention. "Ask him. Ask the lieutenant who did this thing."

Serysta signaled and guardsmen pulled Joh to his feet. "Lieutenant?"

Still wheezing, Joh made an attempt to come to attention. "Yes, my Reinine."

"Did you do this?"

This time he managed to stand straight, pulling away from the guards' support. "Yes, my Reinine. I did."

She frowned. *"Why?"*

Joh didn't answer. Torchay's hands twitched with the urge to wrap them around the murderer's throat again, but he refrained. The Reinine would only stop him again.

With another gesture from Serysta Reinine, the guardsmen dragged Joh off through the rapidly enlarging opening. The Reinine picked her way through the rubble to the healers working over the injured. Torchay trailed behind her bodyguards. He vaguely noticed Aisse moving up beside him, but when she slipped her hand into his, he held on tight.

The two men were awake and sitting up with support. Obed tried to stand, but fell back again when his legs wouldn't hold him. He struggled against the healers, subsiding only when he met Torchay's gaze. "Ilias—" Obed coughed to clear his throat and spoke again. "Kallista—is she—"

"Alive, yes." Torchay wanted to invade the knot of healers working over her, learn what they knew. He had no doubt Obed wanted the same thing, given the obsession he seemed to have with her. With a grimace, Torchay hauled Obed to his feet and supported him to the corner where Stone and Kallista had been moved.

Stone sat against the wall, holding a towel-wrapped chunk of ice from the cellars against the lump on his head. Torchay helped Obed to the ground beside Stone, and Aisse brought him his own chunk of ice. Then she put her hand back in Torchay's, and they waited.

"She is alive," Torchay said after a time, as much to remind himself as to reassure the others. "She has no serious injuries."

"Then why won't she wake up?" Aisse's fingers tightened on his.

Torchay shook his head. He'd done all he could. Didn't Kallista know how much they needed her? Without her, their ilian had no center. She was the one who joined them, made them a whole, gave them a purpose. Their loyalty was to her, not each other. They waited now, four disparate individuals, with nothing to hold them together—except Kallista.

"Maybe it's the magic." Stone cleared his throat and spat, likely spitting the dust out of his mouth. "She shielded us with magic. You know how using it tires her."

"I know." Torchay shifted position, propped a hip against the wall.

"How did you know what would happen?" Obed leaned forward to look past Torchay and Aisse at Stone.

"Know?" Torchay's hands tightened into fists again. Aisse protested, but he paid her no mind. Had there been more than one conspirator here? "Know what?"

"I smelled it burning. You can't mistake the smell of gunpowder smoke." Stone made a face. "There wasn't time to do anything but drop. No cover in the middle of the courtyard."

"You didn't just drop," Obed said. "You knocked us both to the ground, the Chosen and I."

"That's what ilian is." Stone felt the knot on his head and put the ice back. "Looking out for each other. Or that's what they keep telling me."

Torchay's hands relaxed. Kallista was their center, yes, but perhaps the rest of them weren't so separate as he'd believed.

Kallista's eyes snapped open and she struggled against restraining hands. "Obed, Stone—"

"They are well. Aching heads perhaps, but perfectly well." The green-robed naitan urged Kallista back down. "How do you feel, my dear?"

"You're sure? The shield held?" She needed to see them with her own eyes. Again she attempted to rise.

"It seems so, yes." The healer smiled. "You all three came through without much more than a bump on the head. We were a bit concerned about you, however, my dear. You showed no sign of injury, but we could not persuade you to come back to us."

"There's no—" Her hand started toward the place where her child lived, but she didn't complete the motion.

"Your baby is fine. I believe it was your condition combined with the very powerful magic you had to use to protect yourself and your iliasti that caused your lengthy unconsciousness."

"Don't say anything," Kallista begged. "About the baby. I haven't told them yet. I don't want them to find out like this—they'll worry."

"You wish to worry alone?" The healer finally helped Kallista sit up.

"Please, naitan." Kallista clung to the woman's hand.

"It's not my place to share news of this sort." The healer patted her hand. "You have some anxious people waiting to see you." She moved out of the way.

Aisse rushed forward, her youth showing in her haste, and knelt beside Kallista. She grasped both her hands and peered anxiously into Kallista's face. "You are well? Truly not hurt?"

Kallista had to laugh. The other woman's earnestness was appealing. "My head aches, but I'm fine. Help me up."

She pulled on Aisse's hands to rise and instantly Torchay and Obed were there lifting her to her feet. Torchay bent to catch her knees and pick her up, but she stopped him.

Stone was there, hovering behind Aisse as if waiting for her to notice him. Or hoping she would not? He took her hand when she held it out to him and came when she tugged. Kallista took his face between her hands and inspected him for injury, reading the magic as it coiled seductively between them. She tipped his head down and kissed his forehead, then raised it and kissed his mouth, warm and oh, so sweet.

"Thank you," she whispered.

Stone grasped her wrists and pulled her hands away from his face, his expression uncomfortable. "You're the one who saved us."

"You gave the warning." She touched his cheek again, briefly, since it disturbed him, and turned to Obed.

She wobbled, and Obed caught her arm, worry evident in his eyes. Kallista tried to smile, but couldn't. It didn't seem to matter that she had known him just over a single day. He had become important to her. Cupping his face in her hands, Kallista smoothed her thumbs over the marks beneath his eyes and read his magic.

"It was *your* ear." Her eyes flew open, sought out the healer naitan. "His eardrum burst—"

The naitan smiled and nodded. "It's been treated. It will heal."

"Normally?"

"Of course."

Kallista tried to check for herself, but she didn't have a healer's skill at reading nuance. She patted Obed's cheek and started to turn away when he covered her hand with his, holding it in place against his beard-roughened jaw.

"My ilias was given kisses. Do I not deserve as much?" Taller than Stone, or even Torchay, Obed had to bend to bring his forehead within her reach.

She'd only kissed him in the joining ceremony, until now had only touched his hands. She feared the temptation of her dreams. But he was right. He was ilias and she owed him everything she owed the others. She touched her lips to his forehead, and when he raised his head, met her gaze with hope and fear in his eyes, she had to kiss his mouth. Goddess, why did he have to taste so sweet?

Kallista turned away, into Torchay's arms, wrapping herself around him and holding him tight. Now the tears escaped. She hid them in the black softness of his tunic. He tucked her head into his shoulder, his hand cradling it there, and whispered nonsense into her ear until she stopped shaking.

"We have to go, Torchay," she said, soft enough so only he could hear. "We have to leave now."

"Aye. As soon as you can travel." His mouth against her ear made her shudder with longing, but she pushed it away.

"I can travel now."

"But the lads cannot. They've both great lumps on their heads that make them dizzy. A day or two, and they'll be fine."

"It's too dangerous to stay here."

"I'll keep you safe. All of you. Trust me to handle it?" His eyes met hers when she looked up. The same clear, blue eyes she'd known for so long.

"Of course I trust you."

He nodded, accepting her trust with a faint smile. Kallista captured his face between her hands and pressed a kiss to his too-familiar mouth. Less than she wanted, but more than she ought to take, and so piercingly sweet it threatened to bring back tears. Why did this have to be so hard?

The chief healer insisted that Kallista, Obed and Stone all ride back to their suite in chairs. Kallista was grateful the woman didn't insist on stretchers, but by the end of the journey, she wondered if that might not have been the better choice. It could be no more humiliating to be borne through the palace prone on a litter than to fall from the chair in exhaustion. Fortunately, she managed to avoid it.

In the dark hours of the night, Torchay woke her. They were moving to new quarters, back in Winterhold. The last leg of the journey was made with the three marked ones leaning on each other, trying to stay upright with the help of the two uninjured. At the end of it, Torchay and Aisse tumbled the other three into the same bed with orders to stay and rest until they returned, and promptly vanished on some mysterious errand. Kallista couldn't stay awake long enough to wonder.

Torchay wouldn't let her sleep as she wished. He kept waking her from dream-haunted sleep. In truth, she had trouble distinguishing dream from reality. The hard male bodies tucked up against her seemed real enough, but were the kisses? The caresses?

The demon's red eyes rode the darkness. It hunted her. If it found her—she didn't know what would happen, but it would be bad. Only when Torchay lay curled around her, her back tucked into the curve of his body, could she hold the demon out of her dreams. She wondered in her sleep what it meant, but only once.

She was vaguely aware that the healer naitan paid a call. Her hand felt cool on Kallista's forehead. She struggled to wakefulness, afraid the naitan would spill her secret, but she only spoke of magic and exhaustion and rest. Kallista let herself slide back into the dark warmth of Stone's embrace.

It was the lack of touch that woke her. She was alone in the bed, no one beside her. Kallista rubbed open her eyes to the flicker of a single lamp. Obed sat at the table where the lamp stood, working on some kind of papers, his quill scratching as he wrote.

He went still, then laid his pen down and turned to look at her, his dark gaze drinking her in. "Are you truly awake?"

"I think so." Kallista pushed her hair out of her face and rolled to her side. "How long have I slept?"

"Most of three days." He moved to the bed and sat on the edge, reaching for her hand. Kallista pulled it back, afraid of wanting his touch, then hated herself when his face blanked. "The naitan said you pushed too hard, did too much magic. How do you feel?"

Kallista took Obed's hand in hers, trying to make up for upsetting him, but it didn't seem to help much. His face remained just as carefully devoid of emotion as before. "I feel…groggy. Disconnected."

Gingerly, she reached for the magic Obed carried, wondering why it hadn't already gone racketing around through them. It was there, but sullen, sluggish. She stroked mental fingers over it and Obed shuddered.

"I have missed that," he said. "Feeling your touch inside me, knowing I am a part of you. I missed it, though I had it for such a short time."

Obed tucked his cheek into her hand, holding it there against his face, and looked at her. Nothing more. As if he would be content to sit like this as long as she would allow it. It unnerved her.

Kallista cleared her throat. "We need to begin our quest."

"Everything is ready. We can leave as soon as you are well enough to travel. The time was not wasted." He smiled. "Your Torchay is a clever man. No one will know we have gone until we are days from here. No one knows we are no longer in Daybright Tower."

"*Our* Torchay," she corrected. "He is not mine."

Obed's smile warmed. "Of course he is. We are all of us yours. Aisse is a little bit Torchay's as well, and Stone wishes he was no one's, but we are yours first."

And didn't that thought make her uncomfortable?

CHAPTER TWENTY-ONE

Kallista took refuge from her discomfort in action, throwing the covers aside to stand. Obed took her elbow, giving needed support.

"We must go. Right away," she said.

"We will."

But she had to wait through the night and the next day until night fell again before Torchay led them through yet another maze of corridors to an obscure door. It led into a square filled with shuttered shops and teeming taverns. They slipped out of the city in the midst of a merchant caravan and collected their mounts and loaded pack animals at a stable just beyond the gate.

It took almost two weeks to reach Turysh because they rode the entire distance, avoiding the river and its boats. The Tibrans and Obed were so distinctive in their appearance, anyone who saw them would remember. They wanted to avoid notice because no one yet knew who was behind the attack on their ilian. The

Reinine's investigators had discovered that the gunpowder had come from the small stock "liberated" from the Tibrans at great risk and sent to Arikon for scholars and naitani to study. But how the powder had been spirited away and how Joh had come to possess it were questions that still did not have answers.

In addition, Aisse was new to horseback, so they slowed their pace to accommodate her. And that gave Kallista time to practice using the magic from two marked ones.

In Turysh, at the edge of the plain where they would turn north, they took advantage of the city's size and anonymity to hire rooms at an inn on the rough north bank of the Taolind. The barracks and most of the city lay across the river to the south. The ilian indulged in baths, meals cooked by someone else, and beds without rocks beneath. Kallista accompanied Aisse and Obed to the market to replenish supplies, amused by the obvious pleasure they took in haggling over prices. Before dawn, Torchay had everyone in the inn yard mounting up when the first hint of pink touched the sky.

"I still don't see what it would have hurt to get a later start," Stone grumbled, settling into his saddle. "Beds, Torchay. Real beds, for just another hour. Maybe two."

Not that he particularly minded getting up at this hour, but it was a warrior's right to complain. Almost a duty. Besides, it seemed to amuse the others when they bothered to notice.

Obed and Torchay finished securing the loads on the pack mules. They'd banished Stone from the task after the first day when the load he'd tied on slid off the mule's back and bounced along the trail behind it until they got the terrified animal caught and pacified. Baggage wasn't one of his talents.

Everyone was mounted now, even Aisse, who'd finally acquired sufficient riding skills to stop falling off. Kallista wheeled her mount and rode out of the stable yard to the dusty street heading north.

"No-oooo!" The hoarse scream came from nowhere and everywhere, startling the horses into a skittering dance step.

Torchay pushed his mount toward Kallista, taking up a protective position as he searched all directions for potential danger. Obed caught Aisse's reins to help her control her horse. Stone couldn't move, sitting frozen as his mount sidled beneath him. He knew that voice. Its familiarity sliced deep.

"No-oooo!" The shout came again, from the direction of the riverfront.

Stone turned, looked, and his heart ceased to beat in his chest. A tall, ragged man covered head to toe in dirt lurched down the street toward them. He tripped over every obstacle, crashed into everything in his path. When he fell, he crawled until he managed to push himself upright again, never ceasing his limping, lopsided, careening progress toward them.

"Don't go!" he shouted. The creature was all one color, dust dun from his falls in the unpaved street.

Torchay moved his horse between Kallista and the poor wretch, his hand back, touching the hilt of his lower Heldring blade, but he didn't draw it. Stone stared, his heart pounding double time. It was impossible. A thousand impossibilities.

"Khralsh—" He breathed out the word, whether in praise, supplication or sheer disbelief, he did not know. Then he was off his horse and running.

Stone halted almost nose-to-nose with the man, hardly able to believe what his eyes told him. "Fox?" The name was a whisper. A prayer.

"Who's there?"

It *was* Fox. Staring from sightless eyes, scarred, limping and far too thin, but it was Fox. *Alive.*

"It's me. Stone." Filled with wonder, he touched his *brodir's* face.

Fox jerked back, stumbled, and Stone caught him. He pulled

his arm free, before he was quite steady again. "You lie. Stone is dead."

"I thought you were dead too, *brodir*." Stone wiped the damnable wetness from his face with his bare forearm. "I found your body. Your heart did not beat. But here you are. Alive. So can't it be possible I am alive too?"

"It—" Fox lifted a tentative, dirt-caked hand and Stone caught it in his. "Stone?"

He could bear it no longer and threw his arms around his resurrected partner in a back-pounding hug. Blind, lame, scarred—it didn't matter. "You're alive!" He repeated the words over and over.

Finally, when the reality began to sink in, Stone let him go. "What happened? How did you get here? How did you find me?"

"I walked." Fox moved his hands lightly up Stone's arms to touch his face. "Is it really you? What are *you* doing here? Where is this?"

A bark of laughter escaped Stone. "A long story, best told when we have more time." How would he explain everything that had happened? "Come. There are introductions to be made." Stone could feel Kallista's curiosity at this distance without benefit of her magical touch.

"Wait." Fox balked, hanging back. "Stone, no. I can't. I—I have no caste." He pulled away as if unwilling to touch any longer. "I am yours to command, warrior."

Stone wanted to break something, vent his rage in destruction. Had he changed so much in only a few weeks that Fox's words made him feel so? "Can the casteless command the casteless? I was taken prisoner, friend. A prisoner has no caste."

Fox wasn't listening. His face turned away, filled with yearning, his body leaned, he took a step toward Kallista.

Stone glanced over his shoulder at his ilian—his new caste. Would they accept— "Fox?"

He still didn't seem to hear, shuffling forward in his hitching limp, hands out to ward off what he couldn't see. Stone called his name again, caught hold of him, forcing him to a straining halt. *"Fox."* Stone shook him, to no effect. Then he remembered something he'd been told.

"Torchay," he called. "Help me hold him."

At a nod from Kallista, the red-haired man dismounted and hurried over. "What is it?"

"This is my *brodir.* My partner, who was dead."

"Strong for a dead man." Torchay took hold of Fox and braced his weight against the blind man's silent struggle. "What is wrong with him?"

"Other than being blind and lame?" Stone released his grip and moved behind Fox. He brushed the matted hair aside, then had to spit on his thumb to wash away enough dirt to see his partner's neck. The mark was there.

"He's one of us," Stone said. "Marked."

Had the mark, the magic given Fox back his life? Cold slid down Stone's back and he shook the fear away. If the magic had done that, he welcomed it. "Kallista," he called out. "We have a new ilias."

With Torchay on the other side, Stone guided his partner through the increasing traffic on the street to where the others waited, still mounted. They halted well back from Kallista. "This is Fox," he said.

"Your partner who—" Kallista didn't finish.

"Died, yes. As you can see, he's not dead. Could his mark have brought him back?" Stone couldn't stop the shiver that ran through him, but it didn't interrupt his joy.

"We'll not be getting far today, obviously," Torchay said, beckoning Obed down to take over for him. "Let's take ourselves back inside for this. I think we've done enough public magic."

Stone grinned. "Why do you think I stopped him way over here?"

Kallista dismounted, tossing her reins to Torchay. "Aisse, see if we can get our room again. And order a bath."

"I'll order two," Aisse said, sliding haphazardly from her horse. "He's more than dirty."

They left the animals for the inn's stable hands to manage as Kallista led the way back to the large room they'd just vacated. She marveled that she felt so calm. They'd stumbled over yet another godmarked companion, another stranger to take in as ilias, and she felt no more than resigned. Maybe she had used up all her supply of shock and outrage. So many outrageous things had happened over the past two months, one more thing was just...one more.

Inside the room, she stripped off her gloves and turned to wait. Obed stumbled through the door and across the gap to collapse on the chair nearest her, head in his hands.

"What's wrong?" Kallista set her hand on his shoulder after only the briefest hesitation. He didn't deserve her stupid skittishness.

"Couldn't keep up with you." He touched her hand lightly and straightened, recovering from his near collapse. "A blind man with a bad leg cannot climb stairs quickly. I had to leave them behind."

Not that she questioned the wisdom of the One, but how could a man with those handicaps be anything but a hindrance to their quest? Already he was creating problems—and pushing her to blame him for things that were her own fault. She should have waited for Obed. Kallista looked up as Torchay and Stone escorted Fox through the door, Aisse behind them. "You're sure he's marked?"

"You only have to touch him to know." Stone eased his filthy friend into a chair.

Fox struggled to rise. Only Torchay's hands on his shoulders kept him in place.

Kallista rubbed her hands on her tunic against the sudden attack of nerves. "Back away, Stone. If you're not touching him, maybe you won't get caught in it this time."

"I don't mind." He gave her his wicked grin, but she could see his heart wasn't in it. He was more concerned about his friend.

"It won't hurt him," she said, her voice softer with the acknowledgment of his churning emotions. "You know that. Back away. Torchay, you too."

Reluctantly, Stone did as he was bid. Torchay ignored her, returning her gaze with a bland, know-nothing stare. "When you touch him," he said finally, "I'll let go."

Kallista sighed. "At the same time. I don't want you caught in it."

He shrugged. "If it's what they say, I doubt I'll mind it either."

"Don't fight me on this, Sergeant." She spoke crisply, making it an order. After another minute's stare, he inclined his head, accepting it.

Again she dried her hands on her tunic. Would it happen again, like with the other two, that wild rush of near-orgasmic magic? At least this time, it wouldn't be so much like having sex in public. Just in private—semiprivate. Somehow that made her even more uncomfortable.

She'd put it off long enough. With a deep breath, Kallista went down to her knees in front of Fox and clasped his grimy hand in hers.

The magic slammed into her with the same erotic rush as before, but with a difference. It felt familiar, like coming home. The magic raged, sweeping through all the hidden recesses of her soul, making this stranger part of her, except... He was already there.

She knew him. Not his face or his touch, but *him*. The magic snatched away the knowledge, erupting with its expected violence. Kallista rode the pleasure, drawing it out as long as she could, clinging to the familiar taste of this unknown man until their bodies were stretched taut with it. They could not hold it—should not hold such magic, such pleasure, but she did nevertheless. Until the magic itself shuddered.

They screamed, their bodies convulsing in a simultaneous physical release, though only their hands touched. And the magic slipped away, taking consciousness with it.

"Kallista. *Kallista.*"

The name was familiar. And the voice. Because the name was her own and the voice was Torchay's. She wanted to weep, alone inside her skin once more, lying on the floor in a tangle of limbs. "I'm—" She had to reassure him, them, but what to say? "I'm unhurt." That much was true.

"Will you no' open your eyes?" He touched her cheek and she flinched away.

"Don't." And she had to open her eyes, turn her head to see if she'd hurt him. "Not yet. Don't touch us yet. It's still too…"

His face wasn't quite blank, as if he tried to understand.

"Too much," Stone said. He crouched on the far side of Fox, a space away from him. "Too sensitive."

"Yes." Kallista let her cheek rest against the age-smoothed planks of the floor—she hadn't energy for more—and gazed into the dark brown eyes of her new ilias-to-be. They were bound already, the two of them.

"I know you." His hand rose to touch her face, and she remembered. He couldn't see. Those beautiful, melting-brown eyes didn't function.

"Yes," she said again. She caught his hand in both of hers and brought it to rest on her cheek. It was still as dirt-crusted as before, but now she didn't mind.

"But *how?* Who are you? What just happened? How—"

"Shh." Kallista pressed her fingers gently over his mouth, interrupting the stream of questions she sensed were dammed up behind his teeth. "I am Kallista. All will be explained." A smile touched her lips. "But it may take some time. How are you feeling?"

It was Fox's turn to smile. "Tolerable well. Though my trousers don't seem to have fared so well."

"Ah——" Her face burned as she recalled that moment when she had felt his climax as her own. She hadn't thought to consider the physical reality of his experience. "We can remedy that."

His hand shifted, exploring her face. "Are you beautiful, Kallista? But then, how could it matter to me?" His thumb passed across her mouth and she allowed it. "At least you have all your teeth."

He slipped his hand behind her neck to draw her forward, lips parted as if he meant to kiss her.

Suddenly panicked, Kallista set her hands against his chest and pushed. *"No."*

Fox froze, then turned his face away, into the floor. Slowly he separated himself from her, drew his legs up into his chest, wrapped his arms around them and tucked his head between his knees, creating a protective shield around his vital parts.

Damnation. What had happened to him that he would react like this? Bewildered, Kallista looked at Stone as she sat up, accepting Torchay's help to do so.

"He has no caste." Stone's voice held both anger and sorrow. "Because he can no longer be a warrior, he is nothing. In the eyes of Tibre, he should have died, but since he did not…"

Kallista stared from Stone to Fox and back again, unwilling to understand what he seemed to hint at. "Are you saying he thinks of himself as dead?"

"Worse than dead. The dead are honored. Warriors welcomed into the banquet halls of Khralsh. Fox lost that chance when he failed to die. *He has no caste.*"

Stone threw himself back onto his heels and stood to pace. He pushed back the hair that had escaped from his queue, then gathered it in his hands and pulled, as if to pull the frustration out. "How can I explain it so you'll understand? A casteless man is worth nothing—even less than a barren woman, because she at least can give comfort, cook food, create ease."

Kallista glanced at Aisse where she waited near the door. The other woman's face was set, angry, but her anger was apparently not with Stone.

"Anyone can do anything with him, to him, for any reason at all," Stone went on, "because he is *nothing*. Of course he expects abuse. You saw how slowly he drew into himself, because if you wished, you could order him to stretch himself out for your beating, to make himself more vulnerable to the blows. By Khralsh, it's a wonder he's alive."

Kallista touched the godmark on Fox's neck, exposed by his position. He flinched, a movement so small, she noticed only because she was touching him. She stroked her fingers lightly across his mark. "The mark kept him alive. It must have. Nothing else could have done it—kept him alive to suffer."

"It also brought him here, to you," Obed said. "I have felt it, the pull, stronger than any man can resist, bringing me to your side. And now, it holds me here. As it holds him."

"Aisse, is the bath here?" Kallista set her hand on the mat of filthy tangles that was Fox's hair.

"They wait with it outside."

"Have it brought in." She stroked her hand over his head, hoping it would reassure him. "You say you have no caste, Stone, but you did not react like this."

"I lost caste when I became a prisoner." Stone's voice dropped to a near whisper for Kallista's ears only, as servants entered with the tin tub and buckets of hot and cold water. "Among the other kingdoms of the northern continent, I would have been treated just as Fox was. But I was lucky. You Adarans don't have caste. And if I could somehow return to Tibre without this mark and have the language back, I might after a time—if someone didn't kill me first—be allowed to join Laborers caste."

But not Fox. His injuries made it impossible for him to ever fight as a warrior again, to even work as a laborer. How cruel their society was.

"Fox." Should she be harsh? Gentle? How would he respond best? Somewhere in between? "You must get up now and bathe."

He unwrapped himself. "As you require, woman."

Aisse held back Torchay's angry response. "He means no insult. It is all he knows. It is her rank. Woman."

"Her rank is captain," Torchay said, jaw tight. "Or naitan."

"Address me as Kallista." She took Fox's hand to steady him as he stood.

"As you require, Kallista."

Stone took Fox's other hand to lead him to where the tub had been set up before the hearth. It was summer, so no fire was laid, but it was still the largest open space in the furniture-crowded room.

When they halted, Fox could feel the steamy warmth of the promised bath rising to caress his face. He pushed a foot forward until it bumped against the tub, then drew it back, reassured now he knew its location. He reached over his head and pulled off the rag that had once been a shirt.

"I'll go down and see the baggage is unloaded." That was the man with the roughness in his voice, the one who'd been angry when Fox failed to give Kallista her proper rank. How could a woman be a captain? And what was a naitan?

"There's likely something of mine that'll fit him better," the same man said. "He's no' quite as tall as Obed."

"Aisse, go with Torchay," Kallista said close beside him.

So Torchay was the rough-voiced man and Aisse was…the other woman? The one who had explained away his unintended offense?

"See if they have a second tub for the second bath," Kallista went on. "That way he can just step from one to the other."

"Yes, I will," the other woman said, confirming Fox's guess.

Fox shoved his ruined trousers down his flanks, wobbling when he bent to push them off. A strong arm caught him, kept him from succumbing to the damn weakness in his half-healed leg. "Sorry. The leg doesn't hold like it used to."

"No wonder, with half of it missing." This man sounded so familiar, Fox found himself fighting tears. He didn't dare expose any weakness.

"Careful—if you fall and hit your head," the man went on in that cursed, much-missed voice, "you're like to scramble your brains too and we'll both us be in the suds."

Fox went very still. It couldn't be, could it? He had dreamed Stone so many times before, but never had it been real. Now, his mind seemed clear of confusion. Could this be real now? He was afraid to believe it. He wanted to reach out, to speak, but wouldn't. Not until he knew what they wanted of him. Not even then. Not until he knew the rules.

"You're very quiet." Kallista's voice held a warmth he didn't dare trust. "I'm sure there must be a hundred questions bubbling around in that clever brain."

Why would she say that? No one called him clever. Save for one. A dead man. One who haunted his waking hours now, as well as his dreams.

"He doesn't have permission to speak," that damn voice said.

"Oh for heaven's sake—" Now she sounded angry. Fox shivered, despite his struggle not to.

"In the tub with you." The man took hold of his arm, offering too-welcome support. "Step high. The water's hot, but you can stand it. There's a lot of dirt to soak off. Khralsh, you smell worse than you did after that pig dragged you through all the pens at the market when we were twelve."

How could he know that, if he were not in truth...?

"Step down now. Get in. Gods, don't tell me you've lost your wits as well as your sight."

He did as he was told, sinking his feet one by one into the hot water, his mind as unsteady as his balance. Perhaps he was dead. Though Fox had never heard tales of the casteless being ushered into death with the tooth-rattling explosion of the most powerful sexual climax a man could ever know. He forgot to hide his smile as he lowered his bony arse into the water.

"Fox." That was Kallista. Only now did he think to wonder how she knew his name. "Not only do I give you permission to speak, I require it of you. Whether it is a question or a silly comment, I expect you to say it. Beginning with what made you smile just now."

Oh damn. He startled as something plunged into the water behind him.

"I'm just wetting the soap," she said. "Would you rather I wash you, or one of the men?"

She expected him to speak, but did the men? What was their caste, their rank? Who gave the orders? Fox opened his mouth but couldn't force out any sound.

"Kallista is the captain," the man said, his voice gentle. "She commands us all. I know it's impossible to believe, but it's true."

"I can wash myself," Fox said very quietly. He did not know what would give least offense.

"I know." Kallista used a cloth to splash water onto his shoulders. "But can you tell when all the dirt is gone?"

He could only hunch his shoulders at her teasing truth and submit to her washing. What *did* she want of him? What use could he be to her?

"Stone, dip some water to pour over his head. Let's rinse as much of the dirt as we can before we use the soap on his hair."

Fox caught his breath. "*Am* I dead?"

The man laughed. "No more than I, *brodir*." He poured the water over Fox's head.

When he shook it away, Fox spoke. "If it is you, Stone, then I must be dead. We're both dead. But——" Nothing made sense. If he could see, maybe it would help. "Where are we?"

"Not dead, Fox. I swear it." The man gripped his forearm exactly the way Stone would have, making one of his everlasting oaths. "Do I feel like one of the dead? We're deep inside Adara. You spoke to me on the street. Don't you remember?" He let go and poured more water over Fox.

"I thought I dreamed it," Fox admitted. "The last weeks, since I left the camp, it's all been like a dream."

"No more dreaming. No nightmares. This is the reality. We lived, Fox, you and I. Just as we asked of Khralsh. We're the only two who lived, out of all the Tibrans inside the city when the dark magic struck, out of all those in the breach, out of all those on the battlefield below. We lived."

Kallista scrubbed a cloth down Fox's back hard enough to make him wince. Her bare hand followed it, smoothing away the pain with a caress. Did she mean it as one?

"You swore an oath?" She dipped the cloth in the water and squeezed it out over his back, then scrubbed again.

"Yes." Stone answered for them both. "We swore to Khralsh and gave our lives into his hands."

"And so, when all the others died, the One accepted the lives you offered and bound us together for Her purposes." Kallista tipped Fox's chin up and washed his neck. "And that is how you lived."

CHAPTER TWENTY-TWO

"What use can I be to any purpose, as I am?" Fox struggled to keep his voice level and matter-of-fact, but even he could hear the despair in it.

"You're godmarked. You carry magic inside you," Kallista said. "Magic that I as a godstruck naitan can use."

There was that word again. "Naitan—what is that?"

They told him. While Kallista washed his face, ears and arms, Stone told of his own capture and journey to the Adaran capital. While she washed his feet and legs, Stone told of his introduction to Kallista.

"Here." Kallista draped the washing cloth over Fox's hand and placed the soap in his other. "Wash the rest. I'll go see what's become of that other bath."

After wrapping the soap in the cloth to have one hand free for balance, Fox stood to do as he'd been told.

Stone took Fox's elbow to steady him. "What laid your leg open like that?"

"Don't know. Don't remember." Fox dropped the soap in the tub and began to carefully wash the half-healed wound. "They must have thought I'd die of it, so it didn't get stitched. It's healed badly."

"And lamed you in the process." Stone paused.

Fox could almost feel Stone's discomfort like a tangible thing. Why?

"Did it also—"

Fox moved on to wash other tender parts. When Stone didn't finish his question, he prodded. "Also what?"

"Stars, Fox. If I had a woman washing me like you just did, I'd be standing straight up ready for action. I am just from watching her. Did it— Can you still—"

The laughter bubbled up from nowhere, demanding Fox throw his head back and let it fly. He laughed so hard, he lost his balance and fell, slipping through two sets of masculine arms to splash half the cooling water out of the tub.

"Are you hurt?" Kallista called from across the room. "What happened?"

"I laughed too hard." Fox struggled to get his feet under him again. "I'm fine."

"Good. You'll have to get out of the tub and wait while they change the bath. They've only the one tub."

"I fail to see what's so funny about...that," Stone hissed between his teeth. Two men—Stone and one other—hauled Fox to his feet so fast he almost lost balance again.

"Careful." Fox clutched Stone's close-fitting tunic until he felt steady. "And no matter how you might brag, Stone, you would not be standing straight if you'd only just spent everything you had saved. Who's this?" He patted the other man's chest. "Torchay come back with fresh trousers?"

"I am Obed im-Shakiri, ilias to the Chosen One." The man's voice was deep, dark, oddly accented.

"Chosen—" Confusion struck Fox again as he stepped out of the tub. Would he ever understand?

"He means Kallista." Stone draped a towel over Fox's shoulders and handed him another to wrap around his waist. "Don't be too impressed by the ilias thing. We're all iliasti. You too, now, mostly. What do you mean, 'spent all you'd saved'? You mean, just now? When you and Kallista—" Stone fell into silence for a few moments, then whispered a worshipful "Khralsh."

Fox let the men guide him away from the tub, out of the way of laborers working to empty and refill it, and sat in the chair they brought him to. "But—you said when you and Kallista first touched, it was the same as with me."

"Obviously not," Stone said. "It felt good, but not *that* good. It wasn't like that with Obed either."

"How do you know? Obed—you have this mark? Is Stone right?"

"I am privileged to bear the mark of the One, and Stone speaks truth. We did not…spend when this first joining happened."

"We. You mean you and Kallista, or—" Fox collected himself. "Or you and Stone? Or—"

"Wait a minute," Stone interrupted. "Are you saying that *Kallista* did—that she— Too? You brought her *too*?"

"Brought me where?" Kallista said from close by. She moved too quietly. Or maybe Stone made too much noise.

"To paradise," Fox said without thinking.

"To climax," Stone interpreted. "Did he? Just now?"

"It was the magic." Kallista's voice sounded somehow strangled.

Fox heard her retreat and cursed his too-quick wit and the mouth that let it out. Then Stone laughed and the knot in his belly relaxed.

"Damn, Fox, you have got to teach me how to do that." Stone

paused, apparently watching Kallista, for he said, "Stars, she's pretty when she blushes."

"She is beautiful always," Obed said.

And Fox couldn't see it, had no inkling how beautiful she was save the softness of her cheek and the gentleness of her hands on his body. At least he had that. "Stone, how do you know what happened when Obed and Kallista first...touched?"

"Because he didn't touch Kallista. I blocked him, he touched me, and all his magic went through me to get to her. And that's how I know what didn't happen."

Now Fox breathed an awed oath. "So why now? Why with me?"

"Don't know, *brodir*. Goddess knows your skill with women can't be the cause. You haven't got any."

"Chosen." Obed's word was a mere breath, but Fox heard it, turned his face to her presence.

"Maybe it happened because the magic knew me," she said, perching on the arm of the chair where Fox sat. "It was different with Fox. I knew him."

"Do you not know me?" Obed asked.

"I know you now. But then, when we first met—don't you remember that feeling of something shifting? As if you had to be...adjusted. Made to fit. There was none of that with Fox. I knew him already."

"What of Stone?" Obed said. "Did you know him?"

Kallista leaned into Fox, stretched her arm along the back of the chair. He scarcely dared to breathe. "I don't—" she began. "It's hard to remember. That was the first time. I wasn't expecting it. But—I don't remember that shift, that adjustment."

"What do you think it means?" Torchay's raspy tenor was back. "Should you ask Belandra?"

"She doesn't know," Kallista replied while Stone quietly explained to Fox who Belandra was. "She and her ilian were marked at virtually the same time and place. They already knew each other, some of them already pledged to one another. I asked, after Obed. She knew that sometimes the marked were separated and would be drawn together, but she knew nothing of the—explosion when we first touched."

"Do you want to know what *I* think it means?" Stone spoke slowly as if uncertain of his reception.

"Yes." Kallista's finger drawing designs on the back of his neck made Fox shiver.

"I think it's because we were there at the beginning, you and me and Fox. We were all of us together in the city when the God marked us. You were on the wall above the breach, weren't you." Stone didn't ask a question.

"I was."

"When I came to consciousness, I was in the breach. When I found Fox, he was in the breach. At the foot of the ladder as if he'd started to climb. We were there. Trying to reach you. Already bound."

Fox shivered again, this time with the weight of Stone's words.

"The bath is ready." The other woman, Aisse, spoke from a space away—near the tub, perhaps.

By the time the women deemed him sufficiently clean, Fox had heard all of Stone's story, all of Obed's, and most of what had happened since. Stone explained the rules to be followed, and did his best to explain ilian, but Fox still couldn't grasp the concept. He would follow his own rule—that of the casteless blind: Do whatever you're told when you're told, to the best of your ability, and avoid giving offense.

He believed Stone when he promised that no one would beat him without cause, but how could he be allowed to refuse anything? He would do whatever was necessary to stay with this ilian. He had his *brodir* back, alive again. That was part of his reason. But more—Kallista held him.

She might be woman, but she was also captain and naitan. He was nothing. Less than that. He didn't understand most of what they'd told him. But he didn't have to. He was hers.

Clean, dressed in Torchay's extra summer tunic and a pair of Obed's loose trousers, his hair drying into red-gold curls, Fox proved almost more handsome than his partner, despite the just-healed scar cutting down one side of his face. The scar only made him look more masculine. Acknowledging the thought as a bit blasphemous, Kallista still had to credit the One with excellent taste in male beauty.

His face was broad in the middle, narrowing a bit at the chin, with a jutting blade of a nose that rivaled Torchay's. His eyebrows and lashes were thick but fair, their color blending in to the gold of his skin. He was too thin but his frame promised strength once he regained the weight he'd lost. The injury that had lamed him was still raw and red, laid open from hip to knee. It hurt her to see it, but she thought something could still be done to correct the problems caused by lack of treatment.

Had her companions been given her as a test or a gift? *What* kind of test? What kind of gift? Why couldn't the One speak in plain language rather than obscure symbols and images?

When Fox finished the light meal Aisse had delivered, Kallista sat at the table opposite him. "How are you feeling?"

He folded his hands together atop the table, gripping tight when his fingers shook. "Fine. Wonderful."

"Truth?"

"Yes, of course, truth." He took a deep breath and let it out. "I am possibly a bit…overwhelmed as well."

She nodded, then realized he couldn't see her. "Ah," she said. She stretched her hand across the table and laid it over his clasped ones. "Fox, I'd like you to tell me what happened to you after that day in Ukiny. I won't force you if you can't bring yourself to talk about it, but I think it's important."

"What do you want to know?" He spoke into her pause. "I don't remember that day. I don't remember anything until I—"

"Wait. Do you mind the others hearing, or would you rather send them away? Or would you rather tell Stone instead of me?"

He jerked, his head beginning to shake no, then seemed to force himself into stillness. "However you wish it, Kallista."

She separated his hands, taking one into hers and curling his fingers around her palm with her other hand. "I want to know what *you* wish. Do you want me to go, or stay?" She didn't need another worshipper. She already had Obed to deal with.

"Stay," he said. "Please."

"I will then. What do you remember?"

"Pain. And thirst. One of the women giving me water. I couldn't understand anything—their words were gibberish. I think maybe one of the surgeons tried to get her to stop, but she gave me water anyway. I was lying with the dead and dying. They expected me to die."

"Who was it? The woman, do you know?" Aisse had come close while Fox was speaking. His nostrils flared as if he could smell her presence.

"Piheko. She made me understand her name later, in the women's quarters."

"She has a kind heart." Aisse moved away again as Fox turned his surprised face to Kallista.

"Aisse is Tibran," she said. "She ran away. Now she's ilias. You were in the women's quarters?"

"Not at first. Piheko fed me till I could walk again. No one paid me any attention till then—I know because they left me alone— but when I could rise from my pallet and walk, I was noticed. They saw my blindness when I tripped and fell. They spoke and I could not understand what they said. That was the day I lost my caste."

He fell silent, tears welling from his sightless eyes. Kallista squeezed his hand. She didn't know what else to do.

"After they— Afterward, someone carried me to the women's quarters and left me there. The women wouldn't let me in but Piheko still fed me. She gave me a dress to wear and half of an old blanket so I had some cover." His voice was flat, emotionless, as if he told of what happened to someone else, but the tears still flowed.

"A dress tunic?" Kallista was confused.

"Women's clothing," Aisse said. "Only for women. A dress is like a dress tunic, but never with trousers or leggings. So to do sex, is only required to lift the skirt."

"Ah." She understood now. In a caste system where women have little value, clothing a man in something only women wore would show contempt for him.

"While I healed again," Fox said, "I...served. I was beast of burden for the women—blind, deaf, dumb—an idiot. Or I was their pleasure toy. The laborers played games. They liked to trip me, then—"

"Stop it." Stone's chair clattered to the floor as he jumped to his feet. "Do you have to know every damn bloody detail, humiliate him again with the telling? Leave him be!" He stood there another moment, breathing hard, making and unmaking fists, then he spun and slammed out of the room.

The telling seemed to hurt Stone more than it bothered Fox who had lived it. But Fox had been stripped of all pride and will. Stone hadn't. Worried, Kallista weighed her options, horribly few. She could sense Stone's turmoil and wanted someone nearby. "Aisse, go after him. Watch, but from a distance."

Aisse scowled a moment, then shrugged, nodded and slipped from the room.

Kallista looked back at Fox who clung to her hand now with both of his. "When did you leave?" she asked. "How?"

"I don't...exactly know. I remember a need to find some-thing—you, I think—a need so strong it hurt. One day I woke up on the edge of camp. No one cared if I left, so I kept going. I could understand speech, once I left. Folk directed me to the temples, where I was given a shirt, trousers, food. The need pushed me, refused to let me quit, showed me the path when it should have been impossible."

"Do you still feel it? That need?"

"No." He lifted his face for all the world as if he could see her. "I found you. What else do I need?"

Oh, she did not need the weight of this responsibility, did not need to be the center of anyone else's universe. But she had of-fered, the One had accepted, and she could not lay the burden down again until their task was done.

"Thank you for telling us, Fox." Kallista patted his hand and gently disengaged. "We needed to know what kind of healing you might require."

Fox sat up straight, surprise in his expression. Kallista waited for him to ask, to say anything, and when he did not, she sighed. "There may be nothing a healer naitan can do for you, aside from your leg. I know one here in Turysh who can work wonders, even half-healed as it is. Perhaps there is one who can help your sight. We should at least ask what is possible." And perhaps a healer could help mend his broken soul.

It was afternoon before a knock at the door announced the ar-rival of the healer. Aisse answered it and the tall, pale, dark-haired naitan smiled a greeting. As she entered, she looked up at the others in the room and her smile faded.

"Hello, Mother." Kallista tried to smile, but didn't think she succeeded any better than her birth mother.

"Had you planned to let any of us know you were in town?" Irysta set her box of herbals and medicines on the table. "Does anyone actually need a healer or is this one of your games?"

Obed stiffened at the caustic words, but Kallista stilled him with a gesture. She moved to stand behind Fox, resting her hands on his shoulders. "No game, Mother Irysta. Fox was injured in Ukiny just before I last came through Turysh. The wound has healed badly, possibly been reopened and healed again. I ask that you do what you can for him."

Irysta glanced at the others in the room, her eyes lingering briefly on Fox. "Your sedili informed me that you had finally joined an ilian. Your other parents were disappointed that you didn't see fit to have the wedding at home. I told them it was only one more example of your lack of proper family feeling. How was he injured?"

"I don't remember," Fox answered for himself.

Kallista was grateful. She would likely have included some bitter sniping about her mother setting aside her prejudice against soldiers. Irysta would never refuse treatment to anyone, regardless of how an injury occurred, but she would make her disapproval apparent.

"I don't need an audience for this." Irysta waved the others out of the room. "Where is your injury, Fox?"

"On my thigh."

Irysta gestured him toward the bed, opening her box while the three who could leave did so.

Kallista helped Fox to his feet and guided him to the bed. "I assume you want him to remove his trousers before he lies down."

"I can scarcely examine him through them." Irysta looked up. "Why are you still here?"

"Because if I leave, Fox will go into convulsions, and if Obed leaves, he will." Kallista put up her hand to forestall her mother's protests. "I'm sure you don't want to force us to demonstrate. I'm told it's rather painful. Just mark it down as another peculiarity of my unfortunate magic, all right?"

Irysta sniffed, disapproving as always, and turned to her patient.

Kallista moved to stand near Obed. He touched the back of her arm lightly, and when she didn't move away, slid his hand down to clasp hers. Always, whenever she came close enough, he would touch her as much and as long as she would allow it. Not long, most times. But at this moment, she welcomed his touch. She found his unquestioning devotion a comfort.

"This wound looks to have been made by something long and sharp. Like a sword," Irysta said, probing it. "Are you a soldier?"

"I was a warrior once, but no more." Fox spoke through gritted teeth, as if in pain, and Kallista reached for his magic.

Their link was new, forged afresh just this morning since that first terrible day. She could sense only his presence, and that vaguely. Not like Stone's heart beating with hers, or the touch of more than Obed's hand. Kallista gently disengaged from Obed and crossed the room to the foot of the bed. Reaching over the footboard, she wrapped her hand around Fox's ankle. She called a thread of magic to soothe his pain, hoping it would do as she asked. Through the connection of their touch, she could feel the easing take hold.

"Karyl told us your ilian was four strong," Irysta said absently, mind on her own magic as she bent over Fox's wound. "Not six."

How to answer that? She had sent a separate message to Mother Dardra asking her to preside over the addition of Fox to their ilian. She *ought* to invite the whole family, but that would lead to questions and complications and…

"Obed joined us just over a week ago," Kallista found herself saying. "And I would be honored to have you as witness when Fox joins us this evening."

That brought Irysta's head snapping around. She stared at Kallista a long moment, suspicion in her eyes, then turned back to her patient. "For one who resisted family life for so long, you've taken to it with sudden enthusiasm."

"When the One forms the ilian, who are we to deny it?"

"You do understand that your iliasti will expect you to stop indulging yourself with your troops. They'll expect you to be faithful."

Kallista sighed. Irysta would believe what she wished and no amount of protest or explanation would change her mind. "That's not going to be a problem."

Irysta glanced from Fox to Obed behind her then gave her daughter a sour look. "I don't suppose it would be. Still, I had hoped I instilled enough discrimination in you that you wouldn't stoop to snatching beggars off the street."

Kallista swallowed down her anger, leaving it to churn in her gut. "How is Fox? Can you help him?"

"I will not be able to restore complete mobility without surgery, because healing is so advanced."

"How long would it take him to recover? When would he be able to travel?"

"By boat? I'd say six—"

"Horseback," Kallista interrupted.

Irysta frowned. "That's very strenuous. Hard on the legs. No sooner than ten weeks—ninety days—at minimum. More rest would be better."

In ninety days, her pregnancy would certainly be showing. She couldn't afford to wait, unless there was no other choice. "Can you do anything for him now, without the surgery? If he waits, will it make a difference? Can you still help him later?"

"Yes, of course I can help him now. I can restore much of the strength and some flexibility. If he waits longer, I may not be able to recover his complete mobility. It could well make a difference. But then I expect no better from you than to put your own wishes ahead of—"

"How much difference? Between one hundred percent recovery now against fifty percent later?"

"No, not so much." Irysta pursed her lips, thinking. "I would estimate surgery now would restore perhaps ninety to ninety-five percent mobility, while waiting would be...perhaps around eighty percent. Possibly better, but there is no guarantee of that. Without surgery, I might be able to improve his mobility to half of what it was."

Kallista looked at Fox, patted his foot to be sure she had his attention. "What do you want to do?"

"As you require, naitan," he said, eyes pointed toward the ceiling. "Stone has told me of your mission."

"Mission?" Irysta put thirty-four years of disapproval into that one word.

"Orders from the Reinine."

"And you're taking your ilian?" Disapproval *and* shock. Irysta was improving her nonverbal skills.

"They have orders as well." Kallista made her decision. They couldn't afford the time for such a small difference in healing. "Do what you can for him now. We'll do the surgery when we get back."

Now something like smug disappointment joined the other emotions in Irysta's voice and on her face, as if the decision made her unhappy, but she expected no better. "I'll be here."

She gathered a handful of herbs and burned them in the lamp's flame. "Fox, did you lose your vision when you were injured?"

The smoke mixed with her magic, sending him drifting. "Yes," he murmured.

Kallista pulled her own magic back, afraid of interfering with her mother's activity, but somehow he clung, refusing to let her go. She stood in a metaphysical corner of Fox's body, trying to pretend she wasn't there as she watched how her mother hurried the natural healing along, knitting together the severed muscle as much as possible.

It was interesting. Briefly, Kallista wondered if she might be able to do something of the sort now. She had West magic as well as North. Why not East? But she was a soldier, not a healer. Her duty lay elsewhere.

Finally Irysta straightened and dismissed her magic. Kallista could see what she had done, could see where just a bit more binding might—but she didn't know anatomy, didn't trust her own magic, so she left it as it was done. "Will you be at the ilian ceremony, Mother Irysta? You never did say."

"There is a healer at Northside Temple who might be able to do something about his vision."

"She's already been sent for. And you still haven't said if you will come."

Irysta busied herself with her box, arranging the containers inside just so. "Are you certain you want me there?"

"Of course I do. If you want to be there, and if you can keep from—I know I disappoint you. I'm used to it. I've felt your disapproval all my life."

Irysta spoke into the pause. "I don't—I never—"

"Don't bother denying it," Kallista interrupted. "We both know the truth. Insult me all you want. But leave my iliasti out of it. Fox is a soldier, separated by war and injuries from his...sedil, Stone, one of the original four in our ilian. Now Fox has found us again. He is no beggar from the street and he is the brother of my ilias. How can we not marry him too?"

This far from the war, the Tibrans could pass as Adarans from a distant prinsipality, and she would not explain the marking by the One. It would take too long and might call attention. The less attention they drew, the better.

"I am not trying to insult you, Kallista," her mother said with tight-lipped calm. "Or your iliasti. I am merely trying to instruct you on proper behavior—"

"And insulting us by assuming we aren't already behaving that way. Look—are you coming or not? It's up to you. I don't care either way."

"If you don't care about your own birth mother—"

"That's not what I said," Kallista interrupted again, surprised she hadn't already lost her temper and stormed out. "I invited you because you are my mother and I'd like to have you there. But if you can't bring yourself to attend, it's not going to ruin my life. It won't even ruin my day. If you can't be happy for us, that's your problem, not mine."

Where had that understanding come from and why had it taken so long to figure it out? She lifted her hand from Fox's ankle and stared at it. Was it the magic? Or was it that she had an ilian of her own now? That would naturally make her mother's opinions less important than any of theirs. Obed's unconditional approval apparently had its good points.

"The ceremony will be after Evensong at Northside Temple, unless Fox shouldn't be standing then."

"No, no. Let him rest until then, but he'll be fine. You *will* bring him back for the surgery once this…mission of yours is completed." Irysta snapped her box closed and fastened it.

"Yes, Mother, I promise." Kallista moved to the center of the room and gestured for Obed to open the door. "Let me introduce you to the rest of my ilian."

Torchay, waiting just outside, signaled to Stone and Aisse who were downstairs in the public room with the other healer. Introductions were made and Irysta sent on her way without ever saying whether she would come to the evening's ceremony.

The vision specialist determined that nothing organic seemed to be wrong with Fox's eyes. He simply could not see. She agreed that likely it was a result of the magic that had ended the assault on Ukiny, but since no one had done such magic in so many years, she didn't know what might reverse it. She would investigate and with luck know more when they returned for the repair to Fox's leg.

The wedding ceremony that night was utterly unlike the previous two. Mother Dardra, allied with Kallista's blood sisters, had gathered not only the entire family, but all Kallista's childhood friends available. Even Mother Irysta came. The joining, with Obed again providing the bands from his seemingly inexhaustible stock of jewelry, was both solemn and joyous. Once more the magic flared at the end of the ceremony, binding the six of them together. The party afterward spilled out of the inn's spacious public rooms into the streets.

CHAPTER TWENTY-THREE

Their ilian stayed bunched together, moving in a group like a flock of birds, now this one leading or that one dropping behind a pace, but always together. Kallista couldn't move too far from Obed or Fox, and Stone wouldn't leave his resurrected partner. Similarly, Torchay would not leave Kallista's side and Aisse hovered near Torchay, obviously uncomfortable in the bawdy atmosphere of a wedding celebration.

Eventually, they withdrew from the party. The guests who still lingered were too drunk or too intent on their own pleasure to notice. In the room, the ilian was faced with new decisions about sleeping arrangements. Everyone's eyes turned to Kallista, save for Aisse, who slept alone in her own corner, and Fox, whose eyes didn't function.

The weight of the day descended on Kallista in an instant and she glowered back at the men. She was too tired for this. "I'm going to sleep," she announced. "In that bed. The rest of you can sort yourselves out."

They sorted themselves into the same bed with her, all four of them. It made for a tight fit, but they managed without anyone blacking an eye with a flying elbow or getting squashed in the middle.

The first day out of Turysh was hard on everyone, save Obed who hadn't had as much to drink, and Torchay who never seemed to feel the effects of too much wine. They paced themselves to Fox's stamina, which improved gradually with sufficient rest and plentiful food.

Four days out, Kallista called an early halt. It was time to see how much more trouble she would have controlling three men's magic than two.

She sent Torchay and Aisse ahead with the animals, as she didn't want to risk maiming such fine beasts, instructing them to ride until they could no longer be seen. Out here on the subtle undulations of the Adaran plains, they would be miles away before that occurred. Torchay would return in an hour.

Kallista turned her back on her iliasti, trying to open herself to the beauty around her. The plains stretched in all directions, an endless flow of subtle greens this early in the summer while rains still fell. To the west, she could see the purple smudge on the horizon of the Shieldback Mountains, and farther north, swinging closer beyond the Heldring Gap, the Okreti di Vos Range—the arms of God in the old language. The sky curved a smooth unbroken blue overhead. She closed her eyes, searching for that cool, distant sense of the land, of permanence and endurance.

The mountains gave her strength. Through all the lonely years since her magic had burst forth, she had tried to make herself like the mountains, aloof, bearing up under any burden. She had never been so burdened as she was now. She needed that strength, that distance. So she reached out—and found life.

All around her, life swarmed. Quail and grouse, swallows, sparrows, larks, rabbits, lizards, snakes, antelope, boar, mustangs, wolves, foxes and dingoes. Predators and prey. Thousands of creatures living their lives, eating, sleeping, mating, dying. Thousands of hearts beating, demanding she notice, demanding she care.

No, not thousands. Three. Three hearts beating in time with hers, three lives she could not hide from. She couldn't live like this. These men were strangers. She didn't know them, couldn't care about them, didn't want to. The mountains knew how to endure. Again she reached out, desperate for that cool remoteness, that empty peace.

Again, her reach fell short, disturbed by the men clustered near her. "Give me space," she cried, moving to the end of the magical tether.

Empty peace? That wasn't right? Peace was just...peace. She wanted to move beyond that boundary of magic, to step out and let them fall and prove they had no hold on her, that she didn't care what they suffered. But she couldn't.

They disturbed her peace, cut it to ribbons and left it lying in shreds at her feet. She wanted it back, wanted her life the way it was. But when it was that way, she'd wanted something different. She wanted an ilian—which she now had. She wanted a child— she had that too. So why then was she now whining? Because it hadn't happened the way she dreamed it would?

Or because she had to give up her safe mountains and come down onto the dangerous plains to live?

"Kallista?" Stone spoke. "They're out of sight now. They have been for some time."

She set aside her disturbing thoughts and turned to her marked iliasti with a smile. "Then we should begin. We only have an hour before they return."

Stone bowed, accepting her gloves, then stood apart as he had since Obed's arrival. Kallista took her dark ilias's hand and waited for the magic to settle. She'd learned that hurrying the process made it rebel.

"Hold out your hand, Fox," she said, turning to him.

He jumped as if touched by one of her sparks when she clasped his hand in hers, and the magic rumbled through her, twining with Obed's to make her moan. This time, it seemed to calm more quickly, and she reached through the ever-present link to call Stone's magic.

She could taste all three of them in the magic, braided together but still distinct; dark and rich, light and joyous, steady and sweet. She had no free hands left, but perhaps that didn't matter. The magic hummed inside her, quiet, true. For once obedient to her commands. It took the shape she gave it and waited to be released rather than slipping willfully away.

Kallista shaped the scythe in her hands, ordering it to slay nothing with a heart that beat. The feel of all those hearts still lingered. She made the scythe small, only just larger than the space where they stood. She kissed it with mental lips, wished it well, and let it go.

An instant later, a perfect circle of grass and wildflowers around the spot where they stood lay crisp and blackened under their feet. Dead.

Kallista laughed aloud. For the first time since Stone found her, the magic had done exactly what she wanted it to do. No more and no less.

"What happened?" Fox clung to her hand. "Do I smell smoke?"

"It worked." On impulse, she stretched up and kissed his cheek, then kissed Obed's to be fair. "It actually worked for once. Without a fight."

"Don't forget me." Stone came forward to claim a kiss for himself, which she granted without thought.

"I want to do it again. Maybe that was a fluke." She waved Stone back to his place.

"A little hard on the vegetation, isn't it?" he said, retreating.

"It'll grow back. We'll pick a new spot." She walked out of the circle of dead grass, dragging Fox and Obed by the hand until they stood in pristine green. Once more, she called magic, braided and shaped it, then sent it out. Again, the grass blackened and died in less time than it took to draw breath. Kallista laughed, triumphant.

"More kisses?" Stone suggested with his usual cheerful leer.

Why not? She shared them out as before, sweet, playful, seductive.

"What next?" Stone backed away.

Kallista blinked at him a moment. "I haven't a clue. It's been such a struggle to make the magic do *anything*, I hadn't thought beyond controlling it. Learning how to do again what I did that first time it woke."

"Are you sure that you have?" Obed said.

"I don't want to destroy everything within a thousand paces just to test it, but I am confident that the scythe will do whatever I ask."

"Why?" Stone asked. "I mean, why now? What's the difference? Fox?"

Kallista looked up at the blind man, considering. "Possibly." She plucked his magic from the others, testing it with unknown senses. "Probably. His magic contains...order."

"Might have known," Stone muttered. "He's always going on about rules."

"If his magic holds order, what is in the magic I carry?" Obed asked.

Did men think in any terms other than competition? But it was a valid question and the answer might be a good thing to know.

Kallista released the Fox magic and filtered Obed's out. "It feels dark," she said, sipping at it. "Hidden depths behind a wall of illusion—hidden even from yourself? There is…truth in your magic. Or perhaps reality. But it's tucked away deep. As if you're afraid of it."

"I fear nothing." Obed's hand jerked as if he meant to pull away, but he didn't.

"Then you're a fool," Fox said, surprising them all. "Or a man who's never stood in the dark waiting for the cannonade to end so the battle can begin."

"Truth is a frightening thing." Kallista was beginning to see that for herself, much as she would like to deny it.

"What about my magic?" Stone deflected the tension. "Fox has order, Obed has truth. What do I have?"

"Joy," Kallista responded instantly.

Stone laughed. "Joy? What use is that? How will joy defeat demons?"

"How will truth or order?" She shrugged, considering his question. "I have to admit, when it was only the two of us working together, I often thought your magic was having entirely too much fun. I'd will it to do something and it would run away laughing and do what it wanted. Which might be what I asked or might not."

"Perhaps these things are not intended specifically for defeating demons, but for the magic," Fox said. "The order itself doesn't do anything but allow Kallista to control the magic, if her guess is correct."

"It seems to me that it might be a good thing if the magic…enjoyed what it did." Kallista frowned. "Does that make sense? It seems somehow wrong for a thing to enjoy killing."

"But isn't there a kind of joy in doing what you were meant to do?" Fox tightened his grip on her hand.

"It's just magic, not a person," Obed protested. "It's a tool."

"The Heldring swords are tools," Kallista said. "But you can't deny there's a kind of joy about them when they're used as they were meant."

"What about truth?" he asked. "What can it contribute?"

"Truth is always good. How can you fight a battle without knowing what you are fighting against? Where the enemy is disposed and how many they are. It's even more important to know your own strengths and weaknesses." She looked from one man to the other, weighing everything she had just learned. "I'm thinking it's very likely that we four were chosen because of the different strengths we bring to the whole. What one lacks, another provides."

She paused as a thought struck her. "I'll tell you what joy does for the magic. It makes it eager and quick. That's why it was so hard to control, because it moved like quicksilver, so eager to go and do, it wouldn't wait for me to tell it *what* to do. Speed is a good thing, now that there's a little order to hold it back until the shaping is done."

"We four." Stone pointed at each of the men. "Truth. Order. Joy." He grimaced as he indicated himself, apparently not pleased with his own designation. Then he pointed at Kallista. "What's your contribution?"

"Will," Obed said before anyone else could react. "It's her will that gives the magic its shape and direction. Without it, there is nothing."

"See?" Kallista grinned. "Truth. Important stuff." She rotated her shoulders. Sleeping on the ground, even in the middle of a pile of men, made her stiff. "Speaking of direction, I'm wondering if I can aim this magic."

She adjusted her increasingly sweaty grip on the hands she held and called the magic. This time, she shaped and restricted it as before, but when she let it go, she *pushed* it toward Stone. When Kallista opened her eyes—she didn't remember closing them—

she saw a wedge of blackened vegetation widening a short distance beyond Stone before it faded into green. Though she stood in one of the already dead circles, it was easy to see that she stood at the apex of the wedge.

"That's nice to know." She let go of the men to dry her hands. "And when I aim it, it goes farther in that direction."

"Does this magic only kill?" Obed asked.

"Old records say it may be able to put people to sleep or veil their vision."

"Ah, so that's what happened." Fox smiled as if making a joke, but Kallista didn't think he was so amused.

She caught his hand. "If it is, maybe we can fix it." She demanded Obed's hand and when he gave it, called the magic.

This time, she turned it inside out, asking that it restore what had been taken away.

"Are you sure?" Stone murmured. "Don't make it worse."

"No." She restricted the magic, hemmed it in with rules, forbade it to do harm.

"Try," Fox said. "I don't care what happens to me."

"I do. I need your magic." Whispering a prayer, Kallista gave her shaping a gentle *push* toward Fox.

He cried out as the magic shook him, stumbling back, breaking her grip on his hand.

Stone rushed forward to steady him. "What is it? Are you all right?"

"I'm—for a second I saw...I *saw*." Fox stretched a hand toward Kallista. "Dark hair and eyes like the evening sky?"

"Yes," Stone whispered.

Kallista clasped Fox's outstretched hand, felt his shiver as the magic stirred. He whispered an oath, shuddering again.

"Can you see?" She tried to see through the magic, through his eyes, releasing Obed in case that might help her focus better. It didn't.

"No." He shook his head, but didn't sound despairing. *"No,"* he said again, his voice strange.

"I hear a 'but' after that 'no,'" Stone said. "What is it?"

Fox shook Stone's hand from his arm. "Move away. Go quietly—or as quiet as you can, given you move like a constipated plow horse."

Worry shimmered on Stone's face, nevertheless he did as his partner, now ilias, bid, backing away. Kallista could sense no fear through her link with Fox, perhaps more confusion and curiosity.

"You cannot see," she said, just to be sure.

"No, but—"

"I knew there'd be a 'but,'" Stone muttered when Fox fell silent.

"Now you've gone and ruined it," Fox complained. "Shut your bloody hole and move somewhere else."

"What's going on?" Kallista kept her voice quiet.

"I can't see. Everything is as dark as before, veiled, like dusk. But—" Fox turned, his head up. "Obed is there." He pointed at their black-haired ilias. "And Stone has moved—"

He pointed at Stone walking in a circle about them, his finger following unerringly. "Stone is there."

"Your other senses have compensated?" She had heard of it happening.

"I don't think so." Fox frowned. "I can hear them, of course. And smell. That scent Obed wears is distinctive, and if Stone doesn't bathe soon, he'll frighten the horses. But this is something else. I just...know."

"What about now?" Kallista released his hand. "Do you still *know?*"

Fox turned his head, eyes open as if he could see. "It's muted," he said. "But still there."

She touched his elbow, startling him, and slid her hand down his bare forearm to clasp hands again. "Let's see what else you can do. One of you two—" She gestured at Stone and Obed. "Rush us. Fox, try to block him."

The men exchanged glances before Stone waved Obed back. He charged his partner. Fox waited motionless until the last moment, then shouldered Kallista aside, seized Stone's arm as he thundered past and flipped him onto his back. Then he ducked under Obed's near-simultaneous charge. Obed lost his balance, fell half across Fox, and the blind man straightened, throwing Obed atop Stone.

"Bravo!" Kallista laughed. "Torchay will be thrilled to know you can defend yourself."

"I wouldn't go that far," Fox protested. "I knew they were coming."

"And you were handicapped by having to hold on to me. A few more weeks, when I can call your magic without having to touch you, and maybe you won't need touch for this new sense to be clear. We can hope."

Fox turned his face away, but left his hand in her grasp, yielding to her. Emotions were harder to read through the link than the magic itself, or even the body, but Kallista knew he refused to hope.

"So what else can you make the magic do?" Stone asked, dusting grass and ash off himself as he stood.

"I'd like to see what kind of shield I can make, now I've got a way to make the magic behave." Kallista noticed Obed still sitting on the ground, his scowl fixed on Fox's hand clasped in hers, and she stifled a sigh.

Would he be less jealous if she had sex with him, or more? Jealousy had no place within an ilian, but it sometimes happened. And Obed was neither Adaran nor Tibran, but something else entirely. Who knew what his understanding was?

She offered her hand to assist him to his feet and kept her hold when he was upright, but she didn't call magic.

"Well?" Stone said. "Are we making a shield?"

"Not now. I'm tired, and I want the others here to practice the defensive magic. How will I know if I've done it right without someone to test it?"

"One of us could——" Stone broke off as she shook her head.

"I need all three of you." She squeezed the hands she held then let go to pat Stone's face. "If I build the shield with only two, who knows what might go wrong? Torchay will be back soon with the horses. We can wait."

She reached for the gloves in Stone's belt, but he slipped out of her reach.

"In that case," he said with a gleam in his eye Kallista could not like and did not trust, "I think you should work another bit of magic."

"What bit of magic might that be?" She was fairly certain she didn't want to know the answer.

"I don't know about our brother Obed here, but I for one would like to know if you can repeat that...magical moment you and Fox shared back in Turysh with someone else. Preferably me."

Kallista felt her blush burn and turned her back on him, moving away from all three men. "I don't think so."

"Please?" Stone came up behind her and set his hands on her hips, rested his chin on her shoulder. "This kind of abstinence is hard on a fellow. Isn't it, Obed?"

"I will endure whatever discipline the Chosen One demands," Obed said stiffly.

"I'm not trying to discipline——"

"Then why not?" Stone didn't cling when Kallista broke free of him. "What harm can it do?"

She was relieved he'd let her go. He was too great a temptation. They all were. "We've used too much magic. There's not enough left to——"

"So that means you'll try? Another time when there's plenty of magic, you'll——"

"I didn't say that." But oh, she wanted to. Too much. Which had to mean it was a bad idea, even if it was only sex by magic. She couldn't care too much for them, couldn't be afraid to risk them when the moment came. Sharing pleasure didn't have to mean sharing more, but there were already bonds between them. It would be hard to prevent more from developing.

She could feel Stone's desire through the link between them, a conduit that never closed, binding them closer than two humans should have to endure. She didn't mistake either his emotions or his body's sensations for her own, but she could feel them. How much worse would it be when she held similar links with Obed and Fox? Belandra had said to expect the links to form.

Fox spoke. "Someone's coming. Over there." He pointed.

Kallista looked north, the direction their unmarked iliasti had ridden earlier, and saw Torchay at a distance, leading their mounts. "This *knowing* of yours may be quite helpful," she said. "Test it. Find out what you can do."

"As you will it, Kallista."

They continued north, traveling across the broad Adaran plains until they reached the Tunassa River. There they turned and followed the shallow, braided channel northeast. Eventually, it would lead them to the delta swamps surrounding Kishkim and the quasi-legal ocean traders headquartered there.

Daily, Kallista called magic from her three godmarked men, testing it. She perfected the shield magic, though she still couldn't extend it beyond her ilian even to the animals. She tried new spells, many of them suggested by Belandra on her occasional visits. Kallista still didn't understand the rules that commanded Belandra's appearance. They seemed linked to Kallista's progress with the magic, but in no pattern she could discern. Sometimes Kallista wished Belandra would simply go away, but had to admit she was glad she didn't. Annoying as Belandra's eccentricities were, she still provided needful information.

They had reached the thick forest bordering the swamps. The link with Fox allowing her to call his magic without touching had formed the week before. His sense of *knowing* had sharpened just as they'd hoped. Fox could guide his mount on his own and Torchay had begun testing his potential for self-defense.

The link with Obed had only solidified that morning. It took longer, in Kallista's opinion, because he had not been part of that original spell. She could call magic as they rode, sending it to spy out lurking smugglers, Tibran patrols or other predators. The magic had allowed them to keep the pack mules safe from a hunting jaguar, but what would keep Kallista's sanity safe from the magic?

When Belandra appeared as they set up camp that evening, Kallista moved away from the others. She made sure she was in Torchay's view, but waved him back when he would have followed.

"Is there any way to close off these links?" Kallista asked without preliminary, keeping her voice quiet.

"Why would you want to?"

"Goddess—" Kallista cut off the other, more pungent oaths. "Maybe it didn't disturb you, but I like being alone in my mind every now and again. I don't want to break the links, just—a door I can close when I need to."

Belandra frowned, propping a foot on a fallen tree and leaning forward to balance an elbow on her upraised knee. "I've never heard of such a thing, but then, I've never heard of a blind man *knowing* his surroundings without seeing them, or a naitan who could direct the dark veil. Your talents worry me, Kallista. I fear just how great an evil you face."

"The One will grant whatever is needed to defeat it."

"But you didn't wait to be sure you'd collected all She granted, did you? Rushing away from Arikon with your links half formed—"

"Fox still found us."

"What if he hadn't?"

"He did." Kallista began to pace, fighting the urge to shout. "The One brought him to us. She will provide."

"But do you know what to do with what's provided? You must embrace the links between you, and you want to close a door on them." Belandra shook her head, standing straight. "Even if you could learn a way to do it, I advise against it. You need to be able to reach the magic with no more than a thought. If you could close a door, how long would it take you to open it again?

"And what would happen to the marked ones while it was closed? You know how being too far from you affected them. Now the link is established, it could be worse to cut them off from you. Even temporarily. Why is this privacy so important? They can't read your thoughts, nor can you read theirs. Just let them ride in the back of your mind until you need them."

Kallista scraped back the strands that had escaped from her queue. "If they would *stay* in the back of my mind, I would leave it. But they don't. One of them is always pushing himself forward, demanding I be just as aware of him as he is of me." She kicked at the straggly undergrowth in her path. "It wouldn't be so bad if— but they're all *men*. Do you know how often a man thinks about sex? They even dream about it."

"Great Goddess above." Belandra's oath brought Kallista to a halt, and she turned to stare at the dead woman.

"Do you mean to tell me that you aren't—" Belandra broke off to gesture. "Still? With any of them? Have you lost what dregs of sense you might once have had? How do you expect to forge the bonds you must have if you don't—"

CHAPTER TWENTY-FOUR

"Sex has nothing to do with magic." Kallista recognized the lie the minute she spoke it. With most magic, that was true, but *this* magic was somehow different.

"It has plenty to do with trust and caring," Belandra retorted. "For heaven's sake, they're your *iliasti,* not some pack of strangers."

"That's where you're wrong. They *are* strangers, whatever else they are, and the state of my ilian is none of your business."

"Maybe not." Belandra stabbed a finger toward Kallista. "But neither are they strangers. You know them, Kallista. Not just their physical or emotional state. You know their souls, and you're lying to me and to yourself if you say you don't. They're yours, just as you are theirs, and if you want to beat this demon waiting for you, you had better accept that fact instead of kicking and screaming about it."

On that word, Belandra vanished.

"Wait! You only answered one question." Kallista turned in a circle, hunting the other woman. But she was gone.

"Come back, damn you!" she shouted, reaching out with her magic, layering on more and more when she got no response, until she felt as if she stretched across the ocean to Tibre and a thousand years into the past. Still, Belandra refused to answer.

Kallista broke the magic off, and Obed stumbled, almost falling into the fire where Aisse and Stone cooked their evening meal. She turned her back, refusing to move. He wasn't hurt, not badly. Aisse could see to his burn. It wasn't severe enough for even Torchay's care, much less something requiring a healer.

"Is everything all right?" Torchay's rough tenor soothed the raw spots in her soul.

"Fine." This wasn't right either, that Torchay's mere presence could make her feel better. "Belandra left before she answered all my questions."

"Nothing new." Torchay grinned his crooked grin. "You always have twice as many to ask as you're allowed."

"Well, this time, she only answered one." Kallista nursed her feelings of ill use, ignoring the truth that her behavior was more suited to a four-year-old than one thirty years older.

"What did she say?" Torchay leaned back against a tree and folded his arms across his chest, making the muscles flex.

Kallista resisted the strong urge to lean into him. It was only a reaction to the damn links. "Nothing of any importance. You look good in green."

He flushed, looking away. "Then what did Belandra say that wasn't important?"

Annoyed because he ignored her compliment, Kallista spoke without thinking. "She says I should be having sex with the marked ones."

Torchay didn't react at all, and that hurt worse than realizing she'd intended to hurt him, and that she'd intended it because she didn't want to be the only one suffering.

"Then you should," he said. "I don't know why you aren't. It's not as if you don't want them. I see you watching. Goddess knows they want you. Obed would fling himself off a cliff for nothing more than your smile. They all would."

"Stone would demand at least a kiss." Kallista forced the words out, trying to keep things light.

Torchay's smile flickered and vanished. "Likely. So why don't you?"

It shouldn't hurt like this. She was a rock, a mountain. She whirled to walk away.

Torchay caught her arm, held her back. "Kallista—"

She turned on him. "You want to know why? Because if I can't have you, I don't want them either."

"Then have me, dammit." The iron control he kept on his expression shattered and his eyes blazed with passion. He yanked her close, crushing her to him with an arm around her back. His mouth covered hers in a devouring kiss and Kallista responded with equal hunger.

She gripped his face between her hands to prevent his escape, but he showed no sign of wanting one. His tongue plunged deep into her mouth, echoing the motion of his hips as he rocked his rigid erection against her stomach.

Kallista slid her hands up into his hair. Ripping free the cord tying his queue, she combed the braid loose until his waves fell like silk over her skin. She rose onto her toes, needing to bring him closer to the throbbing ache his kiss aroused. Torchay's hand cupped her bottom, providing support.

"Goddess, Kallista—" He breathed the words against her skin, kissing her cheeks, her lips, her eyes. "I love you so much."

"What?" She shoved him away, stumbling back to stare at him. "What did you say?" But she'd heard it.

Torchay pulled in the arms that had held her, that still reached for her after she tore herself away, wrapping them around his stomach as if he'd been gutted again. "I—"

"Don't." She shook her head. "Don't say it. Don't do it. Don't. I can't."

His smile was crooked, tender, tragic. It made her heart ache until she stomped on the feeling, crushed it and swept it away. "I know," he said. "I never expected you to. I never meant you to know. I won't say it again. But don't ask impossible things, Kallista. Don't ask me to stop. That, I can't do."

"Goddess. I can't do this." She turned and ran into the forest, hunted by Torchay's pain. She heard him speak, heard someone come crashing after her, and she ran faster. She couldn't face any of them. Not now.

Nor could she escape them. Torchay trusted the others to stand bodyguard, reluctantly, but he would not let her go off alone in this place. She stopped and waited for Stone. He stopped a distance away, letting his companion approach alone.

"Aisse." Kallista acknowledged her. It could be no one else. She was the only other one not linked.

"What happened, naitan?"

Kallista grimaced. She stepped over the fallen log where she'd stopped and sat down, her back to the camp. Aisse wasn't the only one of her iliasti who had trouble calling her by her name. Fox used it only because she'd told him to and he did exactly what he was told. Obed stumbled over it every time he tried. Even Stone called her "captain" as often as not. It was a symptom of everything wrong with her ilian.

The rest of them seemed comfortable with each other, despite Aisse's continued refusal to "do sex." It was only around Kallista they seemed so constrained. But that was the fault of the magic. Wasn't it?

The magic bound them together, forcing them into a close connection that Kallista fought with everything in her. No one had ever been able to force her to do anything. Adjusting to military discipline had been beyond difficult. She'd settled into it only because she had finally understood the reasons for it. She could remember countless times in childhood when she'd refused to do something she honestly wanted simply because someone told her she *must* do it. Was that what she was doing now? Was this constraint her fault?

Of course it was. If she hadn't reacted so violently to Torchay's confession, she would still be with him. Probably naked. And he would be thinking their lovemaking meant more than it did. Or was she the one wanting to believe a lie, that it meant *less?*

"Kallista." Aisse's touch on her shoulder startled her. "Are you well?"

She shrugged, swiping at her face with the back of her hand. "Well enough."

"Did he——" Aisse stroked her hand down Kallista's hair. "Did he hurt you?"

"No. Never. He would never do such a thing." And now she understood why. She understood his years of devotion, his patience, his concern. It hadn't been duty. "I hurt him."

"But I didn't see you——" Aisse sat on the log beside Kallista, facing the other way.

"Not physically. I hurt him inside, where you can't see. Where——" She couldn't explain it, couldn't care. Shouldn't. "Go to him, Aisse. You like him, don't you? Make it right. Make him——make him feel better." Kallista couldn't do it.

"You want me to do sex with him?"

"No, of course n——" Kallista looked at Aisse. She didn't sound outraged, the way she usually did when someone mentioned sex. "That is, not unless you *want* to. Do you? It's perfectly fine either way, just go. I don't think he should be alone."

Aisse didn't move. "You like doing sex, Kallista?"

Oh, good Goddess, now what? "Yes, I do."

"So why you don't—why don't you? You like Torchay?"

"Yes, I like Torchay." He was her friend and her ilias. But she didn't love him.

"You like Obed and the Tibran men?"

Kallista couldn't help the smile twitching her lips. "Yes, I like Obed and I like Stone and Fox, even if they are Tibran."

"So why? There must be something you don't like if you don't do it."

"I don't like being told what to do. The magic pushes me and I won't be pushed." That wasn't the whole of it, but it was all she'd tell Aisse.

"You like sex and you like our men, but since the magic likes them too, you won't do what you like?" Aisse stood, looking back at Kallista. "That's stupid."

The blunt statement made as the other woman walked away startled Kallista into laughter. Aisse was right. Belandra was right. Even the damn magic was right. But she couldn't just give in, because she was right too. Sex complicated things.

That was obvious just from the struggle she had controlling the links… Control. Was that the key? If she used the magic as Stone wanted, she had to be able to control things better than if she indulged in actual physical sex. Once she got the links under control, maybe she'd know what to do about Torchay. She had to do something. The demon waited. If their ilian was still in this disarray, the demon would win.

Torchay was brushing down one of the horses when Aisse appeared by his side. She didn't say anything, just stood there watching him. He ducked under the tie-rein to work on the other side. Getting away from her silent scrutiny was a bonus.

Aisse stroked a small hand down the horse's neck. "Tell me how to make you feel better."

Despite the hollow ache where his heart belonged and the

burning humiliation piled atop it, Torchay couldn't help smiling. Aisse had as much subtlety as a war hammer. "I'm fine. Why don't you go make sure Obed isn't burning our dinner."

He finished the brushing and moved past Fox who was working on one of the pack mules, to begin on the next animal in line, another mule. He took a step to the left to reach the mule's rump and almost fell over Aisse. "What are you still doing here?"

Aisse looked up at him, her dark eyes full of confusion. "How can she hurt you if she did not strike you? I can't see any injuries, but...you're still injured."

"Goddess, Aisse, did you never care for anyone?" Torchay glanced over his shoulder at Fox. The man was ilias, but still Torchay didn't want to bare his soul in front of him. He didn't want to do it with Aisse, but he could tell she wouldn't leave it alone. Not until he explained something she could understand. She was relentless that way. He drew her away to the end of the picket line.

She lowered her eyes from his face, inspecting him. "Where does it hurt?"

"Here." Torchay touched a closed fist to his gut, to the center of the aching blaze.

Aisse moved his fist aside and touched him there, probing through the coarse cotton of his tunic. "But why?" She frowned up at him again. "There is no wound? Why does it hurt?"

He took a deep breath, closing his eyes against the pain. "Because I love her and she doesn't love me."

"I don't think I like love, whatever it is." Her hand flattened against his chest.

Torchay gave a choked-off bark of laughter. "Nor do I, Tiger aila."

Slowly, her small hand slid across his chest and around his back, until she held him carefully in her arms, her forehead resting against his shoulder. "I don't like it when you hurt," she said. "It makes me hurt too. In my throat and in my chest. Tell me how to make you feel better, Torchay. Right now."

"Oh, Aisse, it's not so easy as that." And yet, her awkward comfort had an effect. He put his arms around her as carefully as she held him. "But this helps."

She pulled back and met his gaze. "I will do sex with you, if you want."

He somehow managed to keep from choking. She was offering this gift to *him?* Despite how she felt about it? Dear Goddess, had she fallen in love with him? Or was it pity? Whatever her reasoning, this was not the time.

"No, little ilias." Torchay brushed her short-cropped hair off her forehead and pressed a kiss to it. He folded her in his arms again, tipping her head against his shoulder. "This is all I want just now."

He held her a long time, taking comfort and giving it, until Fox finished tending all the animals and returned to the campfire. Until Kallista returned from wherever she'd gone, Stone trailing behind. Until the ache in his chest didn't feel quite so hollow anymore.

Aisse didn't love him. Torchay was fairly sure she had no idea what love might be. But they could comfort each other. As the only two unmarked in this ilian, it was natural they would gravitate together. Now, if he could only stop loving Kallista, but he knew that would never happen.

Dawn had broken. Everyone was awake, beginning to break camp. Kallista was returning from the primitive necessary among the trees as she passed Obed on the way out. His awareness brushed against her, flaring into hot desire that rushed through the magic conduit into her mind. It sent her staggering into a tree, so powerful was his passion.

Kallista *reached,* snaring his magic and pulling it tight, pushing back at him all the things he'd sent to invade her. The magic roared, breaking loose to run rampaging through their bodies. She gasped, only the tree where she leaned keeping her upright. She held tight to the magic, forcing it to build. Could she, could they do it again?

Her body and Obed's rode the soaring crest, piling delight upon pleasure upon ecstasy, until finally they broke, spasming in climax. Still she held on, wringing every last tortured drop of release from both bodies, until the magic disintegrated in her hands.

She slumped, clinging to the tree, fighting for breath, unable to move of her own volition.

"Everything all right?" Stone spoke from a few paces away. Fox was with him, but silent.

Kallista considered, then shook her head. She didn't think her voice would work yet.

"You did it again, didn't you? Sex by magic."

She nodded and dragged herself up the tree until her knees were more or less straight. Yes, they would hold.

"Dammit, why is it never me? I want a turn." Stone's voice was supposed to sound teasing, Kallista was sure, but she could hear a definite plaintive note in it.

"Talk to me again," she said through her gasping breath, "tomorrow."

Obed was coming. She could hear his uneven approach through the forest, could sense anger radiating from him. She waved the other two away. "I have to talk to Obed. Alone."

Stone and Fox backed away perhaps a step, and Obed was there. His eyes blazed black fire, his nostrils flared with every breath. "Do not ever do that to me again." His words snarled out between clenched teeth. "If you want sex with me let it be true sex, mouth-to-mouth, skin-to-skin, me inside of you."

"I wasn't the one who started this," she retorted, anger flaring along with the desire his words rekindled.

"I did not touch you."

"You didn't have to! Goddess, don't you understand what being linked like this means? I know exactly where you are and what you are doing every minute. I know what your body feels. When you burned your hand last night, I felt it. When you desire me, I can't help but feel it. I even know what emotions you're feeling when they're strong, like your anger now. Then multiply that times three, because everything I receive from you I receive from Fox and Stone as well."

She threw her hands up in frustration. "What do you expect me to do when you shove your randy state down my throat? I'm going to shove back, Obed. If you don't like what happens, I suggest you get your—your passions under control."

"I did not realize." Obed raised a hand, noticed it was curled in a fist, and struggled to open it. Then he seemed not to know what to do with it.

His anger was fading, and with it, Kallista's anger subsided. She took his hand, clasping her fingers around his thumb.

"I will try to do as you ask." He tightened his grip on her hand. "But know this. I will not again commit the sacrilege of spilling my seed on the ground. I am yours. You know this. I will do anything you ask of me, but please—do not ask this. I do not want it." Holding her gaze with his, Obed lifted their clasped hands and pressed his lips to the back of her hand. Then he released it and returned to the camp.

Kallista let out a heavy sigh. She really should take the time to explore Obed's beliefs, learn what things might offend him. But they didn't have the time now. She trudged up the path to join Fox and Stone, looping her hands through their elbows for the short distance back to camp.

"Obed might not want it," Stone said quietly. "But I do. How about you, Fox?"

"I want whatever Kallista wants."

"Liar." Kallista held on tight when Fox would have pulled away. "Didn't you hear what I told Obed? I feel what you feel. Do you have any moral or religious objections to sex by magic?"

"I have no objections to anything you want from me."

She took a deep breath and let it out slowly. The Tibrans hadn't had him long after he'd lost his caste, but they'd taught him all too well. "I don't need just your magic, Fox. I need your mind and your will. You're ilias now, part of the Varyl ilian. We are your caste now. Do you understand that?"

"I...am beginning to." Half a moment later, he grinned, his face lighting up the forest. "And I have no objections to *anything* you want from me. Especially if it has to do with sex."

They were still laughing when they joined the others.

It took them another full week to work their way through the swamps, past the Tibran lines and into Kishkim's walled streets. While waiting tucked in a sweltering third-floor room near the docks for Obed and Torchay to finish their negotiations for a ship to take them across the Jeroan Sea, Kallista finally gave in to Stone's seductive teasing. She caught Fox in the magic too and brought them all three to a mutual roaring climax.

"Khralsh's bloody hells," Fox gasped, slumping against the wall where he sat on the larger of the two beds. "If I weren't already blind, I think that might have done the job."

"I think it did." Stone slid down to lie on the rug between the beds. "I know I can't see."

"Try opening your eyes." Kallista tried it as she pushed herself up off the tabletop and sank into the high upholstered back of the chair where she sat. "Worked for me."

"You sure?" Stone paused, evidently following Kallista's directive, for he said, "Oh yeah, that works."

Aisse startled Kallista when she sidled up next to her. She'd forgotten the younger woman was still in the room. "That was truly like sex?" Aisse whispered. "You truly enjoy it?"

Kallista worked harder to control her breathing. "Yes, Aisse. Truly."

The little blonde chewed on the inside of her lip. "I wish you could show me."

"Oh, Aisse, I'm not—I don't—"

"With your magic. Not—I know you like men." She chewed on her lip again.

"That's obvious enough, I suppose." Kallista studied her young ilias, trying to find the best response. "What about you?"

Aisse shrugged a shoulder. "I don't like to be hurt. Men hurt."

"Not always. Not all of them. Torchay doesn't hurt you, I know. None of our men have hurt you." Speaking quietly, Kallista emphasized the "our." Aisse had called them that first.

Again she shrugged. "Because I don't do sex with them."

"Why do you sleep beside Torchay now? You trust him not to do anything you don't want, right? He would show you what you want to know, and he wouldn't hurt you. Ask him." Kallista didn't begrudge Aisse Torchay's tutoring, even in this. And maybe it would make up for some of the hurt she'd stupidly dealt him.

Four days later, on the first of Vendra, the last summer month, Obed found a captain willing to transport their ilian to Haav in Tibre. He had no room for their animals, but one of Torchay's kinsmen had arrived the night before to take them in hand. The ship, local but not crewed by Adarans, would leave on the evening tide. They had just time enough to repack their belongings and divide the remaining coin from Obed's supply among themselves.

They were all six crammed into a single, none-too-large cabin. Everyone but Obed became violently ill the instant the ship reached open sea. Torchay recovered first, three days after they sailed, and by the week's end only Fox still moaned in the cabin's single ilian-size bunk.

Kallista feared his blindness was making his condition worse and hoped he wouldn't stay sick for the entire voyage. She could feel his nausea through the link. Eventually, with the help of magic she borrowed from the other two, Fox recovered sufficiently to emerge from the cabin.

The crew had no naitan to control the winds, and though Kallista was tempted to try, she resisted temptation and allowed the captain to use his skill and seamanship. But because of the vagaries of natural wind, the trip seemed endless.

The ilian's close quarters turned small irritations into major faults, creating daily explosions of temper, nursing of grudges and tendering of apologies. Kallista's temper was the loudest, but the others knew how to make their annoyance felt, even Fox who seemed to think he had no right to any emotions. Somehow, the daily struggle to keep from throttling each other bound them closer to what anyone might call a true ilian.

They took the weeks of the journey to teach Stone and Fox a bit of the Tibran they'd lost so they could at least understand orders and identify where they belonged if the ilian was separated. Once Fox was over his illness, he joined the others in the combat training Torchay conducted on deck.

Kallista practiced calling magic, though she didn't work the dark veil, not in the ship's close quarters. West magic disturbed too many people. She played with the winds, hunted stray magics—not many on the open sea—and worked at spreading the defensive shield beyond the members of her ilian. She did *not* practice sex by magic, much to Stone's noisy disappointment and Obed's silent relief.

Nor did Aisse seem to have asked Torchay for any instruction. They slept crowded together on the single bunk, Aisse always on the outside, always next to Torchay, but at least she joined them now. The ilian was coming together, becoming the whole it needed to be if they were to succeed in their task.

On the thirty-third day of Vendra, two days before the advent of the first fall month, the ship made dock at Haav, the major port of the Tibran empire. Haav's docks bristled with masts, golden-skinned laborers with shaved heads swarming everywhere as they loaded and unloaded the ships. A fortress built of rust-red stone loomed over the harbor with three ranks of cannon protruding from its walls.

As they had planned during the long evenings of their trip, Obed and Torchay waited on deck for the assigned Bureaucrat. The Tibran king had apparently learned that treating foreign merchants as if they were members of his own Merchant caste was not conducive to trade. Merchants in Tibre ranked only above Bureaucrats, Laborers and, of course, Women, and suffered occasional abuse from the higher castes. Foreign merchants didn't care to suffer at all. Therefore, a member of the Port Bureaucracy came to each ship and issued various certifications that would—with luck—protect the visiting traders.

"How much longer do you reckon the fellow will have us wait?" Torchay asked, standing at a comfortable parade rest on the ship's deck. He was used to waiting, usually in worse weather than the day's pleasant breeze.

Obed shrugged. "Before nightfall, I am sure. The man is trying to impress us with his importance, which is very small."

"If a person can't push around many folk, he's more likely to push those he can." Torchay had seen it often, especially in the army.

"Your patience is impressive." Obed drummed his fingers on the ship's rail. "Mine is stretched to breaking. I've never liked wasting time. There's too much to be done."

"Peace, ilias." Torchay touched Obed's shoulder and pointed. "Could that be our little Bureaucrat?"

CHAPTER TWENTY-FIVE

The man was far from little. Tall and stout, with a belly that strained the shell buttons closing his black padded vest, he bowled aside the scurrying laborers as he made his ponderous way to the ship. The gangplank bowed slightly as he trudged up it. He took a sailor's hand for support and thudded to the deck.

The captain approached the bureaucrat first, bowing and scraping his way through a sheaf of papers and seals. Then he escorted the local to where Torchay and Obed waited. Stone's suggestion that Torchay wear warrior's red and all of his blades seemed to be a wise one, for the bureaucrat's bluster faded at the sight of him. Torchay folded his arms, flexed his muscles, scowled, and the bureaucrat went pale.

Obed spoke, telling the story they'd agreed upon. Torchay could understand a word here and there, since Obed's Tibran was only fair. The bureaucrat spoke and Obed translated.

"This is Oughrath, Bureaucrat vo'Haav." Obed stumbled over the difficult consonants. "He requires a deposit be made against our potential purchases. Common Tibran practice, though I'm sure he takes a cut of it. When we make the payment, we'll receive our certification and robes."

"Robes?"

"White, to mark us as foreign traders, since we plan to travel inland. Apparently robes work better than mere badges."

"For six of us?"

Obed turned back to fat Oughrath and asked. "Yes," he said when he got the answer. "Robes for our entire party. Even our slaves. We want to protect our investment after all."

Torchay nodded. The Tibrans, including Aisse, would pass as casteless slaves, bought after one of this continent's incessant wars. Kallista would pose as a young—male—clerk. No legitimate trader brought women to Tibre. "Pay him." Torchay pulled a purse off his belt.

"Half now, half when he brings the robes." Obed took the purse and counted out seven gold coins, placing them one by one in Oughrath's sweaty palm. With a last surly glare, the bureaucrat departed.

An hour later, he returned, leading a laborer bearing a bundle of white cloth in his arms. As Fox took each robe from the laborer, Obed gave another coin to Oughrath, and a seventh when the exchange was complete, while Torchay watched, bristling with blades. The bureaucrat handed over a stack of papers, seeming to recite a speech long memorized. Then he was gone.

"What was that last bit?" Torchay touched Fox's arm, directing him toward the stairs.

"Warning us to be sure to wear the robes at all times, especially our slaves." Obed brought up the rear. "If they're caught without the robes, they could be confiscated or damaged."

Torchay muttered a few choice curses under his breath. This "mission" of Kallista's was madness. The whole countryside lay ready to attack if they made one slip. But where she led, he was bound to follow. Not bound as their marked iliasti were, but bound nonetheless. *Later,* she'd told him. *When this ends.* He wanted to hope, but would any of them survive the ending?

In the cabin, they shared out the robes. Torchay collected Kallista's gloves before they left the ship together to find lodging. Without naitani, Tibre had no requirement regarding gloves. They would make her noticeable.

"Stay near the docks," Kallista murmured. "Let's avoid trouble as long as we can."

Obed nodded, leading the way. Torchay brought up the rear, sleeves rolled up to expose the blades at his wrists.

Stone pulled his own sleeves down over his hands and tugged his hood forward to hide as much as possible of the telltale gold of his skin. He checked Fox's hood, then felt a little tingle as Kallista drew magic.

"A veil," she said, "to blur their image of us."

Stone pushed through the crowd after Obed, feeling strangeness stack on top of strangeness as he watched to be sure none of his iliasti were separated from the group or trampled. He couldn't understand anything the locals said, though at the beginning of spring, he'd been one of them.

He'd been one of the Warriors swaggering through town, taking what he wanted. Now he hurried with his head down, looking out for the safety of a blind man and two women, people who would have been beneath his notice before.

If he had not been marked by Kallista's god, would he have shunned Fox when he lost his sight? Stone wanted to think not, but he knew better. He might have made sure Fox had food, clothing, maybe a blanket. But he wouldn't have been able to protect him from the rest of it, even had he wanted to.

As for the women…Stone had never paid much attention to women before, other than as warm comfort on a cold night. He'd never dreamed he could *like* them without sex playing any part.

Obed stopped in front of an open door from which the yeasty smell of beer and garlicky scent of cooking emerged. He looked back at Kallista where she stood just in front of Stone. She nodded, a slight dip of her head, and Obed entered.

Moments later, they'd taken possession of a large parlor and adjoining sleeping rooms on the second floor. Kallista threw off her robe and the sudden appearance of her sweetly curved body in her tight-laced tunic brought a surge of lust skittering through Stone. Though after that long, abstinent voyage, something as simple as the line of her neck beneath her queue or the turn of a graceful hand could inspire lust.

He wanted her. Not just because she was the only female remotely available to him, but because she was Kallista. Even if the women's quarters of every caste in Haav were thrown open to him, he would still want Kallista. He'd never known what a difference it could make, having sex with a woman he *liked*. And that was without even touching. How much better would it be if he ever got to have real sex with her again?

"Stone." Kallista got his attention, pointing toward one of the smaller rooms. "In there."

He was already moving when he asked why.

"Because you're making me crazy. Fox, you too. Follow Stone." She caught Fox's arm and turned him, giving him a little push.

"I should go find us mounts," Obed said, edging toward the door. "For our trip to the capital."

Stone didn't blame Obed for wanting to leave if he didn't want to play. It was the not-wanting-to-play part he didn't understand.

"We don't go anywhere alone." Torchay tossed a robe at Obed and picked up his own. "Not any of us, not ever, as long as we're in Tibre."

"I go—I *will* go with you." Aisse shrugged back into her robe, shoving the knotted ball buttons through the loops to hold it closed.

"Fine." Kallista waved the others off.

Stone shuddered, feeling her reach inside him to gather the magic as the parlor door closed on the departing trio. Kallista paused in the bedroom doorway, watching as Fox climbed onto the bed next to Stone.

"Come." Stone patted the small space between him and his partner-ilias. "You know you'll end up on the floor if you don't. This is much more comfortable."

"We're only doing magic."

"Nothing wrong with being comfortable while you do." He propped himself on an elbow, watching her. "Don't you agree, Fox?"

"I think you should avoid the floor." Fox turned on his side facing her, echoing Stone's position.

She shook her head, a crooked smile on her face as she came through the door, shutting it behind her. "I don't know why I let you talk me into these things."

"Because you know you want to do exactly what we talk you into." Stone scooted his back against the wall, making a little more room. He shivered again as the magic lurched, pulling tighter, when Kallista slid into the space between them. Even with the link that made it possible for her to call magic at a distance, there was still a difference when they touched. More intensity. More power.

She turned to face Fox, and Stone took a chance, leaning in to kiss that curve of her neck that had driven him mad during their time at sea. This time, Kallista shivered, and he grinned, slipping an arm around her waist to pull her back into his erection. Her waist was thicker than he remembered, and she had a little belly on her. The lazy days on the ship had had more of an effect than he realized. He liked the changes. They made her…normal.

"Fox, what are you doing?" Kallista jerked back into Stone. "Keep your trousers on, soldier."

"I am. Just trying to simplify the cleanup." He passed a handkerchief across her to Stone. "One for you, *brodir*."

Kallista sat up as Stone was trying to stuff the cloth down the front of his pants, her elbows and knees transformed into dangerous weapons. "Well, that spoiled the mood." She let go the magic and the delicious tension faded away.

"Not mine." Stone struggled to his knees and twisted around to put himself behind her, thinking hard about how beautiful she was and how much he wanted her in any way he could get her. He didn't know how this connection between them worked, didn't know if he could send her a specific message through it, but he was damn well going to try. If he was only getting sex once a month, he wasn't about to give up his once.

And maybe it was working. She let him move close, relaxed against him when he urged her to. He bent to kiss her neck and she tilted her head, offering access. Stone took what she offered, laying kisses from the curve of her shoulder along the soft pale skin to the hollow beneath her ear. His hands slid forward, touched her sides, moving toward her breasts, but she caught them, set them firmly back on his knees. He didn't protest, because she called the magic again, drawing it from every dimension of his body with a caress so erotic his vision went dark.

Or maybe he'd just shut his eyes. He slid boneless to lie on the bed when she did. She leaned into Fox, kissed him. Somehow Stone could feel it. Not as if he were kissing Fox himself, but knowing how it felt to Kallista when she kissed him. She pulled the magic tighter, making them all three gasp, then she let it go, whipping it higher, faster as they rode it together.

Stone lost all sense of himself, tumbling arse over ears in the wild magic, fighting to hold on, make it last longer. But as before, he was the first to break. He shouted, shuddering as the fierce delight broke over him. His climax triggered the others. Kallista cried out. Fox kept silent but seemed to shake the more violently because of it.

"What," Stone said long moments later when he could see and hear and breathe again, "do you suppose it would be like if we had ordinary sex while you did that?"

"Saints and sinners," Fox muttered, borrowing Obed's oath, his face tucked into Kallista's neck, "I'd never survive it."

Kallista kissed his forehead, then rolled to her back and kissed Stone's jaw. "After, maybe we can try it."

"Why not now?" Stone pulled Fox's arm across Kallista's waist and settled his own above it, just under her breasts. "I don't mean *now* now, obviously, but why wait till *after?* Who knows if we'll still be alive, after? I don't understand what you have against sex, anyway."

She sighed. "It's not that I have anything against sex, exactly…"

"It's us," Fox said.

She twisted toward him and kissed his mouth. "No, I do not have anything against you either. Or Obed. You're all gorgeous. And Torchay, well…"

"So, what is it?" Stone said. Anything that would get him more sex…

"I don't know. Stupidity?" Kallista caught Stone by the throat of his tunic and pulled him in for his own kiss, then squirmed out from between them to stand. She straightened her tunic and smoothed back her mussed hair. She looked as if she would rather discuss anything besides the current topic, but Stone wasn't ready to let it drop.

"Does that mean you're going to start having sex with us? The regular kind?" He pulled the clammy handkerchief out of his trousers. It seemed to have done mostly as intended.

Kallista blushed and looked away. "I…"

"If you don't have anything against sex, and you don't have anything against us, I don't see what the problem is." Did women always make things more complicated than they had to be?

"Because it's not just sex." She began to pace the small room. "Even doing it this way with the magic, it's more than just sex. I care about you and I care about Fox, and every time we…make love, I care more."

"And you don't want to." Fox sat up and swung his feet off the bed.

Kallista stopped and looked at them sitting side by side. She swallowed hard, her eyes haunted. "It scares me," she said finally. "More than facing down the entire Tibran army with all its cannon."

Stone blinked. Kallista, admitting to fear?

She took a deep breath. "But I don't seem to have any choice. I seem to care as much for Aisse even though I don't have any inclination to have sex with her. We're ilian. It doesn't seem to make any difference how hard I fight it. I still care."

All the emotion free-floating around the room made Stone want to pull a pillow over his head. Or make a joke. "So," he said. "Sex? You and me? You and Fox? You and Obed and Torchay?"

Kallista laughed and Stone let out a relieved breath. "I think Obed might object to sharing," she said.

"So maybe Torchay won't. I won't—but you know that." He worked hard to keep his tone light and teasing. "Fox won't either. He has no objection to anything, remember?"

"You're hopeless."

"No, no. I'm *hopeful*. Sex? Please? Often?"

She left the room shaking her head at him to answer a knock at the parlor door. The laborers had arrived with luggage from the ship. She never did answer his question.

Aisse stayed close to Torchay as they walked through the streets of Haav, hood up, head down. The robe that flapped around his calves dragged the ground on her and she liked it that way, liked being covered head to toe, hidden from everyone's eyes. She'd never ventured into this part of town until she'd been loaded on a ship to sail to Adara, never left the warriors' section of town once she'd been assigned there. Her mother had been assigned to Craftsmen's caste and Aisse had grown up running the streets around forge and foundry, past the workshops of weavers, tanners and potters. That was where the Ruler had found her, two years before her coming-of-age.

She forced the memory from her mind. She was Adaran now. Ilian. Safe. If any saw through her disguise and demanded sex, she could say no. Torchay would defend her. Obed too. And they would be overwhelmed and killed for trying to defend her. No Tibran would allow such a thing.

So much pain stabbed through her at the thought, she stumbled. Torchay caught her arm. "Careful, Tiger aila. A slip could expose too much."

"Yes." She would not slip, would not make a mistake. But if it happened, she would give whatever was demanded. She would not be the cause of Torchay's death. Of any of their deaths, for Stone would fight too, and even blind Fox. They belonged to each other.

And somehow, because she knew she could say no, the thought of saying yes didn't disturb her so much. Sex wasn't important enough to die over. She had done it before and could endure it again if she had to. But…was it always something to be endured? Kallista didn't seem to act as if it were.

She sidled closer to Torchay. "You think Kallista is doing magic with Stone and Fox?"

"Aye. Now be quiet. Your voice will give you away." Torchay shook back the sleeves of his robe to expose his blades, and folded back the unbuttoned sides as he followed Obed into the horse market. Aisse scurried to stay between them, kicking the skirt of her robe at every step to keep from tripping over it.

The men moved from trader to trader, inspecting horses, rejecting most, but occasionally coming to terms. Torchay would hand the purse to Obed who would pay. Warriors didn't sully their hands with trade if there was a merchant about to do it for them. Then Obed would hand the lead of the newly purchased horse to Aisse.

Eventually, they had six horses and two pack mules to lead back down the docks to the inn. Obed took the reins to half the animals and Torchay stalked alone. The white robe worn open merely declared him foreign. All else, from the red of his tunic to the red of his hair, blazed out his warrior status and kept all they passed from approaching.

"Torchay…" Aisse skipped ahead to catch up with him, the horses she led breaking into a brief trot.

"Should you be seen talking to me?"

"We're foreign. They expect strangers to do strange things. Kallista says that you will teach me what I want to know."

"Aye, that's true." He slowed his pace slightly, making it easier for her to keep up. "What are you wanting to learn?"

"How sex can feel good."

Torchay lost a step. "You want to learn what?" He seemed on the edge of shouting.

"About sex that feels good. Are you angry? Kallista said it would be all right, but if—"

"She said that, did she?" He did sound angry.

"I asked if she could use the magic to show me, but I'm not marked and it only works if you are, so she said you would do it if I asked you, but if you don't want to—" Aisse resigned herself. She would satisfy her curiosity another way. Or forget the idea. She wasn't entirely sure she wanted to know that badly. "Forget I asked."

"I can't very well do that, can I? Not now you've asked it. And I did no' say I didn't want to." He opened the gate to the inn yard and turned it over to the stable boy to hold as they entered with the new horses. "Hush now. No talking."

They turned the animals over to the inn's horse-groom laborers and went inside. At the top of the stairs, Torchay paused outside the door to their rooms after Obed had gone inside. He moved close to Aisse, crowding her against the wall. "Are you sure this is what you want?"

His height made her nervous, looming over her. His nearness made it worse, but she couldn't get away. She stared up at his face. This was Torchay. He wouldn't hurt her. Aisse nodded, unable to make the motion smooth.

"Maybe you do want it." He touched her cheek and she flinched away. "But you're no' ready to learn it.

"You didn't mind coming close to me," he went on, "but you don't want me moving close to you. You don't want me touching you. If you truly want…what you asked, you've a great many other things to learn first." His thumb stroked across her skin, making her shiver. "Do you want this?"

"Yes." This time she could say the word.

Stone put his head out through the open door. "What are you two doing out here? Aren't you coming in?"

"Aye, we're coming." Torchay slung his arm over Aisse's shoulders and she stiffened, but endured it as they walked in together. "We had a discussion to finish."

"What about?" Stone shut the door behind them.

"Torchay is going to teach me about sex. Good sex." Aisse made herself stay where she was, no matter how badly she wanted to duck away.

"You are?" Kallista's eyebrows went up, but Aisse couldn't tell whether she was pleased or angry.

"Not anytime soon." Torchay took away his arm and Aisse almost sagged in relief.

"You could have asked me." Stone leered at her, trying to make her laugh. "I wouldn't make you wait."

"That's why I didn't." Aisse scowled. "I don't trust you."

"You shouldn't," Fox put in from his chair by the window. "Not when it comes to sex. Stone's technique has always been limited to in-and-out-and-boom. I'm a much better choice."

"Stars, give the man sex and he starts talking as much as a bureaucrat." Stone flopped down in a chair and kicked at Fox's knee. "What makes you such an expert?"

Fox's smug smile made Aisse feel strange. "I have no caste, remember? I was a toy in women's quarters. I learned *many* things about women and sex."

Kallista leaned against the wall and folded her arms, a faint smile on her face. "Aren't you going to offer to teach her, Obed?"

"No." He turned away, said nothing more. Aisse wondered if Obed hurt where no one could see, without a blow being struck. Why did she care?

"I have a teacher," Aisse said to draw attention from Obed. "I don't need another."

She held herself still when Torchay set his hand on her shoulder. He didn't hurt her. It was only a touch, only the warm weight of his hand resting there. It made her feel as peculiar as Fox's smile had.

"So," Torchay said. "Where do we go from here?"

They went north yet again and west, leaving on Peaceday, following the Silixus, a deep, narrow river that changed from brown to green when they moved past the tidal flow. The banks were high, often rocky, lined with tall trees, and climbed higher as they traveled. They rode sometimes atop the rocky bluffs and sometimes down at the river's edge, depending on where the road took them.

Long stretches of it were paved with square-cut stones or hard-fired brick. Twice on their upriver journey, they came upon gangs of sweating laborers with their shaved heads and brown trousers laying the pavement in the roadbed carved out of the forest. At each location, a single Ruler in his teens acted as supervisor accompanied only by a pair of Warrior bodyguards, one as youthful as the Ruler, the other gray with experience.

The workers did not seem to need even this much supervision, laying brick after brick at a seemingly tireless pace. Stone explained that the laborers worked hard because each man knew his caste and role in life, and had the promise of rest after death. Fox added that the promised rest often came early to those who showed too much independence.

Their party of six traveled alone along the great road. Tibre had slightly less trouble with bandits than did Adara due to the regular Warriors' patrols over the entire highway network. Traffic on the road was heavy because river travel on the narrow Silixus was limited to downstream. They had no wind naitani to drive the boats back upriver against the current.

By the next Graceday, they reached the town nestled beneath the cliffs where the Silixus carved its way from the high central plateau in a series of stair-step waterfalls and pools. Here, after goods were portaged by mule train from High Dzawa to Lower Dzawa, they were loaded on the rebuilt rafts to float downriver to Haav and places beyond. The return trip was accomplished by transferring the contents of wagons and carts onto pack mules for the steep climb, then reloading the goods onto other wagons at the upper city. Mule-driving Farmers and their Merchant hirelings tendered fierce scowls at the foreign trader who brought his own transport.

That evening, Torchay and Kallista took their turn at tending the animals in the stable outside the scruffy inn near the lower-city walls. "We should stop here for an extra day," he said, hauling a saddle off the last horse.

"We have to keep going." Kallista dumped a scoop of grain into the bucket for her horse and moved to the next, ignoring the fluttering in her stomach. It wasn't nerves, not entirely. It had taken her a few days to realize the strange quiver was the baby moving inside her. They had to finish this and fast. She didn't know how much longer she could hide her condition.

Should she be showing this much this soon? When she'd decided to keep the baby a secret, she hadn't realized how hard it would be, having no one to discuss it with, no one to share the joys and worries.

"Why? What difference can one day of rest make to this mission?" Torchay touched her arm, and when she ignored him, hauled her around to face him.

The motion dislodged her hood, sending it tumbling down to her shoulders. Kallista took a moment to enjoy the breeze on her too-warm face before she pulled the hood back into place. "Every delay is one more day our people suffer."

"You need the rest." Torchay turned her so the torchlight fell on her face. He took her head between his hands and searched her with his medic's eyes. "I don't like the way you've been looking. You're—"

"I'm fine." Kallista pulled out of his grasp, turned to walk away. "We leave in the morning."

"*Kallista.*" He grabbed her shoulder, dragging her robe half off before he caught up with her and blocked her path. His eyes widened as he stared down at her blossoming body exposed by the open robe and whatever he'd intended to say was forgotten. "Kallista, what in heaven—"

She yanked her robe back together. The stupid knot buttons popped out of their holes just by looking at them. Torchay stepped close, slid his hand through the opening of the robe and set it on her stomach. She didn't stop him. Too late for that, just as it was too late to turn back.

"Who knows about this?" He covered her burgeoning belly with both hands, his voice harsh.

"Me, a healer in Arikon, and now you." She was glad he knew, glad he was the first to know. His hands warmed her, inside as well as out.

"Goddess, Kallista, have you lost your mind? I thought you said the contraceptive spell was working." His hands moved, shaping, measuring. Caressing. "When did this happen? That boy in Turysh? Must have been, big as you are."

She pushed him away, anger searing her. "No, it did not happen in Turysh." She wanted to hit him for making such assumptions, but she had—the baby had grown so fast, she could scarcely blame him for making them. "This child is yours. Or Stone's. That night, after our first wedding, is the only time in months that I've..."

He reached for her again, hooking a hand behind her neck to draw her into a rough embrace. "I don't know whether to kiss you or throttle you. What were you thinking, to hare off into Tibre in this state?"

Kallista let her head rest on his shoulder, allowing herself to take his comfort, to need his strength. She couldn't lean here long, but for a moment, just for a little rest, what could it hurt? "I was thinking we couldn't afford to wait. We have to finish this before I lose my magic. Before any more people die in these damned demon-spawned wars."

Torchay sighed, a long-suffering sound, and tucked her closer. "Why am I no' surprised? You've the patience of a gnat, and you've always been reckless. This new magic of yours has you thinking you're invincible. You're not, you know."

"I know." She wriggled her arms from between them and slid them around his waist. "But we couldn't stay in Arikon. Someone else would only try to kill us."

"Likely." He laid his cheek against her hair. "Still, I wish you'd think now and again about those of us who care for you. You're our center, Kallista. We'd be lost without you."

"No, you wouldn't."

"Aye, we would. We'd survive, maybe even stay ilian together, but we'd be lost."

Her chest hurt and her eyes burned. Was she the one making this so difficult, or was the difficulty built into the situation? She drew back so she could look up at him, the flickering torchlight gilding his fair skin. "I do love you, you know. As my ilias and my friend. My oldest, dearest friend. Can't that be enough?"

He touched a kiss to her forehead. "Aye. Enough, if you'll stop making this harder than it is. We're ilian, Kallista. We're *bound*. You don't have to do it all yourself. Stop keeping secrets. Let us share the burden."

"Easier to say than do," she muttered and Torchay grinned.

"True. But if you work at it, I have faith eventually you'll manage." He kissed her forehead again and handed her the scoop. "Finish graining the horses. I'll take care of the rest and we'll go tell the others."

"*Don't* start babying me." Kallista shook the scoop at him. "I'm not suddenly helpless."

"Now, naitan, you have to give me some space. I've only just learned I'm going to be a father. Takes some getting used to." He chuckled, running the brush along a horse's back. "How d'you suppose Obed's going to react? You think he'll be more—"

A Tibran stepped into the torchlight from the shadowed inn yard. "If you're not going to take her, outlander, I will."

CHAPTER TWENTY-SIX

Kallista whirled, raising the scoop to a defensive position. Torchay went still but stayed on the far side of the horse. She remembered that he understood very little Tibran. He wouldn't want to interfere if it wasn't necessary. Kallista pulled tiny fibers of magic, hoping her men didn't notice. She didn't need them charging out here upsetting things.

"You don't want to do that, sir." She wove the magic into a disguise, deepening her voice, squaring her shape. "I'm no one for you to be interested in."

The blocky Farmer, for he was dressed in green, frowned at her, shook his head and looked again. Then he grabbed her arm. "Don't care if you are ugly. Rulers gave all th' women hereabouts to th' Warriors."

He yanked her against him, hands rough, breath reeking of beer. Kallista choked back the threatening nausea as she drew her blade. The Farmer tried to grope her and unfasten his trousers both at once. His last mistake. Kallista's knife drove deep into his heart. Seconds later, Torchay broke his neck. Blood stained the dingy white of her foreigner's robe as she pulled back her knife and the man collapsed at her feet. Only then did she consider that she might have—*should* have stopped him some other way.

"Hey!" Another drunk Tibran had just emerged from the tavern. "What's going on? What'd you do to him?"

"That's trouble," Torchay put Kallista behind him.

She stepped to the side, unwilling to let him sacrifice himself. "He's drunk," she called in her deepest voice. "Can't hold his beer."

"Then what's that on your robe?" The Farmer scowled as he walked toward them, more Tibrans—Farmers, Merchants and Laborers—crowding in the door behind him.

"He threw up on me." It was the best she could do. She looked around for avenues of escape. They didn't want to be trapped in the stable, but their choices were small and getting smaller by the minute as more men spilled into the walled yard.

"Like hell he did," another man cried. "That's blood!"

Torchay's twin Heldring blades snicked from their scabbard and Kallista drew a second knife for her other hand. Her sword had been packed away as inappropriate for her disguise. She could sense alarm through her links with her marked iliasti—they could hear the uproar as the mob rushed the stable—and sent them a firm *Stay there.* No use all of them getting killed.

She drew magic, ducking behind Torchay and his flashing blades for the time to shape it. She'd never used the veil to render people unconscious, but she didn't want to kill them if she didn't have to. She shouldn't have killed the first man.

"Whatever you're doing, hurry." Torchay backed into the stable doorway. "There's too many of them, even if they're unarmed and unskilled."

Kallista didn't bother responding, too busy with her task. She let the magic go, pushing it toward the gate, and a dozen men dropped in their tracks. Torchay rushed it, Kallista at his back, pulling more magic as she ran. Cries of *"Witch!"* followed her. Something struck her in the head and she stumbled, stunned. A rock? Another hit her and the magic flew free as she fell, and knew nothing more.

Obed bellowed, rushing for the door. Fox tackled him and knocked him to the floor with a crash. "She's not dead," he said, hoping desperately that it wasn't a lie. "She's not dead, and we can't rescue her if we're captured ourselves."

The abrupt cutoff of the magic calling had shaken all of them, even Aisse who had no link. "What?" she cried. "What happened?"

"Something." Fox sat up on top of Obed, holding him down. "Don't know—riot in the courtyard. Kallista—she's *not* dead." He had to believe it.

Stone peered out the window. "Looks like they're taking her. Torchay too. They're both out—unconscious."

"*Not* dead," Fox said again.

"Some of them are coming inside. Looking for us, I'd wager."

The plan dropped full blown into his brain and Fox stood, careful not to step on Obed. He stripped off his stranger's robe. "Hide these. Obed, keep yours on. Stone, you're a Ruler. Have we anything purple?"

"Yes, I think." Aisse hurried to the packs while Obed gathered the white robes and stuffed them under the bed's mattress.

"I can't be a Ruler," Stone protested. "I can't speak three words of Tibran."

"Obed will speak for you. You're a Ruler. You don't sully yourself by speaking to Farmers."

"The landlord knows we came here in stranger's robes."

"But he didn't see any face but Obed's. You came to meet him, to discuss trade."

Fox sensed Aisse hurrying back across the room toward Stone. "Did you find purple?"

"Yes, for a sash or drape. I am his woman?"

"I can't do this." Stone was still protesting. "They'll know. They'll catch us out. You be the Ruler."

"I can hide my blindness if I play Warrior. I can't as Ruler."

Pounding feet and angry voices announced the approach of the mob searching the inn's upper floor.

Fox drew Stone's sword, glad he'd worn warrior's red beneath his white foreigner's robe this day. "Just be arrogant. Aisse, give him a few arrogant words. You know how Rulers act. Be one."

Fists pounded on the door and Fox opened it. The blade in his hand stilled the mob for a second till someone spotted Obed.

"There he is! I told you there were more outlanders here."

"Silence!" Stone roared the Tibran word. He glared at the few rioters visible through the open door, then waved a hand at Obed, gesturing for him to speak.

As he did, Obed glided forward, folding back his robe to show the hilt of his sword. Fox faded away so that he guarded one side of the opening, bare blade in his hand, while Obed guarded the other.

"B-beggin' pardon, Ruler Sir," one of the man began, "but—"

"This foreigner brought a witch among us!" Another pointed an accusing finger at Obed and the shouting began again.

Aisse stretched up and whispered a translation in Stone's ear. He struggled to appear amused by her, distracted from the scene, and hoped like hell that no one could see him shaking. Fox was supposed to come up with sensible plans, not insane ones like this.

The shouting rose in volume and Stone bellowed for silence

again. Then he waved at Obed to go on. Surely he was making up a reasonable explanation. Stone put his arm around Aisse, hoping she wouldn't fling it off because it was him and not Torchay. She let the red-haired man touch her at will these days, not the rest of them. But now she snuggled against him.

Aisse whispered to Stone that Obed explained he had no idea his clerk was a witch, or a woman. He'd merely come to Dzawa to discuss trade with this mighty and wise Ruler and hoped to meet with many others. His explanation mollified some, but not most. Friends of the dead man, no doubt. They wanted to bear Obed off to City Center for questioning. Which meant torture and punishment. They didn't believe his explanations, didn't care about his protestations of innocence.

Stone turned his mouth to Aisse's ear, asked for a few words, and she gave them quickly. Stone released her, advanced on the main protester at the door and delivered a backhanded slap that knocked the man off his feet.

"You dare?" Stone shouted, hoping he remembered the words in proper order. "I am Valor, Ruler vo'Tsekrish. You dare question?" He pointed at the stairs and put on his best Angry Ruler face. "Go! Go now!"

The remaining rioters fell over each other in their hurry to obey. Stone slammed the door shut and fell back against it, his knees taking leave from his body.

"You did it!" Aisse surprised him with an impulsive kiss, then backed away quickly as if afraid he might want more.

"I knew he could." Fox handed Stone his sword.

"Quick thinking." Obed clapped a hand on Fox's shoulder. "Smart thinking. Thank the One that one of us could think."

"All the thinking in the world wouldn't have helped if you three hadn't been able to carry it off," Fox said.

Stone used the tip of his sword set in the floor to push himself upright. "So how do we get them back?"

That would be the real trick, with Obed looking so obviously foreign, Aisse a woman, Fox blind and still half-lame, and neither him nor Stone speaking the language.

"They won't execute them out of hand?" Obed's fear showed.

Stone shook his head. "They'll want to know why they're here, who they're spying for, what they've learned."

"If they think Kallista's a witch, they'll drug her." Aisse sat next to Fox on the edge of the bed. "The drugs stop the magic, make her—she'll do whatever they say."

"Destroy her will." Fox nodded.

"*Destroy* it?" Obed frowned as he paced. "Forever?"

"Not forever," Aisse said. "Till the drugs stop."

"So how do we get them out?" Stone said again. Why didn't they understand that was the only thing that mattered? "We can worry about the rest later. First, we have to get them back, and fast. Before anyone figures out I'm no Ruler. Before they have time to get creative with their questioning."

"Where will they have taken them?" Obed spread one of the robes inside out on the table and took a charred stick from the edge of the fire, using it to sketch a rough box on one edge. "If this is the inn, where is that place?"

Stone took the stick. "We've only been through Dzawa a few times before, but I think City Center is here." He drew another box near the center of the robe and scraped a crooked line to it. "Not far from the lowest pool."

"What about inside?" Obed asked.

"No City Center is *exactly* like another," Fox said. "But they are all similar. There's an outer wall. Beyond it will be Warriors' barracks with women's quarters, the Ruler's house with its women's quarters, prison cells, outbuildings, official government chambers—"

"Draw it," Obed ordered Stone, bracing his knuckles against the table. "Best guess."

* * *

Kallista groaned. Her head pounded as if a hundred cannon were trying to blast their way out. Worse, she felt muzzy, fogged up and— She cried out, *reaching* with her magic, only to recoil as pain doubled her over. She couldn't touch her men, couldn't feel them in her mind. She retched, bringing nothing but a sour taste from her empty stomach.

Once more, Kallista *reached* for them, and once more pain slashed through her. She tried to push past it, ignoring the agony, but the magic wouldn't rise. Nothing answered her.

Someone snatched a handful of hair, lifting Kallista's head for a slap that made her ears ring. Kallista caught the hand before she could be slapped again, using knowledge of pressure points to gain the advantage.

"Don't touch me," she snarled, finally focusing on her tormentor. A woman a few years older than she, tall and square with a face permanently screwed into a scowl.

"Witch," the woman spat. "You'll practice none of your evil here. Your magic is gone, the evil power purged from you."

Kallista turned aside the fear, questing inside for the core where her magic lived. It lay helpless, shriveled and starving, but it survived. The missing links to her men alarmed her more.

"If you attempt magic," the woman said in her cold hard voice, "you will be punished instantly, as you have already discovered. And then your punishment will be redoubled." She twisted her hand free and raised it to strike again.

"You will not touch me." Kallista separated the words, giving them all the emphasis and power she could. She sat up, holding the woman's gaze. Stone had found her light-colored eyes unnerving. She hoped this woman did also.

"Witch." The word was a curse in her mouth. But the Tibran didn't strike a blow. "You have no power here. I will take your evil seed from your belly and destroy it. The Ruler says to wait, let

you give birth and take the child to serve, but I know better. We must destroy it now before your evil spreads."

Kallista rose to her feet, stretching a bare hand toward the woman. She backed away, out of reach, obviously afraid.

"You will not touch me," Kallista snarled. "You will not touch my child. If any harm comes to my child, if you even look as if you are trying to harm it, I will cut your beating heart out of your body and feed it to the wolves. I do not need magic for that."

She snapped her fingers and the woman startled, losing her balance. Her fear gave Kallista an advantage and she took it. She dived across the room, knocked the woman to the floor, then scrambled forward and sat on her. Kallista grabbed her by the hair and banged her head on the hard stone floor.

"Nobody threatens my child." She banged the woman's head again with every word. "Understand? Nobody."

The woman moaned and thrashed her arms and legs, but they had no strength. Kallista struggled back to her feet. What had they done to her? Her magic lay useless inside her, she walked like a drunk on a three-day binge, and she couldn't find her men in her mind. Were they still alive?

A single sob escaped her, but she choked the rest of them back. *Torchay.* He'd been with her when the mob attacked. Where was he now? Was he alive? They'd captured her, brought her here. Maybe they'd brought him too.

Kallista looked around the cell. Tibrans didn't expect a woman to defend herself, much less attack, or they wouldn't have left anyone in here with her. Then again, the woman may not have had authority to be here. She sounded crazed. Kallista knelt to search her, batting away her feeble attempts to stop her, and was rewarded with a key that she hoped would open the door and a long, thin, lethal-looking knife. The woman had intended murder.

Banging the woman's head on the floor one more time for good measure, Kallista put the key in the door and stopped. She was wearing a Tibran woman's dress—thin, flowing fabric that draped over her form. She would blend in, except Tibrans all had gold or yellow hair. Quickly, Kallista ripped a piece of fabric from the other woman's dress and tied it over her dark hair. She opened the door and slipped out.

Where would they have put Torchay?

Torchay bit back a groan as his lurching progress around the perimeter of his cell collided yet again with the stone wall. He just needed to get round it once, to be sure he hadn't missed anything in his blurry visual inspection when he'd first opened his one good eye. The left one seemed to be swollen mostly shut. Tibran merchants and farmers might not be trained to fight a man armed with swords, but they obviously knew how to administer a beating to an unconscious one.

He had to keep moving, keep his bruised muscles from stiffening, had to find a way out of here to rescue Kallista and his child. No matter which of them—he or Stone—had sired it, he was its father. Had they beaten her too? Was she still alive? He had to believe it or go mad.

The cell had no openings other than the barred grille through which they'd shoved him, not even a loose stone in one of the walls. Torchay fetched back up at the entrance and rested his forehead against the flat surface of the rusty bars, peering through at his blades. They lay piled haphazardly across the scarred wood of the table opposite, a full dozen of them. After removing so many, who could blame them for thinking they'd got them all? Doubtless that was why he had one left.

Flexing his aching muscles, Torchay straightened and stretched. The guard sitting at the table looked up from his tankard and scowled. Torchay kept his face blank, reaching his arms to either side as far as he could. The guard grunted and went back to brooding in his beer.

Torchay stretched upward, fingertips brushing the ceiling. He brought his hands down behind his head where, instead of locking his fingers together as he twisted his torso from side to side, he untied his hair to release the thin, sharp blade hidden in his queue.

He slipped it from its leather sheath and tested the razor edge. A small sliver of a knife, it was long enough to reach a man's heart or cut his throat. Now he only required getting the man close enough to do it.

These Tibrans feared magic. Kallista's little display at the inn would have told them they were dealing with magic, but would they know which of them was the naitan? And would this man know how real magic worked?

Torchay leaned against the grille again, shaking his hair down around his face, doing his best to look wild and half-mad. He focused his gaze on the guard and began to recite his ancestry in as ominous-sounding a tone as he could.

Scowl fiercer than before, the guard glanced up for only a second. Torchay spoke a little louder, pointing one hand at the guard and lifting high the one holding his blade, using street-show gestures. The guard glanced at him two or three more times as Torchay started adding buzzes and clicks and other strange sounds he'd once used to tease his younger sedili. Finally the man rose, shouting something, shaking his fist.

Torchay raised his voice, letting a bit of spittle fly, the better to convince the man he was a mad naitan. If the man didn't give in soon, he would have to start his recitation over. The guard shouted louder, but Torchay wouldn't be drowned out. He added a whole-body tremor and the guard's face paled. *Come over here, damn you. Shut me up.*

Finally, at last, the guard scrabbled his sword from its sheath and rushed him. Torchay twisted aside, caught the naked sword in one hand and used it to yank the man hard against the grille while his little blade sliced into the jugular. He searched the dying guard and swore violently. No keys. He looked up and swore again. The man had left the damn keys sitting on the blasted table.

He was not sitting here waiting for the dead man's friends to come find him. One way or another, he would get those keys, get out of this hole and find Kallista. He had the sword. That was a start.

Obed skulked in the shadows outside the stone wall surrounding Dzawa's City Center, praying fervently to the Ruler of Heaven that his Tibran iliasti could get past the guard at the side gate meant for city staff. If either Fox or Stone spoke any Tibran, the task would have been simpler. As it was… He walked closer, listening, watching.

Aisse giggled, pushing Stone upright again. Fox nuzzled her neck. "I promised I would put them to bed. They're so blind drunk they'll never find it without a guide. But when I get them all tucked in, I'll be happy to come back and visit you." She bestowed a smile on the guard that Obed had never seen on the small woman's face, half lust and all invitation. Perhaps too much for their purposes.

"They won't do you any good in that state." The watchman's hands went to his belt, fingers fanned to display what lay between them. "Let 'em sleep it off wherever they fall and tend me now."

Aisse put on a worried face. "Aren't you on duty?"

"Sergeant's already come by. We got lots of time." He reached for her and Fox blocked his hand.

"No," he said in a slurred voice. "Mine."

"Well, I say she's mine and you're in no state to argue with me, are ya?" The guard shoved Fox back with one hand as he yanked Aisse out of Stone's grasp and up against him with the other. Then his eyes went wide and he stared down at the knife protruding from his chest, Aisse's hand wrapped around the hilt.

"You forgot," she snarled. "The female tiger also has teeth."

Obed slipped out of the shadows to catch the man and snap his neck before he could cry out.

Fox took the watchman's helmet and musket while Obed and Stone carried the body into the guard hut and tucked it into the shadows as best they could. The hut was small.

"I am sorry," Aisse said in Adaran when they finished. "I should have done what he wanted. I didn't think. Now we have only until his sergeant returns on his rounds to find him."

"If you hadn't killed him, I would have." Fox settled the helmet on his head. "You should not have done what he asked. You will not. I'll hold the gate against your return."

Stone took the musket from him. Obed held himself still, but would they never cease with their talking? Who knew what suffering Kallista endured while they delayed?

"No, I'll stay," Stone said. "You know when someone's coming—can see around corners. You'll need that to find her. And I'd have killed him too, Aisse."

"I did." Obed seized Fox by the elbow. "Now let us go and find her. Them."

Stone put on the helmet and stood at ease in front of the hut while the others walked across the first courtyard.

"Do you see a building with high slits of windows, or perhaps bars across them?" Fox murmured.

Obed searched the area around them. "Not here."

"Warriors' barracks this way, I think." Aisse turned them to the left. "Wouldn't prison cells be close?"

"Usually. Lead on, Tiger aila." Fox set his hand on her shoulder. "Someone behind the building to our right."

Obed faded into the shadows as heavy footsteps sounded on the paved walkway. Aisse pulled Fox down into an embrace and held it as a Craftsman strode past. When he was gone, they went on, maintaining their lovers' pantomime as Obed slid through the darker night. They passed a Laborer on his way to rest and a woman heading to her own before Obed saw the building they wanted. Fox and Aisse joined him in the shadows.

"How do we get in?" Obed eyed the guards at the doorway.

"Simple," Fox said. "I'm delivering you to lockup. Except Stone was supposed to do this part."

"Vision aside, you don't speak Tibran. How will you—"

"Aisse wrote out orders. At the inn." Fox pulled a paper out of his tunic. "Sound very official. Or they did when she read this back to me."

"What about Aisse? Is she a prisoner too?"

"That's right—you weren't in the room when we worked this bit out, were you?"

"I don't go in," Aisse said. "I will wait here until you have gone inside, then distract the guards so you can get back out again."

"No sex, Aisse." Fox caught her arm. "Kill them if you have to, but don't let them take what you won't give."

"I decide what I give," she snapped, breaking free. "*I,* only I. This is Kallista. Is Torchay. I give if I want. To get them free, I give anything."

Obed's chest felt tight. This woman— He caught her hand and pressed it to his lips. "I honor you, Aisse ilias."

"Use the knife, Aisse." Fox took Obed's arm and shoved him into the moonlight. He sounded angry. Why?

Fox marched Obed up to the prison entrance and presented the forged orders. The pair of guards studied them, peered at the paper, passing it back and forth, and finally admitted them to the building.

"Now," Obed muttered. "Where do you suppose they might have put them?"

"Left," Fox pointed. "Women are always quartered to the left of a House entrance. Why change it here?"

* * *

Kallista sidled down the hallway, all her muddled senses alert for guards. Even if they didn't fear women, they would fear a witch, wouldn't they? She pushed herself off the wall, missing its support as she staggered along. She needed—no, she had a weapon. A knife, right here in her hand. She looked, to be sure it was there, then hid it in her skirt again. She needed to get out. She needed to find Torchay.

She wove through a maze of corridors, trying to remember her path, to keep from passing the same way twice. But it all looked the same, especially after she stumbled into a section of open, barred cells. Even the ragged bundles of sleeping prisoners inside the cells looked the same.

Eventually, she found a corridor that looked different. It had a table on one side piled high with blades and a guard.

Kallista froze half a moment, until she realized the man was dead, slumped on the floor in front of the barred cell, blood pooling on the stones below him. And the blades were Torchay's. She recognized the green-chased over-and-under sheath that held his twin swords. Why were they here? She lurched forward, catching hold of the table before she lost what was left of her balance. Torchay would want his Heldring swords. She could take another of the blades for the weapon she needed.

"*Kallista.* What have they done to you?"

CHAPTER TWENTY-SEVEN

That sounded like—Kallista turned, peering into the shadowed cell, and saw Torchay's face at the bars, looking anxiously back at her. Oh, Goddess, they'd hurt him.

"Torchay, your poor eye." She tottered across to the bars and reached up to touch his battered face, the swollen-shut eye.

He caught her hand, kissed it. "Are you hurt, Kallista? Look at me, love."

She blinked at him, trying to bring him into focus. "I can't walk right. I'm all…fuzzy." A sob caught in her throat. "And the men—I can't find them. The links are gone. Do you think they're dead? And Aisse?"

"I don't know, love. They're clever lads and Aisse is a tiger. They'll have thought of something to stay safe. I'm sure they're all fine." He tipped her face up, lifting her eyelids when they tried to close. "They've drugged you with something. Likely that's interfered with your magic and that's why you can't find them. Are you hurt anywhere else?"

Kallista put her hands protectively over her stomach and the twin blades clanged against the bars. "Oh, here. I was bringing these to you." Torchay took them from her as she went on. "She wanted to hurt my baby. But I wouldn't let her. I hurt her instead."

"Good girl." Torchay moved in the shadows, strapping the sheath on as always so the hilt of one sword sat just over his shoulder and the hilt of the other lay against his hip. "I need you to bring me something else, love. Can you do that? Bring me the keys. They're on the table there, see them?"

"Your poor eye." She wanted to weep, tears choking her throat as she brushed soft fingertips over the swelling. She couldn't see him clearly behind those flat metal straps. She needed to—they needed to get out. She shook her head, trying to clear it.

"Keys, love." Torchay turned her to face the table and pointed past her. "Fetch me the keys, Kallista, and we'll go find the others, make sure they're all right."

"Yes. Keys." Holding her intention firmly in her mind, Kallista swayed back to the table and picked up the keys. She picked up a dagger as well. "You'll loan me a blade, won't you, Torchay? I need one. They took mine away." She frowned as she crossed the space back to him. "I had one. I took it from that woman, but I don't know where it went."

"Of course, love. As many blades as you like." He took the keys and reached through the bars to unlock the door while Kallista turned back for another dagger.

Torchay joined her, replacing as many of his blades as he could in the instant he allowed. "Come along now, love. We've got to be getting out of here. That one's superior will be along again before long." He took her elbow and steered her down the corridor, a naked sword in his other hand, hurrying her faster than her feet would move.

"I feel fuzzy, Torchay. My feet are all stupid. And my head. It feels stupid too." Kallista frowned, stumbling after him. "I wasn't this stupid when I stopped that woman from hurting our baby."

"I imagine the drugs are still taking hold." He paused to peer around a corner and ducked back quickly.

"Kallista, listen to me, love." He caught her face in his hand and turned it up so his open eye blazed blue into hers. Why was he calling her 'love'? He was doing it a lot. "Kallista, you *must* do what I say, do you understand me? You have to look after the baby, and let me look after you. Don't go charging into a fight while you're…fuzzy. Will you promise me that?"

"Your poor eye." She laid her hand gently against his cheek. "Your beautiful face."

"Promise me, Kallista." He hissed the words out with a desperation that got through the haze in her mind.

Promise…? Oh yes. She nodded. "I won't fight unless I have to. Promise."

Torchay slid her hand from his cheek to his mouth where he pressed a kiss to her palm. "I love you," he said. Then he drew his second sword. "Stay behind me, but don't get too close."

He seemed to be listening to something. Kallista dragged a few more fragments of her mind out of the fog to listen and heard footsteps, the rattle of weapons. They grew closer, and closer yet. Torchay stepped away from the wall and spun around the corner.

It took Kallista several precious seconds to gather herself and follow. Torchay fought, one against four, his blades flashing too fast for her fuzzed mind to follow. Only two of the enemy could attack at once in the narrow confines of the hallway. Torchay drove them back a step at a time, but Kallista could see that the beating he'd suffered was taking its toll.

"Go back," one of the rear guard turned the other about. "We'll loop around the cell block and come at them from the back."

"The witch—" The other man hesitated.

"She's been neutralized. She can't work her magic."

Couldn't she? Her men were cut off from her but—

The rear pair of guards fell back, then turned to run. Torchay laughed, attacking harder, but it wasn't a good thing. He didn't speak Tibran, didn't know what they said. She had to warn him, had to help. She'd promised—but that was about fighting. Could she call—

Kallista lifted a bare hand, willing a spark to light. She couldn't reach her men or their magic, but the lightning belonged to her alone. She fought nausea that threatened to double her over, fought pain that near blinded her, but lightning danced from her fingertips. "Torchay, *down!*"

He ducked, and she let fly at the men he fought. One of them dropped. The other screamed in terror, then attacked all the more ferociously. Footsteps, more guards coming. Kallista battled through the pain to call her lightning again.

Torchay dispatched the man he fought, put away a sword and grabbed her arm, ignoring the blue flare coating her hand. He dragged her down the hall, almost reaching the next turn before the guard's reinforcements arrived. He let go and drew his second blade again, pushing her back a pace before he flew at these new opponents.

Kallista looked behind them, trying to force words from her numbed lips, to warn Torchay of the men circling around, but she had no time. She gathered up the spark she still held and threw it lashing down the hallway. The men staggered, screamed with fear, but came on. Once more she *reached* and through the pain, past the lightning, she brushed against a faint sense of *Fox*.

Joy bubbled up, pushed aside the fog for a split second, long enough for her to touch Obed and Stone before the agony broke them apart again. "They're coming," she cried. "Our ilian." And she sent the lightning against the oncoming warriors once more.

Torchay had no breath to answer. Moments later, Obed and Fox came pelting around the corner, taking down two of the guards as they struck. Torchay spun, elbowing Kallista behind him. She screamed as he took a blow meant for her, the Tibran's sword stabbing deep into Torchay's center.

Obed pushed past her, throwing himself into a long lunge that sent his sword slashing through the Tibran. He caught Torchay as he fell. "We must be gone before any more come."

"Yes, gone." Kallista scrabbled Torchay's swords up from the blood-soaked floor and let Fox lift her to her feet. He bent as if he meant to throw her over his shoulder. She stopped him. "No. Might hurt the baby."

Fox froze. Obed, already around the corner with Torchay, called back, *"Hurry!"*

Seizing her by the elbow, Fox propelled her after them. They picked up Aisse at the entrance to the prison, a dead warrior propped there at his post. Stone waited at the gate in the outer wall, another dead guard in the hut behind him. Her iliasti seemed to be littering the ground with dead warriors.

As they rushed through the night-shrouded city, Kallista never quite lost consciousness. She could smell the blood saturating Torchay's clothing, staining Obed's. She heard the clatter of warriors rushing from barracks to City Center. She felt the soft whuff of horses' breath on her hands as they reached the place where the animals had been hidden.

"Up." Fox threw Kallista into the saddle and mounted behind her. "Up the cliff. I know a place, long deserted. They won't expect us to go deeper into Tibre."

Obed held Torchay in the saddle before him. "Do we go on, Chosen One? Or back?"

"On." The fog in her mind seemed to be dissipating, the links with her marked ones solidifying now they were close again. And she *knew,* perhaps as Fox *knew* his surroundings, that if they turned back to Haav, there would be disaster. "Up," she said. "To the place Fox knows."

"I know it," Stone said. "I remember it now. I can lead."

"Then *go*." Obed urged his mount forward. "This one needs rest."

And healing. Please, Goddess, he still needed healing.

The ride seemed endless. Night hid the trail in shadow, slowing their pace until Kallista wanted to scream with fear and frustration. Every second bled another drop of Torchay's life away. The horses stumbled again and again on the steep path, their shod hooves ringing against the stones so loud she feared they could be heard clear to Haav. Cliffs still loomed above when Stone turned off the main path and seconds later vanished from sight.

Fox followed behind the animals Stone led and Kallista realized they were riding along a narrow canyon choked with brush and vines. The horses splashed through a tiny stream trickling along the canyon floor. A few moments more and the canyon walls faded back, opening into a tiny meadow ringed with tall firs and birch. An abandoned way house stood beside a pool, the source of the canyon's stream, fed by another trickle of water split off from the main flow of the Silixus.

The way house possessed only half a roof, the walls beginning to crumble where the roof was missing. But some shelter was better than none. Stone dismounted in front of the building and hurried to take Obed's burden. Torchay's head lolling on his shoulders terrified Kallista. She didn't wait for anyone to help her down, throwing herself from the horse into Fox's arms ready to catch her.

This was her vision. Torchay lying there beneath the broken roof, hands over his stomach, bleeding into the floor on the edge of death.

"No," she whispered, falling to her knees beside him.

"He's our medic," Stone said. "Does anyone else know what to do?"

Kallista called magic, ignoring the lingering pain and nausea. She placed her hands over his wound and tried to see inside him as she had *seen* when her mother healed Fox. But she was linked to Fox. She had no link with Torchay. The magic curled in on itself in distress because it didn't know how to do what she wanted.

"*Naitan.*" Aisse spoke at her elbow. "What can we do?"

"Water. Get me water and start a fire." Kallista drew one of Torchay's wrist blades and cut his tunic open.

Already this reality was different from the vision. He lay on one of the white foreigner's robes, not mounded-up canvas. Kallista had reached him first, not Aisse. And he had no blood bubbling from his mouth.

It still welled from his wound, a slow seeping that gave her hope and frightened her to her soul both at once. The wound was small but deep. Kallista turned him to the side and peered at his back. It didn't go through.

Obed set a skin of water beside her. Beyond him, Stone was laying a fire, Fox holding flint and steel ready to strike sparks. Kallista tore the cloth from her hair and wet it. She needed to wash away the blood, stop it, mend what was torn inside him, but how?

Beside her, Aisse was whispering, praying to the merciful face of the One. Kallista could feel her rocking as she prayed, her arm brushing hers. She almost sent her away, but the others were doing all that was needed. Prayer would likely do more than Kallista could at this point.

Desperate, Kallista pressed her hands over Torchay's wound again with her own prayer, begging for help. Aisse cried out as magic poured into Kallista.

She could see. Exactly where the sword had penetrated, what damage it had done, what she must do to repair it. She *reached*, pulling magic from the men, and spilled it into Torchay. She pushed together torn edges and sealed them, fused blood vessels, sent the blood back into them. She worked furiously, fighting off the death she could feel lurking, waiting for him.

She caught hold of the faint, echoing link she had with Torchay, created at their first wedding and reinforced at the later ones. It was only a shadow of the links she had with the other men, but it existed. With it, she hauled Torchay back into his body and bound him there with ties of love.

Torchay's eyelids fluttered and opened. Kallista caught back a sob.

"K'lista?" he mumbled through barely moving lips. "What's wrong?"

She lifted her bloodstained hands from his wound and saw the raw red of a healing scar. She hurled herself at him. "Nothing. Nothing at all." She held him tight, her tears soaking his shoulder.

For a moment, he held tight to her. Then his hand slipped between them to probe his stomach. "Wasn't I gutted again?"

"Not quite." Kallista swiped at her face, pulling back to let him look. "But nearly."

He stared at the closed wound, then up at Kallista, eyes wide with wonder. "You did this?"

Not even her mother could do this much, not all at once. Irysta could have stopped the bleeding, kept him alive, and day by day, bit by bit, encouraged the healing to take place. Reality penetrated.

Kallista counted *four* links inside her, four conduits for magic. She turned and stared at Aisse. "I had help. From our godmarked iliasti. Including Aisse."

"I? But—" Aisse touched the back of her neck. "There was no—nothing happened, like with the men."

Stone tipped her head forward, turned her toward the firelight. "She's marked, all right."

"But it was quiet," Aisse protested again. "Nothing happened."

"It doesn't have to be splashy or spectacular," Kallista said, fingers combing through Torchay's hair. He nestled into her, his head propped against her thigh. "You're already ilias, already bound. When you accepted the mark, the link was already there. You won't have to worry about moving too far away from me or any of the rest of it."

"Now I'm the only one of us not marked." Torchay didn't move from his spot against Kallista.

"Be glad." She smoothed his hair back off his high forehead and was caught by a yawn.

"Rest." Obed stood. "It will be dawn soon. Can we hide here through the day?" He addressed Stone and Fox.

"No one followed us from the city," Fox said in that quiet, knowing way he had.

"I'll go back to the road," Stone said. "Make sure there are no tracks showing where we turned off. The pack trains don't use the way house. It's from before the stone roads were built, so we should be left alone here."

"Perhaps I can veil the entrance," Kallista offered. "To discourage the curious."

"You can do that?" Torchay tipped his head back to look at her.

"That's why I said 'perhaps.'" Kallista smiled down at him.

They stayed staring at each other a long, long moment. The way they stared, the look on their faces—the same look on both—made Aisse feel all peculiar inside. An odd little ache that didn't hurt floated somewhere between her chest and stomach.

Obed made a strange sound in the back of his throat and turned to walk out. "I'll get the horses settled."

"I'd better get back down the canyon." Stone stood.

"Wait." Fox touched Obed's knee, stopping his exit. "At the prison, Kallista said something. I want to know what you meant."

Kallista frowned. "I'm sure I said a great many things that made no sense at all. It was only when Aisse was marked that the drugs finally left me. What particular saying of mine are you asking about?"

Aisse backed up. She was too close to Kallista and Torchay and that look between them. Fox drew her away from the fire she almost fell into, toward him.

"You didn't want me carrying you," he said, "because it might hurt...the baby?"

Kallista looked away, at Torchay again. He smiled and rose onto an elbow, setting his hand on her stomach, his eyes locked on hers. It made Aisse's stomach hurt.

"Aye." He turned to look at the rest of them, the glow of happiness so bright in his eyes that it made Aisse ache more. "We're going to be parents. All of us."

"And he's already scolded me for coming here," Kallista said. "So I don't need any more from the rest of you. We just need to finish what we came for and get back home so this baby can be born in Adara."

Obed cleared his throat. "Who is the child's father?" His hands made fists over and over, but Aisse didn't need to see that to sense the tension twisting inside him.

"We all are," Torchay said. "All of us, as Aisse will be second mother."

"No, that's not—"

Kallista cut Obed off, but gently. "If you ask about blood ties, Stone sired my child. Or Torchay. One of them. When it's born, the bloodline will be read and we will know. But truly, Obed, it's as he said. You're all fathers now."

For a second longer, Obed stood motionless. Then he whirled and vanished out the door. Stone caught Kallista's glance. Aisse could understand their conversation though no word was spoken. Kallista asked Stone to watch over Obed, and Stone agreed. He ducked from the ancient shelter.

Aisse looked back at Kallista. Torchay had his hand curved over the mound of Kallista's child, smiling up at her as they conversed in low tones. It hurt her to look at them. Not just because of the baby.

Yes, that brought back sorrow, but it was an old pain. Aisse would be mother as well. *Second* mother was better than nothing at all. It wasn't Kallista's baby that made Aisse's eyes burn. It was that look.

She wanted someone to look at her that way. She didn't want Torchay to stop looking at Kallista. She already knew that would never happen. She just wanted him—or someone—to look at *her*.

"I'll get the packs." Aisse stood, turning her back on the...the new parents. That was a word the Tibran language didn't have. "We'll want our blankets. And food."

"I'll help." Fox followed her outside.

Obed had stacked the packs near the building's door and staked the animals on long lines near the pool where they could graze. He was there, brushing them down. Stone was nowhere to be seen, down the narrow canyon, Aisse assumed. She stood beside the packs and stretched, looking up at the stars, in no hurry to go back inside. Fox lounged against the wall behind her, she saw when she turned.

"Was it hard for you to stay in there too?" Aisse rubbed her arms, bare without the foreigner's robe and chilled in the crisp fall night air. Her body buzzed with strange feelings. Was this what the men were always talking about, when Kallista pulled magic? "The way he looks at her, it's...I couldn't stay."

Fox shrugged. "I can't see it."

Oh. Right. Sometimes she forgot that. Aisse frowned at him. "Then, why did you—"

"To help you. With the packs. Or whatever you need." He paused and his hand rose toward her face, hovering scant inches away. "Are you looking at me?"

"Yes."

"Why?" It was obvious he wanted to touch her. Why didn't he?

"Because I don't understand you. I want to. Why are you here, with me? What do you want?"

His hand fell, his head jerked back and bumped the wall. "Nothing. To help." Fox turned his face away. "I'll get the packs."

Had she—had she hurt him without touching him? The way Kallista hurt Torchay sometimes? And Obed? She hadn't meant to. "Wait."

Aisse put out her hand, touched Fox's shoulder as he bent. Before tonight, she had never touched any of the men, except for Torchay, or in combat practice. Fox went still, still as his namesake hiding from hunters.

"Don't go." She curved her hand lightly over the point of his shoulder before pulling it back. "Talk to me, Fox. I want to understand. I—did you follow me out?"

Fox remained frozen, bent before her. "Are you afraid of me, Aisse?"

"No." It was true, she realized. She didn't fear him. Could she do it, put her hands on a Tibran male without fear? Had the magic—had *Kallista* given this to her? Aisse touched him again, curious.

He lowered one knee to the ground, holding his position. "I have no caste, Aisse. All I have is this ilian. Just tell me what you want."

She stroked her hand across his shoulders, tasting the sensations shivering through her, exploring the size and strength of him. Those aspects of a man had always frightened her before. "Would you truly have killed that guard?"

"In a breath."

"Why?" She untied his queue, let his hair fall loose around his face.

"Because you didn't want him and he would have stopped for nothing else." Fox shivered as she traced her fingers along his neck beneath his hair, over his mark. "Because you're my ilias."

"What things did you learn when you were a toy in women's quarters?"

He lifted his head, a smile curving his lips. He captured her hand and brought it to his mouth for a brief kiss. "Would you like me to show you?"

"Maybe." Aisse reclaimed her hand and picked up one of the packs. She could feel her hips sway as she walked to the door, something she'd never felt the urge to allow before. "I'll think about it."

When Stone returned to the hut, Kallista tried to call the veil, to cast it over the canyon. The magic seemed sluggish, reluctant to move, refusing to stretch itself so thin. She had thought the effects of the drugs the Tibrans had given her gone, but maybe they still lingered. Or perhaps the healing had taken more magic than she realized. The healing had been almost complete.

She *reached* for Obed, out with the animals, calling him inside. She could sense the seething jumble of his emotions, but didn't attempt to pick them apart. He deserved all the privacy she could give him.

A few moments later, he stomped through the door. "What?"

Kallista hid her smile. She'd only seen his anger the once. Usually, he hid his true self behind smooth courtesy and elegant speech. She found the change refreshing. "I can't hide the whole canyon. I tried. And I can't hide its entrance from here. But I think I can hide us so that—if the canyon is searched—we won't be seen. But we must be close together."

She could almost see Obed physically summoning his mask. He bowed, accepted the dried meat and bread, the cup of tea from Aisse. "As you will it, Chosen."

Aisse gasped when Kallista drew magic, shivering where she sat next to Fox. Kallista spared a glance and saw Fox murmuring in the younger woman's ear. He would ease her way.

Kallista braided the magic together, marveling at the new skein's richness. Aisse's magic blended perfectly with the others, supporting, strengthening, giving exactly the element needed. The first time, she had needed to see, and she had seen. Now, she needed to obscure vision, and it was obscured.

She whispered to the magic, drawing it close, wrapping herself in its shimmery cloak. When she was sure it understood what she wanted of it, she exhaled, slowly spreading her arms wide to encompass her ilian. A fine, grayish mist floated out and settled gently over the six of them.

"Goddess," Torchay breathed. "You're all fading. I can scarcely see you."

"Truly?" Kallista looked at the others. "You all seem perfectly normal to me. Can you see me?"

"*I* can't." Fox grinned and ducked as Stone threw a bread crust at him.

"I see everyone clearly." Obed filled his cup with more tea.

"So can I." Stone broke off another chunk of bread, to eat this time.

"And I," Aisse said. "But isn't Torchay now—"

"The only one of us not marked." He sounded a bit sour to Kallista's ears.

"But you *can* see us." She pushed him back when he would have sat up.

"Barely." Torchay looked from one to the other of them. "You're transparent. Like ghosts. And if you don't move, you blend in."

"None of the ghosts I've seen were particularly transparent," Stone muttered.

"So, we know the veil works." Kallista wanted to jump up and dance in triumph, but refrained.

"I *can* still see you, even if you're faded." Torchay leaned into her, as if to be sure she felt more solid than she appeared.

"But you're ilias. Without the mark, your link to the rest of us isn't as strong, but you're still linked. You're one of us. So you can see us, if not as clearly as we see you."

"Why can we see him clearly?" Obed asked. "If his link is not so strong."

Kallista shrugged. "Magic." She had no other answer.

"We need to set a watch," Torchay said. "I'll take last—"

"You'll take none at all," Kallista countermanded. "You were nearly gutted again, and while all the holes are mostly closed now, you weren't given back all the blood you lost. You'll spend the day resting."

He scowled at her a moment before he pulled her face down to inspect her eyes. He set his hand over her stomach then, sliding it from place to place until she felt the baby flutter under it. "All right," he said. "I'll rest if you will."

"Agreed." She could wait until he slept, then take care of what needed doing.

But Torchay looked past her shoulder in Obed's direction. "Make sure she does it, ilias."

Obed inclined his head. "It shall be so."

Kallista made a face, but gave in. She had no other choice. She lay down on the bedroll beside Torchay. "No one leaves the hut. The magic is set, I don't have to stay awake to control it, but don't leave the hut."

"Sleep," Obed addressed the others. "I will wake you when it is time."

Stone came to lie beside Kallista, Aisse next to Torchay. But Fox curled up on the other side of Aisse without drawing protest. Kallista, lying close enough to brush Torchay's nose with her own, met his gaze and raised an eyebrow at Fox's action—and Aisse's lack of it. He lifted his shoulder in an infinitesimal shrug.

Kallista snuggled closer, tucking her face into the hollow of his neck. Torchay put his arm around her and they slept.

* * *

Sunlight lay over Aisse's eyes, seeping through her lashes, turning the world red. She shifted, moving forward, away from the sun's rays, and her nose bumped into warm, male flesh. Fox murmured, backed to give her a fraction more room. Aisse followed.

When did she grow to like the way a man smelled? Fox smelled different from Torchay who smelled different from Obed and from Stone. But she liked it. All of it, of them.

Her body still buzzed. It had felt…delicious when Kallista called the magic. Aisse tingled all over, her senses stretched, balanced on some edge she couldn't name. She wanted to wake Kallista, ask her to call more magic, but Torchay wouldn't like it. And Stone would laugh.

She eased closer to Fox, until her breasts pressed against his back. It helped, a little. His breathing stuttered, then fell back into a steady rhythm. Too steady? Aisse stretched closer, until her lips almost touched his ear. "Fox?"

CHAPTER TWENTY-EIGHT

Fox went still, even his breathing stopped.

"Are you awake?" Aisse knew he was, but she asked anyway.

He rolled to his back, eyes open, his expression asking what she wanted.

Her lips brushed his ear again. "Show me what you learned." No. That sounded too much like a demand. "If you wish. Please?"

When she drew back, his eyes still stared at the nothing he could see, but his lips were quirked into a tiny smile. His hand rose, covered her breast, and her gasp made him grin.

"Shh," he breathed, curling round to meld her mouth to his.

Aisse had seen kisses, more of them since coming to Adara and Kallista, but had never done one. Not like this. His lips melted into hers as his hand found the hem of her tunic. He eased it up, insinuating his hand beneath her chemise as well, then stroked his way across her stomach to her breast again, swallowing this new gasp in his kiss.

All of her skin needed touching, needed it so badly it made her squirm, but her breasts somehow needed it more. They needed the heat of Fox's hand covering them, wanted his fingers on their peaks, wanted—*yes,* that—the flick of his thumb.

She needed to be closer to him. Aisse found the edge of his tunic and pushed both hands inside, running them over his stomach and chest and back. If her skin could touch his skin, would it feel that much better? She shoved his tunic up and rubbed her bare stomach against his.

The hard ridge of Fox's aroused member throbbed against her and she recoiled. He let her go, pulling his hand from beneath her tunic, stilling his mouth against her lips. Aisse drew back and looked at him.

He looked like any other Warrior, broad and tall, golden-skinned, golden-haired—though his was brighter than most, touched with red. But he didn't act like any other Warrior.

Aisse hesitated, then brushed her lips across his. They moved, just a little, returning as much kiss as she gave. Still she paused, uncertain, her fingers against his bared stomach.

"I have no caste," he murmured into her ear. "I will do exactly and only what you wish of me."

Truly? In her experience, men became crazed when their members were in the state his was. However, Fox lay still, waiting. For her to decide? He did not *seem* crazed.

Aisse glanced past Fox at Obed standing watch. He stared determinedly away from the sleepers, his hair glinting almost blue in a slash of sunlight. Obed would rescue her if Fox *did* go berserk. But…what *would* Fox do?

A test seemed in order. Slowly, carefully, keeping her eyes on his face, Aisse walked her fingers from his stomach down the front of his trousers. He hissed, almost as if in pain, when she curled

Gail Dayton

her hand over that ridge, but did nothing else. Though his breath came quicker, puffing into her ear and making her shiver. Suddenly curious, she explored, watching his reactions. Strange as it seemed, she'd never actually touched a man's arousal before. The men she'd known had always wanted to do other things with theirs.

Fox made a strangled sound in her ear, and Aisse pulled her hand back. "Did I hurt you?"

"Goddess, no." He gasped for air, stroking his cheek along hers, his words softer than whispers. "Let me show you, Aisse. What I know. You know you can trust me. You *know.*"

Feeling shy and peculiar and still tingly, Aisse nodded, keeping her eyes down, until she remembered he couldn't see what they gave away. Nor could he see her nod. But somehow he knew she had. His lips touched hers again, light and sweet, as his hand slipped back beneath her tunic. He touched her breasts, teasing her nipples into hard peaks. He held back when Aisse wanted to stroke her stomach against his again, but she insisted. She did trust him. And it eased some of the tension throbbing inside her.

His hand left her breasts, sliding down across her stomach to loosen the lacings on her trousers. He slid his other arm beneath her shoulders, holding her in a loose embrace, as if he knew close confinement would disturb her. Then Fox smoothed his hand across the skin below her trousers to touch the tender places between her legs.

Aisse shivered, wanting to push him away and wanting to clutch him closer. She was afraid, but his fingers had found the edge where she was balanced. She gripped his forearm, nails digging in. Fox went still.

"Shall I stop?" He nuzzled her ear, his breath warm as one of his kisses.

"*No.*" She couldn't stay bound up like this. But she was still afraid. "Be soft."

"Trust me." His tongue licked out over her earlobe and she shivered. In the next instant, his fingers probed her folds and brushed over something that lashed her whole body with sparks of pleasure.

Fox caught her cry in another kiss, this one hot and demanding, his tongue stroking along hers the same way his fingers stroked her below. She burned, writhing under his touch. More. She wanted more of this. The tension built until she strained toward him, her tongue plunging deeper into his mouth than his did into hers. Then it burst and she shuddered with glorious delight.

But it wasn't enough. She felt…empty. She pulled her mouth from his. "More."

"Shh." He kissed her, his fingers moving again. But that wasn't right, wasn't what she wanted, needed.

She pushed at his hand. "No, *more*. I need…more."

Fox tried to soothe her, but she wouldn't be soothed. She twisted against him, angry without knowing why. He brought her over him to his other side, away from their sleeping iliasti. "What *more* do you want?"

He settled his weight partly over her, brushing his lips over her eyes, cheeks, nose, as if he used them to see her. Maybe he did. Aisse grabbed his face, matching her mouth to his, lifting into him. That was when she realized it. She wasn't afraid.

Before, when a man had held her down like this, his weight pinning her, the fear had overwhelmed her, blinding her, stopping her breath. But now—she liked his weight, liked having resistance to push against. *"More,"* she growled, gripping him by the hair.

"Do you want me inside you?" His voice a mere breath, Fox slid his leg over hers, between hers, putting pressure where she needed it.

"No. Yes— Will— Is it more?" She arced her body into him. "I need someth— I'm empty. Fill me up."

With one quick yank, Fox had her trousers down below her

knees. His laces took another moment to loosen, then he was lying over her, his knees between hers. Aisse didn't have time for fear to rise before he was inside her in one smooth, deep plunge, filling her as she'd demanded. It felt like…exactly what she needed. Nothing like any sex she'd ever done before.

Fox glided in and out of her on a cushion of liquid passion. No pain. The complete opposite, in fact. Nothing had ever felt so good. She shoved her hands in his hair and held on tight, meeting each of his thrusts with one of her own, until she shuddered again, and Fox went with her.

Aisse lay under him, breathless, weighed down, and utterly content. She ran her hands over his shoulders, wishing she touched skin rather than tunic. They could do it with fewer clothes next time.

Next time? Aisse smiled to herself. Yes. Most definitely.

Kallista let out a long slow breath and tried to will herself back to sleep. Fox and Aisse might not have awakened her with the faint impressions coming through their magic links if she hadn't been on edge already. After everything that had happened, from the attack at the inn until this moment, Kallista ought to be tired enough to sleep for a week.

And she was. But all of it had her unsettled, easy to wake. Aisse had accepted a mark tonight. Hugely important, deserving of more recognition than an offhand comment: "How nice, you've been godmarked…" But Kallista didn't know how or what more should be done. The new marking was only a small part of what disturbed her.

Something else had happened tonight, something beyond the bare events, more momentous than Aisse's marking or Torchay's healing. It had a bit to do with the comfort Fox and Aisse had just found in each other. It had even more to do with Kallista's sheer terror at the thought of Torchay's death. But mostly, it was about the escape from City Center.

Two of them had been in trouble and the other four had worked together to rescue them. If that was not the behavior of a true ilian, then none existed anywhere. It didn't matter how they had begun or what had brought them together. Kallista was tired of fighting the truth. This wasn't just some quasi-military troop assembled for fighting demons. This was her family and she loved them.

The thought still terrified her. So many times the love she'd offered others had been turned aside as insufficient or flawed that she'd stopped offering it. Or tried to. Maybe she'd just labeled it something else, like familiarity. Or friendship.

When it had happened was as unimportant as why or how. It was. She loved. It made no difference in anything or anyone but Kallista, inside herself, and there the changes were profound and unmistakable. It didn't matter if they loved her back, though she knew they did, each in his or her own way. Accepting the truth, ceasing to fight against herself, made Kallista stronger. The love made them all stronger. It bound them tighter together into a whole and maybe, because of it, they would all survive this quest.

Sometime during her musing Kallista slid into sleep. There didn't seem to be any demarcation between waking and sleeping. She lay snuggled between Torchay and Stone, thinking about love and what it meant, while around her the dreamscape began to flow and glitter.

After a time, she sensed the demon, still at a distance, but less of one. They were closing on it. Torchay mumbled something, twitched in his own dreaming, and Kallista soothed him, kissed him quiet. She'd nearly lost him tonight, would have if not for Aisse. She needed them, her iliasti, far more than they needed her. Thank heaven she had not driven them off with her hand-wringing and self-pity.

The demon skipped through the colored glow of dreamfog, spinning itself wide in its search for her. Kallista wondered idly what it thought it would do if it ever found her. What *could* it do, here in the dreamworld?

The twisted wrongness that was the demon shivered past again. When it was gone, looking in another direction, Kallista wriggled free of her men and tucked the fog close about them again, hiding their sleeping forms from view. Then she stepped out into the swirling mists.

"Hey!" she shouted. "You! Looking for me?"

It took a moment for the demon to notice her, or perhaps it had to gather its scattered parts before it arrowed back to loom before her. "You dare?" Its voice boomed through her, vibrating her bones. "Bow before me, puny mortal. Quake in awe at my mighty powers."

"What powers might those be?" Kallista wondered a moment at her lack of fear before she understood. "The One who travels with me is greater than all."

"I will destroy you!" it screamed, so enraged that bits of shadow flew off around its edges to float for a moment before melting back into the whole.

"Possibly." The idea didn't disturb her as much as she thought it should—perhaps because this was a dream. "But possibly I will destroy you. I am coming, Tchyrizel. I am coming for you."

The demon Tchyrizel recoiled when she called it by name. She could only assume the source of her knowledge, but had no doubt it was the demon's true name. It gathered itself, growing smaller, denser, and abruptly a dozen spikes thrust from the demonshadow to stab straight through Kallista's dreamself.

She screamed with the agony of the piercing and opened her eyes with a gasp to sunlight filtering through leaves into the half-roofed way house. Slowing her breathing, Kallista touched one of the places where the demon had pierced her, afraid of what she might find.

"Chosen?" Obed spoke from his post by the window. "Are you well?"

"Yes." She was. Her body showed no consequences of the dream encounter, and she had apparently not screamed aloud or Obed would be more alarmed. "A dream. Nothing more." She frowned. "Isn't it time for Stone to take the watch?"

"Not yet. I'll wake him soon."

Kallista was asleep again before she could figure out what seemed wrong with Obed's words.

Obed woke them all near dusk. Kallista watched him, tasted him through the link. She could feel his weariness. He'd been awake all day, never calling anyone to stand watch in his place. Awake all day and all the night before.

She paused by his side as they were preparing to mount up and leave the canyon, caught his arm. "Don't do that again," she murmured. "Don't lie to me and don't take all the watches. You need sleep as much as the rest of us."

He wouldn't meet her eyes, staring off at the cliffs just past her head. "As you will it, Chosen."

Goddess. She wanted to pound her fists on him until his masks shattered and the man inside came out. *"Kallista,"* she said, her voice low and hard. "My name is Kallista. Not Chosen. Not Captain, not even Naitan. Would it wound your dignity so much to call me by my name?"

Obed looked at her now, his eyes wide, startled. "I did not mean to offend, Chos—Kallista."

"Of course not." She sighed, her hand rising to give his cheek a friendly pat. It lingered for a caress. "Take care of yourself, Obed. I need you."

With a last caress of his tattooed cheek, she turned away to mount her horse. Carefully, she drew off just a trickle of magic from the other three and fed it to Obed, hoping none of them noticed, hoping this wasn't something else that would offend her Southron iliasti's sensibilities. But he needed the strength. She wished she could do it for Torchay.

Just before they left the canyon, Kallista called magic and renewed the veil of shadows around them. This time—because of Aisse?—she managed to extend it to the animals. Could she do it with the defensive shield as well? She would try later.

They traveled by night, cross-country, away from the roads. By day, they hid in the rocky outcrops or narrow water-carved slashes that dotted the rising plateau. Torchay kept their pace brisk. Kallista had no quarrel with that. She could feel time snapping at their heels. They bypassed villages and occasional towns, giving them as wide a berth as would not delay them too much. Warrior patrols thronged the roads and towns, searching for something. Kallista feared she knew what that was.

At last they reached the outskirts of Tsekrish. The building where they hid, overlooking the city, seemed to have once been part of a prosperous estate, abandoned centuries ago though the fields were still cultivated. Only four- and six-legged creatures lived here now.

One river flowed into the Tibran capital set on its high cool plateau. Three rivers flowed out, splitting into a sort of delta far from any sea. The Silixus flowed east and south to Haav. The other two flowed toward the western coast.

The squalor of laborers' huts spilled along the banks of the three rivers, but even in the predawn darkness, lights winked above where the city proper lined both banks of the Unified River, joined by her Iron Bridges.

"There are seven of them," Stone said. "Built by the king that was."

"An unlucky number," Obed murmured. "Falling short of the goal."

"Which doesn't tell us how we can get inside the palace and

find this stupid demon." Kallista couldn't stifle all her grumpiness. She was tired, pregnant and deserved to be grumpy.

"If you'd go to sleep and stop nagging us to death, maybe we'll have a chance to figure it out," Torchay came back at her.

"Why not use the shadow veil and just walk in?" Aisse asked.

"We're close to the demon," Torchay said. "Will it be able to sense your magic?"

Kallista bit her lip. "I don't know. I... It knows we're coming."

Torchay turned and stared at her. "And what makes you think this?" He sounded the way he always did when she'd driven him to the edge. Only now he was her ilias as well as her sergeant, and could throttle her if he wanted to.

She cleared her throat, looked Obed in the eye because she couldn't quite face Torchay, and said it. "Because I told it so."

"Brilliant." That was Fox, not Torchay. "We creep cross-country all this way, hiding from everything that moves, and it still knows we're coming?"

Kallista cut her eyes toward Torchay. No explosion. He stood there in the growing dawn light, hand over his eyes as if they pained him. "It doesn't know *where* we are or *when* we're coming. Why do you think there were all those patrols everywhere? It was hunting us. What happened in Dzawa— My fault, all right? It was my fault, and you do not know how sorry I am."

She put her hand on Torchay's arm, willing him to look at her. She didn't deserve forgiveness for almost getting him killed again, but she wanted it. He patted her hand, his mind obviously else-where.

"If the demon knows we're coming," he said slowly, sorting things out, "why hasn't it caught us yet?"

"I told you, all it knows is that we're coming."

"Yes, but *why*? Why is that *all* it knows?"

She hadn't considered that. Why indeed?

"When did you tell it?" Fox said. "Before we left Adara?"

"No, after Dzawa. I told it that night in the canyon."

"The magic," Obed said. "You were using magic to disguise our appearance after Haav, is it not so?"

"That's right." Where was he going with this?

"And after Dzawa, we traveled under the veil of shadows."

"Traveled *and* slept," Stone added.

"So we lived under the veil of a magic that is a gift of the One." Her dark ilias paused, waiting for Kallista to add up the pieces.

But she couldn't. She was too tired for brain function. "And?"

"And what is it we're coming to fight?" Torchay had obviously caught on.

"A demon." Oh. She blinked as the thoughts clicked together. *Oh.* "So the *magic* was hiding us from the demon because the demon is evil and the magic is good."

"I do not know whether your theology is correct, but it seems to me to be a reasonable assumption." Obed allowed himself a small smile.

"So, Aisse's suggestion was a good one." Kallista fought a jaw-popping yawn and lost. "We just stroll in under the veil, smash the demon and stroll back out again."

"Somehow," Fox muttered, "I have a feeling it won't be quite that easy."

"I have the same feeling, ilias." Torchay clapped a hand on Fox's shoulder, then tucked it under Kallista's elbow. "You need sleep. We'll go into the city as soon as it's full dark."

Kallista yawned again. "Tchyrizel won't know what hit it."

The three Tibrans all went motionless at the same time, staring at her. Torchay instantly moved closer to Kallista, pushing her behind him, as if he'd lost trust in the others, and after half a moment, Obed joined him.

"What did you say?" Aisse finally spoke.

"Tchyrizel won't know what hit it?"

Stone frowned, confused. "What do you mean—*Tchyrizel?*"

"Why?" Now Kallista was uneasy. Not afraid, but...uneasy.

"Tchyrizel is the Ruler's god," Aisse said.

"No." Kallista shook her head. "Tchyrizel is the name of the demon."

"But you said—" Stone took a deep breath. "You said that Khralsh is a face of your One god, and Ulilianeth, the women's god is another face."

"They are."

"What about Huen, the Laborers' god, or Achz and Arilo of Farmer caste?" Fox spoke up. Aisse added the names for the gods of the Bureaucrats, Craftsmen and Merchants.

"Yes, all aspects of the One. You Tibrans split yourselves apart and tried to shatter God, but She is all One."

"But not...Tchyrizel?" Both Fox's hands were curled into fists.

Slowly Kallista shook her head.

"Khral—*Goddess,*" Stone whispered after a long moment.

"No wonder." Aisse looked up at the fading stars.

"We will destroy this demon?" Fox turned his face toward Kallista, his jaw set with determination.

"Yes," she said. "We *will* destroy this demon."

"Good." He held his hand out to Aisse. "We need to sleep."

Kallista smiled to herself when Aisse took his hand. That had worked out rather well, though none of her doing. And height of astonishment, Stone said not one word about it. No teasing, no whining about his turn, nothing. Obviously his partner's comfort meant more than his own.

She drew magic, renewing the veil once more. She was getting rather good at it, as was the magic, falling into shape with no more than a nudge. Kallista held her hand out to Obed. "Stone will take first watch," she said.

Obed still tended to stand watch far more than his share, and they would all need to be in top form by nightfall. Or as top form as they could be, given that one of them was pregnant and another blind and half-lame.

After a moment's hesitation, Obed took her hand and let her lead him to the bedrolls spread in the corner of the tumbledown room. Torchay curved himself around her back, Kallista tucked Obed's hand under her cheek, and they slept.

It was time. The sun had set an hour ago and darkness was upon them. Kallista took a deep breath. They were going into battle, could well be dead before the night's end. The last time she'd been in this situation, Torchay had declared himself her friend. This time...

Her heart cracked open, heat pouring out to sear her with emotion. "I love you," she said. "I love each one of you. Don't you dare—any of you—let anything happen to you. It would break my heart."

She pulled Aisse into a tight hug, then let go of her to embrace Fox, giving him a lover's kiss though they'd only ever been lovers by magic. She kissed Obed the same way, tasting his rich sweetness. He didn't want to be her magical lover and now she regretted not making him the other sort. She lingered a moment more over the kiss when he protested its ending, her tongue teasing his full lower lip, until she set him firmly from her. They had other iliasti.

Stone ended his back-pounding hug of Fox and swept Kallista into a kiss, hot and wild, bending her back over his arm in a silly flourish. She smothered her laugh against his mouth.

"Does this mean real sex after?" he murmured in her ear as he set her upright again.

"Probably." She licked her tongue over his earlobe. "So don't get yourself killed."

"No, aila. Never."

Then she turned to Torchay, took his face between her hands.

"I do love you," she said in a fierce whisper. "The same way you love me, I love you back."

Torchay's hands rose to cover hers then traveled along her arms until he cupped her face the way she did his. "I want to see you, without shadows," he said, "when you say that again."

"Then stay alive. Hear me, Sergeant? You stay alive."

His mouth twitched into a crooked smile. "I will if you will."

She kissed him, putting all her heart in it. At its end, Torchay rested his forehead against her another moment, then stepped back.

Patrols of warriors spread throughout all the streets of Tsekrish after dark. The other castes gave way before them, and Kallista's ilian tried to avoid everyone. The streets seemed relatively quiet, probably because of the extra patrols. Aisse had once mentioned that bored warriors tended to create their own entertainment. Obviously, no one wanted to encounter an entire patrol of bored warriors.

They kept Torchay in the center of their group. They still weren't sure whether his veiling was as complete as the others, since he wasn't marked. Kallista thought he might have protested, except it put him next to her.

They eventually left behind the dusty unpaved streets of the outermost sections of town, crossing over the Laborers' Bridge, the first of the Iron Bridges, into the cobbled streets of the Bureaucrats' Quarter. The bridge wasn't constructed entirely of iron, Kallista noted, but of stone ornamented with iron. Fox confirmed that the other six bridges were the same.

Merchant houses began to appear in the Bureaucrats' Quarter, offering goods, food, drink and other items provided by the higher Craftsmen and Farmer castes. Merchants did not have their own section of the city, but lived in neat brick or wooden houses scattered throughout.

They passed through the narrow warren of streets that made

up the Craftsmen's Quarter of the city, and into the broad brick-paved parade grounds surrounding the rows and rows of Warriors' barracks when Fox tensed.

"Don't tell us someone's coming," Stone said. "I can *see* them coming. Hundreds of them." They all could. Warriors swarmed everywhere.

"Witch Hound." Fox pointed past Kallista's left ear toward the gray stone walls demarking the Ruler's Palace.

"What?" Kallista looked where he pointed.

Past the marching, strolling, laughing, lounging hordes of young, red-clad warriors, Kallista saw a man in bureaucrat's black. He stood hunched over to one side, as if he could not stand any straighter, his eyes blackened holes in a skeletal face. His nose protruded like an ax blade from that gaunt face, the pendulous tip seeming to quiver as he turned slowly from north to south and back again.

"They are real too?" Aisse whispered.

"What's a Witch Hound?" Kallista put a little "captain" in her voice.

"Someone who can sniff out magic." Stone added to his obvious statement before Kallista could lose her temper. "They can tell when magic's being used. They check all the lads when they join caste, search the women at assignment, to make sure no…witches get through."

"But what happened to him?" Kallista shuddered as the Hound's empty eye sockets passed by them.

"A Hound can find magic," Fox said, "because he—or she—*has* magic. The Rulers use them, but they don't trust them. They…lose their eyes first, when they join the Hunt."

"There weren't any in Haav." Aisse shivered and edged closer to Obed, beside her in the rear.

"Not yet." Stone squared his shoulders. "The king's been recruiting more. So how do we get past him?"

"Why hasn't he found us yet?" Torchay drew his lower sword.

The others all followed suit, drawing their Heldring blades. Fox unsheathed the sword bought for him in Kishkim.

"Maybe we're too far away," Kallista said. "There is the whole length of that building between us."

"We used to live in that barracks." Stone tipped his head toward it.

"I prefer my current living quarters." Fox bounced on his toes, adjusting his grip on his weapon.

"Actually, so do I." Stone sounded surprised to admit it.

"Do you know a quiet way to reach the palace?" Torchay reached over his shoulder for the second blade.

Kallista didn't like the way the Hound was acting. His turning had slowed—but only when he was facing them. The rest of the time, he turned faster. He leaned forward, his nose almost vibrating. Kallista unfurled the tiniest thread of magic from the edge of the veil, and sent it spinning out.

Something with enormous, sharp, ravenous teeth snapped the magic up, making Kallista jump. It chomped, drooling bits of magic too small to rescue, hungrily hunting more.

"Too late for quiet." She planted her hand in the middle of Stone's back and shoved. "Go. *Fast.*"

CHAPTER TWENTY-NINE

Stone led out, straight for the palace. "Have they found us?"

The warriors around them seemed oblivious, but the Hound had sensed something.

"Maybe." Kallista kept a hand on Torchay's wrist to make sure he didn't lose them. Had it bothered him, seeing his iliasti as nothing more than ghostly images for the past few weeks? This was not the time to wonder.

The Hound was bowing, speaking urgently to the warrior beside him. Torchay saw it too. "Faster."

Picking up their pace, they rushed down the wide street. No shouts or pursuit followed them, but it didn't comfort Kallista.

"There." Aisse pointed ahead. "Another Hound?"

This one was a woman, also in black, also without eyes, though her lids were sewn shut. Kallista shuddered as her ruined face turned toward them. *Peace,* she thought at the pitiful wretch. *We've come to help.*

A few hundred paces ahead, the gate in the gray walls opened and a squadron of warriors clattered through at double time, heading down the street in their direction.

Another moment, the Hound *looked* at her. Kallista could feel the woman's fear, see the broken places in her soul, but before she could reach out, the fear won. The Hound cried out, pointed.

"This way." Stone turned down a narrower street leading between two rows of barracks buildings, parallel to the palace wall. "There's another gate, smaller. Should be less guarded."

The warrior squadron came down the street after them. At the next cross street, more warriors advanced from either direction.

"They're herding us." Torchay urged Kallista ahead of him.

"As long as they herd us where we need to go, I don't care." But what if they didn't? What if they pushed them away from the palace? They had to get inside. "Is there a Hound with them? With the warriors following us?"

"Behind them," Fox answered. "Far behind. She can't keep up, so they've left her."

"There's one ahead." Stone slowed his pace. "The man from the parade ground."

"We just need a few minutes to let the warriors go past." Kallista glanced over her shoulder.

The squadron filled the street, arms spread, hands touching. Those on the edges ran their hands along the building walls to either side. Up ahead, a door opened and a woman stepped out. Her eyes widened when she saw the warriors advancing, but before she could retreat, a small boy dashed from behind her skirts into the street.

"*Quick.*" Torchay shoved Kallista toward the open door behind the woman. The others were already moving.

Kallista jostled the woman as she passed and *reached* to soothe her alarm. The woman's cry faded, then she shouted at the boy, ran into the street to catch his arm and drag him out of the warriors' path. By the time she got him safely inside, the ilian was halfway across the women's common room.

Despite the urgent need for haste, Kallista couldn't help looking around to feed her curiosity. The room was large, filled with comfortable furnishings in bright colors, red predominating. Women sat or lounged in groups, some of them working on mending, a few of them nursing infants. It was empty of warriors, but Kallista didn't know whether that was because warriors didn't enter this room or because all of them were out on the streets hunting her and hers.

"This way." Stone urged them through the open arch at the end of the room leading to a long corridor lined with doors. Most were closed, but a few stood open to show women in their private chambers, often with small children. Kallista didn't have time for long inspection. Obed hurried her along in her Tibran iliasti's wake with a hand on her elbow.

They passed through a wide, iron-banded door into an entrance hall, currently empty, and from there into an open-ended corridor lined with more closed doors. Warriors' private chambers, Kallista assumed. At the far end of this corridor they found the vacant equivalent of the women's common room. The sturdy battered furniture and faint smell of old beer and older sweat reminded Kallista of the first-year army camps in Adara.

Stone cracked open the door to the street and Fox leaned into the opening. "Clear enough."

"Back to the first gate." Kallista followed them out, Aisse leading the way, Torchay and Obed behind her. "With any luck, they'll have sent all their warriors out chasing us and we can slip inside unnoticed."

Not ten paces from the barracks they'd just left, Kallista felt magic stir. She whirled and saw the woman, the Witch Hound, her broken body stopping in midshuffle as she trailed after the searching warriors. Kallista drew magic.

Peace, Kallista sent again, but this time she *reached* for the woman. The magic unknotted twisted nerves, soothed years of pain, whispered the mercy of Ulilianeth, the strength of Khralsh, the joy of the One who was All. Kallista could feel the ache of the woman's tears—Smynthe, she was called, but she had no eyes to cry them.

She had no eyes, but still Smynthe saw. Kallista waited, let her look, accepting her duty to report them, letting the broken woman make her choice. It would be as it would be. Another long moment, Smynthe looked, never turning her head toward them. She looked at Kallista, at her godmarked ones, at the links binding them together. Then she lifted her face, waved her misshapen hand and urged the warriors on. Away from Kallista.

"Blessed be the One," Obed breathed when Smynthe moved on.

"Blessed be *that* one," Kallista added, calling down more of the Goddess's mercy on the woman.

"To the gate?" Torchay put up a sword, touched Kallista's arm.

"To the gate, the palace, and the demon."

The gate, when they reached it, was far from deserted. The squadron of warriors who'd sallied forth were a small portion of those set to guard. But the Witch Hounds had all apparently gone with them. When Kallista sent threads of magic questing forth, they came back safely, unsnared and untouched.

Stone went through the gate first, veiled in his shadows, sauntering past warriors as if nothing could touch him. Fox followed, then Kallista and Torchay together, with Aisse and Obed behind. They assembled in a courtyard just beyond the guard post.

"Now where?" Torchay spoke quietly. They were well veiled from sight, but perhaps not from hearing. Kallista wasn't sure.

"Don't ask me," Stone protested when all eyes—save Fox's—turned to him. "I grew up here, but I never passed those walls."

"Nor I," Fox said. "We were cannon fodder—meant for the wars, not the palace."

Kallista took a deep breath. She could feel it, that sense of *wrong* that curdled her stomach and shivered her spine. It was close. Far too close for ease, but it wasn't something she could track to its source. Not without using magic.

"I can find it," she said. "But the magic will give us away. The demon knows we're here in Tsekrish, but it may not know we got away from the Hounds or that we're in the palace. If I use the magic to hunt it down, it *will* know."

"What are your orders, naitan?" Torchay tucked her gloves more securely into his belt.

"Let's get as close as we can without the magic." She took a deep breath. "I'd like to get close enough that it can't escape, but I don't know if that's possible. I'm hoping that it wants to destroy us more than it's afraid we can destroy it."

"Your magic *will* destroy it?" Stone shifted his weight back and forth, his gaze flitting from one building to the next, in readiness rather than nerves.

How to answer that? She didn't want to frighten them, but neither could she lie. "I hope so. I believe the One has given us all we need to carry out Her will. But we haven't exactly been able to practice on demons, have we?"

Torchay took Kallista's hand again. "Same formation as before. Stone and Fox lead. Best guess where we'll find the king and this demon of his."

Obed took a moment to drop to one knee for a quick prayer. Stone spit on the pavement. It took Kallista a moment to recall that was an offering to the battle face of the One. She wiped her eyes, offering up her spontaneous tears along with a request for victory and a surrender of will.

"Let's go." Fox bounced on the balls of his feet. "The guards at the gate are paying too much attention to this square."

Kallista fell into formation, following their golden-haired iliasti through palace grounds and past outbuildings until they reached the Ruler's palace.

It stood multi-angled and massive near the center of the grounds, precisely oriented just askew of the cardinal directions, adding to the *wrongness* Kallista felt. She found North, turning to it unerringly as she had for so many years, drawing in its cold clarity. Then, after a brief hesitation, she turned ninety degrees to her left and faced West.

It was *warm*. Comforting and restful, promising answers to questions she didn't know she had, old and wise and welcoming. *This* was what the Barbed Rose feared?

After the first moment of surprise, Kallista opened herself, soaking in the warmth of the setting sun long after it had disappeared beneath the horizon. Almost, she turned again, to the South and the East, but the magic—the *West*—nudged her on.

Turning back to the skewed palace, Kallista pointed her ilian up the wide, stern, gray steps, her skin prickling more and more with every step mounted. They slipped inside behind a young warrior bearing a message baton.

No king had ever found rest or comfort in this place. She doubted any had ever slept through an entire night. The palace hummed with a kind of dissonance that ate at her rational mind, picking at her good sense, clawing at her temper.

Kallista glanced at her iliasti. Didn't they feel it? Better if they didn't. Being the naitan might make her more susceptible to this *wrongness,* but it also gave her more defenses. She didn't draw magic, merely kept the links open and free, ready to draw as they progressed through one echoing, utilitarian chamber after another.

No beauty met the eye anywhere. Proportions were off just enough to keep the open spaces themselves from any kind of functional beauty. The chambers echoed, but they were not empty. Warriors stood on guard at regular intervals, their long, blade-pointed muskets shouldered and doubtless ready to fire. Rulers in purple half capes or waistcoats gathered gossiping in nervous clusters, more and more of them as Kallista's ilian penetrated farther into the palace. Women in filmy red or purple draperies served food and drink, or occasionally, other needs.

"Witch!" The cry pierced the air, rising in pitch and volume as the purple-clad Rulers scattered before the Witch Hound.

The empty sockets were set in a youthful face beneath long tangles of golden hair. He could be no older than twenty, probably younger, his straight strong body clothed in the same soft purple fabric as the women. He hobbled toward them on feet that had been shattered and healed wrong, pointing a trembling hand directly at Kallista. "Witch! Can't you see her? There she is, in the midst of your indulgence, damning you with her wicked, pale eyes."

"I think we've just lost the element of surprise." Torchay drew his second sword as warriors gathered from their posts and advanced. "Use your magic. Find that thrice-damned demon so we can get out of here."

Kallista formed a quick braid of magic and flung it out to seek, small enough it might avoid notice. Then she called back the shadow veil, replacing it with the shield that had saved them from the explosion, solid now and secure.

Women screamed when the six of them suddenly flashed into view. Warriors recoiled, their advance stumbling, as if they hadn't really believed the Witch Hound had detected anything. But they hesitated only a moment.

"Which way do we run?" Stone lifted his sword en guard.

"Run?" Obed's scorn showed clearly.

"We haven't found the demon yet, have we?" Fox retorted. "That's the direction we run."

"And you thought *I* was one for charging cannon unarmed." Stone's feral grin lit his face. "Kallista charges demons."

"But not unarmed." She tugged on the tail of her seeker magic, willing it to hurry.

One set of warriors came to a halt, taking aim with their muskets. Alarmed, Kallista looked the other direction. People—warriors and civilians both—thronged the corridor beyond her ilian. The musket fire would decimate their own people.

"Aim!" one of the guards shouted.

The young Hound was between the ilian and the warriors, oblivious to their activity. Behind Kallista, some realized what was about to happen and began to scatter. The smarter ones dropped to the floor. Kallista did not fear for her own. The shield had stopped crossbow bolts. It would stop musket balls.

She snatched magic, knocked the Hound to his face with it and spread the shield to fill the corridor just as the guardsman shouted, "Fire!"

The shots passed over the tortured Hound's head and hit Kallista's shield. Some of the balls rebounded, spinning back to those who'd fired them. Some imbedded in the magic, hanging in midair. A few stray shots got through around the edges of the shield where it lost strength. But no one died.

"That way!" Kallista turned and ran, away from the firing squad, jumping the people lying flattened in the corridor. Torchay pounded a warrior with the hilt of his sword, knocking him back down. Obed dispatched another who sprang from a niche in the wall.

The seeker magic hummed as it hunted. The palace was so filled with overtones and miasmas left behind by the demon, it had trouble telling the demon from the stench that followed it. Kallista fed a trickle of power to the seeker. It had to be strong enough, but not too strong.

At every intersection, she turned, as long as the turn led inward. Warriors converged, fought to stop them. The shield did not protect as effectively against blades, perhaps because a sword moved more slowly than bullet or bolt. Kallista used her lightning as much as her sword, but reflexively. Her focus was on the magic that sought their prey.

Her ilian whirled around her in a fierce and violent dance, Torchay calling the steps in a voice that grew rougher with every shout. Torchlight lit his hair, caught echoes of flame in Fox's. Aisse brought down more than her share, her ferocity taking the warriors by surprise. Obed was a blur of smooth motion, Stone laughed as he fought and won. Gold and bright, shadow and flame, her iliasti protected her as she did them.

The seeker magic screamed and died. Kallista's body jerked in reaction, slashed through with a quick pain. But she held its thread. She knew where it had died. And what had killed it.

"Come." She charged ahead, blasting a passage through the warriors in her way with the lightning at her command. Her ilian dashed after her, caught almost as unprepared as the warriors she attacked.

Across a central courtyard to the other side, up the broad stairs, through two stark, ugly chambers, Kallista ran. She hauled open a heavy, ornately carved door, stepped inside, and nearly went to her knees under the hate that blasted her.

She groped for the links to her marked ones and called magic, drawing fast and hard, wrapping it around them all, tucking Torchay deep in the center. "My turn," she murmured. "Stay behind me, please."

The six of them together lit up the dark chamber with a pale blue-white glow. Kallista used it to see her way, borrowing a bit of Fox's *knowing* to help. The king was *there*. On his throne in the room's center. And *there*, the demon crouched, slowly taking on a semblance of shape and form.

Its eyes glowed a malevolent, molten black, and it spit hate at her again. Secure in the warmth of her ilian, Kallista let it spill over them without harm and kept moving closer.

"Tchyrizel." Her voice echoed eerily in the gloom. "Release him."

The demon snarled, metaphysical claws ripping at her, at her links. Kallista caught hold. Ignoring the demon's violent struggle, she clung to it, enduring the pain it inflicted as she *reached* into the king. The demon had dug itself deep into the king's soul, burrowed into every part of him.

Kallista called more magic and it came, *through* her iliasti rather than from them. She rooted the demon out of its hiding places, shaking off the pieces that were not demon. Gradually, bit by bit, she pried the demon loose.

It attacked her, biting, snapping, tearing, but the magic somehow held. She would not let it escape. Sweat drenched Kallista's tunic, bruises and scratches made without physical blows marked her body, but her iliasti remained untouched. She managed to protect them from the demon's fury. But she was tiring. The demon was strong. Fighting it took all her ability and concentration. It tore at the shield, rending away bits she couldn't replace.

The demon reached through the gaps it made. Fox screamed, staggered, and the demon's scream echoed Fox's. The magic drove the demonspike from his body. Desperate, Kallista shored up the shield, cutting off the bit of demonstuff, destroying it. Surely she could endure until this was done. She had no other choice.

A few lone strands of the demon still clung to the Tibran king when Torchay cried out. Kallista whirled, saw him convulse, swords clattering to the marble floor with his collapse. The demon had somehow separated him from the others and now hovered over him as if savoring a tasty treat.

"*No!*" Kallista *drew*. The magic came, but she was almost too exhausted to fling it around Torchay, squeeze it between him and the demon. Almost. "You shall not have him."

"Why not?" The demon spoke its first comprehensible words since the battle began. "You do not care about this one. He is not protected. Give him to me and I will let the others live."

"He's *mine.*" Kallista tried to increase his protection, but didn't have the magic to do it.

The demon sank a claw deep. Torchay clamped a howl between his teeth, arcing up onto heels and shoulders in obvious pain. *"No,"* he gasped. "I won't."

"Or," the thing said, "give me the others and I will let you have this one back. They're of no use to me, but killing them will afford me a little fun. I would like some fun."

Kallista swiped away tears with a sweaty forearm, unwilling to waste breath on an answer as she struggled to free Torchay.

"Do it," Torchay rasped as he struggled. "Let me go."

"No!" Other voices echoed Kallista's cry.

"I won't let you have him." She yanked the demon's claw free and it sent three more back in. Torchay twisted, heels drumming on the floor, and the shield shattered. The links shuddered but held. For how much longer?

Her iliasti were weakening. Human bodies were not made to be used as vessels for so much power for so long a time. Aisse's whimper echoed down the link, resonating with the other three. Fox held her up, despite the phantom pain from his phantom wounds. Stone supported them both, though Kallista *knew* his reserves were no greater than theirs. Obed stood in front of them, sword held ready for attack. Tiny droplets of blood trickled down his face, forced out by everything he gave. He held nothing back. None of them did.

Kallista yanked futilely at the demon's grip, at the end of her strength. She could feel it gloating. If she couldn't stop this, they were lost. All of them. Uselessly. She didn't mind so much dying if she could take the demon with her, but could she?

If she didn't, she and her marked ones would only die, but Torchay—the demon would own him. It would send its vile *wrongness* through his mind and heart, destroying whatever it touched. It would take all the honor and loyalty and love that was Torchay and twist it into something dark and ugly while what was left of his soul screamed in silence. Whatever the cost, she would not lose him. Not any of them.

She drew more magic, trembling as she fought to shape it. The darkness of sheer exhaustion hovered at the edge of her vision. Tears blinded her, caught in her throat. Torchay's half-stifled scream tore at her heart.

"Just let him go," the demon whispered. "You have four others. Are you willing to destroy all of them—destroy everything—to save him?"

"Leave him alone!" she shrieked, desperate to hush the awful whispers. "He's *mine.*"

Is he? The quiet voice spoke inside Kallista from the center of her tears. Time seemed to slow, stop as understanding exploded.

Torchay was vulnerable to the demon because he was the only one of her iliasti not marked by the One. And he was un-marked not because he himself wasn't willing to surrender to the purposes of the One, but because *Kallista* wasn't willing to give him up.

She had been afraid that Torchay would love the One more than he loved her—even while she'd been busy denying that she loved him in return. She had been afraid the One would demand his life. And while she was perfectly willing to give up her own life, Tor-chay's life was another matter entirely. She had taken the choice from him, and now the price he would pay was not only his life, but his very mind and soul.

She had other responsibilities as well. Her other iliasti were only four of them. The fate of all Adara, perhaps all of Tibre, of hundreds of thousands of people, lay in her hands. She had risked them all with her selfishness. Her lack of faith.

Who was she to think she knew better than the One God? What right did she have to make demands? How could she think she knew what sacrifices would be called for? All that was required of her was faith, for if she truly believed that the One was God and held all things in just and loving hands, then how could Kallista hold back? After faith came surrender. A willingness to place *everything,* even her most precious treasure, in the hands of the One and to become the tool that was needed for Her work.

"Oh, Goddess." The groan went soul deep as she gave up her beloved to the One who loved them most. "Forgive."

Torchay cried out again as time restarted. Kallista looked, terrified of seeing the demon swallow him up. But the black threads were being driven out through the faint cuts on his skin. His injuries had been more to the soul than to the flesh, healing as Torchay seemed to fill with light, the same light—the same *magic* that filled the others.

The link snapped into place, fully formed. A raging torrent of magic crashed into Kallista, replenishing everything she'd lost in battle and offering yet more. She braided Torchay's stubborn strength into the whole of the magic and *reached* for the king. The demon had taken back all of him.

The veil, whispered the West. *You cannot save him. He's been too long in the demon's grip.*

Acquiescing to the inevitable, Kallista gathered the power. It filled her as it had that day on the city walls above the breach, pouring into every crevice, every part of her. But somehow, she'd grown larger since then. She could hold the magic, from five now rather than two, even with Torchay's booming power added to the others.

She shaped it, named the enemy with a whisper, *"Tchyrizel,"* and threw her arms wide to fling the magic on its way.

It roared out of her, faster than the eye could follow, farther than any walls could contain. The demon screamed, shredding into tatters that disintegrated as the magic onslaught continued. "Zughralithiss!"

And it was gone.

The king lay dead, slumped on his throne, his face peaceful, untouched save for a burn mark on his forehead. It was over.

They had won.

CHAPTER THIRTY

Kallista's knees buckled. Obed and Torchay caught her as she fell. They exchanged a glance, then Obed sheathed his sabre and swung her up into his arms.

"What happened?" Stone asked Torchay.

"Let's get out of this place, and I'll tell you." He pointed at the door. "Back the way we came—or however will get us out of here quickest. Fox and Stone lead."

Kallista tried to pull up a shadow veil around them, but she hadn't the strength. They relied on speed instead, and the confusion that gripped the palace when suddenly all of the Rulers and a good many warriors died where they stood. Corridor by corridor, room by room, they ran. Until Kallista shouted for them to stop, for Obed to put her down. The young Witch Hound, the naitan huddled terrified in the same corridor where they'd first seen him, surrounded by corpses.

She laid hands on the tarnished gold of his hair and kissed his forehead, wanting to weep at his flinch when she did. "Blessings of the One on you, precious child," she murmured. "Come to Adara. To Turysh. They can heal some of your pain there." She wished she could do more for him, help him now, but the magic wouldn't answer.

"Kallista, let's go. Not everyone in the city is dead." Torchay lifted her back to wobbly feet and Obed picked her up again to hurry on.

"He's following," Aisse said, a few paces on.

"We can't leave him." Kallista struggled to get down.

"He betrayed us." This time, Obed held her tight.

"He didn't know any better." Kallista pinched his ear with her fingernails. *"Wait."*

"He can't run on those feet." Fox turned back, threw the boy over his shoulder and trotted on.

"You're insane, you know." Torchay shook his head at her, gesturing at Stone to keep going.

"But you love me anyway." She said it, though she wasn't quite sure it was true.

Until he grinned at her. "Fool that I am."

The palace gates were pure chaos, warriors shouting at each other, giving contradictory orders, brawling, some walking away. The ilian was through the gate before anyone noticed, and the pursuit fell apart before two blocks of barracks passed. Obed and Fox showed no sign that their burdens slowed them, but Kallista could sense their strength leaching away.

"It's not far to the river," she said. "Let me down. I can walk."

"Not as fast as I can." Obed held her closer. "We should take one of the western rivers. They'll be looking for us on the Silixus."

"The Athril's big enough for boat traffic," Stone said. "We just have to be sure to take the center fork. Current's tricky there, they say."

"Can we find a ship? Is there a port at the river's mouth?" Torchay turned in circles as he walked, watching behind as much as ahead.

"There's a port," Stone said. "Djoff. Whether we can find a ship there is another question."

"There will be a ship." Obed descended carefully down the steps to the walkway at the river's edge.

"How do you know?" Stone followed him down.

"I know." Obed would say nothing more, but looked up- and downstream for attackers.

Aisse found a boat. Tied up at a pier, it had been abandoned by everyone aboard save its dead Ruler owner. Stone threw the body overboard while Fox and Obed set their burdens on the benches in the stern. It was a big boat, made for river journeys, long and narrow with a pointed prow. A low, flat-roofed cabin was built into the prow, and a canopy shaded the stern of the boat. The center was open, with oarlocks set on either side for the rowers. The boat was ornately carved, luxuriously appointed, and available.

"Anyone know anything about boats?" Stone asked, standing with the others on the open deck.

They looked expectantly at each other, no one admitting to anything, until Kallista sighed. She slid down the bench to take her place at the tiller. "I grew up in Turysh with the Taolind at my back door. It's been too many years since I manned a boat, but I think I can remember how to steer. Someone look for oars. We'll need them, especially if the currents are as tricky as Stone says."

Aisse calmed the boy—Gweric, his name was—while Stone and Obed located the oars and Torchay cast off the lines. By the time they reached the triple fork in the river, the men had learned the rhythm of rowing, and Kallista was able to steer the boat into the central channel without much struggle. As they left the higher-caste sections of the city, the chaos lessened. Even the lost-looking warriors were no longer in evidence.

"Called them all in to deal with us, likely," Torchay said when Kallista commented on it.

"What happened?" Stone asked, pulling on his oar in pace with the others. "I know you used the same magic as at Ukiny, but how could it kill two men and leave the one between alive? And what happened to Torchay?"

"Later," Torchay said. "When we're safe away."

"That could be weeks," Stone protested.

"The Athril's shorter than the Silixus." Fox splashed water at Stone with his oar. "The coast is closer in the west. And we're in a boat. Won't be weeks."

It didn't take quite a full nine days to reach Djoff on the coast. The city was in almost as much chaos as the capital, everyone terrified. All the city's Rulers had dropped dead along with most of the high-ranking warriors at the same moment on the same black night eight days previously. Kallista and her ilian heard the story from frightened merchants where they sold the boat. Those left were trying to cope but defiance was everywhere. The castes were crumbling. A laborer had dared to strike back when a merchant beat him for his clumsiness. The world was falling apart.

Kallista hid her satisfaction as she followed Obed and Fox down the steep hills to the harbor. Torchay held her arm, steadying her unbalanced gait while Stone and Aisse helped the young naitan Gweric, dressed now in tunic and trousers like the rest of them, down the path.

At the harbor, Obed paused, scanning the scattered masts of those ships that hadn't run before the wind when the Rulers died. Kallista moved up next to him, leaned against his arm, struggling not to pant. It was a long way down from the river docks and she didn't have the stamina lately that she'd had a few months before. "What are you looking for?"

"That flag." He pointed to a bright blue pennon blazoned with a stooping hawk. "Come. We sail with the tide."

Kallista looped her arm through his. "Whose flag is that?"

"Mine. As is the ship." He paused, sought her gaze. "Now yours. I thought to change the flag. A compass rose, perhaps?"

"Whatever you like." She urged him on. "How did you know the ship would be here?"

"I sent orders for it to wait for us."

"No, I mean, how did the ship know to be *here,* in Djoff? Why didn't you send it to Haav?"

"There is another ship waiting in Haav." Obed escorted her up the gangway, moving ahead of her so he could lift her to the deck. "I sent a ship to wait in every port on this continent. When we reach Adara, I will send word releasing them."

Kallista stared at him, mouth open. "You sent... How many ships? All yours?"

Obed signaled to the captain as Torchay, the rear guard, leaped aboard. The crew sprang into motion. "Seventeen ships." He offered his arm again and Kallista took it. "But they are yours, not mine."

Finally he met her eye, his cheeks a dusky rose beneath the tattoos and the natural tan of his skin. "I told you, I am not a poor man."

"Well, yes, but there's quite a gap between 'not poor' and 'stinking rich.'" She blinked as the size of Obed's wealth began to sink in. "Saints and all the sinners."

"Is this safe away?" Stone asked. "Because the minute we leave the harbor here, it's going to be just like crossing the Jeroan, and I want to know what in stars happened back there before I start heaving my guts over the rail."

"Don't be so impatient." Aisse smacked his arm.

"Just explain it, all right? Why didn't the veil magic kill everybody like in Ukiny? And how did it kill people all the way to Djoff?"

Kallista sat on the bench provided for passengers outside the door leading to the cabins in the stern and gestured for everyone to gather. Torchay took the seat beside her, Obed kneeling at her feet. Stone sat on the deck on her other side and leaned his head on her knee, grinning up at her, daring her to order him away. Fox and Aisse sat just beyond, holding hands.

"Now that I've had time to consider," Kallista said, "I believe the magic struck differently because it was shaped differently. Before, at Ukiny, I asked for something to save the people of Ukiny and of Adara. Because we were in the middle of a battle, it struck down everyone who fought against us."

"Except me and Stone," Fox said.

"You were marked. You became part of the magic."

"What about this time?" Stone rubbed his cheek against her knee. "How did you shape it this time?"

Kallista set her hand on his head a brief moment. "I named it. Before I released it, I spoke the demon's name."

"So it destroyed the demon—" Stone began.

"And everyone who worshipped it," Fox ended. "Including a lot of high-ranking warriors."

"All the way to Djoff," Aisse said, "because this time it wasn't only two linked with you, but five. Do you think it killed Rulers in Haav too?"

"Maybe." Kallista shrugged a shoulder. "Torchay's magic holds so much sheer stubborn strength, it wouldn't surprise me if it killed Rulers all the way to Adara."

"Torchay's magic." Obed looked so decidedly unhappy, Kallista held her hand out to him. Why? What was he thinking? He took her hand, kissed it, then let it go.

"What happened then?" Stone asked. "When Torchay was marked? It wasn't much like what happened with the rest of us."

"The demon sank its claws into me." Torchay spoke before Kallista could. "I was unmarked. It left me vulnerable to the demon.

The mark requires surrender. There was one thing I would not give up."

"No, Torchay," Kallista spoke up. "It wasn't your fault. *I* kept you from it. I wouldn't give you up to the One."

He smiled at her, bringing her hand to his mouth for a kiss that made her shiver. "Then why were you marked and I not? You can't think for me, love. You can't dictate my emotions or my decisions. It was *my* refusal. My own…stupidity. I did no' understand that letting you go was the only way I could protect you."

"But…" Kallista paused to think. She was sure she had kept Torchay from being marked. Maybe they both had a part in it. "It doesn't matter now. You're marked like the rest of us."

"What happens now?" Stone leaned back on a braced hand, looking up at her. "We've destroyed the demon. Does that mean the marks go away? Are we still ilian?"

The sails snapped in the wind, drawing Kallista's attention as she struggled for words. "Ilian is family," she said finally. "Bound together to love and support each other and raise any children that may come. It is possible to dissolve these bonds, if the marks leave us." She took Torchay's hand, squeezed it tight. "But, even if that happens, I hope you all stay. I wasn't exaggerating when I said I love you all."

"And there *is* a child to raise," Aisse added. "I stay."

"I too," Fox said quickly. "This is my—my *family*. There are no castes in Tibre any longer, I think, even if I had one."

"I'm staying." Stone made a face. "Though I don't know how much use I'll be raising a child."

"Actually…" Kallista glanced at Torchay who grinned at her. "There will be *two* babies to raise. After we left Tsekrish, on the riverboat, when Torchay did his medical check, he listened to be sure the baby was all right. And he says there are two heartbeats. Twins."

"*Two* babies." Aisse bounced to her knees in excitement.

Torchay cleared his throat. "Not exactly."

All eyes turned to him. Alarmed, Kallista's hands flew protectively to her stomach. "Is something wrong with one of—"

"No." He caught her close in a hug, chuckling. "No, love. Nothing like that. It's just that we'll only have two babies for a short while before Aisse gives us a third."

"Third…" Aisse stared at him, eyes wide with shock. "Third *baby?*" She shook her head, clutching Fox's arm. "No, that is impossible. I am barren. I—"

"Perhaps when the One marked you, She also granted you healing." Kallista stretched a hand toward Aisse who took it and held on tight. "Joy to you, ilias."

"I—are you certain?" Aisse looked as if she'd been struck with one of Kallista's lightning bolts.

"Aye. Your babe should arrive near the end of Mielle, about six weeks after Kallista's two." Torchay grinned. "Joy to you, ilias. Joy to us all." He gripped Fox's hand, then slapped Obed on the shoulder.

Obed knelt on the deck before Kallista without reacting, silent, his face remote. He worried her sometimes.

Kallista leaned forward, touched his cheek. "Will you stay? You never did say."

His expression shut down even more. "Do you cast me off?"

"No, of course not. But I won't keep you against your will."

"Your will is mine, Cho—Kallista."

She gave him a skeptical look, remembering a certain morning in the forest when that had not been true. Obed must have remembered it as well, for he flushed that dark red again, shifting position. "I will never willingly leave you."

Her fingers trailed along his cheek as she drew back. "Good." Kallista took a deep breath. "So. I suppose when we get back to Adara, if the Reinine has no duties for us, we'll need to find a place to live. With our so-wealthy ilias here, we won't even have to worry about finding a way to support ourselves. We can spend our days in idleness."

Torchay's stifled laugh sounded too much like a snort. "I'll believe that when I see it."

"I'm very good at idling." Kallista poked his arm. "You've seen me do it."

"Aye, for a week or two. Then you're jumping out of your skin for something to do."

The sails snapped again and the ship heeled over as the wind broke free of the rocky headland. The three Tibrans promptly turned a bilious shade of green.

"Oh, Goddess." Fox lurched to his feet, stumbling for the rail, Aisse and Stone on his heels.

Kallista's stomach felt none too steady either, but with the breeze on her face and her eyes on the horizon, she didn't need to find the ship's rail yet.

"What of me?" Gweric turned his eyeless face toward her from his post near the ship's mast and guilt dug its talons into her. She had forgotten his presence. "What will you do with me?"

"You've been busy this last week, haven't you?" Torchay said accusingly, moving to put himself between the Tibran naitan and Kallista.

"Adaran?" Obviously she still couldn't tell which language was spoken.

"Good Adaran. Better than Aisse's."

"Peace, Torchay." Kallista set her hand on his arm. "If he can see without eyes, why shouldn't he be able to hear without ears, understand more quickly?"

"I cannot see," Gweric said. "Only all of you. I see the magic flowing between you, weaving back and forth in a pattern. It is beautiful. It is why—how I know you are good. I didn't see it at first, but now I do."

"What *will* you do with him, Kallista?" Torchay didn't relax, didn't move back.

"Turysh, I think. We need to go there for Fox. Maybe my mother can do something for Gweric's feet. After that—" Kallista studied him. Gweric might be able to see her magic, and she might still be able to feel the links, sense the magic that bound her ilian together, but she could no longer reach it. The healer Merinda had told her that pregnant naitani gradually lost their ability to call magic, but hers seemed to have left all at once after the demon died. She could not read Gweric's magic.

"You need to learn how to use your magic," she said. "What you can and cannot do with it. We will have to find the proper place for you to do that."

Gweric looked alarmed. "I—find magic. That is what I do."

"Most naitani can. But all of us have a magic that is our own primary gift. I think it's time you discovered yours."

"I…" He fell silent, motionless.

"Come." Obed rose smoothly to his feet. "I will show you where to sleep. You will not mind sharing with the cabin boy."

As they entered the door beside her, Kallista tipped her head over onto Torchay's shoulder. She was tired of thinking, tired of running and worrying. For just a moment, she wanted to simply *be*.

"I heard you name the demon." Torchay put his arm around her, adjusted her head to a more comfortable position. "I saw it."

"Did you?" She did not want to talk of this now. Determinedly, she shut her eyes.

"None of the others saw it. I might be the last of us marked, but I believe the link between us is closer. For instance, I know you don't want to discuss this."

"That isn't magic. That's nine years at my side."

He chuckled and kissed her forehead. "Likely true. But it was the magic that let me see the demon. And the magic let me hear what it said before it died."

"Oh?" Kallista rolled her head back onto his arm and opened an eye to look at him. "And what did it say?" She truly hoped he hadn't heard.

"Zughralithiss."

A chill ran down her spine at the hissing sound.

"What is it, Kallista? What does it mean?"

She sighed and ran a hand up under his loose hair to his god-marked neck and hugged him tight. "I don't know. Nor does Belandra, except..."

"What?" He tightened his arms around her.

"I fear it means we are not done with whatever the One has for us." Kallista closed her eyes again, breathing in his familiar scent. "It will be on us soon enough, but not right away, I think. My magic is gone until after the babies are born. We have this time to rest, to be together. To be happy. Let's not look for trouble before it comes. All right? Can you give me that?"

"Aye."

Kallista could see the worry lurking behind the smile in his eyes. Torchay was a professional worrier. But he only kissed her and lifted her across his lap.

The future would bring what it brought. Until then, she would be more than content.

GLOSSARY

Adara-the nation occupying the northern half of the continent south of the Jeroan Sea

aila (aili)-Sir or Madam, a title of respect in Adara

Alira River-tributary of the Taolind, descending from the Shieldback Mountains near Arikon

Arikon-capital of Adara at the edge of the Shieldback Mountains in western Adara

Athril River-center, navigable branch of the two western arms of the Unified River

Boren-town where the Alira becomes unnavigable, where the road to Arikon begins

Devil's Neck-impassable isthmus connecting Tibran continent to the Adaran

Devil's Tooth Mountains-the mountains that make the Devil's Neck impassable, habitable only in the lower southern reaches, above the Empty Lands

Djoff-Tibran port on the western coast, at the mouth of the Athril

Dzawa-Tibran city where the Silixus descends from the central plateau to the coastal plain

Empty Lands-an ancient lava-flow desert on the northern edge of Adara, thought to have been created in the Demon Wars 2000 years ago, habitable if one is careful

Filorne—prinsipality north of Taolind, upriver from Turysh; coat of arms: crossed swords, black and silver

Gadrene—Ukiny's prinsipality; coat of arms: blue-and-white ship

Haav—main port of Tibre, at the mouth of the Silixus River, easternmost of the rivers coming out of Tsekrish

Heldring Gap—wide valley in west central Adara, famed for the mines on either flank, and the swords made there

ilian (iliani)—four to twelve Adaran adults joined into a family unit, their version of marriage

ilias (iliasti)—spouse (spouses)

Kishkim—port city west of Ukiny, at the mouth of the Tunnassa River, known for its swamps and smugglers

Korbin—northernmost Adaran prinsipality, just south of Devil's Neck land bridge in the Devil's Tooth Mountains and the Empty Lands, Torchay's home prinsipality; coat of arms: red-and-gold stag

Mountains of the Wind, Mother Range—mountain range that marks Adara's southern border, Mother Range is Southron name; Mountains of the Wind is name used by Adarans

naitan (naitani)—a person with a magical gift

Obre River—westernmost branch of the Unified River, fast and full of rapids

Okreti di Vos Mountains—the name means "Arms of God" in the ancient language; separated from the Devil's Tooth range by a lava-flow desert and from the Shieldbacks by the Heldring Gap

prinsep (prinsipi)—the ruler (male or female) of one of the once-independent governmental units now joined together to create Adara

prinsipality—the province ruled by a prinsep

prinsipella—the offspring (male or female) of a prinsep

Reinine—the priestess-queen chosen by the collective Adaran prelates and prinsipi to rule Adara; a lifetime appointment, but not hereditary

Shaluine—prinsipality north of Turysh, between Taolind and Tunassa Rivers; coat of arms: gold lion

Shieldback Mountains—a western mountain range separated from the Mother Range by the Taolind and Alira River valleys and from the Okreti di Vos Mountains by the Heldring Gap, where Arikon is located

Silixus River—important transport river in Tibre, easternmost of the three branches of the Unified River, the only one that empties into the Jeroan Sea

Taolind River—Adara's major river, leading from northern coast at Ukiny southwest deep into the interior

Tibre—the nation made up of most of the continent north of the Jeroan Sea

Tsekrish-capital of Tibre, on the high central plateau where the Unified River breaks into three

Tunassa River-secondary river, north of the Taolind, rarely navigable, empties into Jeroan Sea at Kishkim, runs southwest to northeast

Turysh-Kallista's hometown, at the confluence of the Taolind and Alira Rivers, also the name of a prinsipality, coat of arms: green tree surmounted by a gold crown

Ukiny-port city on Adara's northern coast, at the mouth of the Taolind River

Unified River-flows into Tsekrish from northern mountains, once considered sacred

THE TEARS OF LUNA

A shimmering crown grows and dims and is always reborn. Luna has the power and gift to brighten dark nights and lend mystery to the shadows. She will sometimes show up on the brightest of days, but her most powerful moments are when she fills the heaven with her light. Just as the moon comes each night to caress sleeping mortals, Luna takes a special interest in lovers. Her belief in the power of romance is so strong that it is said she cries gem-like tears which linger when her light moves on. Those lucky enough to find the Tears of Luna will be blessed with passion enduring, love fulfilled and the strength to find and fight for what is theirs.

A WORLD YOU CAN ONLY IMAGINE ™

LUNA™

www.LUNA-Books.com

THE TEARS OF LUNA MYTH
COMES ALIVE IN

A WORLD AN ARTIST CAN IMAGINE ™

Over the next year LUNA Books and Duirwaigh Gallery are proud to present the work of five magical artists.

In January, a print created by
IAN DANIELS
was featured in *Shadows of Myth* by Rachel Lee.

If you would like to order a print of Ian's work, or learn more about him please visit Duirwaigh Gallery at www.DuirwaighGallery.com.

For details on how to enter for a chance to win this great prize:

• A print of Ian's art

• Prints from the four other artists that will be featured in LUNA novels

• A library of LUNA novels

Visit www.LUNA-Books.com

LBDG11042TR

GUARDIAN OF HONOR

Robin D. Owens

With their magic boundaries falling and terrible
monsters invading, the Marshalls of Lladrana
must follow ancient tradition and Summon
a savior from the Exotique land....

For Alexa Fitzwalter, the Marshall's call pulled
the savvy lawyer into a realm where she barely
understood the language, let alone the
intricacies of politics and power.

Torn between her affinity for this new realm
and Earth, will she return home if given the chance?
Or dare she risk everything for a land not her own?

Visit your local bookseller.

LUNA™

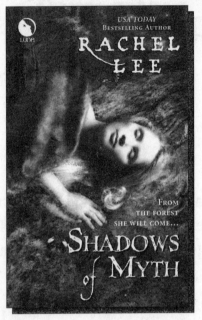

BRINGS YOU THE THIRD
POWERFUL NOVEL IN

LINDSAY
McKENNA's

SERIES

Sisters of the Ark:

Driven by a dream of legendary powers,
these Native American women have
sworn to protect all that their people
hold dear.

WILD WOMAN

by *USA TODAY* bestselling author
Lindsay McKenna

Available April 2005
Silhouette Bombshell #37

Available at your favorite retail outlet.

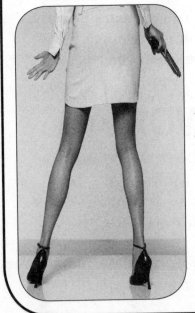